Early Praise for THE FIDDLER'S

"Peterson is a natural-born storyteller, and *The Fiddler's Gun* is a sly, soulful, instant classic." —Allan Heinberg, Executive Producer, *Grey's Anatomy*

"*The Fiddler's Gun* is an exciting, rollicking adventure that will touch the depths of your heart as its characters wrestle with human frailty, failure, love, and the quest for redemption. You will love this book, and you'll read it over and over." —Travis Prinzi, author of *Harry Potter & Imagination*

"Redcoats, pirates, orphans—and Fin Button, a passionate and savvy young woman who is a treasure all by herself. Here is high adventure that feels like truth. Three huzzahs for A.S. Peterson: *The Fiddler's Gun* is an achievement." —Jonathan Rogers, author of *The Wilderking Trilogy*

"Like a vivacious child, it grabs your attention and runs away laughing, urging you to give chase. Don't start this book when you have something important – like sleeping – to do; I guarantee, it won't get done." —Paula K. Parker, BuddyHollywood.com

"Peterson has lovingly crafted a work of historical fiction which begs the question, "Can this really be a debut novel?" With dogged fidelity, he captures the spirit, manners, and social conditions present during the American Revolutionary War. We meet colorful, credible characters who navigate the high seas of life and love, dependence and independence, war and peace, truth and consequence and despite forays into ostensibly dark places, *The Fiddler's Gun* carries a steady pulse that is beautiful, lyrical, and redemptive." —Curt McLey, ThePhantomTollbooth.com

THE FIDDLER'S GUN

FIN'S REVOLUTION: BOOK ONE

A. S. PETERSON

RABBIT ROOM
— PRESS —
NASHVILLE, TENNESSEE

Published in Nashville, Tennessee by Rabbit Room Press

940 Davidson Drive

Nashville, Tennessee 37205

Cover artwork by Evie Coates

Edited by Kate Etue

Library of Congress Control Number:

2009911581

ISBN 978-0-615-32542-2

ISBN 0-615-32542-4

Printed in the United States of America

09 10 11 12 13 — 6 5 4 3 2 1

For my family—

without whom I'd be unfashionably sane.

"...the story of any one of us is in some measure the story of us all."

—Frederick Buechner
The Sacred Journey

The Beginning

THE TROUBLE WITH PHINEAS Michael Button began the moment she was born. She had the expected two ears, two eyes, one nose, and dimpled cheeks, but in her father's mind there was a problem. He had twelve children, daughters all, and was convinced that number thirteen would be his long-awaited son. So on the twenty-fifth of September, 1755, when he drew another baby girl from the womb of his long-suffering wife, he declared the discovery of an unacceptable mistake. He held up the little squirmer by a leg and inspected it with great suspicion, turning it first one way and then another as if peering at the child from differing angles might produce a change in its gender.

After a long and uncomfortable spell of dangling the child by a leg and harrumphing in displeasure, he handed it over to his wife and asked, "What's that, then?"

"What is it? What *is* it?" Matilda-Mae Button screamed at him.

"Twelve of them you had already and still not got it right. We ain't keeping this one." He nodded, walked away, and scarcely gave the child another thought for more than twenty years.

To her meager credit, Matilda-Mae Button didn't give up quite so easily as her husband. She named the child after its father, hoping she could trick him into thinking she'd fixed it. And then she went so far as to whisper in the child's ear tales of what a good boy she was and lies of what a fine man she'd grow to be. It was a conspiracy of conviction she visited upon her daughter in hopes of talking her newborn child out of the way she'd been made in the womb. Raising twelve other daughters was trouble enough, though, and trying to fool number thirteen into a son eventually grew tiresome.

Upon the morning of the seventh day of her life, Phineas Michael Button crossed the Savannah River into the Georgia colony. She was swaddled tightly and tucked deep into the arms of one of her twelve sisters, who were, in turn, tucked into the back of a covered wagon. In the front seat, her parents argued in whispers and hushed exclamations. They'd arrived in the town of Ebenezer and the discovery of an orphanage had generated a decisive mood in their father and a quarrelsome one in their mother. Many words flew in both directions between the two, but it will suffice to say that when the wagon clattered its way out of Ebenezer that morning, the orphanage had gained a child and the wagon had lost one. The Buttons left behind a bundle of red curls and unwanted promise, and Matilda-Mae uttered a silent prayer that her thirteenth baby girl would somehow know a full life in spite of her unkind beginnings.

The Baab sisters of the Ebenezer orphanage were ready and willing to answer that prayer and see it through, but time has a way of leading a person along a crooked path. Sometimes the path is hard to hold to and people fall off along the way. They curse the road for its steep grades and muddy ruts and settle themselves in hinterlands of thorn and sorrow, never knowing or dreaming that the road meant all along to lead them home. Some call that road a tragedy and lose themselves along it. Others, those that see it home, call it an adventure.

PART I

FOUNDATIONS

Chapter I

"G IVE HIM A WHOP on the head!"

Danny Shoeman and John Cooper were up to no good. Again. Nine-year-old Owen Sheffield was cornered behind the stable, out of breath, and whimpering in the path of the beating he seemed certain to catch in the form of a "whop on the head." To a boy like Owen—frail, timid, and endlessly awkward—a confrontation with two menacing sixteen-year-olds was nothing less than a sign of the apocalypse, the end of the world, the coming of a reign of tyrant gods bent on his destruction.

Luckily for Owen, Fin Button was within earshot and this was just the sort of trouble she hoped for when she crawled out of bed each morning. She peeked around the corner of the stable and her lip curled into a grin. Seventeen years at an orphanage will teach a person either to get along very well with all manner of people or to fight like a heathen. Fin had never been one to get along, so boys like Danny and John had taught her how to fight. Even as a small child, Fin was more likely to run with the boys than play dolls with the girls, and she learned all manner of indecent behavior in their company—cussing, for instance, and climbing and spitting and how to throw her fists and make her punches count. It was just horseplay at first, but eventually there were real fights, usually over disrespect shown to one's mother. For orphans, the esteem of one's mother was elevated to something approaching sainthood and the hope of a parent's good intentions was the holiest thing a child could possess. As such, the tainting of it caused all manner of boyish violence.

In her younger days, Fin lost her share of fights and slunk around the orphanage with plenty of black eyes, fat lips, and bloodied noses, but she didn't take well to losing. Once it was apparent to her that the boys had weight and power as their advantages, she claimed speed and surprise as hers. In time she learned that whoever threw the first punch usually won the fight, and she hadn't lost one since. The boys learned that getting cross with Fin Button was a sure way to invite a fist in the eye, and by the time she was sixteen most people avoided her like they would an angry hornet's nest.

"What you think, John? Should we beat him, whip him, or pound him?" said Danny.

Owen Sheffield opened his mouth to protest his doom but was so alarmed that he failed to form even a comprehensible word and only managed to gurgle. Then he tried to faint his way out of the predicament. He'd heard playing dead was a sure way to escape bear attacks, so he rolled up his eyes, shuddered, and went limp.

Danny and John broke into a fit of laughter. It was this laughter that disguised the sound of Fin Button walking up behind them; it was also this laughter that turned Fin's face red with anger and wound her arms tight, ready to throw. The laughter stopped abruptly when she spoke.

"I got a whop for the both of you," she said. Before Danny Shoeman could turn around to see who was speaking, he had an earful of knuckle and a gut full of Fin's dirty, skinned knee. Surprise and speed. She left him lying in the dirt, sucking for wind, and turned on John Cooper, who quickly appraised the situation and decided that running was his best option. Fin didn't allow it. She shot out her hand and jerked him by the ear so hard she nearly snatched it clean off.

"Ow, ow, ow, ow . . ." said John as he bent around and followed his ear back toward Fin, and then, "Oof!" as she kicked his legs out from under him and he flopped to the ground next to Danny.

After that the three of them went to yelping, scratching, and biting like dogs in a pit. Owen Sheffield cowered out of the way. At first he was too afraid to do anything but keep clear and be thankful Fin had come to his rescue, but soon he gave up his cowering and began to cheer for her. "Stick him again, Fin!" he shouted and, "Look out behind!" And when he saw that Fin was in danger of letting the boys get the best of her, he jumped in among them and latched himself fast to John Cooper's left leg until Fin knocked him cold in the dust and could turn her full attention to putting Danny down.

To the smaller children, Fin was a legendary figure. She was their caretaker, their guardian, their savior. When the young men her age, her friends at play in earlier years, began to speak in deeper voices and fuss about their sprouting beards, they saw she wasn't really one of them and shunned her. The girls wanted little to do with Fin either, so stuck between the children and being alone, Fin took the younger generation on as her flock. She would tolerate no mistreatment of the younger orphans by the likes of Danny Shoeman and John Cooper.

It didn't take long for Sister Hilde to follow her nose to the commotion. Once Hilde detected the outbreak of a fight within her realm, she descended on it like bird of prey. She flew across the courtyard and seized hold of Danny Shoeman's arm as it travelled through the air toward Fin's head.

"Cease! Cease this very moment!" Sister Hilde ordered. There was a brief moment of silence in which all the involved parties did, in fact, cease all movement and stood perfectly still in contemplation of each other. But then, as if upon some unseen cue, each of them burst into shouts of accusation and denial. Sister Hilde's nose quivered in anger. "Silence! Explain this madness, Danny Shoeman!"

"It wasn't my fault, Sister Hilde. She started it!" said Danny, pointing at Fin.

Fin feigned shock.

"They was picking on Owen and was going to knot him up. I wasn't going to stand and just watch," explained Fin.

Sister Hilde had scarcely even noticed John lying on the ground. When he groaned and wiped his bloodied nose with the back of his hand, she snapped her fingers and ordered him up. "John Cooper, get up from there this instant," she said as if the discovery of a boy awakening in the dirt at her feet were a perfectly natural, although unsatisfactory, occurrence. She rounded back on Danny, "Do you expect me to believe that Phinea started this fight, Danny Shoeman?" Fin smiled like an imp. "You should be ashamed of yourself. Go get cleaned up, it's nearly time for dinner."

"But—" he protested, still pointing at Fin.

"Enough!" Sister Hilde aimed a bony finger at the dorm and Danny sulked off.

"You, Miss Button," she considered Fin for a moment, "are a shameful and continual disappointment. Is this how a young woman behaves? You're seventeen years old and look at you! You're a monster, you filthy child."

Fin bristled and clenched her fists. Sister Hilde knew very well that Fin was no child. She used the word like a weapon. Hilde scowled down her nose and shooed Fin away in disgust. "Get yourself ready for dinner." She turned to appraise Owen Sheffield. "Are you hurt, child?"

"No ma'am."

"Then what are you waiting for? Go!"

Sister Hilde Baab was the slight old crone who held the day-to-day run of the orphanage firmly in her grip and sent orphans running for cover when she'd flick her gaze their way. Years before, when Sister Hilde first came upon the newborn Phineas Michael Button, she made up her mind that a girl with a man's name wasn't proper and lopped off the *s*, leaving naught but Phinea behind (she was similarly dismayed when the children shortened "Phinea" to "Fin"). Despite an unfriendly demeanor and shrewd tongue, Sister Hilde's nose was her deadliest weapon. Same as the rest of her, it was long, pointed, and gnarled like an old tree, striking out first in one direction, then shifting midstride to head in quite another, then finally changing its mind again and heading back the way it had gone to begin with. When she was irritated, it twitched back and forth and turned red. When she was mad, it dove down and depressed her nostrils, making them flare out like crab apples. Children claimed she could even point with it, and the last thing a child wanted was to look up and find Sister Hilde's nose pointing at him. Wherever Hilde was, somewhere else was always a better place to be.

A monster and a filthy child. Not a suitable description as far as Fin was concerned and yet more accurate than she wanted to admit. The older she got the clearer it became that she wasn't what people expected of a young woman. Whenever Sister Hilde accused her of not acting her age, she knew exactly what she meant, yet she refused to surrender her own ways to Hilde's all-encompassing authority. In the seventeen years since she was abandoned at the orphan house, Fin had grown into a freckled mess of red hair, spindly limbs, and boyish features. Although Sister Carmaline often whispered that a pretty face might lurk beneath the smudges of dirt and tangled hair, Fin didn't care to find out. She was one of the boys, and the sisters' insistence that she was nearly a grown woman wasn't about to change that.

In defiance of her orders to wash up, Fin snuck through the front door of the chapel and climbed the ladder to the tower. Bells for calling the Lord's worship were too costly for the small town, and the tower was empty save nesting birds, cobwebs, and deep shadowy corners in which to sulk, pout, or hide. Fin considered it her domain.

She settled into the cleft of the bell tower and considered swatting the dirt off her clothes. She decided against it, solely for Sister Hilde's sake, and looked out over the walls. The vast pine and oak forests of southern Georgia spread out around her, broken only by the meandering line of the Savannah River. Somewhere to the east, she imagined, it met the Atlantic, but she'd never been to the sea and the imagining was all she had. The smell of dinner was on the air and the sun was setting behind her. The long shadow of the bell tower stretched out across the walls and reached beyond the boundaries of the orphanage. Fin closed her eyes and let part of herself go with it.

Chapter II

"FIN!" CALLED A VOICE from below.

She ignored it.

The voice called again and a shadowed figure stepped into the courtyard. Fin raised two fingers to her mouth and whistled. Peter LaMee looked up and followed the sound. Like his form crossing the courtyard, Peter was vague and difficult to define. He held his words close and was content with his silence in a way uncommon to a boy of seventeen. While Fin always had an opinion and a need to voice it, Peter was a quiet companion, a good listener. They were two sides of a coin—one a stark profile and the other an obscure symbol of the minter's affiliation. She gave another short whistle and Peter LaMee clambered up the ladder into the tower.

"Sister Hilde is going to skin you," he said.

"I've had it with her and her waggling nose." Fin didn't move. She maintained her solemn consideration of the countryside. "I'm not hungry."

"She won't let us eat till we're all at the table. You know that." Fin knew. That was precisely the point. Fin's lips lifted into the slightest grin as she pictured Sister Hilde sitting at the table fuming over her whereabouts. But it wasn't fair to the rest of those waiting to eat, and she knew that too.

"Fine." Fin sighed with irritation. "Let's go."

Inside the dining hall the sisters, Brother Bartimaeus, and twenty-four orphans stared hungrily at two platters piled high with roasted pork and a kettle of stewed carrots. When Fin moseyed in and made her way to her seat, she was pleasantly satisfied by the distinct twitch of irritation in Sister Hilde's nose.

"Miss Button, thank you for joining us," said Hilde. "You will see me after the meal. Let us pray."

For the next twenty minutes the room was full of the *smack-smack* and the *mm-hmm* of well-enjoyed food. Brother Bartimaeus ate quietly with a grin on his face while Sister Hilde paid more attention to the orphans' table etiquette than to her own plate. Sister Carmaline, on the other hand, ate every bite as if she feared it might be her last.

Carmaline Baab, Hilde's elder sister and the official headmistress of the Ebenezer Orphan House, was a terrifically fat woman who somehow managed to stay plump even during lean years when others starved. She didn't glutton the food (that anyone ever saw); people just figured the Lord himself had set her ample dimensions and all the failed harvests and dysentery in the colony wouldn't lighten her. Her cheeks were as rosy as new-picked apples, and the chubbiness of her face made them bunch up against her eyes so that she looked to be forever squinting out at a world that was too bright. Everywhere she went she bobbled along humming hymns while orphans scurried here and there trying not to ogle at the vastness of her.

When the sounds of dinner died down, Sister Carmaline stood (a state confirmed by the slight vertical elongation of her orb-like physique) and waited for the room to quiet. Fin jabbed Peter with her elbow and rolled her eyes. Carmaline always had a speech.

"Thank you for your attention, children. And thank you, Brother Bartimaeus, for another heavenly dinner." Nodding heads and smiling faces concurred. "Before we adjourn to our beds for the evening, I wish to discuss a few matters."

Several orphans rolled their eyes and were each dutifully ignored by Carmaline.

"I'm sure you took note of the elderly gentleman about the yard earlier today with Sister Hilde and myself. He was, as some of you may know, Brother Bolzius, the mayor of Ebenezer, and he was most impressed with the level of order and cleanliness we demand. In fact, he was impressed enough to make a small proposition on the behalf of the town."

At this, several napping boys sat up to take closer notice of the goings-on.

"Mr. Bolzius has seen fit to provide the town with a new chapel and wishes to build it here on our grounds."

This impressed almost no one.

"He will provide all the necessary materials, and the architect, Mr. Thom Hickory, will oversee construction. However, a detail of able young men chosen from our orphanage will be the chief laborers. You'll all do well to understand that such work may one day lead to an apprenticeship, and that to a fruitful life beyond our walls."

The eyes of every boy in the room widened with excitement—as did Fin's. Hands shot up around the table and waved furiously.

"Order! Hush! Hands down!" snapped Sister Hilde.

"Sister Hilde and I will consider whom to send to Mr. Hickory in the coming days, so it would behoove the lot of you to be on your best behavior." She paused to let that sink in, then continued, "Now to the next matter of business. Brother Bartimaeus," she nodded his way, "has requested that we provide him an assistant. Though he denies it, I continually assure him that he is getting old."

Bartimaeus grumbled something unintelligible in his defense.

"Having someone around to help with the daily preparations of food and cleanup after meals will be a relief for his weary bones," explained Carmaline.

This not only impressed no one, it seemed to terrify everyone. Children shrank back into the shadows, desperate not to draw any attention that might warrant their being chosen. A doom of endless dishwashing and pot scrubbing was a horror thought to be visited only upon children in the lowest reaches of hell.

"We will consider this appointment for the next few days, so I once again suggest that you behave to impress. You are dismissed to evening chores, and I will see you all in the morning."

Carmaline bobbled out the door and Hilde took command of the room. "Miss Button will to tend to the dishes this evening."

Fin knew it was coming and didn't look surprised, though she did afford Sister Hilde the appropriate glare.

"The rest of you, off to your chores. I want horses fed, water hauled, and floors swept within the hour. Dismissed!" Hilde clapped her hands together and a flurry of bodies whisked dishes to the cleaning trough and left Fin staring at a mound of scrubbing to be done.

"A word, Miss Button," said Hilde when the hall was emptied.

Fin clenched her teeth and turned with her eyebrows stuck up.

Hilde ignored Fin's obvious irritation. "You'll do well to learn a thing or two while you attend the dishes. No man will have you as a wife the way you are. The sooner you learn your place and learn your work, the sooner you'll be married off and away. Mind me, Miss Button. It is the way of the world."

Fin's inclination was to teach Hilde a thing or two about the world by way of a sharp cuss and a right hook. But she bit her tongue and kept her hands.

"Yes, ma'am," said Fin with a sarcastic smirk that set Hilde's nose aquiver. Hilde narrowed her eyes briefly before turning on her toe and marching out of the dining hall with a sniff.

When Hilde was out of sight, Peter stuck his head through the door.

"Want some help?" he said.

"No, if she catches you helping she'll give me more work. I'll see you in the morning."

She gave him a crooked smile and rolled up her sleeves as he walked out the door. She didn't mind the chore so much. At least it was quiet.

Building a new chapel sounded like more fun than she'd had all year. Working with her hands and being out in the sun with the boys—that was where she belonged, not sitting in sewing class with the girls where the sisters would have her. Who wanted to sit around knitting blankets and spinning yarn when you could be outside building a new chapel?

"At it again, eh, missy?" She jumped at the sound of a voice from behind her.

"Good Lord, Bartimaeus! You nearly scared me to death."

He chuckled in his breathy, creaking way as he rolled up his sleeves and began drying dishes as Fin got them clean. He was tall and wiry and bent like a fishhook as his shoulders bowed down under the weight of his years. Whatever hair he had in youth had weathered to silver and long since ceased to cover his head in any meaningful way. Now it just hung on above his ears like moss clung to an old oak. His sun-darkened skin covered him like aged leather and was parted everywhere by creases that gave the impression someone had drawn a map on his hide; Fin wondered if there might be buried treasure to find if she studied him long enough. His arms and hands seemed to bear more scars and fading tattoos than original material, but for all his battered coarseness, his way was smooth as water. When he spoke, his voice seeped out like the groan of a ship's timbers.

"What did you think of Sister Carmaline's speech?" he asked. "Could be good work for one that's willin'." He threw his towel onto his shoulder and placed the dried dishes into the cupboard.

Fin shrugged. "At least there will be something to show for it. I haul water from the well fifteen times a day, I sweep floors, wash linens, and feed pigs, and for what? So I can get up and do it all over again tomorrow?" Fin had a mind to spit at something, but didn't. "But this? This has results."

"Aye, cookin's got results you can taste! It's nice to see the fruit of your labor. Never tire of it," he said. "Nothin' does me so good as the table rounded about with mouths at the feast." He wiped his face with the towel and laughed to himself. "You see that Danny Shoeman tonight? Boy can jabber away like a bothered chicken but he shut it up quick when the pork hit the plate, cain't he?" He looked at Fin and lowered an eyebrow at her. "There's some power in a pig when it's roasted up right, missy. Power, see here?" Then his face opened up into a smile and he smacked his lips.

"I was talking about the chapel," Fin said flatly.

Bartimaeus smacked his lips once more then wrinkled up his face and frowned at the dish he was holding. "Oh, hmm. 'Course you were." He returned to drying the dishes.

Fin shifted back and forth on her feet in the awkward silence. She'd managed to embarrass the old cook. She felt she ought to make it good somehow but was almost as out of practice at apology and tact as she was at the spinning wheel.

"You run along now," he said. "I'll finish this up, and if Sister Hilde bitches hellfire about you being done so soon, you tell her to come deal with me. Go on." Bartimaeus waggled his arm at her. She hesitated a moment but decided not to give him a chance to change his mind.

THE NEXT DAY THE boys at the orphanage turned on their charms for the sisters. Changes from the daily routine didn't come nearly often enough to suit most of them, and the prospect of building a new chapel set even the most mischievous boy straight as an arrow. Danny Shoeman came to breakfast in his Sunday best—not that it was significantly better than his Monday worst. Elroy Snell sat next to Sister Hilde and served her plate with the greasiest grin he could muster; he even cleared her place and offered to wash the morning dishes. Some argued that the sisters schemed up the entire situation just to see what sort of behavior the orphans were capable of when they put their minds to it.

All this was preposterous to Fin. From where she sat, milking a cow, she saw boys all over the courtyard being overly courteous and working three times harder whenever Sister Hilde walked by. It made her sick. When she spied even Peter going out of his way to smile at Sister Hilde, she'd had all she could stomach. She picked up the nearest hard object—a horseshoe— and lobbed it at him in irritation. It barely missed him, and Peter's smile turned down into a grimace.

"What was that for?" he demanded.

"You know bloody well what it was for, Peter LaMee. You've never in your years smiled at that woman, and now you're selling your smiles for a few nails and a hammer. You should be ashamed, acting like the rest of these buggers."

"Can't hurt to try," said Peter with a mystified shrug.

"If that's what it takes, you can count me in for another summer's worth of hauling water, milking cows, and spinning silk. I'm not going to prance around here like a grinning idiot, and it'll be a cold day in August before I turn a smile at that old bat." She was milking the cow so hard that Peter winced for fear she might pull a teat right off.

Around the corner came Sister Hilde. As she passed, Fin gave a good, sharp yank on the teat in her hand. The cow groaned and kicked a hind leg out, narrowly missing Hilde. Hilde's nose shot up and quivered directly at Fin.

"Miss Button, I suggest you be more careful or you'll have more than dishes to wash this evening." Her nose attempted to calm itself as she spoke. "Mr. LaMee, I hardly think Miss Button needs you here to distract her."

"Yes, ma'am," said Peter and hurried away out of sight.

Hilde put her hand on Fin's shoulder and leaned down. Fin's eyes transfixed on Hilde's quivering spike of a nose, and she devoted all her attention to making sure she didn't laugh.

"Miss Button, I hope you don't have any convoluted notions of going to work on that new chapel. Stone and wood work is no place for a young woman, even one so coarse as yourself." Fin flashed her eyes at Hilde, all thought of laughter now gone. Before she could protest, Hilde raised a finger in warning. "Ah-ah, I'll hear none of it." For a moment, Hilde looked almost happy, and then she straightened up and stalked off around the corner of the stable.

Fin gritted her teeth and glared at the cow. "Next time kick her right in the chin, won't you?" she said. The cow swished its tail.

Hilde seemed to hate everyone, but she held out a special place in her dark heart for Fin. It would be trouble enough convincing people she could do a man's work, and Sister Hilde intended to make sure she never got the chance.

Fin leapt up and ran to the chapel. She flung open the door and climbed the ladder into the bell tower. No one could see her here. It was the one place she felt was her own. The sisters were too old or too large to make the climb, and the other children knew it was against the rules.

The empty bell tower lifted her above the walls. A boundless green country rolled out before her, a world free of sisters and rules, a world where she imagined she could do as she pleased and be who she was and no one could tell her how to dress or talk or act. How she might ever enter that world and make it her own was a problem she hadn't yet solved.

Chapter III

Fin spent the following week in a mischievous pout, a mood that manifested itself in a number of misfortunes befalling Sister Hilde. On Tuesday morning, Hilde discovered her shoes mysteriously filled with cow dung. She shrieked in anger and threw open the closet to fetch her second pair and shrieked again, finding them treated the same. Despite the intense scouring she gave her footwear before breakfast, she was accompanied the rest of the day by the odor of fresh manure—not to mention the squish of wet shoe.

On Wednesday, curious misfortune struck again when the hogs escaped their pen and ran amok, soiling the freshly hung linens, pulling many of them down and dragging them about the yard. Hilde stood amid this porcine calamity shrieking demands like a general and waving her nose at any orphan in sight until the riotous pigs knocked her legs from beneath her. She landed squarely on her rump and came snout to snout with a great, swarthy hog that nuzzled at her cheek and licked her shuddering nose. Hilde wrestled the beast to the ground and dragged it back to the pen in a feat of determination and anger that quite impressed the on-looking orphans.

At other times during Fin's pout, acorns, pecans, and cypress balls fell with astonishing accuracy to connect with the top of Sister Hilde's head. For reasons unexplainable by orphans, these only seemed to fall when Hilde wandered near the front of the chapel and directly under the bell tower. It was also in odd coincidence that Fin managed to be out of eyeshot whenever any such malfeasance occurred. Sister Hilde could find no proof of any culprit however, and Fin, though primely suspected, stayed safely out of the cook pot. Such small but total victories gradually succeeded in lifting Fin out of her pout and into more of a satisfied sulk.

Peter tried to cheer her spirits, but Fin used his attempts as opportunities to induce him to join her plots against Sister Hilde. It was Peter who kept lookout while Fin stuffed Hilde's shoes with cow-pie and loosed the hogs, and it was Peter who lured Hilde into the target area while Fin lobbed her missiles from the bell tower.

On Friday after evening chores, Fin stepped out of the dining hall with a scandalous glint in her eye. She slipped across the courtyard, keeping a sharp look around to see that Hilde wasn't watching and darted into the barn. She emerged moments later carrying a rusty claw hammer and a handsaw, and then dashed back across the yard to hide in the shadows under the awning of the chapel door.

In the dusk, amid the chirping of insects and the clamor of twenty-five orphans readying themselves for bed, there came the less natural sound of metal scraping on wood. While the lamps of the orphan house were being snuffed, Peter stepped outside the door and looked around. The sound of metal on wood came again and he cocked his head to one side, listening, before stepping away from the door and walking toward the chapel.

"What are you doing?"

Fin jumped and held the hammer up as if she was ready to throw it. She was kneeling in the grass beside the front door of the chapel and had managed to work the first of the three front steps loose. When she realized it was only Peter, she smiled and motioned for him to be quiet.

"This is going to be the best. If I take off the steps and saw through them a bit from the bottom, then I can put them back on and the next person that tries to climb up, they'll snap and fall right through and I've got a whole pot full of hogslop hidden behind the dining hall so I can pour it underneath, so when Hilde goes in for prayers before breakfast . . . it's going to be great."

Fin barely suppressed a cackle as she went back to prying the second step up with the hammer. "How'd you know I was out here?" she added as she rocked the hammer back and forth.

"Heard Delly Martin upstairs complaining that everyone was in bed but you. Hilde will be out looking any minute."

"That little girl needs a lesson in keeping her mouth clapped shut."

"This is a bad idea, Fin." Peter was shaking his head.

"I'm full of bad ideas."

Peter knelt down. He reached out and put his hand on the hammer to stop her.

"Have you thought that someone could get hurt? Hilde's not the only one that says prayers before breakfast. What if Carmaline walks into this? What if it's Owen?"

Fin's shoulders slumped. She sat still and contemplative for a moment then wrenched the hammer away from Peter and continued her work. "You telling me what to do now, Peter? Thought that was Hilde's job."

"You know I'm not. But I'm worried."

Fin stopped working and snapped her head up to look at Peter. "You're worried? What have you got to worry over? You'll find an apprenticeship soon, or go to work on a farm, or join the army, and you'll be out of here and away from Hilde and her chores and rules, and her ever-waggling tongue. But what about me, Peter?" Fin shrugged at him.

Peter didn't answer.

"What's going to happen to me? I'm seventeen, but I'm not like the other girls—you know that. 'It's a matter of a man and a marriage,' isn't that what Carmaline tells all the girls? All they want is to get married off and spend the rest of their days sitting in skirts and mending holes in a husband's pants. I don't know how to want that, Peter."

"So what do you want?"

Fin didn't answer and instead continued tearing up the step. Peter sat down beside her. He reached for the hammer once more but Fin pulled back. Peter didn't withdraw. She hesitated and ground her teeth and then gave the hammer over and crossed her arms.

"I don't need looking after, you know?" said Fin.

"'Course you don't," said Peter. Fin could see his smile in the dark and gave him hers in return. Then she shook her head.

"I suppose this was a pretty terrible idea, huh?"

"The worst."

They broke into laughter and tried to muffle their amusement in the darkness but the sound may as well have been a siren to Hilde's ears. She followed the commotion to its source and set her bony hands upon her hips, looming over Peter and Fin for some time before either saw she was there. When she spoke, both of them lurched upright and wide-eyed.

"Do you care to offer an explanation for this, Mr. LaMee?" said Hilde.

Fin opened her mouth to claim her part but Peter elbowed her in the ribs and lifted the hammer up so Hilde could see it.

"Sorry, Sister Hilde. I meant to tell you earlier," said Peter. "I noticed the step boards were loose and wanted to nail them back down before someone got hurt. Fin was just helping me."

Hilde narrowed her eyes at the both of them. Her nosed ticked from side to side as she considered Peter's explanation. Before she could make any judgement Peter bent down and hammered the step back into place while Fin nudged the saw out of sight with her foot.

"There. All done," said Peter. He stepped up onto the step and tried it with his weight.

Fin could hear Hilde's breath whistling in her flared nostrils as she considered the scene.

"To bed. The both of you, before I choose to see more than darkness allows."

Neither argued.

ON SUNDAY, SISTER CARMALINE declared that an announcement would be made at breakfast. She didn't say what the announcement might be, but everyone was sure the topic was the selection of the chapel detail. Boys laid odds on who might make the list and bet slingshots, knives, and the odd bear's tooth. John Cooper, Danny Shoeman, and Peter LaMee were heavily favored.

Breakfast all but disappeared as soon as Brother Bartimaeus laid it on the table. The excitement of the day dictated that this was a meal to be quickly done with and swept aside. It would not do to bother tasting it as it went down, not when there were more important matters to be gotten around to.

Sister Carmaline, of course, held no such anxiety. She enjoyed each bite of her bacon, eggs, two biscuits, and an orange just as thoroughly as ever. The orphans, having long since dispatched their food, wrung their hands and stared at Carmaline in silence. By the time she finished and called the room to attention, they were on the edge of bursting.

"Children, I am happy to announce that Reverend George Whitefield is to be our guest today and will preach our service." Her face lit up as she passed the news. "Reverend Whitefield is a great man and his patronage is an immeasurable blessing. I expect all of you to be dressed properly and to have your finest behavior on display. Tomorrow we shall make our choices for the chapel detail—and for Brother Bartimaeus's assistant. I assure you that anyone causing an embarrassment today will certainly find dismay come tomorrow. Am I understood?"

Heads nodded and "yes ma'ams" answered.

"Good. Dismissed!"

Reverend Whitefield had been instrumental in the finances of the orphan house and he visited whenever he was in the colonies. He always tended to be going on about God choosing people and folks being predestined for such and such, but Fin never cared much for sermons, and his talk about people not having a say in their own lives was more than enough to make her wrinkle up her nose at the whole affair. If there was anything she couldn't stand, it was other people telling her what to do—even if other people happened to be the Lord.

Sister Carmaline, on the other hand, claimed that Reverend Whitefield was the greatest Christian of the age, and if the crowd at the orphanage that morning was any indication, most of Georgia agreed. Folks began arriving soon after breakfast, and within the hour the entire courtyard was packed.

The orphans busied themselves putting on their best clothes, and Fin was as anxious as the rest to get outside and join the excitement. She and the sisters parted ways, however, on the meaning of "best clothes." To Fin it meant nothing more than her usual trousers, shirt, and bare feet. To the sisters, it meant the frilly blue dress they forced her into whenever they wanted to impress people. Fin loathed it.

After a healthy amount of glaring at the offending garment, her desire to join the excitement of the crowd outside won her over and she put it on with a grumble. She felt preposterous. The way the other girls were forever brushing things, and powdering things, and primping things utterly confounded her. On occasion she did find herself having the merest concern for her appearance when Peter was around, but she tried her best to ignore the feeling and usually succeeded quite well. The matter of the dress, however, brought it to her mind and she quietly wondered what he would think of it. Then she cursed herself for the thought and promised not think such foolishness again. She jabbed a wretched bonnet onto her head and ran out the door.

The courtyard was choked with people of all shapes, sizes, and smells. Plumped and powdered women in hoopskirts and endless petticoats stared down their noses at lesser-dressed folk, while black-coated gentlemen calmly batted away farmers, smiths, and anyone else they suspected might be untidy or of lowly account. These were in the minority, however, as most of the crowd were plainly dressed in various shades of brown and were smiling, shaking hands, and chatting away with country-folk they hadn't seen since glory-knew-when. Fin pushed her way through them toward the chapel trying in vain not to be seen in the dress.

At last, she gained the chapel doors and slipped inside to find her usual spot. Peter was already there, dressed in a black suit. She plopped down beside him and he eyed her up and down.

"Nice dress, Fi—" A sharp elbow in the side shut him up. He winced and fretted under his breath, but on the subject of the dress, he wisely chose to stay silent.

People continued to pack into the chapel until children were standing on the benches just to see the podium. The windows were open, and the crowd outside crammed their faces through to get a glimpse of the goings-on. Fin half expected someone to tear the roof open and lower down a cripple.

After a good deal of grunting and grumbling in the crowd as Sister Carmaline plowed through, she popped out at the front and stepped to the podium.

"Good morning, brothers and sisters in Christ," she said, beaming with a hostess's pride. "I am honored to welcome the esteemed Reverend George Whitefield back to Ebenezer today." An eruption of claps, whistles, and amens peppered the air before she could continue. "Before Reverend Whitefield delivers us the Word, I'm pleased to welcome the choir from the Bethesda Church in Savannah to bless us with song."

She removed herself to the side and a double file of men and women clothed in black robes with wide white collars took to the stage. The choir director stepped to the front of the assembly and raised his baton. There was a moment's pause and the first notes began. The sound that came from the choir was unlike anything Fin had ever heard. She'd never cared for Sister Carmaline's vespers, much less her singing, but as the weight of the choir's hymn rolled over her, she felt small and exhilarated like a leaf caught in a summer wind.

The gathered crowd joined the choir. Men's thundering tones rumbled forth while the soft voices of women and children soared bright and clear. The sound was tremendous and Fin feared for a moment that it might bring down the chapel. It ended, and for what seemed a long time, there was no sound at all.

Then from somewhere outside, a commotion erupted. The crowd chattered and everyone looked around in search of the cause. Sister Carmaline bounced forward and called the chapel to order but few heeded her. The murmurs of the crowd indicated that someone was on the roof of the dining hall. Fin and Peter pushed their way toward the door, and Sister Carmaline was still trying to call order to the service when they broke free of the chapel doorway and plunged into a sea of people that clogged the whole of the courtyard. People sat aloft in the trees and on top of the fences and filled every open space. On the roof of the dining hall Fin spied an elderly man with silvery hair and black, flowing robes.

"My friends! I deem the chapel is too small to house the many ears that have come. The Words of Life are not uttered for those that got here first, rather they are best fallen on ears that have never before come at all." It was Reverend Whitefield.

He began his exhortation and his voice carried across the crowd as if he were speaking to them each alone rather than to a multitude. He didn't endeavor to speak to the church-going so much as to the drunken and tattered on the edges of the crowd, whose dirty faces streaked clean by rivulets of tears gave testimony of their gravest sins.

"I am the chiefest of sinners," said the Reverend as he closed, "and the least of all saints. I want to be converted from a thousand things, and from ten thousand more. Lord God, confirm me. Let neither spark nor flame of hell warm the feet of a man the Lord God has chosen. Before the sun was set in the sky, before we were formed in the womb, he ordained the calling of the faithful. Come now whom he calls and be born a new creature. Lord God, *revive!*"

In droves, people went to answer his call, down to the Savannah River to let baptism carry away their sin. Fin and Peter went, too, and Reverend Whitefield himself plunged them beneath the cleansing flow.

Fin watched Peter come up from the water. His face was radiant, yet she felt she saw him grow apart from her in some way. It seemed he was standing a step more distant than he had been only a moment ago. She reached her hand out to him, almost dizzy with the illusion of distance. He took her in a hug, but when he let her go she was stiff and withdrawn.

"Fin?"

She tried to manage a smile.

"What's wrong?" said Peter.

"He said God chooses us before we're born."

Peter wrinkled his brow.

Fin looked away. "Just like my parents. They wanted a boy. They didn't want me. What if he doesn't want me either?"

She walked away and pushed Peter's attempts to comfort her aside. By the time she reached the dormitory she was already pulling off the dress.

CHAPTER IV

SISTER CARMALINE PLACED HER fork neatly onto the empty plate before her and wrestled her bulk out of her chair to call the room to attention. Rumor had it that a list of names for the chapel detail was under Sister Hilde's watchful protection. The room was quiet before Carmaline could finish asking it to be so. Everyone was anxious to have the news. Everyone except Fin.

"We have made our choices carefully in light of the hard work and responsibility required and have selected five of you to assist Mr. Hickory. Take care to understand that your work for Mr. Hickory is in *addition* to your usual duties and chores." Carmaline turned and nodded to her sister. "Sister Hilde, if you please."

Hilde stood and produced a list from her apron. She cleared her throat and began to read. "Danny Shoeman, Lachlan McEwen." At the proclamation of each name, murmurs of assent and dissent rose and fell. "Hans Richter, Thom Nodger"—the rest of the boys in the room held their breath— "and Peter LaMee."

Peter grinned at Fin and she half-smiled back at him. She knew Hilde would have her way, knew better than to entertain the thought of being chosen, but some treacherous depth inside her held out hope of things known better and betrayed her to disappointment.

"Mr. Hickory tells me that from time to time additional assistance will be needed. That assistance will, of course, be chosen from whoever is most willing and deserved of special privilege." The list disappeared back into the folds of Hilde's apron, and she took her seat. Fin's spirits rose at the promise that she might still get the chance to go to work as a "special privilege," but she quickly squashed them back down.

Sister Carmaline rose again and waited for silence. "You five may present yourself to my chamber after lunch to be introduced to Mr. Hickory. Is there anything else to be attended to this morning?" she looked around the room. Brother Bartimaeus cleared his throat at Carmaline. "Ah yes, Miss Phinea Button, you will report to the kitchen immediately following dismissal to attend to your new duties."

Murmurs, jeers, and sounds of sympathy bubbled around the room. Fin only stared at her plate in silence. Peter tried to wrap a consoling arm around her shoulder, but she pushed him away.

Sister Carmaline excused herself while Hilde ordered the children to chores. Fin sat at her place as, one by one, the other children exited. Peter was the last to leave her. Of course, he would be. Able to find no words that might be of help, he gave up and left her staring.

She raised her eyes when the room was quiet, thinking it empty. Brother Bartimaeus was sitting across the table looking at her.

"You'd rather be out with the boys, eh, missy?"

Her brow wrinkled a little more.

"But from where I'm sittin' it looks like I got me a fine, strong, and able set of arms and legs to help me out. Could even say my work just got lopped in half. Now that's somethin' worth grinnin' about, see here?" He grinned at her, but she refused to unwrinkle her face. "What you say we get this place cleaned up so we can have some fun?"

Fin was determined not to like any part of the situation, but she did her best to avoid outright meanness and gave herself over to cleaning up the dining hall as best she could. Washing dishes was a task she was certainly no stranger to, and they worked at it in silence. Fin scrubbed and Bartimaeus dried. By the time they were finished, Fin was soaked from the sloshing water and feeling even more miserable then when she started. Without a word, she snatched a broom from the corner and began sweeping out the room. Bartimaeus crossed his arms and leaned himself against the kitchen doorway to consider her while she worked. She glanced at him repeatedly, wondering why he was just standing there, but all he did was frown back. Finally, being watched so closely had worked on her long enough, and she stopped, leaned the broom against the table, crossed her arms in mockery of him, and glared.

"What?" she demanded.

"Stow that broom and come in the galley, or kitchen, as old Hilde would say." He winked at her then turned and walked out of sight into the kitchen. She snatched the broom up and muttered under her breath as she put it away.

"Somethin' I want to show you," he said. He turned around and motioned to the wall, spreading his arms out wide as if he were welcoming it. It was covered in shelves from the floor to the rafters and every one was filled with tiny bottles, vials, pots, and wooden boxes. "You know what those are?" he asked and raised an eyebrow at her.

Fin shook her head.

"Well, I'm goin' to tell you, see here? These are bits what a cook can make a little magic with." He picked up a small wooden box from the nearest shelf, opened it, and breathed deep of the contents. "Aaahh, rosemary." He handed the box to Fin. "Go on, get a good smell of it." She looked inside at the small pile of long, thin, grayish-green bits and smelled it cautiously. Its pungent odor instantly reminded her of the smell of chicken cooking for Sunday dinner.

"Smells like chicken," she said.

"Well, no. It don't smell nothin' like chicken. But it does smell like dinner, don't it? That's because I use a pinch or two when I *cook* the chicken. Now see here, all these little pots and boxes got spices and herbs. Sage, bay leaf, peppercorn, orange peel, thyme, see here? And this is what we goin' to make magic with." The creases of his face spread out and refolded themselves into a giant smile. "Throw a chicken in the pot without the right magic and you get plain ol' turd chicken. But throw in the right mix of this and that and—*ooowwee!*" He slapped his knee. "Mouths a-waterin' from here to Charleston."

Fin gave in and smiled.

"Now see here, we got work to get done for lunch and dinner, so let's get to it."

Bartimaeus rattled on for the rest of the day about what spice to use, and how much, and for what sort of meal. He never tired of talking about cooking, and to Fin's surprise she didn't get bored of listening. He showed her the garden and made himself hungry just talking about how to tell when the various cabbages and peppers and beans were ready to be plucked and cooked. Then he took her to the barn and used a poor Charolais calf as a model to teach her where all his favorite cuts of beef came from.

"Right yonder," he patted the calf's shoulder, "that's a roasted piece of heaven just waitin' to happen, missy. Little bay leaf, little salt, add some carrots and taters. Yes, ma'am. Sunday dinner in the flesh, ain't you, darlin'?" He was talking to the calf and seemed to have momentarily forgotten Fin was there. Fin was thankful the calf didn't understand what he was saying. He spoke so enthusiastically about his craft that Fin couldn't help but be drawn along by him, and by the end of the day she was nearly convinced that she might enjoy her new chores.

Bartimaeus gave her the duty of mashing potatoes for dinner to go with a stew he was stirring up out of nothing more than a few leftover pork rinds and some onions. When she was done, he dipped a spoon into the bowl and sampled her work. He closed his eyes and smacked his lips as he chewed, then frowned and sampled another mouthful.

"Well?"

"Best damned taters I ever ate. Bloody well done, missy." Fin completely failed to mask her delight at his language. "Pardon me, Miss Button. Taters made me forget myself. Don't go lettin' on to Hilde about that, see here?" He winked at her.

That evening after Sister Carmaline said grace over the dinner, Bartimaeus stood up and addressed the dining hall.

"Miss Button here made the taters and done a fine job on her first day in the galley." Hilde cleared her throat and exchanged a stern look with Bartimaeus. "Kitchen that is," he amended. "Well, thank Miss Button if you like the taters, see here? She done a good job." He sat down and Fin was glad of it. She was blushing.

After dinner she found Peter behind the chapel lying on his back, shirt off, covered in sweat, and apparently ready to go to sleep right there on the ground if he could get away with it. She kicked him.

"Fin!" he said with no small bit of irritation. "Don't touch me; it hurts everywhere." He groaned.

"Hurts? What did they do? Beat you?" she teased.

"We spent all day making bricks." Fin turned green with envy and narrowed her eyes at him. "Playing in the mud might sound fun, but I can tell you that after about six hours, fun it ain't." He attempted to sit up, failed miserably, and groaned as he settled back to the ground. "I don't think I'm going be able to move tomorrow."

Fin laughed and sat down next to him. "How many bricks do you have to make?"

"Only thousands. How was the kitchen?"

"Hate it. I like Bartimaeus though. He's funny." She paused and then added, "I'd rather play in the mud," with a devilish grin.

"I'll trade you," Peter said.

She smacked him on the leg. "Stop fooling around."

"I'm going to bed," said Peter and groaned as he tried to stand. "If I can get up, that is." Fin tugged him to his feet, and he limped off toward the dorm house.

"Goodnight," she called after him, and Peter grunted back weakly before stepping through the doorway.

Fin was tired but not sleepy. She looked around to make sure Hilde's nose wasn't watching then headed around to the chapel door, ducked inside, and climbed up to the bell tower. She was surprised at how hard it was to remind herself that she didn't like working in the kitchen with Bartimaeus. He was so different from the sisters. Fin sensed in him a hint of rebellion that intrigued her. Tattoos on his arms, muttered curses on his breath, magic in his kitchen—he was full of things the sisters never let on about. If she couldn't be out in the sun with Peter, at least Bartimaeus was good company while scrubbing pots. A small consolation to be sure, but small was better than none at all. It would have to do.

CHAPTER V

WEEKS PASSED AND THE blank spot on the ground that marked off the site of the new chapel grew into a foundation. Peter progressed from making bricks to actually laying them, and Fin, though constantly looking for reasons to sneak out to the chapel site to see what was going on, was taking to Bartimaeus with increasing fondness.

She and Bartimaeus took long walks through the countryside each morning under the pretense of looking for wild herbs, and this was the high point of Fin's day. Though they would often bring back some root or herb, the primary and unspoken reason for these walks was simply to get away from the bustle of the orphan house for a while, to walk and to talk, and to enjoy the quietude of small company. Most days, Bartimaeus prattled on about the movement afoot to declare independence from England. Fin didn't much understand all his talk about Stamp Acts and taxation and representation but she tended to be very keen on the idea that the Crown had no business telling Georgians what to do.

"Why should we even care what King George says? If someone I didn't know told me to give them money, they'd have a knuckle in their ear," said Fin, indignant.

"Aye, and me too. But what if that someone was twenty feet tall, breathed fire, and ate your children if you didn't pay him his due, eh? The king's a king, missy. Got hisself armies and navies and gov'ners and what all to see he's listened to. He's a stranger but he's no vagrant, see here?"

"We should just kill them all then."

Bartimaeus chuckled. "And who'd be doin' that killin'? And who'd be killed? There's no army but the king's, and half the British in the colonies is friends and family to them that you'd have dead. Nasty business it is."

"Well they've no right telling us what to pay or what to do."

"I reckon if you asked the king yourself he'd tell you God give him the right by makin' him king. But more'n that, it was the king what built the roads and raised up the towns. Was the king what give the land to the folks to live here in Ebenezer. Folks round here got long memories and few are anxious to do wrong by them that done right."

"Have you ever been to England?"

"Yes, yes, I've been," he said, "and don't wish to go again." He frowned and looked somewhat ruffled.

"You've been on a ship then? Tell me about ships—and the sea! I've never seen the ocean." She could hardly contain her excitement.

"Ah, the sea," his eyes focused on some far distant past and the wheels of memory creaked to life inside him. "I remember first lookin' on it and thinking I'd come to the edge of the world. So far, so wide, and so *perfect* it was. My young eye couldn't fathom the distance of it. I was nineteen when I saw it first and twenty when it took me for its own, on a merchant ship, out of Charleston, carried me across to far London and a new world—the *Old* World, see here? After London, the sea became my life and in those young days my Eden, all green and blue, and God himself walked and talked with me across that foamy deep."

His eyes darkened, and refocused on some angled space where the wheels of regret screamed and strained.

"It's different now, see here, the blue and green they gone; turned cold, a grey waste what leads to poison shores and a broken beauty. Now life's just," he waved his hand in the air, "a walk among ruins." His eyes swam back to the present and stared into the shadows.

"What happened?" Fin whispered. "Bartimaeus?"

"Things I wish had *not*." He said it with finality. He was done speaking. He turned quietly, without looking at her, and headed back toward the orphan house. Fin stared after him a moment then caught up, and they walked back in an uneasy silence.

For the rest of the day they labored with few words between them. Whatever had been stirred up in Bartimaeus had rattled him and left him quiet and dark. Fin felt guilty that she'd brought up the questions that caused his dour mood, but all attempts she made to smooth it over or lighten his spirits resulted in little more than downcast eyes and indistinct mumblings about not having time to talk. She was frustrated not only at him but at herself. She wanted to make things right but didn't know how to go about it.

After dinner, Bartimaeus approached her looking very much more serious than he normally did. "Miss Button, somethin' I'd like to show you. Sister Hilde wouldn't approve I reckon." He was almost whispering. "About sundown make your way to the river. Careful not to let Sister Hilde see you." Fin nodded. She was baffled, worried, and a bit excited.

Once the dining hall was clean, Bartimaeus gave her a wink and shooed her out the door. She found Peter sitting on the chapel steps waiting for her as he did every day.

"Dinner was good. Did you cook it?" Peter asked.

"Thanks and yeah, sort of . . . well, no. He tells me what to do but then ends up doing it all himself. I think he enjoys it too much to let it go." She laughed. "He's in a weird mood today." She told Peter about their talk in the woods and then about her secret meeting at the river.

"What do you think it is?" asked Peter.

"I haven't got the faintest clue. You should come. Just follow and be quiet."

"You sure that's a good idea?"

"Terrible idea—but when has that ever mattered?" She grinned at him and Peter gave in. "It's probably just an old toadstool you can only find at night or something like that." She waved and ran out the gate toward the river. Peter waited a moment then shook his head and followed.

When Fin got to the riverbank, she spotted Bartimaeus. He had a small fire lit and was sitting on a log with a black carrying case lying next to him.

"Safely escaped Sister Hilde, I take it?"

Fin grinned.

"Now, let's see here," he said as she sidled up next to him on the log. He picked up the case and set it on his lap. "You remember that little bit I was runnin' on about earlier? Goin' to sea and all that?" Fin nodded. "Well, that hauls up a whole lots of stuff that I came here to get away from, hurtful stuff you see, and you think I might not know it but I see a sort of hurtin' in you sometimes. I'm thinkin' you might have some old angry stuff tucked away over the way Hilde and the good Lord treat you sometimes, maybe about your folks too." He patted the case gently. "This here is what I wanted to shew you, is what old Bartimaeus learned to do with all that hurtful stuff. Learned long ago you got to *put* it somewhere. Got to get it out from inside you and *put* it somewhere. That stuff can eat you up from the insides. Eat you up till there's nothin' left but hurt."

He cocked his head to one side as if listening for something then spoke into the darkening woods. "Peter LaMee, that you?" he said with no anger or worry. Peter stepped out from behind a tree; his face was flushed red with embarrassment. "I should to have known you'd be followin' after Miss Button. You come on up. I expect she goin' to tell you what I say anyhow, might as well get it from my own mouth. You come on up." Peter came up and sat down next to Fin. She rolled her eyes at him, thinking she'd taught him better how to sneak without being caught.

"I'm sorry, Bartimaeus. We tell each other everything," Fin said.

"Now that's alright, ain't nothin' goin' on here that ain't good for you both." Fin breathed a sigh of relief.

"Now then," he said and carefully thumbed up the latches on the case. He opened it and Fin and Peter leaned forward to see what was inside. The box was lined in red velvet, and the bottom half was molded to hold its three habitants. The first was a violin, glowing lusty red in the firelight. It was the most delicate and graceful thing Fin had ever seen. The curves and luster of it were stunning, feminine. The second object was the violin's bow, long and elegant, strung with white hair. The third object in the box was a Spanish blunderbuss, made of dark red wood and adorned with silver flourishes. The handle was engraved with an ornate *B* and embellished with festooning swirls and curves. It was as beautiful as the violin but graceless and menacing, its barrel flared out like a mouth yawning open into a scream.

"Now, see here, you got to put that hurt someplace, and this is where old Bartimaeus learned to put his." He lifted the fiddle out of the case and caressed it.

"It's beautiful," whispered Fin.

"Aye," he said and crooked it into his neck. He drew the bow across the strings and the instrument moaned a forlorn note. "Beautiful, that's what you got to do with that hurtin', you got to turn it beautiful." He closed his eyes and began to play. He rocked back and forth on the log and let the song come out of him. He poured all his pain into the void of the violin and gently worked it out, turned it to beauty. Fin and Peter sat mesmerized by the music; they'd never heard anything like it. It was sweet and sad and felt like a lamentation. Neither could say a word. Fin's face flushed red and her eyes glistened with held tears.

Bartimaeus lowered the violin. "Now missy, don't you cry. You didn't have no idea I had that hurtful stuff when you was askin' me about them way-back days. I brought you here to show you I could get rid of it, see here?" Fin wiped her tears and nodded.

"What's the gun for?" asked Peter.

Bartimaeus's face darkened. "That's where all that hurtful stuff ends up if you don't get rid of it. Got to get rid of it. You don't and it might just get rid of you, see here? I keeps it there to remind me. I put it down the day I got this here fiddle. Swore I'd never take it up again. Done too much hurtin', got to turn that hurt to beautiful, see? Otherwise the hurtin' turns hateful and the ole hand-cannon there like to wake up and do terrible things . . . *terrible things*." The way Bartimaeus said it made Fin shiver.

"I reckon I rambled on enough for one night." He put the fiddle back in the case and closed the lid. "You two run along now. I'm gonna sit here and think things out a bit. You go on, get some sleep."

Fin and Peter said goodnight and walked back up to the orphanage. When they got to the top of the hill, Fin turned around and looked back down toward the river. Bartimaeus was silhouetted against the fire, standing still as an oak, his head bowed. She turned and walked on to bed.

Chapter VI

DESPITE HER GNAWING CURIOSITY, Fin avoided broaching the subject of the sea or the black case with Bartimaeus for a few days. He went on teaching her his herbcraft and cooklore with the same old cheerfulness, but she sensed that it would be best to give him time before prying him further. Fin decided that Monday after dinner was probably time enough, though, and when she ran off to the chapel for classes that afternoon she was preoccupied with things she intended to ask Bartimaeus after dinner.

"You may put away your books," said Sister Hilde to the class. "Today we are going to discuss something that is becoming increasingly important. Henceforth, we shall devote each Monday's studies to this new curriculum. Let us call it Contemporary Happenstance." She looked pleased with herself and was also pleased to find the class paying more attention than usual.

"Can any of you tell me what is going on in the world outside our little town?" She scanned the class for answers and Fin stuck her hand up. Hilde ignored it. "*Exactly.* You haven't an inkling. The world is moving very quickly outside our gates and it is time that you understood it. Can anyone tell me what taxes are?" She scanned the room. Fin shot her hand up again. "Miss Button?"

"When the British take money that's not theirs."

"I see your work with Brother Bartimaeus has more than his cooking rubbing off on you. Taxes are monies collected by the government for the purpose of funding the needs of the country. Now, some people here in the colony of Georgia feel that the Crown of England is due little money from us, and to that effect, this past week in Savannah most of the merchants have stated their intent to boycott—refuse to buy—any British goods.

"Can anyone tell me what effect this might have on us?" She scanned the room. No hands.

"The overall effect is tension between the colony and the Crown. There are many here and elsewhere in the colonies that advocate independence. It is entirely possible, children, that there is a war coming." The threat of war wasn't something new, but that Sister Hilde had now spoken its possibility aloud gave it a substance it hadn't had when it was nothing more than rumor and hearsay. "Our proximity to Savannah could have serious consequences for us. It is this situation that I wish to help you all understand on our coming Monday afternoons. Any questions?"

Danny Shoeman raised his hand.

"Yes, Mr. Shoeman."

"If there's a war, do we get to kill the British?" he said. Several other boys whooped their approval.

"The question, Mr. Shoeman, is rather: if there is a war, do the British get to kill *you*?" Hilde raised an eyebrow at him. "God save us all if it comes to war. Now, let us begin with the idea of representation. A proper understanding of Contemporary Happenstance is impossible without a proper understanding of the terms, ideas, and philosophies that drive it."

She spent the rest of the afternoon talking about the Magna Carta and Parliament and other such things that would have put most of the class to sleep had she not been so vigilant a watchman. Fin was fascinated and couldn't wait for a chance to talk to Bartimaeus about the new class.

When Sister Hilde dismissed them, Fin caught up with Peter in the courtyard.

"Bartimaeus says there's war coming for sure. He thinks the Brits got no business with us at all and we need to go independent, even if he won't say it," she said.

"Don't really see that it has a lot to do with us. I never seen any British around here," said Peter with a shrug.

"Oh, come on, Peter. Do you expect to spend your whole life in Ebenezer? When we get out of here, do you really want to be under the thumb of some king all the way across the ocean?"

"Never really gave much thought to leaving. Why would I go anywhere else?"

Fin balked. "Peter LaMee, if you think I'm going to stay my whole life in this town, you've got a block of wood between your ears."

"What does my staying have to do with you?" Peter asked.

Fin tried to put together an answer to that question but couldn't. When she attempted to open her mouth to speak, her trembling bottom lip interfered. A knot swelled up in her throat, and she felt the sting of ready tears in her eyes. She wouldn't have it, though. A white flash of anger erupted in her mind and before she could untwist her emotions or get a word out, Fin reeled back and threw a punch. A perfectly baffled Peter LaMee received the blow squarely in the chin and Fin left him lying in the dirt.

AFTER DINNER, FIN WASHED up the dishes and swept the floor, then approached Bartimaeus as he was wiping down the dinner table. He looked at her out of the side of his face and knew she was up to something. He raised his eyebrows and made a beckoning motion with his hand.

"Well, get it out, missy. You been hem-hawin' all day about somethin', so I suppose you best let it out before you pop."

"You remember the fiddle you showed me?"

"Oh sure, ain't had to play it much lately, got all that stuff turned out," he said.

"Could you teach me?"

He stopped what he was doing and looked at her for a long time, considering the request in his mind. "I was right about that hurtful stuff you got, eh?"

She shrugged.

"Miss Button, it would be my pleasure. But, see here now, Sister Hilde, she don't like my fiddlin', calls it heathen music. I got no idea why some music might be fit for the Lord's ear and some ain't, but I wasn't never one for followin' rules much, so I do it anyway." He chuckled. "Now I'll be happy to teach you, but we got to be quiet about it, see here? We can sneak the ole fiddle out when we goes on our walk for some herbs."

"Thank you Brother Bart!" She ran to throw her arms around his neck, but he backed up and stopped her short.

"See here, you can't be callin' me that, missy. Don't no one call me Bart no more and that's the way I like it. Bartimaeus is the name my folks give me, and I got no reason to go changin' it."

With a confused look, she acquiesced and finished delivering her hug. As she walked out the door, she threw one last smile back at Bartimaeus and saw him staring after her in serious consideration. It made her feel uneasy.

The next day, Fin was able to think of little more than getting through breakfast so she and Bartimaeus could take their walk.

Just outside the gates, the new chapel was taking shape in earnest. The boys worked day in and day out laying bricks and mortar. With each brick the walls seemed to rise out of the ground as if the new building was sprouting from a seed of stone in the earth.

In the short time that Peter had been working on the chapel, he'd managed to make quite an impression on Mr. Hickory as a hard worker and quick learner. He was also starting to make quite a different impression on Fin. The hard work had changed the boy of a year ago into a darkly tanned and tightly muscled young man, and some days she found herself sneaking out to the work site not to see how the chapel was coming so much as to watch Peter work bare chested in the sun. Fin found that more and more often she felt self-conscious when Peter's eyes were on her. Brushing her hair and washing her face weren't things she ever did unless the sisters ordered her to it, but lately she discovered that she had the uncontrollable urge to do so anytime she was likely to see Peter.

When breakfast was finally over and the kitchen was clean, Fin and Bartimaeus slipped out into the woods. They walked and talked until they came to a small draw near the river with a fallen cypress to sit on. Bartimaeus opened his case and lifted out his fiddle. He laid it into the crook of his neck and played a few notes. Then he tuned it up a bit and lowered it.

"Alright missy, now let's see here." Bartimaeus held the fiddle out. Fin took it and held it gently with her fingertips. "Put her up to your neck . . . uh huh . . . right there. Now hold the bow . . . uh huh—" before he could say anything else Fin slid the bow across the strings and made such a screeching racket that every dog for a mile around perked up its ears and sniffed the air in alarm. "Whoa, missy! Hold on now. If we do this, you got to listen to me."

"Sorry," she said and squinted in embarassment.

"Here, put your fingers like this . . . now pull the bow easy, loosen up . . . can't be makin' the beauty when you all tightened up like that. Relax, missy." Fin put her excitement aside and did as he said. She pulled the bow across the strings and the fiddle sighed a note. "There you go, that's right. Now then, let me have that back so I can show you how to do."

For the rest of the morning Bartimaeus immersed himself in the long process of teaching her to tame wild sound into music. Fin hoped she'd be playing like Bartimaeus by the end of the day but was a little daunted at how hard it turned out to be. Fin wasn't one to give up easily, though. She resigned herself to keeping with it and meant to make Bartimaeus stick to his promise of teaching her, no matter how many mornings it took.

At dinner, Fin relayed the entire experience to Peter.

"Don't let Sister Hilde catch you," he whispered, throwing a cautionary glance toward Hilde. Her nose seemed to be quivering ever so slightly at the suspicion that someone was talking about her.

"Don't worry. Bartimaeus could deal with her anyway," Fin assured him. "How was work?"

"Mr. Hickory says that after the chapel is finished he wants me to apprentice with him in town."

"Really?"

Peter shrugged unenthusiastically. "He's already spoken to Sister Carmaline. She told him it would be fine."

"What's wrong with that?" Fin couldn't believe he wasn't excited.

"I've never been away from the orphanage. Going to live in town . . . it's just different is all."

"Living in town?"

"That's what he wants. I'll go live with Mr. Hickory, and he'll teach me all about carpentry and stonework. He doesn't have any sons. I think he wants me to take over his work one day."

Fin knew she ought to be happy for Peter, but she didn't like the thought of not having him around. If Peter left the orphanage to live in town she'd rarely be able to see him unless she took to sneaking out—and that was liable to end up as more trouble from Sister Hilde.

"It'll be like you've got a real family, Peter. You'll love it," she said. She tried to sound optimistic but had the distinct impression she failed. Peter just shrugged.

WINTER CAME ON HARD enough that year to put the chapel work to rest and life slowed down for a while. Peter enjoyed his extra leisure time and spent much of it reading books borrowed from Sister Carmaline. Fin continued her daily fiddle lessons, and by the end of the year, she felt rather good about her newfound talent. The weekly Contemporary Happenstance classes continued, and Sister Hilde kept them all up to date on any news she heard during her supply trips to Savannah. All of the unrest seemed to be up in Boston, and folks in Ebenezer had little real concern for any of it. After all, the British weren't killing people; it was just a legal mess over taxes.

The boycott in Savannah had produced one effect, however, that did increase the tension in town—protests and the growing independence movement had spurred the Royal Governor to send out British patrols. Every week a small detachment of red-coated soldiers marched through town. Some of the townsfolk greeted them and waved while others spat or stopped what they were doing to afford them grim stares. Fin didn't know what to think. The fancily dressed men parading through the town with muskets held at the ready were quite a sight to see, but it made her skin prickle. It was as if the entire colony was under the watchful eyes of an ominous Sister Hilde clothed in red.

When spring finally came around, Peter was anxious to resume work on the chapel and the sisters were equally anxious to get him and the other boys out of their hair for most of the day. On Peter's first day back to work, Fin ran out to the chapel site to find him. She spotted him talking to Mr. Hickory and stood nearby, bouncing on her toes in anticipation as she waited for them to finish.

"Ready to get back to work?" Mr. Hickory asked.

"Yes, sir. Been kind of bored the last few weeks."

"Good, good. I figure with a little luck we'll be about done here by fall. Got them other boys working on pews down at the woodshop right now," he said and motioned off toward town. "Let's get to it, got bricking to do yet, and the sun'll be sinking before you know it." Mr. Hickory pointed to Fin, who was bobbing up and down like an excited puppy. "Think this little lady's wanting to talk to you," he said to Peter.

"Peter! I want to show you something!"

"I'm scared to ask." Peter rolled his eyes.

"Come off it! I've been working on it all winter and, well, when can you meet me down at the river?"

"Not until after dinner," said Peter with a look toward Mr. Hickory.

"Ok, I'll see you there." She grinned and ran off to the dining hall, leaving Peter feeling like he was going to end up in trouble.

Before dinner, Fin found Bartimaeus poring over a pot of stew and muttering that it didn't taste quite right. She stood at the door considering him for a moment then ran in and hugged him.

"What are you working on?" Fin asked.

"Stirred us up a pot of stew for dinner. Used some of that old pork from last night." He dipped in a spoon and sampled it. "Not got the spice just right yet, though; not sure what's missin'. Taster ain't as good as it used to be," he said and chuckled.

"Let me see." She plucked the spoon out of his hand and tasted it. "Just needs a little pepper is all." She reached for the pepperbox.

"See here now! That's my, missy."

She threw a few pinches into the pot and stirred it. "Try this." She dipped the spoon and handed it to him.

"Hee hee, you got the touch, Miss Button, got it right on the spot." He smacked his lips and went back for a second sample. "*Mm-hmm*. Yes ma'am indeed, you have *got* the touch."

The winter had taken its toll on Bartimaeus. He was slowing down. It took him more effort to lug the pots up to the stove, and he'd more and more often ask Fin to reach things on top shelves because he couldn't stretch so high as he used to. Watching his age wear him away made Fin sad. But more than sad, it made her necessary. When she first started working with him she felt out of place and underused; he'd been the one doing most of the work and seemed happy enough to be doing it. Now their roles had turned. Necessary wasn't something she'd ever been before, and she didn't think she could bring herself to leave him even if Sister Hilde ordered her to.

"How you comin' with that fiddle now that you been practicin' all on your own?" he asked.

"Wonderful, if you must know. I've composed something for Peter," she said with a bit of a blush.

"Oh, indeed? My songs not good enough, eh? Got to go to makin' up your own, see here!" he balked.

"He hasn't heard it yet. I'm going to play it for him tonight."

"You two be careful now. Woods ain't no place for two kids runnin' around at night."

"The woods are safer than Sister Hilde."

"Heh, maybe they are, now, maybe they are. Let's get to work on the biscuits. Dinner will be here before we know it."

Stew was never a big favorite with the children but it went over without complaint. Sister Carmaline took the opportunity to announce that with the foreseeable completion of the chapel, plans would soon take shape for the dedication ceremony and the first Sunday service. She and Hilde were both very excited.

After dinner, Fin made quick work of cleanup, grabbed the fiddle case, planted a kiss on Bartimaeus's cheek, and disappeared through the door before he could get a word out. When she got to the river, the sun was just starting to slink out of sight behind the trees, and she found Peter skipping stones on the bank.

"Bet you can't skip one all the way across," she teased him.

"Bet you can't either."

"You're on," she said. She set the fiddle case down and kneeled to find a perfect stone.

"You're mad, you know that?" said Peter.

"We'll see." Fin found the stone she was looking for. She stood up and stretched her arms. "Ready?"

Peter shook his head and chuckled. "Ready when you are."

"You first, Pete."

Peter turned, slung his stone, and watched it fly. *Plink . . . plink . . . plink . . . ploop.* It stopped about twenty feet short of the far side. "Your turn."

Fin made a big show of eyeing the angle and winding up then let fly the stone. *Plink . . . plink . . . plink . . . plink . . . crack!* It landed in the rocks on the far side. She looked supremely satisfied.

"Do you ever lose?" said Peter shaking his head at her.

"Not if I can help it. Maybe I'll let you win next time." She smiled at him then grabbed the fiddle case and ran up the bank. She sat down between the knees of an old cypress tree and opened up the case. Peter dropped down beside her as she lifted out the fiddle and bow.

"You have to promise not to laugh."

"And why would I do that?" said Peter with a grin.

Fin smiled at him and shrugged playfully. "If you don't promise, I won't let you win next time."

"Alright, no laughing," he said though he looked as if he might burst into laughter at any moment.

She played a few notes and tuned up the fiddle, then, satisfied, looked at Peter. "I made this up for you. If you laugh I'll knuckle in your lip."

Peter grinned at her and nodded. She began to play, but she was nervous. Her hands shook and the notes came out unsure of their places. As she continued, she began to relax and the music smoothed like the river after a stone's ripple. The song was a juxtaposition of two melodies: one light and dramatic, the other slow and steady. She wove them together into a tapestry of sound that stumbled and wavered until at last it found its way into beauty.

All thought of levity now gone, Peter listened in simple awe. The last time he heard her play, he was reminded of Sister Carmaline's unbearable vespers singing, but the sounds Fin formed now were sublime. Her eyes were closed and her face was lost in the playing. She rocked back and forth with the rhythm of the bow, and the melodies of her song danced and entwined, one around the other, until the sun crept away and the gathering dark won the night. The final note hung in the air for a golden moment like a whisper between lovers, then faded away to silence.

Fin lowered the fiddle and looked at Peter. He was lost in shadow. A glimmer of moonlight caught in his eyes and gave him away. They sat in darkness for a long time, silently looking at each other, neither willing to break the spell.

"Do you like it?" Fin whispered.

Peter didn't speak. He leaned forward in the darkness and found her face with his hands. And he kissed her. He'd wanted to kiss Fin Button for as long as he could remember. She always moved too fast or he too slow. But not now. They moved together.

"I've been waiting for that for ten years, Phinea Button."

"Why'd you wait?"

"You never stay still long enough for me to catch you."

She leaned forward and kissed him again. "I should be still more often."

Fin carefully placed the fiddle back in its case. The moonlight glinted off the silverwork on the handle of the old blunderbuss and caught Peter's eye.

"Hold on," he said, "let me see that."

"Don't, Peter!"

"Why not?"

"Bartimaeus made me promise."

"Promise what?"

"Not to touch it. He said if he caught me with it he wouldn't let me use his fiddle anymore."

"I only want to hold it," said Peter as he bent over the case.

"Peter *don't*," she pleaded.

Peter reached out and ran his finger down the barrel.

A shiver trickled down Fin's neck, and she pulled his hand away. Then a cry rang out from the direction of the orphanage. Fin and Peter turned to look and saw people running. Someone was shouting in the dark. Fin snapped the case shut and they ran up the hill.

Outside the front gates of the orphanage, a man on horseback was waving a piece of paper in the air and a crowd of people had gathered around him.

"Damned Redcoats! They've started it, they've *started* it," he cried.

People were filing out of houses all over town and coming to see what the commotion was. The orphan house had emptied, and the sisters stood at the gate. Brother Bartimaeus spotted Fin and hurried over to her.

"Calm down, man! What have they started?" said a voice from the crowd, and Mr. Bolzius stepped out. "What news and what proof?" he demanded.

"A massacre in Boston, sir! Brits opened fire on a crowd peacefully gathered." He handed the paper he was waving about to Mr. Bolzius.

"It's all there in *The Georgia Gazette*, the bloody Brits have started murdering honest folk in Massachusetts—only a matter of time now," he said looking at the mayor to see if his message was clear.

"I see." Mr. Bolzius handed the paper back to him with a worried look. "Thank you, good sir. Now if you please, leave us to our thoughts and our beds."

The gentleman on the horse didn't like Mr. Bolzius's reaction. "Can't trust them, you hear?" He began shouting to the crowd again. "Don't trust a one of them. You hear me? War's coming. Coming *soon*." He looked around madly. "*Coming to Georgia!*" He spurred the horse and it jumped into a gallop. The crowd parted, and he rode out of town toward Bethany to break the news there. As he faded into the night, the crowd broke into a chatter of questions, worries, and fears. Fin and Peter looked at each other, speechless. Bartimaeus stared down the road after the messenger with worry in his eyes.

"Do you think it's true?" Fin asked Bartimaeus.

He didn't answer right away. When he did, he didn't turn to look at her.

"I expect it is. Was bound to come to it sooner or later."

"What are we going do?" asked Peter. Bartimaeus considered it.

"Nothin'. We do nothin' except go about our business like always. Might come a time when we got to decide what side of the fence we sit on. Lord willin', we won't. We do nothin', see here?"

He turned and walked back through the gate. Fin and Peter followed and ran to bed before the sisters could think to wonder why they'd run up from the direction of the river.

THE NEXT DAY THE community was buzzing with what-ifs and what-to-dos. Mr. Hickory told Peter that several fistfights had broken out the night before between loyalists—"Tories" he called them—and a few of the more outspoken continentals. One of the loyalist families had even started moving out of their house in town to make a permanent home of their farm in the country. "Didn't feel safe anymore," they said. Sister Hilde made use of class time to inform the children of the news and assured them that Boston was a very long way off and they had no reason to feel in any danger in Ebenezer.

Fin was uneasy about the whole thing and had to push down fluttery feelings of excitement. She told herself there was nothing *exciting* about the possibility of war in Georgia, but the more she thought about it, the more ashamed she felt that she really *was* excited.

While she and Bartimaeus washed the breakfast dishes, she fired question after question at him. "Who decides if there's going to be a war?" "Where do you think the British will attack next? Savannah?" "Do we all get guns if they come to Ebenezer?" "How many British do you think there are?" "If there's a war, do you think King George will come fight? And if we kill him do you think we'd have to find someone to be king of Georgia?"

Fin had more questions than Bartimaeus wanted to give answers to, and by the time the dishes were done, he'd gone quiet and dark.

"If it comes to fighting here, in Georgia, will you fight?" she asked.

Bartimaeus looked at her with a sharp eye and considered it.

"These bones too old for fightin', missy. Push comes to shove, I'll hold my ground but I won't be runnin' off with the young fellers."

"Have you ever had to fight before?"

"Fight? I done plenty, I reckon. Never for no cause or such, just young man's foolery." His tone told Fin he didn't want to talk about it, but she didn't let that stop her.

"Like battles? Indians?"

"That's all dead now, missy. I'm dead to it. Different man now," he said. "Leave it be." It was an order.

Fin pressed him, "You always do that. Why can't you just tell me?"

"I said leave it *be*!" He turned away from her and walked toward the door.

"I don't want to *leave it be*! I want to know you, who you are, who you were."

He spun to face her and his eyes changed. It was as if that hurtful place he loathed to look upon was now right in front of him and he exploded upon it.

"*Piracy and pillage*! Is that what you want to hear? *Murder, rape, rum, and ruin*? That's who Bart is! That's who I was!" He was raving. The creases of his face spread to an unclenched visage of anger. "I killed men, women, and children. English, Colonist, French, Spaniard, Moor, Turk—you name it, I killed it, missy. This what you wanted?" Fin shrank away. "Don't be scared *now*! You ain't heard the worst of ole Bloody Bart. Laid down with a whore, he did, then cut her throat cause *he didn't want to pay*! Killed his own friends for gold and a gallon of rum."

He flung open the old fiddle case. The morning light fell on the blunderbuss inside. Its silverwork gleamed as if freshly wakened. Bartimaeus grabbed the weapon and flourished it.

"Me and ole Betsy here done our bloody work from Mexico to Mediterranean and left a trail of tears and blood that leads straight to hell, missy! Straight to the burnin', fiery *pit*! You happy now, Miss Button? This what you wanted to know?"

Fin was shaken. She backed against the wall and slid to the floor in tears.

Bartimaeus threw the gun—Betsy—down on the table in disgust and sat with his head bowed, breathing heavily. The only sound in the room was of tears and regret.

"I'm sorry, missy," he whispered. "I'm so sorry."

Fin stared at him and cried. She huddled against the wall as if trapped in a cage with a wild animal.

"Was Reverend Whitefield that found me." He spoke softly and kept his eyes to the floor. "He was preachin' outside London. Must have been ten thousand folks come to listen. More people than I ever saw in one spot. Listened to him for a bit, and it reminded me of the talks my mother used to give. All that about sinnin' and redeemin' and repentin'. Sounded like foolishness to me, maybe 'cause I was drunk. Don't know why, but thinkin' about my dead mother started me to cryin'. Next thing I see is Reverend Whitefield bendin' over me, tellin' me to *stand up*. So I done like he asked, and he told me it weren't like a man to lay drunk while he was preachin' the Word, and if I was ever to be a man I'd have to *stand up* like I just done, only to keep *standin'*. Couldn't never lay down, he said. Told him I couldn't do that, and he says, 'I know, son, but God will pick you up when you fall.' Told him there wasn't no God where I live, and he said I best find a new place.

"That's how I come to Ebenezer, see? Reverend Whitefield told me he knowed of a place needed a good *standin' up* man to help out, a place there weren't so many temptations for a man with *layin' down* troubles. Told me the Good Lord chose all us sinners to be saved way back in the old days, and all the devils in hell wasn't goin' to come between God and a man he done chose. Figured I might as well stop puttin' devils between us if that was the case.

"And so, here I am. Put away ole Betsy and spent the last of my money on a fiddle I seen layin' in a shopwindow in Charleston the day I set feet off ship and sea for the last time." He finished and wiped his hand across his forehead. His face was familiar again and loving. The creases and wrinkles of his face relaxed back to their places, but it seemed to Fin they ran deeper than they had before.

"How did you know he chose you?" she whispered.

"Oh, I don't know. When the reverend went to tellin' me, I wasn't in no place to do much arguin'."

"And what if God didn't choose us?" she whispered from the shadows. "Does that mean all the angels in heaven can't stand between us and hell?"

"What's this talk? See here, you got no place thinkin' like that, missy. If ever there was a little miss I'd say God chose, it'd be you."

Fin didn't answer. Chosen was what she wanted to be more than anything. Not chosen to do chores or work with Bartimaeus but chosen to simply belong.

"I been standin' up for nigh on twenty years now." He smiled. "Got lots of help along the way, from the Reverend, from Mr. Bolzius, from the sisters, and maybe you don't know it, but this last year you been helpin' me stand up too." He offered her his hand and she took it. He pulled her to his chest and hugged her.

"I'm sorry, Bartimaeus."

"Don't you be sorry, now. Don't you be sorry. Sometimes we got to look in the dark to see how bright's the dawn." Bartimaeus released Fin and gently pushed her away. He reached out and grabbed up Betsy from the table and put the gun back in its case. Then he lifted the fiddle and cradled it in the crook of his arm. "I reckon I got fiddlin' to do. Got to turn it beautiful." He smiled and winked and walked out into the morning.

CHAPTER VII

IN THE WEEKS AFTER the horseman's proclamation of war, the townsfolk met British patrols with more suspicion than ever. People came to dread the sound of their stomping boots and the rattle of their shouldered muskets. Families called children indoors and watched from behind drawn curtains as they marched through town armed with threatening glares and unspoken accusations.

The walls were up on the chapel, and all the major stonework was complete. Mr. Hickory kept Peter busy through every daylight hour, honing his carpentry skills as they raised the roof and bell tower. Swinging around in the high rafters looked a world of adventure to Fin, but she didn't mourn the missing-out as much as she used to. She enjoyed her days spent with Bartimaeus and jumped at any opportunity to play the fiddle down at the river or to sit quietly in the bell tower of the old chapel so she could look over the walls and see Peter dancing among the trusses of the new. Sometimes he'd spy her watching from his perch and smile at her across the gulf between.

In addition to offering him an apprenticeship, Mr. Hickory had invited Peter to his house for dinner on several occasions and Fin didn't have any trouble admitting she was jealous.

"I don't see why I shouldn't be able to come with you."

"It wouldn't be proper," Peter protested, though he couldn't point out why. "It's a family dinner, Fin. If you came—"

"What? I'd embarrass you because I don't powder my nose and wear a bonnet?" She planted her fists firmly on her hips and Peter eyed them closely, sensing she might let one fly at any moment.

"No, Fin. It's just—I don't know. Look, maybe next time, alright?"

Without answering, she spun on her toe and walked away. A passel of younger children parted before her like chased geese as she stomped her way back to the dining hall.

Whenever Peter was absent from the dinner table, Fin usually found out later that he'd been invited to the Hickory's "at the last minute." Foolishness if ever she heard of it.

As summer tumbled into autumn, the chapel was all but finished. The tower and steeple had been painted white, and the interior was furnished with pews enough to seat nearly two hundred people. The sisters were in a constant state of excitement about the coming dedication ceremony, and even Sister Hilde beamed with pride when the subject came up. Reverend Whitefield promised to preach on the first Sunday of its opening, and Bartimaeus, especially, was looking forward to seeing his old benefactor again.

To Fin's dismay, the completion of the new chapel meant the time had come for the dismantling of the old. The boys that had previously occupied themselves with the business of construction turned their labors to the reverse. Day by day Fin watched the old chapel wither away. It was first gutted and then stripped of its cypress board-and-battens until all that remained were the beams and rafters of a sad skeletal framework. On the day before the old chapel's final destruction, Fin and Peter stole away to the barely recognizable remnant of the bell tower to honor their secret place with laughter and call out of memory its role in so many of their pranks and games.

"Remember when Hilde caught you fishing during Sunday vespers?" asked Peter. He was smiling, and his eyes were quick and bright. The reminiscence transformed his usually reserved nature, and Fin sensed a lilt in his voice that she rarely heard.

Fin threw her head back and cackled. "She was going to switch me for calling her a smelly fishwife!"

"And you ran all the way up here from the river with her chasing you and trying to swat you with your own fishing pole!" Peter laughed and made mock swatting motions at Fin.

Fin doubled over in laughter, wheezing and breathless. "She couldn't climb the ladder, and you should have seen how her nose waggled while she screamed at me."

"And you were making faces at her the whole time!" They laughed until they were red-faced and could hardly breathe.

Fin calmed her laughter at last and wiped her eyes to look out at the new chapel. She and Peter were suddenly quiet and a wave of melancholy filled her and slowed her breath. "I'm going to miss this. It's the only place inside the walls to find any quiet."

"You'll have the tower in the new one. They don't have bells for it either."

"Then why build a bell tower?" Fin rolled her eyes.

"Mr. Hickory says when you build a thing you build your purpose into it, and sometimes you have to let others finish it. That church will be there for a hundred years and in time someone's bound to find a bell to crown her."

"It won't be the same."

"I suppose it won't, but the new one is even higher. You can see for miles from up there. Just wait, Fin. You'll love it."

She didn't reply, just gazed off into the evening. Peter shifted closer to her and took a deep breath.

"You remember what I told you about Mr. Hickory and his offer?"

"I remember," she said.

"He's asked me to start after the dedication."

Silence sat between them like an intruder.

When Fin spoke she was almost whispering. "You're leaving, Peter LaMee." It wasn't a question.

"No, I'm not, Fin. It's just into town."

"You're leaving me for your own world, Peter, to start your own life. And

I'll be here, cooking chickens and wishing I wasn't. There's nothing for it, Pete. I'm never leaving this place. I'll be right here, under Hilde's thumb, right where she wants me. And you'll be," she waved her hand at the horizon, "out there." She turned her head and refused to cry.

"Fin—" Peter started, but she kept on.

"I understand, Peter. I've been watching orphans leave here my whole life and never once saw one come back. Not really. It'll be the same—you'll come for dinner once or twice a week at first, then once or twice a month. Then I'll hear you've married some girl from Savannah, and then I won't hear any more at all." Fin looked away from Peter again and raised one hand to wipe her eyes.

"What if I married some girl from Ebenezer?"

Fin gave a start and laughed, "Like who?"

He didn't answer at once and she ran through a list of all the girls she knew in town, trying to picture each of them with Peter. Each one she imagined seemed more preposterous to her than the last. As she ticked down the list in her head, she realized that Peter still hadn't spoken and was patiently watching her.

"Who else, Fin?" he said.

She balked at him with her jaw hanging to her chest then he grabbed her up and kissed her. She took his face in her hands and laughed and kissed him again, and again, and again.

THE NEXT MORNING, FIN arrived at the dining hall before dawn to prepare breakfast, and she found Bartimaeus bent over the dinner table, rubbing it furiously with a rag.

"Bloody spots . . ." He was muttering at the table as he tried to eliminate the scuffs and stains on the finish. Fin put her hand on his shoulder.

"Let me do that. You go on and get the fire started."

He acquiesced with a grumble. Fin swiped the rag in the wax and rubbed it across the surface of the table, obscuring the finish with a cloudy film. She picked up a clean cloth and buffed the wax off to bring out the luster of the wood. She could see her reflection in the table: it rippled and distorted with the subtleties of the wood, almost (but never quite) a perfect picture. She thought that if she rubbed hard enough and long enough that maybe she could force a true reflection to reveal itself.

She and Peter decided not to make any mention of their intentions, at least not until Peter had worked with Mr. Hickory long enough to settle into his new position. Fin didn't mind the wait so much, but the thought of being cooped up in the orphanage without Peter depressed her. The promise of living together with him, on their own, was motivation enough, however, for her to endure a hundred nose-wagglings and cook a thousand chickens. She would wait. However long, however hard, she would wait.

She finished off the table, not having cleared the marring on her reflection to any noticeable extent, and went to help Bartimaeus cook.

After breakfast, she sat on the porch and watched the last of the old chapel brought to the ground. With a thunderous tumult, the bell tower came down in a heap of rubble, and her corner of solace disappeared forever.

Chapter VIII

THE SISTERS WERE IN a fury of activity preparing for the first Sunday in the new building. They sent out invitations and argued over what songs they'd sing and fussed about the order of the service and even made sure a reporter from *The Georgia Gazette* would be in attendance. The town council decided to name the new building the Jerusalem Lutheran Church, and the naming lent it a certain weight that it lacked when it had been a simple chapel. As word spread that the Reverend Whitefield would speak on the day of the dedication, people began to arrive from hill and vale all across Georgia. For a week prior to the ceremony, Fin and Bartimaeus worked night and day to ensure they had food enough to feed the multitude.

Two days before the big event, though, Sister Carmaline received ghastly news. Reverend Whitefield had died. On the very day he was to set out for Georgia, he had been "called home" as Carmaline would say. She was a wreck trying to think of how to break it to the crowds and was certain she'd be lynched when the news broke. Bartemeus hadn't taken it well either. When he heard, he walked out of the dining hall, and the sounds of fiddle-play floated up from the river for the rest of the afternoon.

The night before the ceremony, Sister Carmaline was in terrible a state at the dinner table. "Land o' Goshen! What will we do? There will be a riot!"

she worried. She didn't eat a bite. She sat and patted her chest and rocked back and forth and prayed for help.

Midway through the meal, a rapping at the door quieted the room and Hilde answered. A handsome white-haired gentleman strode into the dining hall, removed his hat, and bowed.

"I should be delighted to speak with Sister Carmaline Baab," said the gentleman.

Carmaline fanned her faced and patted her heart and bade him leave her be.

Hilde rolled her eyes. "How may we help you, sir?" she said.

"Ma'am, if you will permit it, I would speak in the Reverend Whitefield's stead."

Carmaline ceased her hysterics and eyed him up and down in bafflement.

"Well, a stranger off the streets will never do," said Hilde rather shrewdly. "Are you even a preacher?"

"Yes, ma'am. I'm afraid I am," said the gentleman without the slightest hint of being offended.

Carmaline resumed patting her chest and rocking back and forth and raised one hand to her forehead and warned the gentleman of her worries. "The crowd will riot, I fear, when they find they've come all this way for a common preacher instead of the Reverend himself." She paused herself again, and turned to look at the gentleman. "What did you say your name was, sir?"

"John Wesley, ma'am," he said with a bow.

Sister Carmaline fainted.

If the sisters held George Whitefield to be the greatest Christian of the age then second place surely went to Reverend John Wesley. Though the Reverends Wesley and Whitefield had virulently disagreed on more than one point of faith, they accounted each other friendly rivals. Sister Carmaline suspected that were these two pillars of Protestantism ever thrust into the same space that blows might come of it, but Reverend Whitefield's passing had rendered the thought moot and she was elated that the Reverend Wesley had arrived to rescue her from certain lynching.

Early the next morning, Fin was once again made to put on a dress. She scowled about the courtyard, muttering curses and looking awkward until she spotted Peter dressed in a suit and preening like a rooster. Though Fin thought he seemed gentlemanly and more handsome than any man in town, she rolled her eyes up and told him immediately that he looked preposterous.

"You're one to talk." Peter chuckled as he eyed her dress and bonnet. Fin threw him a sarcastic smirk, clenched her fists, took a deep breath, and calmed her urge to rip the bonnet off her head and feed it to him.

They walked out the gates and up to the steps of the new church. There was a wooden scaffold erected to the right of the door that reached as high as the steeple atop the tower. Fin wondered why they hadn't taken it down for the opening day, but when she asked Peter he just shrugged.

The interior had remained strictly off limits to everyone except those working on the final details. Even the windows had been curtained against peeking eyes, and Fin was eager to see the inside of what Peter had spent the past year and a half working on. They walked through the doorway and the brick exterior opened up into a shining white sanctuary. Towering windows pierced the walls, and the space between them was a canyon of light filled with carved oaken pews. The ceiling seemed as high as the sky to Fin; she'd never been in anything of such size before. The centerpiece of the great room was the organ and its brass pipes climbing from the floor at the center of the dais to the ceiling high above. Fin looked around in awe.

"It's beautiful, Peter!" she said. He led Fin to their seats, and they sat down to await the ceremony. The crowd streamed in and packed every corner of the room until an usher announced the room full and they opened up the windows to let people outside lean in to see what they could.

Mr. Bolzius stepped to the pulpit and led the congregation in an invocation. Then Peter stood and walked to the front where Mr. Hickory and the other boys of the work crew joined him.

"I wish to recognize the men without whom this building would not have been accomplished." Mr. Bolzius motioned to Mr. Hickory and his workers. The young men on the dais bore little resemblance to the boys Carmaline and Hilde had chosen a year and a half before. They stood taller and their shoulders filled the coats that once had swallowed them. "Danny Shoeman, Lachlan McEwen, Thom Nodger, Hans Richter, Peter LaMee, and the architect and chief builder himself, Mr. Thom Hickory." Applause erupted. Mr. Hickory took a deep bow and Mr. Bolzius continued. "Gentlemen, we are in your debt. May the beauty of your hand be a pleasure in the eye of the Lord."

The organ bellowed as the men returned to their seats and Mr. Bolzius led the congregation in song. The people, both outside and in, sang together, and for miles around music filled the forests and fields. When the singing ended, Mr. Bolzius introduced Reverend Wesley. He took the stage amid a murmur of questions and stepped to the lectern.

"What many of you have heard is truth. Our Brother, Reverend Whitefield, walks with God this morning. I pray you will grant me leave to speak in his stead this Sunday bright."

Nods of assent crossed the room and courtyard and the reverend commenced his dedication.

"Many years ago, as he was led to the stake, John Huss proclaimed, 'Today you burn a goose, but in a hundred years will come a swan whose voice you will not be able to still.' I say that today a swan is born. Today, out of dirt and mud, out of brick and tar, there rises a beacon that shines in the wilderness. Let no man still the voice that here is given cry, and let no man throw down that which the Lord builds up. A mighty fortress is my God, which no man on earth may assail. Amen."

Peter rose and walked out of the building, leaving Fin to wonder where he'd gone while Mr. Hickory went to the left of the dais and stood beside an object cloaked under a sheet.

"By labor of fire and forge, we find here that which is given to surmount the steeple and proclaim our purpose to far eyes lifted." He motioned to Mr. Hickory, who withdrew the sheet and revealed a large white swan atop a glimmering pike. "Behold the swan that rises."

The congregation clapped and amened.

"Good people, we shall remove ourselves to the courtyard to view the final crowning."

The crowd bustled out the doors, and Fin was swept along with them, wondering where in the world Peter had got to. She looked up and saw a rope hung from a series of pulleys and beams stretching out to the steeple from the scaffold. Danny and Hans carried out the swan and tied the rope fast around it; then Lachlan and Thom hauled on the rope and the swan rose above the crowd. As it ascended, the crowd's eyes followed it in silence. Then Fin spotted Peter atop the steeple. Peter leaned out, took hold of the pike, and maneuvered it into the socket atop the steeple. The assembly slid into place with a victorious clang, and the crowd erupted in applause.

As Peter made his way back down, a wagon trundled into the courtyard, and Sister Carmaline hurried over in a fury to shoo away the culprit of such inconsideration. She launched into a sound berating, but the wagon driver patiently ignored her and handed over a letter. Carmaline tore it open and read it then hurried over to Reverend Wesley and thrust the letter at him.

Peter made it back to the ground and joined Fin with a questioning look. "What's going on?"

"I don't know" she shrugged.

Reverend Wesley read the letter under his breath, his eyes widening as he did so. Then he called the crowd to attention.

"My friends, it pleases me to read you this letter sent from Mr. Jonathan Hickleby of New Hampshire." He began reading in a loud voice. "Dear Sirs, it is with my sincerest condolences that I greet you. You will, no doubt, have learned by now through quicker means of our brother, Reverend Whitefield's, recent translation into glory. It was in my house he spent his final hours and, until the very end, he was determined to honor his engagement with you for the dedication of your new church building. When at length he spied God's plans were otherwise, he bid me see this final cargo delivered thence. May this bell crown your tower and call all Christian men to worship with its toll." The wagon driver flung the cover from his cargo and revealed a newly founded bell gleaming bright in the morning sun.

"It seems Reverend Whitefield has the final word of the morning," smiled Reverend Wesley, and then, too low for most to hear, almost a whisper, "Well done, old friend."

Sister Hilde beamed like Fin had never imagined was possible while

Sister Carmaline sat down heavily on a bench and fanned her face lest she swoon.

Peter ran to the wagon to join Mr. Hickory and the rest of the building crew. They placed lifting timbers below the bell and called for help to lift her. Men from the crowd ran to their aid, and together they carried the bell to the scaffold and tied ropes fast about it. Ten men it took to hoist her up. The crowd watched with glee as it found its mark and men aloft swung her into place inside the tower. The sounds of rapping hammers echoed in the tower as the bell was secured in its housing, then Danny Shoeman jumped up, grabbed the tolling rope, and pulled down with all his might. The sharp peal rang clear, and people below shouted and cheered. Again and again Danny pulled the rope. No slow, mournful toll for those in death, but a victory chime for life renewed.

CHAPTER IX

ON A TUESDAY IN early October, Peter left the orphanage. The anxious leaves had turned in spite of the summer hanging on past its due, and in the morning heat, Peter packed for the move to the Hickory household. To Fin it seemed a thousand miles away. She met his departure in a fitful and somber mood and nothing Peter said could alter it.

"I'll only be down the road. You can nearly see it from here."

Fin didn't answer. They stood outside the orphan house as the sisters waited at the front gate to send him off.

"We've got plans, Fin. It won't be long."

"Why should we wait? I want to come with you."

"It's too soon. Mr. Hickory barely has room even for me. We have to wait."

Fin wasn't consoled.

Peter turned away and gathered the last of his belongings from the doorstep. When he turned again to face her with his pack slung across his shoulders and a bundle of tools and clothing in his hands, he was different. He was no longer just an orphan, no longer her constant companion. He was a man, with a place in the world, with a skill, with a home waiting for him, even if it was only five minutes' walk through the gates. And he was leaving her behind, inside the walls, alone.

Fin reached out and touched his arm. She wanted to embrace him and kiss him, but the sisters were watching. Though she would happily risk their scolding, she withheld herself to spare Peter. "You're my way out, Peter, my only road. You know that?"

Peter moved closer and gave her his smile as Sister Carmaline called out for him to come.

"I know it, Fin, and I'll be waiting. Down at the end of the road."

Sister Carmaline called out again and he went. At the gate, Hilde and Carmaline hugged him and kissed his cheeks and waved him off while Fin slunk into the shadow of the orphan house and watched in silence as he walked down the road and dwindled out of sight.

In Peter's absence Fin felt almost completely alone, and only Bartimaeus helped to fill the empty spaces in her days. He cheered her with his good humor and they took any opportunity to slip away from the orphanage and convene on the riverbank to play the fiddle. Fin had quickly surpassed him in technical skill, but she never tired of hearing the complexity of his playing or the emotion he funneled into it. They learned from each other and often played deep into the night, sneaking back into the orphanage by moonlight to escape Hilde's attentions.

Peter stopped by for dinner often. The sisters were always happy to have him, and his visits were a relief to Fin. After dinner they snuck out the gates to walk by the river until the sun went down.

"How long, Peter? It's easy for you, you don't have to deal with Hilde, and all those kids. I'm going crazy!"

"I don't know how long, not yet. I've only just moved in. I can't ask them to take in you too, not yet I can't. Be patient, Fin. Trust me."

The argument ended as they always did, with Fin stomping off mad. Often she claimed there was some girl in town she didn't know about, and Peter would be left dumbfounded.

To Fin's daily dismay, Sister Hilde had started a new crusade to turn her into a proper woman. Hilde waggled her nose about wearing the proper clothes and speaking in turn and sitting up straight and holding her hands in her lap, but Fin was old enough now that threats and lectures bounced right off her. Hilde's failure to encourage any noticeable transformation put her in a constant state of aggravation and was a prime source of amusement for Fin.

Late that November, Bartimaeus informed her that she'd be coming with him on his supply run to Savannah, and Fin was ecstatic. Sister Hilde was quick to point out, though, that Fin would be going exactly nowhere unless she was dressed properly. Fin could do nothing but agree and smolder.

The next morning, Fin arrived at the dining hall in her only dress with a smile on her face. Bartimaeus raised one suspicious eyebrow at her quiet submission to Hilde's demands, but he didn't say anything. They loaded the bolts of silk they were to sell in town and mounted the wagon just as Sister Hilde arrived to inspect Fin.

"Good heavens, child, button that up. All the way to the top!" Fin obeyed without a word. "Now go inside and manage that hair. You're not going anywhere with that tangled mess. If you can't manage it, then tie it back and hide it with a bonnet for goodness' sake." Fin started to protest but bit her tongue and ran off to do as she was told. After a few minutes, Fin came back with a bonnet on, trying her best to look like she belonged in it.

"Better. A fine woman you may make one day, Miss Button, if you'd just put your mind to it. Now, you two be careful and I'll expect you back by sundown."

"Yes, ma'am," said Bartimaeus. "You'll find bacon out for breakfast and a stew in the pot ready to warm up for lunch and dinner. Don't burn my galley down." Hilde frowned and waved them off. Bartimaeus snapped the reins and the wagon lurched down the road into the rising sun.

When they had passed the last house in town and gone around a bend in the road, Fin jumped up and cursed Bartimaeus's ears numb while she unbuttoned her dress in disgust. Underneath it she was wearing her usual shirt and plain britches. She threw the dress in the back of the wagon and plopped back down with a sigh of relief. Bartimaeus chuckled.

"You forgot the bonnet," he said quietly. Fin gave a little scream as she ripped it off her head and threw it behind her. She and Bartimaeus broke into laughter.

Fin had never been further than walking distance from New Ebenezer and Savannah was a new world for her. Over a hill from the west they came rolling, and the city spread out below like a picnic set upon a green blanket. The smells of salt and fish from the harbor met them on the wind, and they descended the hill into the city proper where cobbled streets added the clack and rumble of hooves and wagon wheels to the clamor of the city's voices. Fin's wide eyes couldn't drink enough of all the color and commotion. Men in coats and black hats walked arm in arm with ladies under parasol shades. Shop windows filled with guns, porcelain dolls, fine clothes, china dishes, and ornate furniture lined the streets. Here and there, a drunken sailor sang and swaggered into an alley, and everywhere wagons wheeled cargo from far and wide to fill the holds of waiting ships bound for business across the Atlantic or south to the Caribbean.

It wasn't the city that stopped Fin's breath, though. It was the wide blue sea beyond. It rolled in blue-green swells to the horizon and was dotted everywhere with ships of all kinds coming and going, all turning the wheels of commerce.

The smell of fish and filth grew stronger the closer they got to the harbor. It nearly overwhelmed Fin, but Bartimaeus was breathing deep of it and smiling. He pulled the wagon up in front of a storehouse and jumped to the ground.

"Now, see here, missy. I got to go in and take care of business. Got to see what price this here silk will bring. Don't rightly know how long I might be, so you go on and have a look around but don't stray too far, and you come runnin' back directly if there's any trouble."

Fin nodded wildly and jumped out of the wagon. She took in the scene like a hungry man eats, sampling a bit of one thing then moving quickly to taste another. It was all new and full of wonder, the sounds of the harbor, strange people, clothes, smells, even colors. Most of the buildings on the street were storehouses, many with wagons in front loading goods in and out. She saw men unloading sacks of dry goods, bolts of fine cloth, piles of tobacco, and crates of exotic shipments from across the sea.

She struck out southward hoping to find her way to the seaside to glimpse it up close. At the first crossroads, however, a commotion up the side street drew her attention. There was a small crowd gathered and shouting in front of one of the buildings. She ran up to the next block to get a better look. As she drew closer, the shouts became clearer.

"No justice. No peace," the men were chanting with their fists in the air. The target of the protest was the large building in front of them. It was an official-looking building with white pillars spread across its face and high, arched windows girding its walls. Two British soldiers clad in red and white, with muskets at the order, guarded the double door. Farther down the street, a merchant shingle hung above an open door. Tondee's Tavern, it read. Men were pouring out of the building and joining the crowd, raising the volume of its chant to a roar.

"No *justice*. No *peace*!" The crowd's fervor grew in waves. The guards began to look nervous, and one of them turned and entered the building. He returned moments later with a British lieutenant and resumed his post. The lieutenant addressed the crowd.

"Stand down! Order will be kept here." The mob ignored him. If anything, his demand seemed to intensify the crowd's clamor.

"NO *justice*, NO *peace*!"

Fin didn't want to worry Bartimaeus, so she turned and ran back down the street to find the wagon.

"Bartimaeus, there's a protest! People are shouting!" she said as she ran up, out of breath.

Bartimaeus was unloading the last of the silk bolts from the wagon. "Protest, eh? What you say we find some news and see what the upset is all about. We're done here. Got a good price, and the shipper say he'll bring him a boat up river next month so's we can load it from our back door. How's that for good dealin's?" He winked at her and swung himself up into the wagon seat. Fin climbed in beside him. He snapped the reins and they headed off up the street. When he turned the corner, the mob was blocking the road. The crowd had grown to several hundred people, all shouting in unison.

"NO JUSTICE, NO PEACE!"

"You stay here, missy. I'll see what I can learn, don't you go nowhere, see here?" He gave her a stern look and hopped out of the wagon. She watched him drift around the crowd, appraising people until he settled on a target and approached him. They exchanged a few words, and Bartimaeus came back looking worried.

"Man says the Royal Gov'ner got some politician locked up in the jail house for talkin' independence. Folks ain't none too happy about it."

A fancily dressed man in a white wig—an official of some sort, Bartimaeus surmised—came out and tried to calm the assemblage, but whatever words he said were lost in the din of the crowd and he retreated back into the building. Four more British soldiers came out and posted themselves, flanking the door.

Then there was a loud crash followed by the high, bright sound of shattering glass. Men were throwing stones at the building, breaking the windows.

"We best get home," said Bartimaeus.

The soldiers at the door shifted nervously in their boots as the crowd became more and more restless. Men began to hurl stones at the soldiers and the chant intensified.

The lieutenant came out onto the steps and shouted at the crowd again. The crowd answered with more anger. He turned his head and gave an order to the soldiers. They raised their muskets. They backed against the wall and took aim. The roar and zeal of the crowd didn't slacken at all. They pumped their fists in the air and more stones flew.

"*NO JUSTICE, NO PEACE!*" they cried.

A flash of fire and smoke exploded out of a musket. In the crowd, the chant turned into screaming. *Whoom, whoom!* Two more musket shots. The front of the building was obscured by smoke.

"*Hya!*" cried Bartimaeus and the wagon jumped to life as people scattered. "Hya! Hya!" he snapped the reins over and over, urging the horses on as people fled. *Whoom,* came the sound of another shot. Where the crowd had been, there were three men lying on the ground, wounded and crying out for help, while through the clearing smoke she saw soldiers reloading as another fired his ball into the fleeing crowd. *Whoom!*

Then they were too far down the street to see. As they rumbled out of town, Fin heard only screams and the echoing of discharged muskets.

Bartimaeus drove the horses without mercy. Fin feared he might run them to death. His eyes were wide and wild, filled with rage, as if at any moment he might turn the wagon around and charge back to town to exact some desperate vengeance. He saw in those short murderous moments flashes of the man he'd been and visions of what he might be driven to again, and so he drove the horses mad to escape his own fearful intent. Fin saw it all in his eyes, the turning back, the fear of what he might do, the war he fought to master himself, to keep *standin' up*. She reached out her hand to comfort his unrest, half-afraid he might snap at it like a rabid dog, but when she touched him, gently on the shoulder, she felt the fear subside, and she saw again the man she knew and loved.

Bartimaeus pulled the horses up and stopped in the road. He breathed deeply with his head down. Fin put her arms around him.

"Damn them," he whispered.

THEY ARRIVED BACK IN Ebenezer just before nightfall. The courtyard was empty and voices from the dining hall told them dinner was afoot. They unhitched the horses and Fin stabled them as Bartimaeus tended to the wagon.

"I'll tell them," said Bartimaeus as they entered the dining hall to join the others. The room hushed. Sister Hilde knew with a look that something was wrong.

"Bartimaeus, what is it?" she said.

"Protest in Savannah, crowd gathered outside the jailhouse and the English fired into them." Sister Hilde covered her mouth in horror and gasps filled the room. "At least three shot down that I saw. They were still shootin' when we cleared out of town."

"Are you alright?" said Sister Carmaline. "Phinea, are you hurt?"

"We're fine, but who knows for how long. The Whigs won't stand for it. There'll be more killin' before it's done. I'm goin' to warn Mr. Bolzius before trouble starts in town. Folks bound to find out soon." Bartimaeus hurried out the door.

"Phinea, are you alright, child?" said Carmaline as she hurried over and inspected Fin physically from head to toe. "My Lord, my Lord."

"I'm alright," said Fin.

"Thank the Lord, child," said Carmaline, hugging her.

Sister Hilde stood at a distance and appraised Fin as she might a sick horse. "Get some food before it's cold," she ordered, making no mention of Fin's change of clothing.

THE NEXT DAY THE entire town was abuzz. There were many comings and goings on the road outside the orphanage, and townsfolk often hurried into the courtyard to speak with the sisters only to hurry out again moments later. The air was filled with tension, and all the children felt it.

Fin couldn't stand having the story bottled up inside her and was determined to see Peter and tell him all about it. He would be around to call on her after dinner, but she wasn't satisfied to wait. When lunch was over, she cleaned up as fast as she could and told Bartimaeus she'd be down at the river practicing fiddle. After a quick look to make sure Sister Hilde wasn't watching, she slipped out the gate and ran down the street to the edge of the town looking for Mr. Hickory's house. She only knew its whereabouts from Peter but found it easily enough by the sawhorses and carpenter's tools lying about.

She snuck around to the back to see if she could spot Peter. He was eating lunch at a picnic table with Mr. Hickory and his wife. Fin hid in the bushes and waited for him to look her way. Each time he looked up between bites, she waved to catch his attention. Fin had nearly decided he must be blind before he saw her at last. He nodded her way and she dove out of sight behind the bushes. A few minutes later, Peter casually walked into the tree line.

"What are you doing, Fin?"

"I wanted to talk to you."

"It's dangerous to be out like this. Who knows if the British might be coming here next?" He sounded worried.

"I was there, Peter. I saw the whole thing."

"You were there?"

"Me and Bartimaeus were in Savannah, and we went to see what the protest was about. They just started shooting! It was awful. Someone needs to show those damned redcoats that Georgia doesn't take to folks just up and shooting people. I think Bartimaeus might do something—he was really angry."

"What do you mean, 'do something'? What would he do?"

"I don't know. When they started shooting it was like he wanted to jump out of the wagon and go—hurt someone. He didn't, but—" she didn't finish, didn't want to. "What if there's a war, Peter. Will you go?"

Peter looked startled; he'd never considered the idea. "What are you talking about? Go fight? I don't know," he said.

"I would," said Fin. "There needs to be a war. The English have no right pushing us around. The colonies should go independent. *I'd* go fight," she said half to Peter and half to herself.

"You're not going anywhere, Fin."

She glared at him. "And who are you to tell me where I'll go? British don't tell me what to do, and neither do you, Peter LaMee!"

"I didn't mean it like that. I mean we've got plans here. I'm not going to mess that up by getting killed in some war, and I'm not going to let you either." She softened a bit. He wasn't trying to control her, just protect her.

"What if we did something together, Pete? If there's a war, I mean. We could be like a team. I could dress like a boy, and we could join the militia!"

Peter looked at her askance and gave an uneasy chuckle. "You're mad, you know that?" She wasn't kidding and Fin sensed it was unsettling him. She let it drop.

"Head back to the orphanage, Fin. It's not safe out here. Half the families in Ebenezer are moving out to the country. There could be trouble in town. There's lots of folks loyal to England. Mr. Hickory says independent is the way to go, but war ain't the way to do it. Says it'll come if we just settle down and let the Good Lord do his work. I don't know. I do know I'd feel better if I knew you were safe back at the orphanage, where Sister Hilde can keep an eye on you." He said the last part with a teasing smile that brought him an insulted look from Fin. "Don't worry, I'll come by tonight after dinner."

"Alright, see you then," she said and sprinted off toward the orphanage. Peter stared after her until she was out of sight.

CHAPTER X

THAT EVENING AT DINNER, Sister Carmaline declared that, due to the civil unrest, orphans would no longer be allowed outside the gates. It didn't escape Fin's attention that Sister Carmaline was looking right at her during most of the announcement. After the others were dismissed, Sister Hilde stayed behind and cornered Fin.

"Miss Button, do not think we are so blind as to have missed your frequent excursions outside the walls. While we have had some measure of tolerance of late, you can expect that to now cease. It is far too dangerous for a young girl, even one such as yourself, to be out without proper supervision. Do not disappoint me, Miss Button," she ordered and left.

Fin was half-shocked and half-infuriated. Sister Hilde had known she was sneaking out. She had known and not said anything. That was most unlike Sister Hilde—or Carmaline for that matter. Was she hoarding up evidence to prosecute all her crimes at once? Maybe she was bluffing and only suspected Fin's ventures beyond the walls. Certainly if she knew, she would have come down like a hammer the instant she found out. But found out or not, they weren't about to stop her from seeing Peter tonight, or any other time she wanted to. The nerve of that woman to try to keep her cooped up in here like one of her precious chickens. The sisters were terrified of everything in the world outside of the orphanage, it seemed, and the latest news had done nothing to ease their paranoia. This might make life a little more difficult, but it wasn't going to bring it to a stop.

Fin finished her chores and headed out the door. Bartimaeus stopped her.

"I'd be careful, missy," he said

"Careful about what? I can't leave the walls, in case you missed it."

"I won't go stoppin' you. You're old enough now to make your own decisions. Just remember, you'll have to abide the consequence if Hilde catches on." Then he turned and left, leaving Fin to her choices.

Fin considered it for a moment—a small moment. The notion of ceding defeat to Sister Hilde was more than she could stand. She walked out to the gate to wait for Peter.

As she reached the gate and saw Peter coming up the road, a voice spoke from behind her.

"Mr. LaMee, may I help you?" Sister Hilde said, walking up from behind.

"I come to walk with Fin a bit, if that's alright," said Peter. Fin began opening the gate and Sister Hilde's hand came down on the latch.

"I'm sorry, Peter, but Miss Button is restricted to the grounds for the near future."

"He can come inside then, Sister Hilde. We just want to talk," said Fin.

"I think not. It's far too late for visitors. It is nice to see you again, Peter, perhaps some other time. Come along, Miss Button."

"I'm not going anywhere," said Fin incredulously.

"Indeed?"

"Fin, don't make a fuss," Peter said.

"You've got no right to tell me I can't talk to Peter. He's lived here all his life and has every bit as much right to come inside as you do."

"Miss Button, I suggest you leave off this nonsense before I become *irritated*," said Sister Hilde as her nose began to rise.

"Go on, Fin. We'll catch up later," said Peter. He eyed Sister Hilde with a worried look, but there was no stopping Fin now.

"This is ridiculous! Go to bed, you wicked old bat, before *I* get damned well irritated. I'm sick and tired of listening to your constant threats of extra chores and switchings and God only cares what else. Haven't you got anything better to do than follow me around? Haven't you got any children of your own to nag? But, oh, of course you don't, and you're not my mother either, so you can take your bonnets and your rules and your nose and carry them right out of my life!"

Fin's mind was full of a hundred other insults and thoughts she'd like to voice, but she stopped. She'd gone too far and she knew it. Fin had hurt her. Hilde turned away and walked back toward the headmistress's chambers.

"She didn't deserve that," said Peter flatly.

"I'd better go," muttered Fin.

"Things will be back to normal before long; don't worry about it. I'll see you."

Fin smiled at him as best she could and watched him turn to leave. He paused a moment and turned as if to say something more.

"Go on," she whispered and waved him off. He nodded and walked away.

Fin went to bed and lay awake a long time wondering what Sister Hilde's vengeance would be.

As Fin walked to the dining hall the next morning, the weight of what she'd said to Hilde pressed down on her. Very rarely had she ever directly defied Hilde and never so plainly as she had last night. She was convinced Hilde had deserved the tongue-lashing, but no matter how she tried, she couldn't convince herself to stop feeling guilty. Why she should regret speaking rudely to Hilde was beyond her reckoning. Certainly Hilde had been rude to her often enough, so why now such remorse when she only gave her a taste of her own venom? Thinking about it irritated her.

When she arrived at the dining hall, Bartimaeus was in the kitchen stirring up breakfast. She retrieved the beeswax from the cupboard and went to work polishing the table without speaking to him. There seemed to be more nicks and blemishes on the surface than she'd ever seen before. No matter how hard she scrubbed at some of them, they refused to disappear. She expected Sister Hilde to stride into the room and descend upon her at any moment. She couldn't think of anything Hilde could do that would be worse than punishments she'd served a thousand times before, but she couldn't escape the look on Hilde's face as she'd yelled at her. What horrible fate would Hilde devise for such offense? Fin didn't dare imagine it, and she became furious at a particular scuff on the table that refused to buff clean. She scrubbed it so hard her fingers hurt, and then she began to beat on it.

Bartimaeus yelled from the other room. "Too late to get it clean now, missy. Best get them dishes set out."

Just as Fin finished setting the table, Sister Hilde entered the dining hall. Hilde said nothing. She simply sat and waited for the meal to commence. Fin tried to erase any trace of guilt or worry from her face and scurried to the other room to find something to do.

Throughout the meal, Sister Hilde was silent and avoided any eye contact with Fin. Fin tried her best to act as she would any other morning. She did not intend to let Hilde detect an inkling of the guilt she felt.

When the meal had finished, Sister Carmaline dismissed the children. "Excuse yourselves please, and ready yourselves for morning prayers. Miss Button, will you please join me in my chambers once your work here is tended to?"

That was it, the hammer stroke, the knell of doom. Fin quivered. Sister Hilde exited the room without acknowledging Fin's presence.

Fin took to her cleanup with the slow, heavy steps of a man led to the gallows.

"Cheer up, missy. She can't kill you." Bartimaeus said and smiled at her. She hadn't mentioned the confrontation to Bartimaeus. She was ashamed of what she'd done and was afraid he'd think less of her for the knowing. But clearly he had heard, probably from Hilde herself. He was right. She couldn't kill her, but death might be an easier doom than whatever Hilde had in mind.

Finally, she could put off the meeting no longer. She trudged to the headmistress's chambers and rapped on the door.

"Come in, Miss Button," called Sister Carmaline through the door. Fin pushed it open and stepped inside. Carmaline was sitting in her rocking chair next to the fireplace patiently considering her knitting. Sister Hilde stood quietly, her back to the door, looking down into the black-sooted hearth.

"Shut the door behind you please," said Carmaline in her usual cheerful voice, without looking up. Fin did as she asked, shut the door, then stood before her and waited. She stared intently at Sister Carmaline, hoping that by some miracle Hilde would continue looking into the fireplace. She didn't want to have to endure her gaze.

"Miss Button, how old are you now?" asked Carmaline, though she knew perfectly well.

"Nineteen."

"Nineteen years old." Carmaline paused to look up and appraise Fin before continuing. "Nineteen years, and it seems the extent of what we have managed to teach you has been to dress like a vagrant, disregard our rules, and speak vulgarities and insults to your elders."

Fin risked a glance at Hilde; she was cold, unmoving, her back to the room, staring into the fireplace.

"Sister Hilde and I have spent nearly twenty years of our lives attempting to train you to survive in this world, attempting to raise you up to become a proper woman, capable of making a home and marrying a suitable man. But it seems we are failures." She paused again but didn't look up.

"I am at somewhat of a loss as to what to do, Miss Button. My sister feels that we would do well to turn you out to reap the benefits of your meager skills and graces. What do you think, Miss Button?"

Turn her out? Let her go? Suddenly Fin was confronted with the reality of it. It was what she'd wanted all her life, to get away, to be on her own, to make her own decisions. And now, faced with it, she was paralyzed. She wasn't sure she was ready. What would Peter think? The timing was all wrong.

"I'll go if you want me to," she stammered, defiant, not meaning a word of it.

"And where would you go, Miss Button? To Peter? I think not. Peter is a good lad and well employed, but I very seriously doubt he is prepared to risk his job and his future for an ill-mannered girl with nowhere else to go. Do you know, Miss Button, that I have seen your like before? Girls like you, with their minds set to make their way in the world, invariably make their way no further than a harbor-town brothel. Is that what you think to do?" Carmaline looked up briefly. "No, I should think not. But no harlot ever went out searching for her end. The end finds the harlot when all other doors are shut."

She looked up to appraise Fin once more, and then, thoughtfully, went back to her work before continuing.

"Well, Phinea, despite what my sister thinks, I have hope that you may yet be turned from your reckless nature and one day may be fit for a fine man and fruitful union. Therefore we will not turn you out." Fin let out her breath. "However, there will be changes made." Fin didn't like where this was going. "From here on you will no longer be working with Brother Bartimaeus." Fin opened her mouth in protest but Sister Carmaline pressed on. "We will afford him a new apprentice. Henceforth, you will be under the direct supervision of Sister Hilde." Fin's eyes nearly popped out of her head. "You will assist her in the supervision of chores and the other daily workings of the orphan house. You will not be permitted out of her eyesight until such time as trust enough is built that Sister Hilde deems it appropriate."

"Sister Carmaline—"

"Furthermore, all contact with Peter LaMee is forbidden."

"You can't do that," Fin whispered.

Sister Hilde turned and glared at Fin. "I can indeed, Miss Button. Your relationship with Mr. LaMee has done nothing but lead you to mischief. Mischief which is, as of this moment, at an *end*," Hilde hissed.

Ignoring Sister Hilde, Fin threw herself at Carmaline's feet and begged. "Sister Carmaline, please! You don't understand—" Carmaline ignored her, concentrated on her knitting.

"*Silence*, girl!" spat Hilde as she jerked Fin up by the arm. Fin ripped her arm away and backed toward the door.

"You can't do this . . . you can't do this . . ."

"Miss Button, may I suggest that you calm down and collect your thoughts. We have nothing but your best interests at heart and you will do well to heed the decisions of your elders," said Carmaline, perfectly calm.

"I can't, Sister Carmaline please—" Fin cried.

"My dear, I'm afraid you have no choice."

There it was. No choice. It echoed in Fin's mind. This is what they wanted. All her life lived inside walls and defined by their choices, never hers. Her father chose a boy and cast her aside. The sisters wanted her to clean and cook and chose her for Bartimaeus. Only Peter had ever chosen her as she was and as she wanted to be, and now Hilde wanted to take him away as well. *No choice*, said Carmaline. All her life's fears converged on those words and she backed away, flailing at them like a fire set to burn her. No Peter. No Bartimaeus. No fiddle. No choice.

She flung open the door and ran. Bartimaeus was in the courtyard and he tried to stop her, but she flew past him to the gate. She raised the latch and cast one look back. Sister Hilde was standing at the edge of the headmistress's chambers staring at her with a look of perfect satisfaction on her face. Fin threw open the gate and ran headlong into the morning. No choice but to run.

She ran down the road—to Peter. Peter would convince Mr. Hickory to let her stay. They could be married today; she could be away from the sisters forever. Peter would know what to do. She could barely see the road through the tears in her eyes, but at last she found Mr. Hickory's house. Peter was in front of the house sawing logs. The sight of him was like water on her parched tongue.

"Peter!" she sobbed. "Peter!"

Peter caught her as she was slipping to the ground exhausted. "Fin, what's wrong?"

"Peter . . ." she couldn't manage to say anything else.

He shook her, worried. "Fin, tell me what's going on."

"They said I couldn't see you again."

"Who? Who said, Fin?"

"Sister Hilde." Mr. Hickory was standing nearby, watching, with a worried look on his face. Fin was sobbing. "I left, Peter! I left."

"Left? Left the orphanage?" he asked.

"I can't go back, I can't stand it anymore."

"Fin, listen, you have to go back. You can't stay here. Just go back and apologize. Sister Carmaline won't let Hilde turn you out."

Fin looked at him, unable to believe what he was saying. "I can't go back Peter, I can't."

"Fin, you have to. Remember our plans? We just have to wait a little longer."

"I can't go back, Peter."

"Fin—" he said, imploring her to go back.

Fin pulled herself to her feet. "I won't. I *can't*. Peter, please!"

Peter cast a look at Mr. Hickory. When he turned back he lowered his head close to hers and spoke softly into her ear. "Fin, we talked about this. Wait a while longer."

Fin pushed herself away from him and ran. Peter had betrayed her. Peter wanted her back at the orphanage, behind the walls, locked up and looked after. Peter didn't understand. She ran from him, from all of it, into the woods. Away from people and choices, walls and control. She ran through the trees and brush, briars bit at her legs, tore her clothes, brought bright blood to thatch her shins like ribbons. Roots pulled at her feet and bit into her soles, but she was beyond the pain and ran.

At last, she met the river. She fell on its bank and sobbed into the rolling waters. She was trapped and Peter had turned her away. She hadn't seen that coming, not Peter. The tears came like a tide and she let herself float away upon them.

Hours later, when the crying had dried, sleep found her and laid her to rest on the muddy bank. She dreamed of her fallen bell tower and in her dream it rose high over the earth, and from her lost corner she saw the sea shining on the horizon like a beacon.

Night came and Fin awoke in its cooling dark. She sat up and felt the sting on her legs where the briars had torn her. She stood and felt a sharp pain in the bottom of her foot. She touched it with her hand and found a deep gash. In her mind, she heard Sister Hilde berating her for going barefoot outside her room and she muttered curses at herself. She winced as she touched the wound.

She limped to the water's edge and waded into the river to rinse the mud from her clothes. The water was cold and clean. In the moonlight, she could just see the outline of herself in the reflection and it brought back the memory of the day. Running from the orphan house. Peter turning her away. No choice.

Fin washed herself of the muck and spooned a handful of water onto her face Maybe Peter was right. Hilde couldn't really keep them apart forever. If Peter could work and sweat day after day for them to be together, was it really so much for her to tolerate Hilde for a few more weeks or months? She couldn't work with Bartimaeus, but that didn't mean she'd never see him. Perhaps she was just being foolish.

Fin waded back to the bank and limped her way through the woods toward the road. Her clothes were wet and clinging, and though the night air made her shiver, her head, at least, had cleared. If Peter wanted her to, she'd go back. She'd suffer it for the promise of Peter. Fin thought of the pleased look Sister Hilde would give her when she admitted defeat, and it made her ill. But she would suffer it for Peter.

She fumbled her way through the dark, looking for the road. Almost at once, she felt the cut on the arch of her foot reopen and begin to bleed. Moonlight broke through the treetops here and there, but little of it reached the ground to light her way, and the night had a strange way of elongating distance. A stone's throw in day felt like a mile alone in the dark, and her aching foot made the crossing no easier. When she reached the road, at last, she breathed easier and wondered if Peter was looking for her—if anyone was. Surely someone would have worried after her by now. As she turned east toward town, she heard footsteps approaching from the west. She strained her eyes in the dark to see who was coming. Peter perhaps, but the darkness was too deep.

"Peter?" she called into the night. There was no answer, just the sound of footsteps coming closer.

"Hello?" she called out again. Her instinct told her to run, but she pushed the feeling down and assured herself she had nothing to fear.

Then something glittered in the dark, a shiny wisp bouncing in the moonlight. Out of the veil of night came two men, dressed in red coats, white trousers, and black tricorne hats. British soldiers. The moonlight glanced off their muskets as they bobbed up and down in the dark.

"You there! Hold!" barked the man on the right. He lowered his musket at Fin and approached her. Fin considered running but her damaged foot wouldn't allow it. She held her ground and stuck her chin out defiantly.

"What business are you about this hour?" he said. His voice was rough, confident, accustomed to commanding the attention of men and it expected its orders followed. The other soldier leveled his musket at her and peered through the dark, trying to see if she was man or woman, armed or innocent.

"No business but my own," said Fin.

"What's this? A girl? After midnight? Stalking out of the woods?" He looked back. His companion shrugged at him. "Speak up! You're one of those Whigs, I'll wager, lying in ambush for honest king's men."

"I'm headed home. I was sleeping down at the river—"

"All alone, eh? Put up your hands where we can see you aren't armed," he ordered.

Fin stood still, defiant, considering it.

"Up!" he barked and jabbed his musket at her. She put her hands up. "Check her," he said to his companion.

The other man slung his musket over his shoulder and moved toward her. Fin backed away, and he caught her by the wrist and wrenched her around so that her back pressed against him. He ran his hands down her sides and then paused and chuckled. His hands began moving again, but slowly, softly, lingering. Fin tried to wrest herself free, but he jerked her back and held her to him. She felt his breath on her neck.

"We got a fresh one here," he whispered to his friend. His hands continued their search. Fin closed her eyes and thought of playing the fiddle.

"Tie her," said the man pointing the musket. He was laughing. She was glad she couldn't see his face. The man holding her wrapped one arm around her waist and reached with his other for some unseen lashing. Fin took her opening. Speed and surprise. She spun around, freed herself from his arm and struck him in the face. Then she ran. The wound on her foot erupted in a fountain of agony, but she ignored it and flew. Seconds later, she heard the soldier's labored breathing behind her. His hands snatched at her and caught her by the arm. He flung her to the ground. When she rolled over to kick at him the butt of his musket crashed into her cheek.

FIN WOKE TO THE crackle and pop of a campfire. She felt its warmth on the back of her legs and heard voices, the same voices from before. One was low, rough, throaty, the other smooth, metered, and precise. She couldn't make out words, only tones and mild laughter. Her senses swam in and out of consciousness. Her mouth was gagged with a salty, foul-tasting cloth. She tried to open her eyes and felt a dull ache in her left cheek where the musket had struck her. She couldn't see out of her left eye; it was swollen shut. Through her right eye she saw that it was still nighttime and she was surrounded by woods.

"Rum's run dry," said a voice behind her.

"Good, let me sleep," said the other.

"Sleep then, you old sot," the smooth voice said. She heard the hollow clunk of a bottle thrown into the woods. Fin tried moving her arms, but they were tied behind her. She tried moving her feet. They moved freely, unbound. She could run.

"Oy, is our lassie waking up?" Fin froze. She heard a rustle, then footsteps. A boot struck her in the lower back and she cried out.

"She's awake now." They both laughed. "What do you say, lass? I'll forgive you for our scuffle, if you forgive me," said the sharp, calculated voice, dropping to a malicious whisper.

Fin rolled and tried to get to her feet. The soldier standing over her put out his foot and knocked her to the ground like a broken chair. They laughed at her. She fought for her feet again.

"Ha! She's trying to run home," he said and kicked her over again. "Oops."

Fin cried out in frustration and tried to gain her feet once more.

"Oops!" he kicked her to the ground again. The two men burst into laughter. Fin bellowed through the gag in rage. The soldier bent over and grabbed her by the neck, pushed her face into the ground, and whispered in her ear, "That's the spirit, lass!" She struggled against him, and he drove his knee into her back, knocking the wind from her lungs. "You'll tell me the name of every Whig in this blight of a town before I'm done with you, lassie. But before we have our little talk, we got to soften you up a bit. Jog the memory so to speak."

Fin tried screaming, but all she could manage was a muffled moan through the gag. She kicked at him and rocked back and forth, trying to escape his hands. The more she fought, the more he laughed. In her mind, fear mingled with rage and she couldn't separate the two. No choice, nowhere to run, no one to help, only fear, fury, and, somewhere over the horizon, madness, lurking like a wolf.

"Ho, she's a live one!" said the rough, low voice. Fin felt the cold line of a knife on her flesh. She kicked and moaned, pulling at the bonds tying her hands. The rope cut into her wrists. She felt the knife bite into her lower back as she struggled, but she didn't care.

"Damn it, girl! You'll gut yourself if you don't mind your squirming," he spat.

She felt warm trickles of blood running down her side where the knife had pierced her, but still she kept fighting. The man swore and struck her in the temple with his fist. Her vision blurred and her thoughts swam around in her head like fish in the river, near—far—clear—dim.

He threw her over onto her back. She tried to scream at him. Only a ragged moan obeyed. She told her limbs to kick at him, but they didn't listen. She rolled her head to the side and looked into the fire. She focused on it, stared at it, tried to escape into it in her mind.

Then she saw a figure in the flame, rippling in the air, a man like a storm. He moved like floodwater churning through a gulley. He swirled and flowed out of the fire and raised his arm. She heard voices shouting. The rough-voiced soldier was grabbing his musket. The flowing water-man moved toward him, his hair like the foam of an angry river. A blunt, flared muzzle exploded into the soldier, and a crimson flower bloomed from his back. He staggered backward and collapsed into the fire. The blaze licked around the dying soldier and began to consume him. The watery figure moved closer. His features swirled like the wrinkles of a wave raising up for its plunge to the shore, and she knew him. She barely felt the joy through her pain, but she knew him.

Bartimaeus. He'd come for her.

The soldier that had been on top of her was yelling. Bartimaeus drew a kitchen knife from his coat and slashed at him. The knife painted a gaping red stripe across his face, and the soldier staggered back, screaming. Bartimaeus launched at him again with murder and vengeance to work, but the man turned and fled into the woods.

Bartimaeus knelt to cut Fin's bonds. His creased face bent and twisted like a squall: now fury, now thunder, now cool, cleansing rain. He pulled the gag from her mouth and she inhaled a precious breath like no other since she'd been born. Then she screamed—no words, no thoughts, just pain and release. Bartimaeus cradled her in his arms and held her like a babe. He too was shaking with tears and rage.

Beside them on the ground, next to the fire, lay the blunderbuss—Betsy. Smoke flitted out of her barrel like breath in winter.

Chapter XI

FIN AWOKE ON A bed in the headmistress's chambers. She was covered with thick woolen blankets and warmed by a fire. Sister Hilde sat stone-faced in the rocking chair near the hearth with her Bible laid open in her lap, reading quietly. From outside the room, Fin heard the warm sounds of children gathering for a meal, small feet stomping on wood, the scraping of chairs on the floor, the voices and sounds of home.

Fin dared not speak. Sister Hilde hadn't seen she was awake yet. Would Hilde be angry with her? Would she tell her to leave now that she was rousing? Fin was afraid of the answers.

Her entire body ached. The swelling around her eye seemed to have gone down, but her cheekbone throbbed dully. Her temple pounded with each heartbeat.

The soldiers. It came back to her in spurts and explosive images. Running. The butt of a musket. The cold edge of a knife. The fire. Bartimaeus's eyes as Betsy woke. Oh, Bartimaeus. He'd killed a man. *Terrible things*. He'd brought back Bart, the man he used to be—and Betsy. He'd *lain down*. She couldn't bear it. Twenty years *standin' up*, he'd said. Now he'd brought himself low for a foolish girl and her pride.

Oh, Bartimaeus. Did his fiddle hold notes enough to assuage such grief? She couldn't imagine it did. She couldn't keep silent any longer and began to cry.

Sister Hilde's face lifted from her reading. She stood and placed the Bible on the mantle then sat down on the edge of the bed. Fin tried to roll over and turn away, but Hilde pulled her up into an embrace. She held Fin tight and rocked her. Fin looked up. She could hardly believe it. She had never imagined Hilde harbored a thimbleful of caring in her.

"I'm sorry," cried Fin into Hilde's bony breast.

"Hush, child," she whispered.

Their embrace was long and difficult. Years of bitterness had spread a gulf between them too vast to span in so short a time.

Hilde laid Fin back on her pillow and without speaking stood and left the room. Fin tried to remember the last time she'd actually touched Hilde. The only physical contact she'd ever had with the woman had been that of a disciplinary sort. How strange to be caressed by a hand that had only ever brought pain.

Fin heard the door open and the rhythm of quick steps on the wooden floor. Peter ran into the room and straight to the bed. Fin smiled through her aching face at him. He picked her up and kissed her. She didn't care that it hurt. She'd go through pain a thousand times for such kisses.

"I'm sorry I told you to go back. Me and Bartimaeus were looking for you all night!" He was talking so fast she could barely make out his words.

"You were looking for me?" she asked softly. Peter had been looking for her. Of course he would have been. But knowing it, hearing it out of his own mouth—she needed that. He had looked for her.

"Mr. Hickory said to let you go, said you just needed to cool off. But when I went to see you at dinner they said you hadn't come back. We spent all night looking. I went door to door through town asking, and Bartimaeus, he searched the woods." He stopped long enough to kiss her a few more times and Sister Carmaline appeared at the doorway, squinting a big smile at them. "Fin, there was so much blood, I thought you were dead. Bartimaeus came into town carrying you and there was so much blood. Are you alright?"

"I'm fine," said Fin, hoping maybe he'd put her down soon. It was really beginning to hurt.

"You won't be getting out of that bed for a few more days if I have anything to do with it, Miss Button," cautioned Sister Carmaline.

She heard footsteps coming through the front door again, soft and slow. Bartimaeus slid through the bedroom doorway and worked his creases into a smile. He looked different—*was* different. Not on the outside, something on the inside had changed. He looked like he had aged years since she'd seen him smile last. Picking up Betsy again had hurt him. She smiled back and said nothing.

"You all get to the table now so I can get Miss Button here some dinner," he said. Carmaline tugged Peter out of the room. Bartimaeus ducked around the corner and brought back a tray piled high with roasted turkey, okra, potatoes, and peach cobbler. He set it down on the night table and looked at Fin.

"Can you sit up? Lyin' down won't do."

Fin risked it and pushed herself up against the headboard; it wasn't pleasant but she managed to make it look painless. Bartimaeus nodded with satisfaction and placed the tray on her lap. She appraised it hungrily while he sat down in the rocking chair next to the fire. She wanted to say something to him, to thank him. But somehow, thanks didn't seem sufficient. She looked at him, sitting there, smiling at her; she searched for the words to let him know how she felt but when she tried to speak, he stopped her.

"I know, missy. You just eat up now, see here? Old Bartimaeus like to keel over dead the last two days with no help. Got to get you back up and runnin' around," he said. Fin smiled at him and dug into her dinner with fury.

THE NEXT MORNING FIN decided that, despite Sister Carmaline's assurances to the contrary, she was not going to stay in bed any longer. Whether it hurt or not, she was getting up. She swung herself out of bed and groaned as her muscles protested; they were aching and sore. Sharp pains flared in her lower back. Her midriff had a thick bandage wrapped around it to protect the wounds where the knife had cut her. When she stood up, the cut in the arch of her foot throbbed and she shifted her weight quickly to relieve the pain. It hurt, but it wasn't so bad. She'd be limping for a few days.

She looked around the room for her clothes and failed to find them. Unfortunately, Sister Carmaline had laid out a plain blue dress for her. She scowled at it but was in no mood for stirring up trouble. The least she could do was to put it on. She slipped into it and washed her face in the basin on the night table. Looking up into the mirror was a mistake, though. Fin hardly recognized herself. Her cheek and left eye were a dull, greenish-yellow color; the other side of her face was black and blue from her hairline above her right eye to her ear and down to her jaw. Colorful—but not anything she wanted to get used to. She ran a brush through her hair to give it some semblance of order then went outside.

The sounds of a normal day at the orphanage greeted her. Kids running and yelling, animals lowing and braying, Sister Hilde off in the distance scolding someone, and the smells of the kitchen binding it all together. The place didn't feel as confined as it had only a few days ago. Odd, that. Three days earlier, this had been the worst place she could imagine. Now she couldn't think of anywhere she'd rather be. All that was missing was Peter. He'd be back at work with Mr. Hickory, no doubt.

She stepped off the porch and made for the dining hall. Inside, Bartimaeus was sitting at the table whittling away at carrots.

"Up and about already?" he said, raising an eyebrow. "Didn't expect you'd stay down long."

"I've had enough bed for a week," she said.

He motioned to the kitchen. "Go get you a knife and help me peelin' these here carrots."

Fin retrieved a knife and pulled up a chair next to him. She had questions but didn't know how to ask.

"Hmm?" he said without looking up from his carrot. He knew her mind.

"You killed that man," she said with a wince.

His creases deepened. "Reckon I did."

"I remember the other man yelling. But I don't remember what happened to him," she said and looked at Bartimaeus.

Bartimaeus tended to his carrot in silence. He finished and placed it on the table. "I cut him. Didn't kill him. He run off into the woods." He fixed his eye on her. "Was more worried about seein' to you than I was about seein' to him." He wiped the knife on his shirt and picked up another carrot. "So I let him go. Reckon these old legs too stiff to give much chase anyhow."

Fin thought about it as she peeled her carrot. "Will he come back?" she asked.

Bartimaeus stopped and looked across the room at the wall. "Reckon he will. They was king's soldiers. I expect they'll want to find the man that killed one of them."

Blood rushed from her face.

"What are you going to do?" she demanded. "You can't just stay here and let them come!"

Bartimaeus turned, looked at her. "If they come for me, then I'll go. I told you, I been *standin' up* twenty years now. All them years I wondered why the good Lord spared me the gallows. Most of old Bart's friends swang for the hangman—but not me. Always wondered why. But the other night in the woods I learnt somethin'. Lord kept me back, just for that one night. Reverend Whitefield told me the Lord done chose us afore we was even born. I reckon I was chose to be in them woods." He laid down his knife and smiled at her. "Now that's done. Lived more years, and better, than I ever deserved, and it's time for old Bart to pay for all the hurtin' he made."

Fin's shock turned to anger. His casual attitude infuriated her. He might be perfectly willing to go rot away in some jail, but it was a long way from acceptable as far as Fin was concerned. She slammed her knife down on the table and limped out of the room. Bartimaeus stared after her for a moment then resumed his carrot work.

She stopped in the courtyard and leaned against the wall of the dining hall. The short exertion of hurrying out of the room had exhausted her. The soldiers would return. They'd take Bartimaeus away. She needed to do something, anything. Circumstances beyond her control were about to take away one of the only people in the world she loved and there was nothing she could see to do about it. Walls. Closing in again.

She needed her bell tower. She needed to get above the walls and see the trees. But it was gone. The new chapel had locks on the doors. She limped out the gate and down to the river. She wished she had brought the fiddle, but she couldn't stand to go back for it. If she saw Bartimaeus, she would yell at him, tell him to run, to get away. But she knew he wouldn't listen. Stubborn man. How dare he sit there in his kitchen and wait for his own doom, a doom crafted by her foolishness. She dropped to the ground under a large cypress. It was the same spot where Bartimaeus had first showed her his fiddle, and Betsy. Her entire body ached, and she could feel dampness on the bandages; she'd torn the wounds open. They were bleeding. She pulled herself up against the tree and set her mind to finding a way to save Bartimaeus. Pain and helplessness were not options.

After hours of trying and failing to think of a solution, she made her way back to the orphanage. The best she could come up with was to convince Bartimaeus to leave Ebenezer, if only for a while. Maybe whoever came for him could be persuaded that a traveler had killed the soldier, not a resident. It was the best plan she could muster.

When she got to the gate she looked down the road and what she saw made her heart drop into her stomach. There were red-coated soldiers at Mr. Hickory's house. One was on horseback, an officer, and he was talking to a group of townsfolk in the street. Fin couldn't believe it was happening so soon. She opened the gate and ran to the dining hall. Bartimaeus was there setting lunch on the table. Her body screamed with pain from running.

"Soldiers. Bartimaeus, you have to hide!"

Bartimaeus stopped what he was doing and looked at her calmly. "I'm done hidin', missy. When they get here I'll be goin'."

"No! You have to hide or run or leave! You can't let them take you!"

Bartimaeus looked at her and smiled. "It's alright, missy. This place don't need me no more."

"What about me? I need you! You can't just let them come. *Do something! DO SOMETHING!*" she shouted at him.

Bartimaeus came around the table and took her by the shoulders. "See here, you and Peter goin' to do just fine. This is my choice, missy. It's *my* choice. If I run, then what? Old man hidin' in the woods and folks' barns? Waitin' around for the man to come knockin'? And when he does, what am I to do? Fight? Run some more? No, missy."

Fin beat on his chest. *"Do something! Please, Bartimaeus, do something!"* she cried at him. Bartimaeus didn't try to stop her. Her fists hit him again and again and again. He closed his eyes and accepted the blows like kisses.

Outside a man's voice shouted for the gate to be opened. The soldiers were here. Fin heard Sister Carmaline bustling out of her quarters, shooing off children and demanding to know the meaning of the order.

"If you don't do something, I will," said Fin. She clenched her jaw and looked him straight in the eye. "I won't let them. I'll stop them."

Bartimaeus turned deadly serious. "You'll do no such thing. You got to stay out of this." He grabbed her firmly. *"Look at me!"* She looked up at him with a face set in stone. "You stay out of sight, you hear?"

"I won't let them take you," she said coldly. She had to do something.

Bartimaeus's eyes flashed with fear or anger, she couldn't tell which. He looked around the room then gritted his teeth. Fin was too startled to resist when he pushed her into the kitchen. He slammed the door and turned the lock before she could realize what he was doing.

Fin rattled the door threatening to rip it off its hinges. "BARTIMAEUS!" she screamed.

Bartimaeus walked out of the hall.

"BARTIMAEUS, *NO!*" she bellowed.

The soldiers were at the front gate. The officer had dismounted and was speaking with Sister Carmaline. Bartimaeus walked straight to him.

"I'm the man you're lookin' for," he said.

The officer looked back toward his men. A soldier with a bandage covering his face stepped forward. There was a slotted opening in the dressing so that one eye could peer out. The eye glared at Bartimaeus and the man nodded. "That's him."

"Shackle him," said the officer, and two men came forward with chains. Bartimaeus held out his wrists and they clasped the manacles around them. Sister Carmaline covered her mouth with her hands and wept. In the background, the muffled screams and banging from the dining hall went ignored. Fin was trying to tear the door apart.

Carmaline and Hilde watched in tearful silence as the soldiers reformed their detail and, with Bartimaeus stumbling along in tow, began their march back toward Savannah. When they passed out of sight, Hilde turned to investigate the commotion coming from the dining hall. She threw open the door to the kitchen and stormed in.

"What in the name of heaven!" she swore.

Fin pushed her aside and ran through the door. She could catch them. She could stop them. If she didn't get him back now, she'd never see him again. She ran through the gate, ignoring shouts of protest from Hilde and Carmaline. Her foot felt like it was on fire. The wounds on her back were bleeding freely, but it didn't matter. The troop of soldiers was already on the edge of town. Bartimaeus was stumbling behind them in chains. He fell and they kicked him, jerked him to his feet, struck him. She opened her mouth and tried to scream, but her lungs hadn't the will. Arms reached from behind and pulled her off the road. She struggled against them, furious, wailing a silent cry.

"Let me go!" she begged.

It was Peter. "Fin, let him go. There's nothing you can do. Let him go." She tried to hit him but his arms held her fast.

"Let him go. There will be a trial. He'll be back, Fin," Peter assured her.

That seemed to calm her. It at least give her a reason to stop fighting. She went limp and Peter lowered her to the ground. She didn't have tears left. She stared down the road. Peter picked her up to carry her back to the orphanage, and she lost consciousness in his arms.

WHEN SHE AWOKE, SHE found herself back in her own bed in the orphan house. The thought of Bartimaeus's case going to trial comforted her. At least he wasn't just going to disappear. A judge would have to hear about the way the soldiers treated her, what they planned to do with her, and how Bartimaeus had rescued her. The court would acquit him. It was as simple as that.

Fin had no idea what day or even what time of day it was. She lay help-less, without the energy or will to move. Sister Carmaline came in several times to check on her, and Fin simply rolled away and ignored any inquisition. Her dreams were of red coats and cruel intentions, and her waking thoughts tormented her with the hundred ways she could have prevented it all from happening.

In the evening, Carmaline came in with food and refused to leave until Fin had eaten. Fin sat up and took the tray Carmaline offered her. The food looked grey and tasteless. All she could do was pick at it.

"Miss Button, I am going to talk," said Sister Carmaline. "Whether you are listening or not is up to you, but I will not leave until I have finished."

Fin ignored her and continued nudging her food, eating the odd bite.

"You have been through an horrific amount of misfortune these past days and we all feel deeply for you, dear." She paused to determine if she was having any effect on Fin, there was none at all. "However, this is a home with rules and order, and I must insist that we've seen the end of your screaming and running about. Many of the children are positively terrified of you, and I cannot say that I blame them. Now, I fully expect you'll require a few days to mend. When you are feeling up to it, we are greatly in need of you. Sister Hilde has been doing the cooking of late, and the travesty on your plate is evidence enough of her lack of . . . finesse. In Bartimaeus's absence, I hope you will be able to fill in . . . until he returns." Once again, she paused, and once again, Fin ignored her.

"Now, about Bartimaeus." This time Fin did show a flicker of interest but promptly covered it up by taking another bite of her food. "I plan to ride into Savannah tomorrow to visit the courthouse. I expect at the very least to return with a date for the trial so that we may all attend to show our support. I also intend to secure the services of a lawyer."

"I'm going with you," said Fin.

"My dear, I know you and Bartimaeus are close, but you must leave this to me. You are in no condition to travel."

Fin wanted to protest but she lacked the will. She set the food tray aside, rolled toward the wall, and pulled the blankets up over her head.

Fin rose before dawn and solemnly slid into her hated blue dress. She washed her face, tied back her hair, and capped it with a bonnet. She stared into the mirror wondering who the person staring back at her was. Bonnet and dress, prim and proper. Most of her face was marbled with the green and blue of bruises born and dying, but there was no mistaking the flared outlines of a properly attired young woman. It was the person Carmaline and Hilde always tried to wedge her into—a total stranger. But stranger or no, she determined to abide it for the sake of her intentions. She made a last scowl at the mirror, then turned and walked down to the stables.

She manhandled the wagon out of its berth in the barn and fetched the horses to tack and hitch. When Sister Carmaline bobbled out of her chambers just as the sun was peeking into the world, Fin was sitting patiently atop the wagon waiting for her. Fin didn't look at her, she just sat there, back straight, hands folded in her lap, looking out the gate and down the road to Savannah. Sister Carmaline stopped at the bottom of her steps and considered the situation. There would be no removing Fin from the wagon without a great deal of grief and noise. Shaking her head back and forth, Carmaline waddled across the courtyard and clambered up into the wagon seat. She busied herself adjusting her girth into as comfortable a position as the seat would allow then took the reins in her hands.

"Phinea Button, you are a stubborn wonder," said Carmaline without looking at Fin, and then she snapped the reins and they rolled out the gate.

They didn't speak during the ride. Carmaline hummed hymns and Fin sat stone-faced, thinking about Bartimaeus. Surely, they wouldn't have beaten him. What did they feed a man in jail? Did they let him wash or attend his faculties in private? She had no idea what he was going through and was terrified to find out. How long would it take him to come to trial? How long would the trial last? How long until he was back at the orphanage and her world returned to normal? Questions and fears galloped through her mind as the horses plodded slowly toward Savannah where answers lay waiting.

By late morning, they were trundling into the city and Fin's wringing hands belied her anticipation. The streets were choked with folk on foot, coming and going like ants. The crowd grew thicker as they neared the city center, and several times Fin considered jumping clear of the wagon to carry on by foot. The wagon made such slow progress in the narrow streets that, at last, Carmaline determined to livery the horse and wagon and walk the final distance.

But even walking, they made difficult headway. The crowd all streamed in the same direction. Something was happening, and many onlookers were anxious to find good ground from which to eye the spectacle.

Carmaline found a man standing still long enough to accost him and inquire about the bustle and stir.

"Pardon sir, could you kindly tell me what all the commotion is about? We are making for the courthouse and never have I seen so much business in the streets," she asked sweetly.

"Hanging today. Been a long while since the last one. Folks come out to see him dangle," said the man. "Good day, ma'am." He hurried away.

"Thank you," said Carmaline to the man's back as he walked away. "Come on, Phinea. Let's be done and home, away from this dreadful business." She grabbed Fin's hand and pulled her along behind.

When they reached the city square, Carmaline bumped people out of the way with a barrage of pardon-me's. Fin could just see the top of a gallows pole erected in the center of the square, but there wasn't any victim yet to mount it. As she climbed the steps to the door of the courthouse, Fin craned her neck around to get a better look at the gallows. It was a wooden platform about six feet high with a small stair leading up the right side. On top stood the fearful pole with a cruel arm hooked over to swing the noose. The platform was surrounded at the base by a score of red-coated soldiers holding the crowd at bay. Sister Carmaline pulled Fin through the doorway, and the din of the crowd muffled to a low rumble.

The anteroom of the courthouse was a large chamber with a high ceiling and was trafficked to and fro by men in black coats and white wigs. Two soldiers flanked the door with muskets held at the order. Sister Carmaline looked about for some idea of who to speak with, finally approaching a tall, willowy man topped with a powdered wig and begging his pardon.

"Good sir, could you assist me?" asked Carmaline.

The man gave her an agitated appraisal and replied, "How may I help you, ma'am?"

"A friend of ours was taken into custody by soldiers, and we've come to learn of his whereabouts and charges," explained Carmaline.

"Very good, ma'am. You will need to speak with the clerk in the room right over there." He motioned to a door at the far end of the hall, then bid good day and continued through another door at the opposite end of the room. Fin followed Carmaline in the direction of the clerk's office.

The office was much smaller than the entry room and held three desks set against the walls and piled high with paper, books, and ledgers of various sorts. Behind each desk sat a man, hunched over and scratching furiously with a quill. None looked up at the entry of the two women. The scritch-scratch of the quilling and the smell of ink filled the room.

"Excuse me," ventured Carmaline, and the man nearest popped his head up and peered at them through spectacles. He said nothing as he looked them over and scratched at his cheek with an inky finger.

"We are here looking for a friend of ours. He was taken prisoner by soldiers in Ebenezer two days past—" said Carmaline.

"Name?" ordered the inky-fingered man.

"Bartimaeus Gann."

"Gann . . ." he muttered and began rummaging through the papers stacked on his desk murmuring the name to himself, then stopped suddenly and fixed his eyes back on Carmaline.

"Gann?" he asked.

"Yes sir."

"*Bart* Gann?"

"Yes."

"You're a friend of Bart Gann, you say?"

"Yes sir, he is our cook at—"

"Ma'am, if you're looking for Bart Gann, you've only to step outside and view the gallows pole," he said.

"I'm sorry?" said Carmaline, confused. Fin froze.

"Ma'am, Bloody Bart Gann—the pirate—is going to hang this very day at noon."

Carmaline's face turned white. "No, no you're mistaken. Our friend, Bartimaeus, was brought into custody only two days ago. We've come to find a date for trial and find a lawyer," said Carmaline.

"Trial? Ma'am, he admitted, by his own mouth, his crimes and felony. He's been wanted for hanging some twenty years by the Crown. The judge spoke his end last evening, and today it carries out. Now, if you please, I have work to attend." He dismissed them and bowed his head back to his scratching.

Fin's blood ran icy cold. Her mind reeled. She turned and fled out the door. From the steps, she could see that three men now mounted the gallows. One was standing at the rear of the platform, his head cloaked in a black mask cut through with eyeholes. The second was a red-coated soldier standing by the steps, holding his arms out in front of him and reading in a loud voice from a curled parchment. The third was Bartimaeus. He stood bent and wrinkled below the arm of the gallows pole and round his neck circled the hangman's noose. His face wore no expression.

"For the crimes of Piracy, Murder, Mutiny. . ." As the soldier pronounced each crime, the roar of the crowd swelled. They stomped their feet and raised white-knuckled fists. In the distance Fin barely registered the tolling of the noonday bell. ". . .you are hereby ordered to hang by the neck until dead. Have you any last utterance before such sentence be made sure?"

"Bartimaeus!" shouted Fin. She ripped off her bonnet, sprinted down the steps, and flung herself into the crowd. She flailed her arms, pushing and pulling people, trying to make her way to the foot of the gallows. "*Bartimaeus!*" she cried again as she swam through the masses of humanity come to watch the villain swing.

Bartimaeus turned his head and saw her then. His face melted into something of both a smile and a look of deep mourning. Fin reached the rank of soldiers at the base of the gallows and tried to claw her way past, but they held her fast. She looked up from behind red-coated shoulders and cried out to him.

"I'm here, missy," he spoke softly down to her. "I'm *standin'* right here."

Then he turned to the soldier that read the decree and nodded. The hooded man stepped forward and stomped on the floor near Bartimaeus's feet. A slight board snapped below him, and Bartimaeus plunged to ruin. The rope pulled his neck into a long unnatural shape. He trembled a moment then stilled and swung in the wind.

Fin screamed amid the gasps and cheers of the crowd then slipped to her knees and tore at the ground.

SISTER CARMALINE BEGGED THE Royal Governor not to put the body on display to be eaten at by crows, and at last, he agreed. British soldiers threw Bartimaeus's limp body into Carmaline's wagon, and Fin climbed in and laid her head on his breathless chest. With no words to say between them, Sister Carmaline and Fin rolled away home.

They buried him under a green cypress on the south bank of the Savannah River. Men and women from the whole town wide came to see him laid to earth and sang hymns to waft him heavenward. Fin knew no song or speech to mend the loss and no embrace could break her stony face.

Peter sat at her feet when all was done and offered the solace of company since no words reached her. For a long time they remained that way. Fin stood stone-like, her eyes transfixed upon the meager planted cross, the last witness to a man's earthly passing. Peter sat next to her in the grass, quiet and still.

Again and again, Fin saw him fall, saw the rope snap taut, heard the cruel jeers of the crowd. And his face, she couldn't escape it, looking at her to the end, smiling and sad. He should have been blaming her. She sent him to die. If he hadn't come to rescue her, he'd be here with her now, playing the fiddle and laughing his creaky laugh. It was her fault. And yet he smiled.

Fin didn't move; she was afraid that if she did, she'd crumble. Peter stood and walked away. She wanted to turn, to stop him. She wanted him with her. But she couldn't bring herself to move or call out to him. Then he was gone and the sun was sinking behind the trees. The shadow of the grave marker stretched across the ground like the cold, incriminating finger of a ghost. It inched closer until she backed away out of its reach.

Then from her left, movement. Peter returned, holding the fiddle out like a gift. Bartimaeus's fiddle. Fin took it and caressed it. Then she reached out and took the bow as well. Peter's eyes quietly pleaded with her, urged her to create something beautiful out of the twisted knot of pain she clung to.

She stretched out her arms and began to play. Sound eddied out of the fiddle on a wave of notes as long and deep as grief itself. She poured all her broken pieces into the song and offered them up, struggling to weave notes enough to mend a heart so finely shattered. The song lifted her, lightened her, each note siphoned out bitterness and in its place left something as pure and sweet as rainwater. Her song rose and spiraled and sailed as a cool wind blew off the river and carried leaves, whirling, into the air like dervishes wrapping her in a tree-fallen lament.

When she lowered the fiddle Peter reached out for her and she welcomed him. She didn't crumble after all. He bore up her timbers and held them fast. Fin laid her head against him and found rest.

"How long, Peter?" she whispered.

"Soon."

Chapter XII

THE DINING HALL FELT colder and smaller to her now that Fin had to tend the meals alone. It was eerily quiet and devoid of the muttering and chuckling she'd always known it to hold. Every corner and doorway held a memory, and each time the floorboards creaked she turned, half-expecting Bartimaeus to step out of the shadows and tell her it had all been a dream. She knew better, though, and reminded herself that although mourning was well and good, there were people counting on her to have a meal ready.

She tried to shake away the melancholy by fetching the beeswax to polish the table. It had more scuffs and pockmarks than sheen. She remembered when the finish was as clear as a mirror, many meals ago. Even the waxing didn't restore the shine like it used to. In some ways it made it more beautiful; it looked aged. In other ways it just looked old and used. She did the best she could and headed back into the kitchen to start the meal.

Biscuits and bacon were the course of the morning, and when the sisters came in at daybreak, she felt a dash of pride at the looks of surprise and approval they gave her. The children followed soon after, and within the hour, the meal had gone from pan to plate to belly, and not a crumb or gristle was spared. Fin felt the work and routine of the day begin to take hold and anchor her; it drew her back to shore from within the current of grief that threatened to drown her.

Peter promised he would talk to Mr. Hickory about finding a plot of land for them. He didn't think the timing was right, but he was as anxious as she was to start a life of their own. Fin contented her mind with work, but she knew herself well enough to know that time would make monotony out of routine and she'd end up clawing at the walls sooner or later. Peter knew it too.

At the end of the week, Peter came with good news. Mr. Hickory had agreed to talk to Mr. Bolzius on their behalf. In the days that followed, Fin was almost happy. She put body and soul into her work, and no one heard any complaint from her lips.

She petitioned Sister Carmaline and won permission to walk in the woods each day after lunch to forage for herbs and spices. This gave her a chance to visit Bartimaeus's grave, and with each visit she found more good memories to take comfort in and felt less sting from the bad.

She often took the fiddle along and played by the river, although she knew Hilde would forbid it, and each time she raised the lid, the sight of Betsy laying in the case made her wince. It brought memories of Bartimaeus back to her. She tried not to think of him but failed much of the time. Little things brought him back when she least expected him: spotting an herb in the wild, hearing a wisp of music on the wind, seeing a ship on the river and thinking of the sea. But she refused to touch the weapon. It was wholly evil to her. It was the instrument of Bartimaeus's fate, and she loathed the sight of it. At times she thought of removing it, getting rid of it, but she feared seeing the empty imprint of it in the case would be worse. So there it lay, asleep and in wait.

A few days later, Peter cantered up the road on horseback trying his best hide a smile. Fin knew the moment she saw him that he had news.

"There's something I want you to see," he said and offered her his hand. She took it and he hauled her up into the saddle behind him.

"Where are we going?"

"Just hold on." He dug in his heels and they galloped off down the road.

Two miles outside of town, Peter turned off the road and they made their way through a stand of trees and out into a broad clearing. Half the open space was plowed in rows and the other half was fresh, wild grass. Peter pulled up the reins and jumped down, then helped Fin off.

"That's the edge of Mr. Hickory's property there, where the field ends," he said and pointed to the plowed rows. "And this"—he motioned at the uncut grass between the field and the trees—"is where ours begins."

Her mouth fell open in a joyous gape. She stepped up on her toes and planted a kiss on Peter's cheek, then turned and ran, laughing, through the field. Peter stood back and watched her. She was beautiful: red hair wild, dancing in the green field, arms out, twirling, jumping, laughter like music. It was the first time she'd been so carefree since Bartimaeus had gone. She fell down and rolled in the grass and Peter ran out to catch up with her. She was lying on her back looking up at the sky.

"Ours, Fin," he said as he lay down beside her, "Only two acres, but it's all ours."

"It's beautiful, Pete." She rolled to face him and propped herself up on her elbows, her smile was wide and bright.

"I'll start building a house in my free time. I figure two months, three at most, and we can move in."

"Two months?" said Fin, her smile faded for a moment.

"We're almost there."

They spent the rest of the daylight pacing off dimensions, pointing and planning the house and field. By the time they climbed back onto the horse to ride home, Fin's cheeks ached from all her laughter and mirth. It felt like years since she'd been happy.

When they got back to the orphanage, they announced their engagement to the sisters. Carmaline made a big show of hugging and kissing and blessing them, but Hilde had little to say. Fin expected as much. The next day, Carmaline cornered Fin in the dining hall and measured her from head to toe, stating her intent to make the wedding dress herself. She put her hands on her hips and explained in clear terms that she would hear no argument whatsoever about whether or not Fin intended to wear a dress at the wedding. She even claimed that the Bible stated that women must wear dresses at weddings, though she was hard put to find the exact scripture. Fin hadn't actually given any thought to the wedding itself. Other girls might fancy big engagements and laced dresses, but Fin was more concerned with the wedding night and her freedom thereafter. Sister Carmaline prattled on and on about decorations and banquets and a hundred other things that flew out of Fin's mind as soon as they'd flown out of Carmaline's mouth. Fin simply went about her business as usual and left the details up to those who cared.

The two months that Peter expected it would take to build the house was an eternity of waiting for Fin. She kept herself busy with her duties in the kitchen, and each day when she finished, she'd run down the road and out to their plot of land. Often she'd find Peter there. He had started cutting timber immediately, and inside the first month managed to frame out the makings of what Fin thought was the most beautiful sight in the world: their home. It was simple, only two rooms, a bedroom and common room, and it would have a long porch down the front and east side. When she found Peter there, she helped him with the work—planing and jointing lumber, sawing logs. Anything she found to do filled her with deep satisfaction. Other times, when Peter wasn't there, she daydreamed, imagining what their lives would be like: children playing in the grass, crops at harvest, Peter coming in after a day's work and taking her in his arms. The frustration of the waiting was her constant companion, and she longed to be rid of it.

Meanwhile, tension in the countryside was rising. Calls for independence filled the papers, and more and more people were taking sides on the issue. Fin, of course, was for independence, but many of the people in town clung to their old loyalties. It infuriated her. Most of the townsfolk had come from Germany, and why they would side with the English once they got here was beyond Fin's reckoning. British troops became a common fixture on the roads from Bethany in the west to Savannah in the east, and they posted official notice in town that citizens were to provide boarding for the king's men at need. Several times a week the familiar sight of six or seven men in redcoats came plodding through the town, their eyes always full of suspicion. They terrified Fin. She never wanted to come face-to-face with another soldier as long as she lived.

Sister Carmaline approached her one afternoon and asked how she liked her work in the kitchen. Fin answered with a shrug. She enjoyed it as much as one could expect.

"What would you think of staying on here as our cook?" asked Carmaline. Fin didn't understand what she was asking. "You'll be moving outside of town soon. That means we'll be out of a cook and I, for one, am not anxious to see Hilde back in the kitchen." Fin shivered as she remembered the meals Hilde had cooked while Fin had lain wounded in bed.

"But I'll have work to do of my own," Fin said.

"I know that, dear, but we'd compensate you. You'd be able to take home food for Peter and yourself. Keeping a home is hard work, and I'm offering you the chance to ease some of that by earning your way."

"I don't want to stay here forever, Sister Carmaline. I can't."

"I know, Phinea, and I wouldn't expect you to stay forever. Just until we—you—can train up someone to take your place. Delly Martin is of an age now that I think she'll make a fine helper."

Fin took a deep breath and agreed. The sisters deserved that much.

Everything was falling into place. The house was nearly finished, and Sister Carmaline declared the wedding date would be set for the Sunday following its completion. Fin was mad with anticipation. She swore the sun mocked her by stretching days out longer than they ought to be. Nights, she barely slept and considered that the legions of chirping insects keeping her awake were quite possibly in collusion with the treacherous sun. She pestered Peter constantly about when the house was going to be done, but his deliberate nature demanded that every detail be perfect and nothing be rushed. She wanted to choke him.

In late autumn, Peter declared the end in sight, and Fin wasted no chance to run out and help him finish. Peter put her to work nailing down the floorboards of the porch while he sat in the shade of a water oak carving table legs with a spokeshave. As Fin pounded in one nail after another, she smiled to herself, remembering how she had longed to work on the chapel with the other boys. That all seemed so far away and silly to her now, and yet here she was after all, hammer and nails, building a house and revelling in it. She entertained the brief thought that at last she'd won out over Hilde's restrictions and constraints but she knew at once that the part of her that cared was gone. This would be her own home, she her own woman, and not for spite or pettiness but for the love and life she wanted to share with Peter.

She pounded in another nail and stood up. The porch was nearly done. Another few hours of work and she'd be finished, but a look at the sun told her she'd already stayed longer than she ought have. Dinnertime was sneaking up, and she was needed back at the orphanage to prepare it.

"Peter, I have to go," she called to him.

Peter put down his tools and walked to the house. He stepped onto the porch and stamped his foot on the board she'd just finished nailing down then studied the whole of her work with his bottom lip pushed out in concentration.

"Suppose that'll do," he said.

"I guarantee it'll do better than you could've done." Fin playfully elbowed him in the ribs.

"Hmmph." Peter grinned. He reached out and pulled Fin to him. Fin dropped her few extra nails into her pocket and put her arms around his neck.

"How long, Peter?"

"Just until Sunday."

Fin marveled that three days could seem so far away. She stretched up on her toes and kissed his cheek.

"I've got to start dinner. I'll be back after and I'll bring you something."

"As long as it's not your stew."

She pulled back and narrowed her eyes. "If it is, you'll eat it and like it."

Peter laughed. "I suppose I might."

"See you in a bit. Wait for me, okay?"

"I'll wait. I always do."

Fin walked to town eager to be done with dinner and back with Peter. The day was chill and she was glad when she stepped back into the warmth of the dining hall. The sisters were about the business of the other orphans. Fin could hear Hilde in the distance berating someone for running in her presence, and it made her smile.

She'd become efficient at the preparation of meals and her hands began their work out of habit, leaving her mind free to wander. She found herself imagining nights alone by the fire with Peter, and children, and a life forever free of the orphanage.

She'd almost finished cooking when she was startled out of her reverie by the sound of harsh voices in the courtyard. Fin peeked out a window and saw a detail of six soldiers milling about and calling for whomever might be in charge. Sister Carmaline wobbled out of her chambers and hurried to meet them.

The man giving orders had a scar running across his face from temple to temple. The scar passed over both eyes; one was pale and blind, the other glared around, wide open, its lid removed by the knife that cut him. Periodically, he scrunched up his cheek in order to close the eye in a lidless blink. Fin knew at once who he was. It was the man Bartimaeus had cut, the man who fled into the woods, the one who had put his hands on her.

Fin listened at the window to trying to hear what was going on. She couldn't make out words, just broken sounds. Carmaline was talking to the scarred soldier and she didn't look pleased with what he was telling her. Then Carmaline turned and caught up her skirts in her hands and huffed toward the dining hall. Fin rushed to the door to meet her.

"Phinea, the soldiers demand we grant them room and board. How soon can you feed them?" asked Carmaline, her face flushed with anger.

Fin balked. "Sister Carmaline we can't! That man, he's—"

"He's prepared to take what he wants by force and burn our home if we don't accommodate him. Now, do as I say, child!" ordered Carmaline.

Fin's mouth worked for words. She couldn't believe what was happening. Carmaline hurried out the door and waved the soldiers to follow her into the dining hall. Fin ran into the kitchen to escape notice. She listened in horror as the door opened and boots clomped in. She heard the clatter of muskets being propped against the wall as they came through the door. Chairs scraped the floor and men's voices filled the room.

"I'm starving," said a voice from the table.

"The food will be ready soon," said Carmaline before she hurried into the kitchen.

Fin was backed up against the wall. She looked at Carmaline and shook her head back and forth. She couldn't go out there. He'd see her. He'd remember. She couldn't.

"Phinea, hurry up! These men are hungry and we've no reason to make them more so," said Carmaline. "I'm going to fetch Sister Hilde from the chapel and prepare beds. Get the food on the table and everything will be fine."

Without looking at Fin again, Sister Carmaline hurried out of the room and left the building. Fin was alone with them—with him.

From the other room she heard their voices, grumbling and fussing at each other.

"Get on with the bloody meal!" one called out.

She had to move, had to act. She tried to shake off her fear and called back, "Almost ready, just few minutes." She gathered her wits and went to check the stew. It was ready. She hurried to the oven and removed the loaves of bread. The voices in the other room were restless and growing angry. She looked around for bowls and her eyes fell on the fiddle case. Betsy was in there. She should load Betsy just in case he recognized her. At least she'd be ready this time. She softly plucked the case from under the cupboard and placed it on the tabletop. She lifted the lid and Betsy stared up at her. The engravings on the barrel seemed to smile. Fin reached out slowly, hesitant to touch it. She knew how to load a musket, knew how to shoot one; Peter had taught her. But she'd never shot a blunderbuss. They didn't call them "hand cannons" for nothing.

The barrel was over an inch in diameter, and it wasn't made to load with a single ball like a musket. It was made to scattershot anything that was packed into it: rocks, metal, salt, anything you could find. She looked around for something to load it with. She ran to the shelves where the spices were kept and shook the tins and bottles, looking for something hard enough to be dangerous.

"What's going on in there!" called a voice from the other room.

"Just finishing up," she called back.

She couldn't find anything. Then she remembered. She put her hand in her pocket and brought out a handful of nails. She picked up Betsy, dumped powder from the horn into the barrel, dropped in the nails, then tore off a piece of her shirt and stuffed it in as wadding. She pulled out the rod and packed the barrel. It was done. She lay Betsy back down in her case, closed her eyes, and tried to slow her breathing.

"Where's the bloody food?" called an angry voice.

"Coming!" shouted Fin. There was nothing left to stall over. She was going to have to go out there. She closed the fiddle case.

"Well, looky here," said a sharp, cruel voice from the doorway. It was him. It was him, and there was no mistaking the recognition in his eye. He scrunched up his face to blink then came into the room. Fin couldn't move. He was grinning. The sounds and smells of that night came back to her in terrifying flashes. The smell of his companion burning on the fire. His sharp cry of pain as Bartimaeus's blade scarred him.

"What's going on in there?" called a voice from the other room.

"Quiet!" shouted the scarred soldier without taking his eye off her. The eye winked at her again and looked her up and down, his smile widened.

"Unfinished business we got, eh?" he said, almost a whisper. Fin backed up against the table. He advanced. Two quick steps and he had her throat in his hand, squeezing it until she could scarcely breathe.

"What's wrong, lassie?" His voice was lowered but cruel. "No sport left now that your old man ain't around to blind me other eye?" He heaved his words out on billows of rotten breath. Spittle flew from his lips. Fin closed her eyes. It was happening again. "Make a sound and those men will arrest you and everyone else in this traitor's nest of a town."

Her hands searched the tabletop for Betsy. The case was to her left. She reached out her hand, but she was too far away; she couldn't reach it. Then her right hand felt something long and cold. A kitchen knife. She found the handle and thrust the knife into his chest. His good eye bulged and rolled madly. His mouth opened and closed, gasped for air. Then he fell forward onto her and she suppressed a cry as he slid to the ground. She dropped the knife and it clattered on the floor. The soldier rolled onto his back and clawed at his chest, working for air. She heard a sickening wheeze from the wound. Hellish, liquid sounds escaped his mouth.

"Sergeant?" called a voice from the dining hall.

They'd be coming through the door any second. Fin threw open the fiddle case and grabbed Betsy. There was no turning back now. She would not hang like Bartimaeus. She hurried to the door and peeked out. The soldiers had all set their muskets against the wall next to the front door, at least ten feet from the nearest man and fifteen feet from her. Five soldiers. One shot from Betsy. One shot each from six muskets—if she could get to them in time—if they were even loaded. It was madness. She stood at the doorway while her mind raced to think of another option. But there was no time. The scrape of a chair on the floor and the clomping of boots coming toward the kitchen made the choice for her. A shadow fell in the doorway, a man was coming. Fin took a long breath and stepped out into the dining hall.

The approaching man stopped in his tracks. Confusion spread across his face. Fin stood in front of him and slowly raised Betsy.

"What—" the soldier took a step back and Fin pulled the trigger. Betsy exploded into the dining room. The redcoat in front of her collapsed instantly. Two more at the table fell back screaming, one with a hole in his neck, the other bleeding from his chest. Fin threw Betsy aside and ran for the door. One dead already, three dying.

One of the two soldiers at the table, snapped out of his shock and realized Fin was heading for the muskets. He raced her for the door. Fin got there first, picked up a musket, and thrust the bayonet into the man's belly. He opened his mouth in a silent, agonized plea. She pulled the trigger and the musket blew him back onto the table. She threw down the weapon and picked up the next one. The last soldier was still sitting at the table with a look of horror and surprise on his face. He was no older than Peter. She leveled the musket at him.

"No." He said it softly and put his hands in the air.

But Fin was lost. She pulled the trigger.

One of the wounded men groaned and spat blood onto the floor in front of her. Shouts were coming from the courtyard. She could barely see through the smoke in the room, and the acrid tang of gunpowder was sweet in her nostrils. The man on the floor cried for help. Fin picked up another musket and put it to her shoulder. The wounded man pulled himself up and braced himself on the table with one hand. With his other hand he drew a knife from his belt and pointed it at her. He twisted his face into a hateful snarl that vanished in smoke when Fin pulled the trigger.

The door opened behind her and she turned. Sister Carmaline was in the doorway, peering into the smoke-filled room. Fin emerged from the haze like a ghost. Her face blank, her hands and clothes splashed red. Sister Carmaline looked at her in horror and then her eyes fell to the floor and saw the dead. She rushed in to examine them. Sister Hilde ran into the room and looked around.

"What have you *done*?" shouted Hilde. "What have you *done*?"

Outside in the courtyard the younger children were crying. Several of the older boys were running up to the dining hall to get a look at what had happened. Sister Hilde turned and herded the children away. Fin walked across the dining hall and picked up Betsy.

Sister Carmaline looked up from one of the dead men. "Are you hurt, Phinea?"

Fin didn't answer. She went into the kitchen and put Betsy away. She latched the case, picked it up, and walked to the door.

"Phinea, where are you going?" said Carmaline.

Fin stopped.

"They'll come for me, like they did for Bartimàeus," she said. "I'm leaving." Then she walked out the door. In the courtyard the children stared at her open-mouthed. She walked passed them and through the gate.

People were coming out of houses all down the street and edging their way toward the orphanage, trying to see what the gunshots had been about. Some stared at Fin in her blood-spattered clothes. Others rushed passed her.

When she passed Mr. Hickory's house, he was standing outside.

"You hurt, Miss Button?" he called to her.

She didn't answer and walked away. Peter was waiting. Mr. Hickory stared after her then turned and jogged down the road toward the orphanage.

What have you done? Sister Hilde's words. Her life was ruined. She couldn't marry Peter. She couldn't live with him on a farm outside of town. Not now, not anymore. She'd murdered six men. Six British soldiers. If she didn't leave, they'd come for her. If she hid, they'd tear the town apart to find her. This was what Bartimaeus felt—and he chose to stay. Fin couldn't do that, wouldn't do that. This is what it's like to be truly alone, she thought, to be empty of hope, cut off, lost, with no road home. This is what it feels like to be abandoned by God. All the devils in hell between.

Fin reached the spot where the road turned off toward a green field surrounding a freshly built house with a nearly finished porch, and she stopped. Peter was down there. He was waiting for her. But how could she explain it to him? What could she say? She couldn't bear to see him, to see the look on his face when she told him she had to leave. She didn't want to see that beautiful green field that until an hour ago nurtured the seeds of her future and dreams. She wanted to forget that she'd ever been happy. She wanted to forget that Peter loved her. She wanted to forget that she'd ever stood in her bell tower and seen the trees stretching across the world to the horizon, and she wanted to forget she'd ever longed to go out and see what lay beyond it. She was alone and empty, and so she ran. She turned east and fled into the vast Georgia wild.

PART II

ACROSS THAT FOAMY DEEP

Chapter XIII

IN STAGGERED THROUGH A grey world of leaf-barren trees, each step carrying her farther from the riven life behind her. She kept near the roads and hid in the hollows or behind trees when a rider or wagon passed. Each time she heard someone approach, she expected soldiers, but none ever appeared. Night came on and still she walked, by moonlight, shivering in the damp and cold. When the moon passed out of the sky, she settled down onto a stone jutting out of the hillside and attempted to sleep, but couldn't. She opened the fiddle case and lifted the instrument to her neck. She tried to play, but her shaking hands wouldn't allow it. She wanted to find a way, like Bartimaeus, to turn pain into beauty, but she scarcely believed the world held beauty at all, much less that she could create or add to it. She laid the fiddle back in its velvet cradle and latched the case, and soon dawn began to warm the sky.

She climbed to her feet and picked up the fiddle case then crested the hill to look down on the waking city of Savannah. She intended to lose herself there, to drown her old life, to forget. If there were any beauty left for her, she would find it in forgetting.

With the lightening of the horizon came sounds on the breeze, first of knockers-up rapping with their poles and calling the city to life, then of bells and wagons on cobblestone and roosters crowing. The city awoke by slow degrees as she descended from the hills, and when she reached the first cobbled streets it had come fully awake. But all the wonder it stirred when last she saw it was gone. Now the city was a nightmare of suspecting eyes and threatening glances as if she wore her crimes upon her like a brand. The sight of soldiers induced beads of sweat to her face no matter how often she told herself they could not know. In her ragged clothes she drew distasteful stares from tidier, more properly dressed folk, and she felt a degree of relief when she emerged at last from the town proper and onto the clamoring waterfront.

The streets bustled with commerce. Sailors sang cadence as they muscled capstans and loaded their holds. Wagons and horses weaved and darted up and down the streets like ants on a broken mound. Vendors hawked everything from fruits to firearms, and laborers loaded and unloaded goods from the world across. Men of all colors, smells, and tongues busied themselves around her: black men with downcast eyes and broad backs, hairy white men with taut round bellies tanned dark by the sun, long-coated gentlemen with monocled eyes and stuffy airs. Shirtless sailors called out orders from toothless mouths and hefted crates with their sinewy, tattooed arms. The only things most of them seemed to have in common were a lack of couth and a precise command of vulgarity.

Hundreds of ships clogged the harbor. Their thousand masts jutted into the sky like the withered trees of a dead forest. Great merchant vessels lined the piers, and men heaved crates, pallets, and sacks filled with sundry exotics out of every hold. Others ships lay at anchor in the harbor and ferried goods to shore by smaller vessels and barges. The smells of salt, fish, and sweat ripened the air. This was the life Bartimaeus had known when he was young. Fin devoured it. She was drawn to it as if from among the crates of mysterious cargo she might reclaim his company from the stuffy closet of grief.

She set down the fiddle case next to a lamppost and sat on it to observe the comings and goings around her. At first, everything appeared chaotic, but gradually she began to see patterns emerge from the madness. Spectacled clerks counted goods and scurried between the dock and their shipping companies to deliver accountings of what was loaded or unloaded. Sailors delivered their goods to warehouses as directed by the proper dock masters;

then most visited the shipping offices for pay. Couriers delivered mail in marked satchels. Captains argued over and paid docking fees and money-clerks received them and scrawled the collections down. Pickpockets strolled casually through the crowd, bumping into people and begging pardon with sly grins. For hours, she watched and tried to imagine her own place out among them all.

When night came, she ducked beneath the dock and looked for a place to sleep. Ragged forms lurked in the darkness. Men gaunt as the dead and clothed in sackcloth huddled in shadows and stared at her with empty, inhuman eyes. Some cried out to her for food or money, but most simply studied her as she passed and muttered to themselves in madness. Rats, dogs, and other unidentifiable creatures scurried over her feet and between her legs as she stumbled through the black forest of barnacle-encrusted pylons beneath the quay. Here and there, refuse chutes descended from the pier above and vomited their waste into rotten piles of decay. Two dogs circled each other, snapping and biting as they vied for some rotted pound of meat.

At length, she curled up into a depression in the filth and tried to sleep but did little. She wondered if Peter was looking for her; surely he would be. More than anything she wanted to open her eyes and see him standing over her, bending to take her up and hold her and bear her home. He didn't come, though, and she couldn't even cry for him. Her tears were gone, swallowed up by the numbness of despair. When sleep did come at last it was haunted by dreams of murder, and morning came without renewal.

For a week, Fin lived the unlife of a vagrant. Her only food was what she scavenged in alleys or refuse piles. Nights beneath the docks gave her solitude but offered no rest. She prayed for death if only to suffer no more of life, but that too was withheld her.

Without work she had no money, and without money, no food, no board, nothing. In a world without family, friend, or love, only engagement to the beast of commerce sustains life. She needed to find purpose again; she needed to find work.

On a moonless night she stepped out of her clothes and washed in the briny filth of the port. She scrubbed herself and her clothing with handfuls of sand, and when the morning came she went up to the streets. She looked far from what the sisters would consider presentable. Her pants were torn at the knees and too short to cover the tops of her tattered leather workboots. Her shirt, once white, was stained and mottled brown and hanging open at the left shoulder, but as she considered her homely state she noted that she bore a distinct similarity to many of the sailors trafficking the streets. For once in her life, she fit in.

Work was less likely to find her than she was to find it, she reasoned, so she worked up her not inconsiderable gumption and went forth. She'd forgotten what day it was, and the first person she spoke to told her it was a Tuesday.

"Sir, I'm looking for work," she said to a friendly looking sailor walking off the pier.

"What you asking me for?" he said. "Check at the shipping office if I was you."

That made sense, she supposed. The waterfront street was a solid line of shipping offices as far as she could see in either direction. She walked the length of the street looking at each door and into each window, hoping to find some sign of welcome or notice of help wanted but found none.

She picked the door of a building that looked less seedy than its neighbors and cautiously stepped inside. The room was full of crates and barrels and a group of businessmen huddled around a table in its center. When she entered the room they ceased their talking and raised their heads to look at her. Her voice caught in her throat, and for perhaps the first time in her life she couldn't think of what she wanted to say. In embarrassment, she retreated out the door as the men laughed at her and turned back to their discussion.

Back on the street, of course, she remembered precisely why she'd gone in but decided against venturing back for another try. She walked on to the next building and knocked on the door. When no one answered, she tugged at the handle and found it locked. She moved on to another building, one with an open door, and went in. An old man with white-filmed eyes lounged back in his chair behind a desk and addressed her general direction.

"Mr. Sotherby! Your wife, sir! She has been three times to see you this morning and gone away in a state, I'm afraid."

Fin was only other person in the room.

"I'm sorry, I think you've mistaken me for someone else. Pardon me." She hurried back out the door as the man called after her.

"Mr. Sotherby! Mr. Sotherby! What shall I tell your wife?"

The next three doors were locked. The fourth opened below a shingle that read "Smithers and Jouncey Shipping Co." Inside, a plump clerk scribbled away at some unknown business behind a desk topped with manifest documents. Stacks of paper and what appeared to be boxes of stacks of paper filled the room. Dates and names adorned the sides of each box, and by a quick glance around she noted that they had been collecting for quite some years indeed. She approached the desk and opened her mouth to speak.

"Excuse—"

"May I help you?" The man promptly interrupted her without looking up from his scribbling.

"I'm looking for work and—"

The man tilted his head up slightly as she spoke and peered at her over his glasses before cutting her off. "No work."

"Well perhaps you could refer me to—"

"If you are looking for a contract aboard a ship, I'm afraid you are far out of luck. You haven't the constitution or muscle for the work, and I doubt, from the look of you, that you've ever set foot on a ship in your miserable, scrawny life. *No* work."

He stared at her over his glasses and flicked his eyes toward the door.

"But—"

"*No* work!"

Fin wrinkled her forehead at him and removed herself back out onto the street. She came to an abrupt stop as she collided with someone. The someone seemed to be the man now lying on the ground, sputtering curses and smelling of rum. He was skinny, pale, toothless, and very nearly pickled in alcohol.

"Ahhh," he groaned as he climbed his way to his feet.

"I'm sorry, sir. I didn't see you," Fin tried to beg pardon.

The man started and spun once around looking for the source of her voice and then had to contend with a bit of wobbling before he managed to focus on Fin.

"What the bloody drink are you think you doing?" he sputtered in a grammar only the drunken can master.

"I was just coming out of the build—"

"Ye scrawny rat, don't know who you're messing about!" He made a show of putting up his fists and nearly succeeded in throwing himself back to the ground. He'd have done just that had not a monstrous hand clamped him around the neck just as he was about to fall. A dark, hairy man the size and demeanor of a bear had come to his rescue but didn't look any too pleased about it.

"Tommy, you drunken dog. Leave off the locals and get to the *'Snake*! We haul anchor in the hour and you've work to sober up to," he growled at the skinny drunk.

"Let off me, Jack. This kid tried to rob me, he did. I'm about to shew him me robber-knockers!"

Jack growled under his breath, picked him up by the scruff of his neck and threw him over his shoulder. He marched off down the street with Tommy kicking and hollering to be let go. Fin was amused by the affair until she saw Tommy had got himself free of his captivity and was running full gait back toward her. He barreled down the street yelling a cacophony of curses and vulgarities at her. Fin made up her mind that she'd heard and seen quite enough. She set her case down and stepped to the side. In his drunken state, Tommy forgot to slow down as he approached his target, and she threw her fist into the side of his face as he stumbled past her. That ended the commotion. Tommy crumpled onto the cobblestones and lay silent on the street.

"Robber indeed," Fin muttered as he began to snore. She turned around to find a hulking obstacle barring her way. She had to crane her neck and back up a step in order to see his face. It was the man Tommy had called Jack—and he didn't look any too pleased with her either.

"You just ruined the most worthless sailor I ever had the displeasure to bark an order to. I ought to box your ears and throw you in the brack."

His face was so ugly it made Fin wince to look at it, and the way he had it scrunched up in anger didn't help the condition. His eyes were set too far apart, such that Fin thought he must see all of what was happening on either side of him as well as in front, and his mangled, pudgy nose was so covered with sun-baked skin that whenever he moved his head too quickly little flakes of it floated off like snow. Thankfully his beard covered the remainder of his unfortunate face. He looked to have three teeth, more or less, and the rest of his appearance could be summed up in two words: large and hairy. Everything about him was over-big and covered in short, curly, black hair—hands, fingers, neck, ears—every visible patch of skin seemed to be sprouting.

He worked his face around for a moment while he nudged Tommy with his foot. Then he looked at Fin again, and she suppressed the inclination to turn and run.

"You know what a press gang is, kid?"

Fin shook her head.

"It's me," he said. The monstrous man chuckled under his breath, a sound that navigated its way through the caverns of his chest and came out like a muted rumble. "You're replacing Tommy." He picked Fin up and threw her over his shoulder. Fin gave a yelp and hollered to be unhanded.

"Quiet down, kid, afore I have to gag you," Jack barked.

"Mister, if you want me to work for you I can walk on my own. Work is just what I was looking for."

Jack put her down and considered her.

"You're a mite scrawny, but willing work scrawny's better than forced work fat, I always say. Was you robbing Tommy?" he asked.

"No, sir."

"Well you are now!" He slapped her on the shoulder and laughed like a thunderclap. Fin just stared at him. "Stealing his job. Robbing him his berth on the 'Snake . . . ah, never mind." He waved his hands at her. "What's your name?"

"Fin Button."

He stuck an enormous right hand out. "Jack Wagon."

Fin put her tiny hand in his and he shook it around.

"Enough jabberin'. There's trouble with the locals tonight, and we needs to get seaward in the hour." He slapped Fin on the back, spinning her around, and walked off down the street. Fin had to jog to keep up with him.

"Mr. Wagon!" Fin called after him, but he ignored her. "Mr. Wagon, what sort of trouble?"

Jack inclined his head toward her, but didn't speak. Then he pivoted on the toe of his boot and turned onto a pier. Fin scrambled to keep up. He stopped in front of a gangplank running out to the deck of a black and tan ship. Its three masts speared high into the sky and gulls circled above.

"The *Rattlesnake*." He hooked his thumb over his shoulder at the ship. "Let's go, scrawny."

Fin took a deep breath and trotted across the plank. Jack followed after with a single bound and hollered orders and curses down into a hatch. His yelling caused quite a commotion, and in seconds, muttering sailors popped out onto the deck and scurried about the ship, untying ropes, climbing the rigging, and doing all manner of shipboard work.

"Where's Tommy?" yelled a voice down from the tops.

"Ruined in the gutter he is, damn his blood!" shouted Jack up at the voice. "This bony lad laid him out with a single whop." Jack slapped a hand on Fin's back, and all the sailors on deck stopped what they were doing and turned to look at her.

Fin opened her mouth to inform Jack that she was no "lad" but stopped and thought better of it. Every man on deck had his eyes trained her way, yet it seemed it hadn't occurred to a one of them that she was anything other than what Jack had just named her. She gulped once, snapped her mouth shut, and slouched her shoulders down so her chest was less likely to give away what her clothing and boyish nature conveniently hid.

"Say hello to your new mate. We're rid of Tommy once and for good." Jack pointed a meaty finger at Fin. "Now get yourself to climbing, Mr. Button! Knut needs help aloft with the lines and sail."

Fin looked up. Some forty feet above her, a man in the rigging of the mainmast waved down. She waved back and clambered up into the ropes as if she was born to it. When she reached the top, the man looked at her in confusion.

"Never heard of a name like Button." He looked at her sideways and narrowed one eye.

"Call me Fin. Can't say as I ever heard a name like Knut before either," she said, grinning at him.

"Tommy Knuttle. Already got a Tommy on the 'Snake though, so's they call me Knut." He frowned as he spoke of himself and talked a beat slower than most folk.

"There's no Tommy anymore, though. Mr. Wagon said I'm replacing him."

Knut's frown deepened.

"So does that mean I can call *you* Tommy now?" Fin asked.

Knut scratched his head and rolled his eyes in thought. "I'm Knut," he declared. He nodded and looked at her to make sure she understood. "Grab hold of that rope over there. Don't know why we got to get to sea a day early, but I don't cross Jack, no sir."

Fin followed Knut's lead closely as he showed her how to ready the top sails, and after a few minutes they had the work done and climbed back down to the deck. The ship was unmoored and floating out into the harbor. Jack stomped about the deck bellowing orders as he pointed toward work and kicked the nearest sailors in the proper direction. Knut tapped Fin on the shoulder and motioned her to follow him. He led her to a spot far aft from where Jack's attention was focused.

"Jack's the captain?" Fin asked.

"Glad you asked me and not him. He'd belt you in the head for saying it. Jack's the first mate. He likes the ordering and stomping, but he ain't one for stiff-neck work like captaining." Knut frowned and cast a nervous glance around. "Don't think Jack and the captain likes each other none."

"So who is the captain?" Fin asked.

"Tiberius Creache," said Knut in a whisper. He looked around again and checked over his shoulder, as if afraid he was being watched. "I don't think the captain likes me none neither."

Without warning, the rumble of distant cannon-fire split the air. Fin flinched at the sound, and Knut dove to the deck and covered his head with his hands. The rest of the crew gathered along the rail see what was going on. To the north, where the Savannah River emptied its waters into the ocean, three British frigates had arrayed themselves across its mouth. They were throwing a volley of cannonshot at what looked to Fin like a cloud of fire coming downstream. It took a moment for her to realize that the blaze was a ship. *B-b-b-boom*! Another volley erupted from the British cannons, and bits of fiery debris exploded from the blazing ship where the guns found their mark. Collision was imminent. Two of the British vessels came around and fled seaward. The third wasn't quick enough. The flaming ship plowed into her amidships, and Fin heard the cracking and splintering of the hull even as far away as the *Rattlesnake*. As the two ships sank into the estuary, thick pillars of smoke rose to mark their graves, and Fin lost sight of the calamity as the *Rattlesnake* rounded the shoulder of South Carolina.

"*That*, gentlemen, is why we're a'sea today and not tomorrow," shouted Jack across the deck. "Got word midday about British plans to seize supply boats upriver. Talk at the tavern said the local militia aimed to put a stop to it. Bad news to stay in port when the locals get riled. We head for Philadelphia to trade what we got, and the captain claims he's got business with some politician. Now set watch above and get below before I find a swab to keep you company!"

So began Fin's life on the sea. Knut showed her to the berthing and found her a spot to swing a hammock next to his. She had nothing to call her own except the black fiddle case she carried away from a bloody kitchen in a world shrinking behind her. As the wind blew her north aboard the *Rattlesnake*, she felt the pain of all that had happened slipping away. This was the sea; this was what Bartimaeus had loved. She wanted to forget every-thing life had given her up to this moment, save two things: Bartimaeus and Peter. Peter would wait for her. She'd come back. She'd come back for him once she'd seen a bit of the world and the war. Once the British were gone she could return home safely. He would wait.

She spent little worry over the notion that she was going to have to hide the fact that she was a woman. She hadn't tried to deceive anyone, but her breeches, short tangled hair, dirty face, and boyish chest had taken care of it for her. No one seemed to have thought twice about her. She considered for a moment whether she ought to be offended but quickly brushed the thought aside. The only person she'd ever cared to look female for was Peter, and it was just as well she keep it that way.

The sail north to Philadelphia was a four-day venture, and it proved four of the longest days Fin had ever known. She soon learned that the *Rattlesnake* was no vacation from chores and duty. To the contrary, there were more of both than ever, and as the newest crew member, she was assigned all the least desirable tasks: swabbing decks, pumping the bilge, dumping the latrine, and working the hardest (which is to say, latest and most boring) watches.

Fin didn't complain though. She loved it, loved the purpose in it, the challenge of it. It was hard work, "man's work" as Sister Hilde would say, and while the other men aboard looked forward to drinking and investigating the local womenfolk when they hit shore, Fin could think only of sleep and rest.

Knut was her companion in nearly every chore and duty. Many of the crew mocked his awkward speech and thought him slow in the head, but Fin took a liking to him right away. Though he was clearly older than her by years, he worked long and steady and never spoke ill of anyone. She came to think that he looked like a twig. His limbs were overly long and skinny, and where they jointed together they bulged like knots. His sun-darkened skin and scars made him the color of fallen leaves, and she worried that if he fell asleep in the woods he might never be found. Fin took to his gentle way and enjoyed his companionship. Knut seemed more than happy to have company that didn't push him around.

Few of the rest of the crew would afford her any attention or entertain any of her questions. She recognized the pattern, though; it was the same at the orphanage. She'd seen time and again that when new orphans arrived they'd have to endure a period of shunned isolation until they achieved some untold quality that made them one of the crowd. At least Knut eased her transition.

He also provided Fin with a hearty education on shipboard life. He showed her to the galley for meals and explained the meanings of many various bells, whistles, and flags. He patiently drilled her on the tying of knots and told her when to report for watch duty and when to try to sleep— something that was scarce as the ship was badly undermanned.

"The '*Snake* used to have eighty crew," he said. "But only got forty now."

"Why not more?" Fin asked.

"Some people don't like the captain none." Knut shrugged.

"Why not?" she asked, but Knut wouldn't answer.

She pieced together from conversations that the *Rattlesnake* had been in Charleston not long ago loading tobacco bound for trade in England when the captain changed plans and sailed for Savannah with a half-empty hold and no explanation. They'd been in Savannah ever since, and the captain hadn't been seen at all until the day Fin came aboard. There were rumors of every sort: that the captain had a mistress, that he ran afoul of the law in Charleston and needed a quick out, that he was secretly spying for the Continental Congress. Theories haunted any space where two sailors spoke, but by far, the most popular was simple madness. Most of the crew thought him insane. Fin didn't know much about seaborne commerce or the basic activities of captains, but it took little time for the rumors in the air to color her perception of him.

Jack, on the other hand, while not the captain of the *Rattlesnake*, was certainly the one that kept it running. He seemed never to rest. At all hours of the day and night he barked orders and stomped across the deck inspecting lines, knots, rigging, brass work, and anything else he found that needed daily maintenance to keep the ship running fleet and sure. Though he was a harsh master, the crew loved him. Jack expected excellence, and the crew worked to achieve it. He'd snarl insults and spit fury at a man who did his job half-hearted and then grin and smack him on the back once it was done proper. He hadn't spoken to Fin since the day he pressed her into service and Fin wasn't anxious to garner his attention—she already had all the work she could weather.

Fin was scrubbing the poop deck on the second day underway when the door to the captain's quarters opened and Tiberius Creache stepped out into the world to appraise his ship. He was tall and older than she'd expected. Great locks of curly grey hair cascaded out from under his black tricorne, and his face was hawkish and severe with deep-set eyes and a hooked nose. He was dressed gentlemanly in a red topcoat and fine, white breeches, but his eyes conveyed nothing gentle; they peered across the deck as if searching for a mouse to pounce on.

Jack climbed up the steps and greeted him but received no recourse for his courtesy. Creache continued inspecting the ship and sailors with his gaze. Fin stopped scrubbing for a moment and watched him until his hawkish peering found her looking back. He narrowed one eye at her, and she returned to her scrubbing.

"Who is that?" he said. His speech was smoothly metered and menacing. Fin didn't need to look up to know whom he was talking about.

"New tar, sir. Picked him up in Savannah to replace that no-gooder Tommy," said Jack. "Name's Button."

"I see," said the captain. Then he turned and stalked back into his quarters and wasn't seen again before the ship saw Philadelphia.

CHAPTER XIV

THE *RATTLESNAKE* SAILED UP the Delaware, and when it came upon Philadelphia in the afternoon of the fourth day Fin was breathless at the city's size. She had thought Savannah a great metropolis, but compared to Philadelphia it was little more than a country by-water. Streets and buildings stretched as far as she could see in every direction, and there were an uncountable number of ships, some coming, some going, most sitting still in between.

As they drew near the pier, Jack commenced barking orders and the crew prepared the ship for mooring. Fin and Knut climbed aloft to pull in the sails. Their size lent them to easy climbing, and in the past days Fin had spent more time up in the ropes than down on solid footing. Once the sails were secure, Knut called her down but she ignored him. She climbed up to the highest yardarm and stared out across the cityscape. From so high up she could see across the rooftops for miles as she tossed side to side with the rolling of the ship. Fin smiled. It was like looking out at the forest from her old bell tower. She felt for a moment as if she were home. Then, like a thunderclap, an order barked up from Jack broke the spell. She shimmied down and hurried back to work as the *Rattlesnake* came to rest and settled at the wharf.

The crew moored the ship and Jack ordered the holds opened up. They spent the afternoon unloading the little they had aboard and delivered it to the proper warehouses as directed by the dock master. When the work was complete and accounts were settled, Jack delivered the paperwork and monies to the captain and returned with pay for the crew. It was the first money Fin had ever had, and the few coins, no more than a pittance to others, were all riches and finery to her.

When Jack released the crew to go ashore, she prodded Knut to find her some paper and a pen. The rest of the crew laughed and sang and headed down the pier into town while Fin sat, scratching away with a quill, writing Peter to let him know she was safe. Knut didn't seem anxious for the company of the rowdy crew, so he sat down and waited patiently without asking to whom she wrote or why. Fin wrote little more than that she was safe, she was working, she'd be home soon, and Peter ought not to worry about her. When she finished, she folded it up and hopped to her feet.

"Let's go find the Philadelphia postmaster."

Knut shrugged and pointed toward the city. "It's down that away. I been there with the captain before." He ambled across the plank and down the pier.

Knut was a reliable guide. He remembered just where the postmaster's office was. After dropping a few coins for post, he and Fin wandered the town. A few blocks from the pier they spotted three shipmates bartering for the services of a painted prostitute on the steps of a run-down brothel. Fin frowned at them and winced at the sight of the prostitute teasing the sailors; she wore an eye patch—and had more eyes than teeth. She didn't know who to feel more sorry for, the whore or the sailors. *The end finds the harlot when all other doors are shut.* Fin turned away thinking she'd kick in a few doors before she walked through that one.

"Where should we go, Knut?"

"I don't reckon. Mainly I just stay on the 'Snake 'less the captain or Jack needs me." He shrugged with a frown and Fin shook her head. She couldn't decide if he was daft or not. Sometimes he was as quick as a whip, and other times she swore he was as dumb as a plank. Dumb or not, he was the only friend Fin had made, and she wasn't going to spend the evening cooped up on ship and alone.

"Tommy Knuttle, you and me are going to have some fun," she told him with a determined nod.

"Fun?"

"And we can start right there." Fin pointed at a sign swinging over the door of a tavern down the street. TUN TAVERN it read. She grabbed Knut by the arm and dragged him toward it. He didn't protest, but he didn't seem to like what he was about to be pulled into either.

When they got to the door, Fin pushed it open and stomped in as if she'd been in a hundred portside taverns and knew just what she was doing. The tavern was dimly lit and smelled of beer and sweat. Crowded tables cluttered the room, and laughter, shouting, and the singing of several different songs, all at once, livened the air. For reasons she couldn't quite put a finger to, Fin felt right at home. She dragged Knut by the collar to the nearest open seat and sat him down beside her. The man next to her was as fat as an ox and gave her a stare of appraisal before hefting his drink and returning his attention to his fellows across the table. Fin stared around at the place wondering what to do next.

A stubbly bald man bobbled up to her. "Drinks?" he asked as he wiped his hands on his filthy apron.

"Yes—uh, two," stammered Fin.

"What whets your fancy?" he said impatiently. Fin didn't have the least idea what her fancy was nor why it might need whetting. She looked to Knut. He was busy cleaning out his ear, oblivious to the conversation, no help at all.

"What do you—"

"We got the finest beers from all across the colonies. Also got a few from old Ireland and even a cask of German dark just in if that's your taste. We don't suffer an English draught, though, if that's what you're thirsty for."

Across the room, a gaggle of noisy patrons whistled and banged their empty mugs on the table. The waiter waved to calm them down then raised his eyebrow at Fin. "Not got all night, sir. What'll you have?"

"Have anything from Georgia?"

"Georgia? Let's see now . . ." He rolled up his eyes and scratched his pate in thought. "Yes sir, I believe we got a bit of a cask left from nearabout

Macon. A thick stout it is, like the folk that made it, or so I hear," he said with a chuckle.

"Two of those please," said Fin.

He nodded and hurried over to the table where the men were shaking their empty cups at him. Knut was staring across the room. He had discovered the spectacle of a drunken man alternately dancing and falling down as people cheered him on. Knut grinned, a rare condition.

"Georgia?" said a gruff voice from across the table.

"Excuse me?" said Fin. The man across from her was red as a beet. By the count of empty mugs and bottles in front of him, Fin thought he might be trying to pickle himself as well.

"You from Georgia?" he said.

"Me? Yes, sir."

"Heard about that woman you got down there. Good stuff, I reckon."

"Woman?"

"That War Woman!" He grinned as he said it. "That lady what killed them English. My kind of woman!" The other men at the table agreed and laughed.

"That kind of woman like to bowl you over and feed you to her biddies!" said the man next to him.

"She can bowl me any way she like!" said the red-faced man as he picked up his cup. The others chuckled then knocked their mugs together and took a long draw.

"I haven't heard about her. What happened?" asked Fin. Her stomach was fluttering.

"Thought you said you was from Georgia, mister."

"I am. But I've been at sea and—"

"Woman down in Georgia, six British was ordered to seize her house. She invited them in, they says. Sat them all down for supper. Then killed every one of 'em in cold blood. Right at the dinner table. 'The Georgia War Woman' they calling her—ain't seen her have you?" he finished with a chuckle.

Fin's head felt like it might pop. He was talking about her. He had to be.

"Did she have a name?" Fin asked.

"Aye, what was it now. Odd name it was." He picked a flake of dried skin off his ear as he thought about it.

"Phinea Michaels," said the man next to him. "Locals give her right up, damned Tories." Fins face went white. The sisters must have withheld her last name to protect her. "British won't let this one go. They'll get hold of her family; she'll turn herself in if the damned Tories don't do it for the money first."

"What money?" Fin asked.

"A thousand pound is what money. Alive or otherwise."

The waiter returned and plunked down two pints of foamy beer in front of her. She picked up the drink and gulped at it. When the bitter hit her she nearly choked it back up. She'd never tasted beer before. The men across the table laughed.

"Easy, boy. Don't waste good beer on a weak belly. Where's that paper?" The man craned his neck and shouted around, looking for the newspaper. Someone from another table yelled back, wadded up a piece of paper, and threw it in Fin's direction. The red-skinned man across from her caught it, unwadded it, and smoothed it out on the table.

"There she is," he said and passed the piece of paper across the table. She took it from his hands and tried to look calm. It was an issue of the *Philadelphia Gazette*, and the headline said "Georgia War Woman Slays English." A crude woodcut print depicted a shorthaired woman impaling a soldier on a bayonet. Ebenezer, the orphan house, the sisters, they were all there, all in the paper. Fin was mortified. She wanted to run out the door and keep on running until she was back home, back with Peter. The last line read: "Reward of one thousand pounds to be paid by the Royal Governor for the capture or killing of Phinea Michaels." A thousand pounds. She couldn't go home. Ebenezer had as many folk loyal to Britain as not; someone was sure to turn her in. But what if the man was right, what if the British threatened people close to her, or worse—hurt them, imprisoned them? She folded up the paper and stuck it in her pocket.

"You said the British would do something to her family? I didn't see that in the article," she said to the red-faced man.

"It don't? Hell, I can't read. That's what I heard though. Damned English want to make an example, stretch her neck where folks can learn about the *kindness* of King George, I reckon. People been talking about it all over." He paused and scratched his cheek. "What you so curious for? You know something about her?"

"No, I used to live nearby. But I haven't been back in ages." Fin tried to shrink from sight and took another sip of her drink. She glanced at Knut. He was studying her as if she were a strange animal.

"You alright, Fin?" he said.

"I'm fine. Look, there's Jack."

Jack and several other sailors from the *Rattlesnake* had just walked through the door and were clearing drunks away from a table so they could sit down.

"Let's go join them, come on." She scooped up their mugs and walked over to the newly cleared table. She plunked the drinks down and settled herself across from one of the sailors, a man she knew only as Bill. The other men at the table eyed her and Fin felt they were silently considering whether or not she ought to be there. Fin looked around for Knut and discovered him standing back from the table, deep in thought.

"Sit down, Knut," said Fin.

Knut shook his head and frowned.

"Knows better than to sit, he does," said Bill from across the table. "Bad luck to have an addlebrained half-wit about." Several of the other men laughed in agreement. Fin noticed a look of disapproval on Jack's face, but he didn't disapprove enough to say anything.

"The half-wit is the one thinks his luck is in another man's head," said Fin.

"Eh?" said Bill, looking confused.

"Hard of hearing? I'll say it again. You say your luck's bad due to Knut, and I say you're the half-wit for thinking it."

Bill's face turned dark, and he inclined an ear toward Fin. "Don't think I heard that just right, swabbie. 'Cause if I heard that right, I'd be obliged to knuckle in your noggin'." Bill leaned across the table and raised an eyebrow.

"Careful, Bill! Jack say he knocked in old Tommy with one whop!" called out a sailor from down the table. The others erupted in laughter, and Knut squirmed in his clothes. Fin's blood was beginning to boil. If there was anything she couldn't stomach, it was folks getting down on people who couldn't stand up for themselves.

"I said," she leaned in toward him, "I think *you're* the half-wit."

Bill pushed back from the table and stood up hard enough to knock his chair over backwards behind him.

"Best clear back, boys. I'm about to box this youngun's ears."

Bill walked around the table. Fin squared off with him, threw up her fists, and grinned. Her grin seemed to produce a sort of growling sound inside Bill's chest.

"Fin, let's go," said Knut from behind her.

"We ain't going nowhere, Knut."

Fin winked at Bill, and he charged her. She stepped to the side and laid her fist into his face the same way she'd done Tommy in Savannah. Bill fell to the floor. The men at the table laughed and cheered and the bartender yelled for peace, but all the noise disappeared when Bill jumped back up. Fin blinked in surprise, and he threw his fist up under her chin. She sailed through the air and landed on her back atop the next table over, sending patrons scattering for cover. Now Bill was the one grinning. Fin scrambled off the table and noticed that her jaw didn't seem to close in just the same way it had before. Jack shook his head in exasperation.

"Ain't done with you, boy," growled Bill.

Fin wasn't amused anymore. She rushed at him, and they set to throwing fists and hollering one at the other. Bill's hands felt like hams clubbing her each time he connected, but her small size and quick feet provided connection was rare, if painful. Bill, on the other hand, couldn't seem to avoid Fin's fists no matter what he did. Later, he would swear she had help because two hands alone could not have hit him so many times in so short a span. It didn't take long. Bill hit the ground with a thud and didn't move until the sun came up. The sailors cheered and laughed, and Jack sat shaking his monstrous head.

Fin turned to Knut and ordered him to sit. He did.

She sat down beside him, and Jack hollered at her down the table, "Button, if you don't quit off beating on my crew, we'll have no one left to run the *'Snake* at all." Fin laughed. "Bill was buying the drinks tonight. So you just inherited Bill's . . . bill." Fin opened her mouth in protest, and Jack raised an eyebrow to silence it.

"Fair enough," she conceded.

Jack winked back at her, then stood up and cleared his throat. "Gentlemen, those of you that ain't yet met, this here is Fin Button." Jack nodded toward her, and Fin gulped her drink to hide a blush. The others at the table shouted hellos at her. "Button, this is Ned Smithers." Jack motioned to a blond-haired man with a big, toothy grin. "Next to him is Flanders Topper, also known as the Boot Snuffler—we won't get into that." Topper was a small, plump man with a bulbous nose and looked to be covered in dirt from hair to foot. He rolled his eyes at Jack and nodded at Fin. "Far side o' the Snuffler, we got Fred Martin and Art Thomasson." The two men grunted at Fin in between guzzles from their mugs. "And over here we got Tan Bough." Jack hooked his thumb over his shoulder, and from behind him, Tan glanced at Fin through a tangle of sandy-brown hair. He acknowledged Jack's introduction with the slightest smile and turned away.

"'Course, you and Bill Stumm already met." He motioned at Bill lying on the floor. "Now I don't expect no more trouble amongst me own crew," said Jack with an air of finality. The men at the table nodded and were soon singing old songs and drinking as if nothing had ever interrupted them at all. Bill lay peaceful as a babe near the foot of the table.

Fin nursed her swelling lip and wiped her bleeding nose off on her sleeve then got up and angled her way around the table toward Jack. He was huddled over a drink, talking with Tan. Jack spied her out of the corner of his eye and held up his hand to Tan. They stopped talking and looked at her.

"Jack, could I talk to you?" Fin asked.

"Look like you already are."

"In private?"

"Nothing I want to hear can't be heard by Tan and the rest. Get on with it," he barked at her, irritated.

"I heard there's trouble back home, in Georgia. And I was wondering—"

"Don't even think of trying to weasel-worm your way off the 'Snake, mister. I like you good enough and you got the jerk to be a fine sea-hand one day, and them's scarce nowabout with the war afoot. So forget about running off and go sit down." He narrowed his eyes at her. He was crouching to pounce if she gave him a reply he didn't like.

"No sir, I don't want to leave. I was just wondering if we'd be headed back down to Savannah any time soon. I'd like to check up on friend and family as the case might be."

"It's the captain decides what we do, and where, and when. Not me—and damn sure not you. The devil alone knows the captain's mind, so you best tend your work and leave them matters be, Mr. Button." Jack wrinkled his brow and was silent a moment. "But if we land back in Savannah, come talk at me, and I'll be sure you get the time you need to check on your kin." Jack turned back to Tan and resumed his former conversation without waiting for Fin to reply. She walked back to her seat next to Knut.

She was desperate to know if the sisters and Peter were safe. If that man was right about the British using people close to her as leverage then she'd never forgive herself if any hurt came of it. But if she went back, they would be looking for her. She sipped on her beer, which was beginning to taste quite good, and considered her thoughts in silence.

"You alright, Fin?" She turned and Knut was looking at her with a worried face.

"Just thinking about home," she said with a tinge of sadness.

"Don't remember my home," said Knut.

"Don't remember? How can you not remember your home?"

"Don't know. I forget lots of stuff. Reckon that's why they call me Knut."

"You said they called you Knut because it was short for Knuttle." Fin looked at him curiously. Knut thought about it for a moment while scratching his ear.

"Oh yeah, I forgot," he said. He shrugged and gulped down the rest of his drink while Fin shook her head in amazement.

After another round of drinks, Fin began to ease into the company. The men laughed and told sea stories and poked fun at one another, and soon she was laughing easily amongst them and wishing she had more to add to the conversation. They passed the hours in comfortable fellowship, and even Knut seemed to relax eventually, though he never spoke.

Men poured into the tavern until the entire space was jammed with the drinking and the drunken, and as the hour grew late a man shouted for attention and banged a stool on the floor. The singing stopped and people wheeled around to see what the commotion was about.

"Quiet! Quiet please!" The man was in military uniform and held one hand in the air, calmly attempting to call the room to attention until the din of the day's leisure quieted and all eyes attended him.

"What in bloody hell are you dressed up for?" called a voice from the crowd.

"For those of you that don't know me, my name is Robert Mullan and this is my establishment you are enjoying." The man smiled and a great many mugs raised and sloshed about in salute.

"Cheers to the master of the house!" they called and drank. Mr. Mullan waited patiently to regain the attention of the room.

"I have here some business that I should like you to attend," he said and cleared his throat. "The Continental Congress has ordered the formation of two battalions of marines, and they have seen fit to award me a captaincy. I have been appointed to persuade such men as are hardy seamen and fearless in battle to cast in their lot with my marines to seek our fortune on the high seas of this new War for Independence." The crowd wasn't impressed, as evidenced by the chorus of *boo's* and various thrown objects that found their way through the air to Captain Mullan. Undeterred, the captain calmed the room again and continued. "I beg you, hear me out! Only yesterday, I spoke with a man who cast in his lot with a privateer who promised him only his share of what British fare they fouled. I offer that same promise of equal share in loot and booty, in addition to the many benefits of service to the Congress, including monthly pay, provisions, and clothing." Around the room eyebrows lifted as the quiet of thought encroached.

"If we throw in with you, we get paid to kill British and still get a privateer's share?" shouted a man on the far side of the room.

"Aye, indeed. A corps of marines to harass the British trade, nettle their navy, and be an angry thorn in the side of King George until he leave us be." This brought nods, murmurs, and a smattering of cheers. "Those that would aid the cause and cast in with me make your way up to place your name."

To Fin's surprise, Ned Smithers and Fred Martin stood up from the table. Jack's eyes popped wide, and he slammed his fist down hard enough that the cups on the table jumped into the air like startled frogs.

"Sit your arses down!" Jack growled at Ned and Fred.

"Now look here, Jack—" said Ned.

Jack slammed his hand onto the table again. "SIT!" he bellowed. Fred started to sit back down, but Ned glared at him and he stopped mid-sit, not certain where he wanted to end up.

"Jack, that sounds like a right good offer to me, and you got to admit that Creache ain't been on the right side of the business stick lately. Not that none of us took much of a care for him to start—"

"You two listen here, and listen good," Jack interrupted. "I don't give a damn what this fancy officer is offering. The 'Snake ain't gonna lose the two of you to it. We're working a slim crew as it is, and I'll be buggered if I'm gonna let you walk away. I'll knuckle you cold, carry you back, and chain you to a cannon if I got to."

"Jack's right, Fred," said Art Thomasson. "You ain't never been one for fighting anyhow. Quit fooling around and sit back down."

Fred eyed Art and Jack in consideration then looked at Ned for guidance.

"Come on, Fred. I'm tired of Creache's ill temper. This has the sound of a good turn to me. But if you stay or come, I'm out all the same." Ned turned to Jack with rising determination, "You can have the 'Snake, Jack, right along with the serpent at her helm."

"By hell, you will not!" snarled Jack.

Tan reached out, put a hand on Jack's shoulder, and whispered to him in a calm voice. "It's their choice, Jack. Leave them to it."

Ned stepped away from the table. Fred made up his mind and made to follow, but Jack had different plans. He leapt up and charged after Ned like an angry bull.

"Here we go," muttered Tan with a sigh and a slight grin. Then he took a deep breath and charged after Jack.

Jack caught Ned and tackled him so hard that Fin was afraid he'd be crushed like a bug. Fred, on the other hand, seemed to have lost all ability to reason. He was darting around the room, trying to hide from Jack, when he tripped and fell headlong across a table of half-soused Irish. The Irish didn't appear to be mad at him; they actually seemed quite pleased to be given an invitation to the melee and they took to clubbing Fred about the room like a beanbag.

While Ned and Jack were squared off and trading punches, Tan latched himself onto Jack's back and crooked his arm around his neck, trying to choke him into unconsciousness. It wasn't having any effect that Fin could see. Captain Mullan tried to yell over the din for order, but for all the crowd knew, he was cheering them on and it wasn't a minute before every fist in Tun Tavern was flying.

Fin and Knut stood back and enjoyed the show until a short, hairy man with one arm bowled them over into a tall, bald man with two arms and they were obliged to join the ruckus. Most men took Fin for granted due to her size, but they soon learned better with her fist in their eye.

As sailors kept by long bouts of shipborne boredom do, they bloodied each other with a sort of grim amusement. Tables and chairs flew about, splintering here and there on heads or hinds, and despite all the broken knuckles and noses, there didn't seem to be an angry man in the room, save Jack Wagon and Captain Mullan. The Irish however, far surpassed amusement and appeared to be in the throes of pure glee—much to Fred's misfortune. Through it all, Bill lay snoring peacefully at the head of the table right where Fin had dropped him.

Tan remained latched fast to Jack's neck and was tossed side to side, thrown into walls and tables, and rolled over on the floor more than once, until at last he succeeded in felling the giant. Jack tumbled to the floor with a resounding thud, and Ned breathed a heaving sigh of relief that he'd managed to survive. With Jack down and out, the life quickly died out of the rest of the combatants, and soon the room was full of groans and deep breath. Captain Mullan stood at the head of the room muttering and swearing about his broken tables and disastrous recruitment meeting.

Ned regained his breath and staggered around the room nudging unconscious bodies with his foot looking for Fred and finding only groans. Tan lay on the floor in exhaustion, and next to him, Jack lay in a tumbled heap showing no signs of waking in the near future. To Fin's amazement and delight, the Irish had regained their table and resumed drinking while they compared bruises.

"Fred?" called Ned, and from the direction of the Irish table came an answer. Fin looked closer and there was Fred seated among the crowd of red hair and freckles with a smile on his face as his newfound mates admired his many whelps and bruises whilst pouring him drinks as fast as he could empty his cup.

"Over here!" he called. "This here's Ned Smithers. Ned, meet the O'Malleys. I can't keep the first names straight, but they all answer to O'Malley so why complicate matters?" The men at the table erupted in laughter. Ned wasn't particularly amused and threw a nervous glance at Jack, who was still lying in a heap on the floor.

"Come on, Fred. Let's throw in with the marines and find us a spot farther from Jack. He'll be no friendlier when he wakes."

Fred turned his attention back to the O'Malleys and rapped his mug on the table to get their attention. "Let's throw in with Captain Mullan there and knuckle in some British on the gov'ner's ticket!"

Fred hardly had time to finish speaking before the whole O'Malley gang jumped up and carried him toward Captain Mullan's table on their shoulders, cheering and singing all the way. Ned followed after, rolling his eyes. When they reached the head of the room, Captain Mullan stopped his swearing and wasted no time showing them where to sign. As the O'Malleys, along with Fred and Ned, shuffled out of the tavern, Fin couldn't help but feel a twinge of pity for whatever British managed to find themselves in the path of the Continental Marines.

"Come on, Knut. Let's see if Jack's alright."

Fin walked over and knelt beside Jack. He seemed to be fast asleep and no worse for the wear.

"He'll be sore at me when he comes around," said Tan, sitting up and wiping his brow. "But me and Jack been friends a long time. He'll get over it." Tan looked at Fin with curiosity. She got nervous every time he looked at her, as if he somehow knew her secrets. Surely he didn't, but she couldn't shake the weight of his stare.

"How will we get him back to the 'Snake?" asked Fin.

Tan chuckled. "We don't. Would take ten of us to pick him up, much less carry him back. He'll come round soon enough. Till then, leave him lie." Tan stood up, moved to the nearest table, and took a seat. Fin and Knut joined him as he called for a drink.

"Knut, was I dreaming or did I see you giving a few licks?" asked Tan.

Knut's face turned red and he lowered his head.

"He can take care of himself more than people think," said Fin.

"You don't have to tell me. Knut was a hell of a boxer once upon a while ago. Things change though, I reckon." Tan considered Knut, as if trying to decide what else to tell. Fin didn't know what to make of the information. She looked at Knut, but he refused to meet her eyes.

"What do you mean?" she asked.

Tan didn't answer the question. "You two had best run along. Jack will come to afore long, and he's not likely to be pleasant company when he does."

Fin decided he was right. She didn't like the thought of being too close when Jack woke to find his crew two sailors short to the new marine battalion.

"I'll see you back on the 'Snake." She smiled at Tan and then nudged Knut, "Come on, let's go find some food."

They hurried out of the tavern, and Fin felt Tan's eyes on her back as she left. They walked to the *Rattlesnake* in a thoughtful hush, Knut quiet at her side. Her hand made its way into her pocket to feel the small wad of paper hiding there, the *Gazette*, with her face on the front page.

Chapter XV

J ACK'S WHISTLE CALLED THE ship to muster. The crew groaned their way out of sleep and dozens of bloodshot eyes squinted up into the morning light. Curses ascended like prayers muttered to the rhythm and clomp of feet climbing topside. On deck, Jack's spirit showed no signs of a hangover. He hollered and stomped as lively as ever, kicking the odd buttock into sobriety and calling down hellfire to burn away sleepy eyes. Only the black and blue of his face gave away the night's misadventure.

"Get up here, Button! Move your feet, Art! Where the bloody hell is that Knut?"

"I'm here, Jack," stuttered Knut from behind.

Jack jumped in surprise. "Yeah, ain't you always," he grumbled. "Captain wants to talk to the lot of you. Someone get back down and drag Tan out of bed. Anyone seen Topper?" A few hungover sailors shrugged.

"Seen him hanging out a window at the Scarlet Lady about midnight," called Art. "From the look of the lass he was sugarin' on, he'll wish he was dead." Art laughed and several others joined him.

Jack muttered and fumed and chewed at his beard.

After a few minutes, Jack was satisfied he'd gotten everyone there was to get. It turned out Topper wasn't dead after all, just sleeping in a barrel of dried mackerel. He smelled as if he'd bathed in a whale, and taken in combination with his normal odor, the effect was staggering. Jack made him stand downwind then blew a couple of short toots on his whistle to let the captain know he was ready.

The door to the captain's quarters opened and out stalked the old hawk with a lecherous smile curled behind his whiskers. He walked to the balustrade and looked down at the crew gathered below. As he scanned the deck his smile melted away and he narrowed his eyes at Jack.

"When I ask to speak to the crew, I mean I wish to speak to *all* of them, Mr. Wagon."

"Aye sir, wish I could say different, but this is all of them." Jack wasn't barking now, he sounded sheepish, something Fin hadn't thought possible.

"Perhaps you can explain to me why my crew appears to have vanished into the night?" Creache's tone was sharp, his voice cold and angry.

"The war is recruiting folks, and some of the men decided to jump ship." Jack winced.

The captain considered the situation quietly, taking time to glare at everyone present in turn. "Men that desert my crew will reap the benefit of their shallow loyalty. The price of desertion is dearly paid." The captain's eyes fell on Knut and lingered. Knut looked down at the deck and shrunk out of sight behind the mainmast. "I suggest the rest of you consider that." The captain scowled down at them until he was satisfied that his threat had taken effect.

"Some of you have wondered at my decision to leave Savannah so quickly and so lightly laden." He pulled a folded parchment from his vest and held it up for all to see. "This is the reason. I have been to a meeting with a political contact and have acquired a Letter of Marque." Several of the men raised their eyebrows in surprise; most looked confused, including Fin. "I see from the looks on your ill-educated faces that some of you have no idea what that means—which is, of course, no surprise. This letter grants the *Rattlesnake* license to seize any British vessel as I see fit. I may claim it and its cargo as my own, provided I pay a thirty-share to aid the Continental Congress in its war." The captain lifted his chin and preened with satisfaction.

Seizing and claiming sounded a lot like piracy to Fin. She glanced around at the rest of the men and saw mixed reactions. Tan was grinning from ear to ear. Jack looked troubled. Knut was busy twirling a bit of rope around his foot. Topper was still standing downwind; his eyes were closed and Fin was sure he was asleep standing up.

"This letter makes the *Rattlesnake* a privateer, and it will make us very rich men. The Atlantic is ripe, and this war is the season of its harvest. I aim to reap a lion's share. Whatever we lay claim to will be divided equally among the crew."

"I didn't sign on the *'Snake* for fighting, captain," yelled Art Thomasson.

"Fighting? Who said anything about fighting?" The captain smiled nervously. "Our quarry is the British trade, not her navy. All we need do is scare the daylight out of them and claim our reward. All very peaceable, I assure you."

The prospect of a merchant crew simply handing over cargo and ship without any fuss seemed slight to Fin, and Art didn't look convinced either. Bartimaeus had been a pirate; was this how his descent began? Nonsense, she told herself. This was perfectly legal, and even if she didn't appreciate being forced into the situation, she did like the sound of causing the British some trouble. The sooner the war was over, the sooner she'd be safe from British bounties, back home with Peter. If seizing merchant ships for Captain Tiberius Creache would quicken that end, then she was more than willing.

"We sail with the tide, make ready the ship. Mr. Wagon, I trust we'll not have any more deserters?" said the captain.

"Not if I can help it, sir."

"If you cannot 'help it' then perhaps we will find a new first mate." Creache looked down his nose at Jack like he was scolding a wayward child.

"Aye, sir." Jack turned to the crew and barked orders to get underway.

Fin and Knut swung their way up into the rigging, and the rest of the men took to setting the *Rattlesnake* free of its moorings. In short time they were creeping away from Philadelphia and back toward the blue Atlantic. Fin once again forgot her worry. She enjoyed working the ship more than she could have dreamed possible, and not even her misgivings about the captain could ruin it. The ropes, the sails, the serpentine knots, even the language of the work delighted her. She cherished words like *stanchion, clew, fiddle-block, gudgeon*, *leech*, and *luff*. She rolled them around in her mouth and fell in love with them before she ever knew their meanings. She spent the rest of the day bouncing around the ship learning all she could from any man willing to teach. Every time Jack turned around she was working at something different. He was so used to kicking the lazy out of sailors that he hardly knew what to make of Fin's unending delight in the ship's work.

By sunset, the ship was running wide open and Fin climbed up to the crow's nest to relish the day and find some peace away from the men. She felt like she was back at the orphanage again. Chores always needing done. Jack stalking about putting boot to buttock like a larger, hairier Hilde, and her hiding away above it all, trying to see what was waiting over the horizon. She missed Peter, though, and Knut was a poor substitute. Knut was a good friend, if a quiet one, but there wasn't any fire in his company.

Fin closed her eyes and imagined the woods near the river, Peter walking next to her, the sounds of him moving, breathing, his voice. She could see him in the moonlight as she played the fiddle, could see him rocking back and forth with the rhythm. She wanted that quiet place again more than even the sea and all its freedom. Then the memory of musket fire splintered her solace. The sounds of Bartimaeus and Betsy, the sounds of soldiers dying at the dinner table, the sounds of her life, her dreams, being torn away. "War Woman" the *Gazette* had named her. It sounded ridiculous, *was* ridiculous, but what had she expected? She killed six men. Now she was going to have to live with it. The only way back, the only way home, to Peter, to that beautiful green field in the country was to win this war. Independence, taxes, politics—meaningless. She just wanted to go home. Tiberius Creache had provided her with a way to assist in achieving that goal, a way to help win the war. She'd kill a hundred more soldiers if that's what it took.

Knut's voice floated up from below, calling her to dinner. Fin called back and descended to the world at hand.

WHILE THE *RATTLESNAKE* PROWLED north along the coast, the crew passed the time talking up the change of occupation. Some men were ecstatic about the prospects of a privateer's life, often to the point of blood-thirst. Bill Stumm, for one, became an intolerable braggart about all the British he intended to kill and how. Others, like Jack, didn't care for the business at all and meant to follow orders as necessary but had no intent of violence if it could be avoided. The two opinions formed an unspoken division in the crew—those who relished the captain's Letter of Marque like a lusty treasure on one hand and those who eyed it warily on the other. Fin was torn. She had no reservations after she'd thought it over, but the company was much better on the conservative side of the issue. She liked Jack and looked up to him. She had the feeling that Tan looked forward to the challenge of privateering but he was cautious and sided with Jack. Knut had no position, of course, except that of staying out of trouble, which to him meant staying clear of Bill and his ilk. "Don't think Bill likes me none," he'd say, often to himself. Fin didn't care for Bill and the company he kept either, so it was just as well she kept her thoughts of privateering to herself to avoid the risk of alienating the few friends she had.

Since she'd bested Bill in Philadelphia they had not spoken, and he harbored a festering dislike for her. Knut was right about one thing: Bill was trouble, and staying clear of him was good counsel. Wherever there was discord on the ship, Bill was sure to be at the center of it.

Five days after leaving Philadephia, the *Rattlesnake* spotted the first prize of her new career: a small merchant ship bound for Boston and flying British colors. Creache stood at the rail and peered through his spyglass, grinning like a tiger. The ship was several miles off yet, and he ordered the *Rattlesnake* to come around and close on her from the windward.

"Mr. Wagon, payday is in front of us. Load the guns and arm the crew." He snapped the spyglass closed.

Jack turned to the crew and shouted orders, "Topper, take your crew and see to the guns! The rest of you, to the armory!"

Every man on deck jumped to life and headed below. Men followed Topper to the gundeck or Jack to the armory. Fin ran to her berth and pulled out the violin case. Her heart thumped inside her chest like a war drum. She lifted the lid and stared down on the fiddle. She remembered how it sang in

Bartimaeus's hands. She had been afraid to pick it up since leaving Georgia, afraid she wouldn't remember how to play it. It wasn't the fiddle she'd come for, though. Fin could hear the other thing calling to her, whispering for her to pick it up. She moved her eyes and there it lay, crouched in its case, smiling up at her—beautiful, wicked, laughing. Betsy.

Through the walls, Fin heard Jack yelling. She heard the clang of metal and the beat of running feet. Topper was shouting orders, loading the cannons. Fin grabbed Betsy, thrust it into her belt, and ran for the armory. Tan was there, issuing musket balls and powder. Fin took what she needed and grabbed a rusty cutlass.

"Know how to use that thing, do you?" said Tan. The other men were sweating and dire with worry, but Tan had a grin on his face that Fin sensed could break into laughter at any moment. At first she thought he was making fun of her, but she was wrong. His grin wasn't a mockery, it was an exultation, a challenge thrown in the face of violence and whatever peril they might face.

"I can manage," said Fin with confidence, then she turned and ran up onto the deck. The captain was at the helm staring at the British ship with greedy eyes. The other sailors arranged themselves along the rails. They loaded muskets and stared around at each other with worried looks. Fin looked for Knut and found him port astern peering down the barrel of a pistol as if it was a spyglass.

"Give me that, Knut," she said and snatched it out of his hands. Fin quickly loaded it and handed it back to him. "Know how to shoot it?" Knut nodded. "Good—careful where it's pointing though," she added.

Fin turned to her own protection. She stuffed Betsy full of musket ball and packed the barrel, then stuck it into her belt and looked around. The other sailors had finished loading weapons and were, one and all, looking intently at the British ship as it drew closer.

"Alright, boys," shouted Jack, "do this right and no one gets hurt. All we got to do is scare 'em good. Just 'cause you boys got guns, don't mean you got to go firing 'em, hear?" Fin hoped it would be that easy. Jack walked to the hatch and called down, "You ready down yonder, Topper?" A muffled voice called back and Jack nodded. "All's well, captain. We're ready."

Creache smiled.

"Loose a cannon across her deck, Mr. Wagon," he said.

"Aye aye, sir" said Jack. "Alright, Topper, send her a hello from the 'Snake!"

Once again a muffled voice answered from below. Fin glanced at Knut and saw he had his fingers plugging up both ears. Then Topper sent his greeting. *FOOM!* The ship shook and smoke poured out of the portside gunwale. A cannonball stabbed a hole in the British ship's mainsail and splashed into the water on the far side.

Creache threw up his spyglass and peered through it. Jack turned to the captain, awaiting orders. The rest of the hands on deck stared at the prize and clutched the rail, white-knuckled.

They were close enough to make out the sailors on board the other ship now and could read her name as written on the stern, the *Whistle*. Fin studied the ship and saw men about the deck, working in the rigging, taking in sail.

"They're stopping, they are," said Jack, half to himself, half to the crew.

"Take in sail and prepare to board," ordered the captain.

The crew jumped into action and brought in the sails. Art was at the helm and aimed the *Rattlesnake* up alongside the *Whistle*. Jack called for grapplers. On the portside, men brought out hooks and hurled them at the rail of the *Whistle* to pull her in close. The crewmen of the 'Snake were silent and kept one hand on their pistols while they tended tackle and hooks with the other. On the deck of the *Whistle*, its captain paced the quarterdeck while his men stood about. Fin was surprised to see they looked more curious than scared or angry.

There was a dull knock as the two ships bumped together, and Jack ordered a plank laid across the rails. Creache walked across the plank and hopped down onto the deck of the *Whistle*, followed by Jack.

"I demand to know what this is all about!" said the captain of the *Whistle*.

"About? This is about money," said Creache and smiled. "I am Captain Tiberius Creache, and I hereby claim this vessel and her cargo."

"Are you mad?" balked the *Whistle*'s captain.

"Indeed," said Creache. "But my state of mind bears little influence to our present situation." He produced a document from his coat and waved it in front of the other captain's nose. "This Letter of Marque grants me leave to seize any British ship and cargo that I so choose—mad or not," said Creache with an evil smile. "Therefore, if you would—what did you say your name was?"

"Burleson. Captain Burleson," said the man amid his obvious fluster.

"Very good. Captain Burleson, if you would please order your men to transfer your cargo to my hold, we shall keep this transaction civil." Creache looked pleased with himself.

"By God, I will not!" protested Captain Burleson. Creache's eyes narrowed to slits. He drew his pistol and leveled it at the man's face.

"Much like my madness, I assure you that God is of no relevance to our situation. If you insist, however, I will arrange for you to discuss it with him personally. Then, *by God*, I will have your hold and scuttle your ship." Creache little more than whispered it, but even the waves seemed to have hushed. Every ear heard him and fingers all around crept closer to trigger and blade. "Choose, captain, before my madness makes up its own mind."

The *Whistle*'s captain stood quivering for a moment then spoke decisively. "Do as he says! Open the holds!" His men paused, considering whether or not he meant it, then they hesitantly began to obey. Creache didn't move. The barrel of his pistol never wavered from the other man's face. For over an hour, they stood staring at each other, Creache occasionally smiling and chuckling to himself.

The *Whistle*'s crew transferred their cargo and stores to the *Rattlesnake*, while Fin and the rest of the crew stood at the rail with guns ready, making sure no one stepped out of line as the hold was ladened. The tension was thick as fog. Fin was consciously aware of every drop of sweat on her face, every slap of the waves against the hull, every breath of the men around her. Knut, beside her, shifted from foot to foot in nervous agitation.

At last, the transfer was complete. Jack turned to the captain and nodded. As quickly as he had drawn it, Creache holstered his firearm and smiled widely at the captain in front of him.

"Thank you for your generosity, captain, and good day." Creache turned and trotted back across the plank. Jack followed and barked orders to loose the *Whistle* from her hooks. Creache disappeared back into his quarters and the *Rattlesnake* eased away.

Fin looked back and saw the crew and captain of the *Whistle* standing stone-still on deck. They looked positively boggled. Fin smiled. Maybe the privateer business wasn't as bad as she'd feared. The seizure had gone smoothly, no blood drawn, and now they had a full hold of imported goods to sell for profit. Mad or not, Creache may indeed make them rich. Jack ordered the arms returned to the armory and soon the sails were full again, and the *Whistle* dwindled into the horizon.

In the following days, Creache set his sights on seven more unwary merchant ships, and each time he managed to seize the cargo without the loss of a single life or even a drop of blood. The men couldn't have been more pleased and scuttlebutt aboard began to claim that Creache might not be such a sore captain after all.

When they moored in Philadelphia again, two weeks after the *Whistle*, they had a hold full of imports from Britain to unload. For two days they wheeled 'round the capstan to lift up the ill-gotten fare and wheeled it 'round again to lower the crates to the wharf. Fin, too small to offer significant help at the capstan, fetched and delivered their take to warehouses up and down the waterfront. After Creache paid the Congress its share, the take was so large that he easily made good on his claim of riches by paying each sailor his due in bags of coin so large that Fin thought she'd have to spend half of her's to even lift the sack. She bought some well-fitted boots, new trousers, a cedar sailor's trunk, and a leather vest that better concealed the secrets beneath her shirt. She ate well and drank well and spent money, for which she had little use, on frivolous things. And she took time to write, to tell Peter she was safe and sure.

In late April, they had news of the Revolution. George Washington had chased the British out of Boston. Thomas Payne published *Common Sense*, and Fin bought a copy just like myriad others and steeled her will with its denouncement of monarchy and justification of democracy. The Americans were at war, and Fin felt she was moving in earnest toward the end of her sojourn.

The advent of open war raised the stakes for the *Rattlesnake*, however. The Royal Navy was thicker along the coast, and the *Rattlesnake*'s reputation as a menace to the Crown grew with every ship she seized.

In late fall, they got underway from Charleston and prowled the coast along the Carolinas in search of a prize. Long days passed without sighting a target, and the crew grew restless in the downtime. Fin lay in her hammock on the gundeck, lazy in the heat of the day, while Tan and Jack sat nearby playing cards and Knut slept, leaning against the bulkhead. Bill and several other sailors had gathered at the far end of the deck. They were laughing and discussing their plans for the next port call.

"Button, don't never play cards with Tan," grumbled Jack. "He cheats."

Tan looked at Fin and rolled his eyes. "You can't stand another man to have good luck can you?"

Jack harrumphed. "Don't start with me, Tan. I'm right—and you know it."

"You mean about me cheating or about Creache?" asked Tan

"Hmmph, both."

"What about Creache?" asked Fin.

Tan put down his cards turned so he could face her. "Jack's got himself all worked up like a woman because he thinks Creache's luck is due to run out." Fin opened her mouth to protest his comment about women but remembered herself and snapped it closed. "Now, you'd think our fair and hairy first mate here might congratulate his crew for such a job well done." Jack was patiently ignoring him. "But you'd be wrong. He prefers to think the only reason we're still safe and unbloodied is the good captain's run of luck."

"You done yet?" asked Jack.

"Can you believe that, Fin? Just another superstitious sailor." Tan had a big grin on his face. He enjoyed teasing Jack and drew it out for all it was worth.

The truth was that it wasn't just Jack: many of the crew thought it was only a matter of time before their luck ran out. They'd come away too easily from all the ships they'd boarded. Not once had the business come to violence.

"Have you been on a privateer before, Jack?" Fin asked.

"No. But I was on the *Dancing Susan* when she was taken by pirates off Martinique. It was no peaceful business, I can tell you. Half the crew was dead or bloodied before it was done. Bad business it is. Fifty men on the deck of a ship, all with blades and muskets, and every one trying to kill the other, and cannons blowin' holes the size of kegs in the bulkheads. Bad business; worst there is. So we're a privateer, you say? For British eyes we're no more than pirates and thieves. We've been lucky. And sure as the sun goes round, lucky don't stick for long."

Fin expected Tan to tease him again but he didn't—his grin was gone. It had become suddenly quiet, and Fin looked around to see that the other men had all stopped their business to listen to Jack. Even Bill Stumm and his regulars were listening.

"Your deal, Jack," said Tan. Jack dealt the cards and people resumed their previous conversations.

The schism that had been created when they'd turned to privateering had widened, and though unspoken, it was plainly written in the company the men kept. Those that had taken to the new work readily and wantonly were the captain's men through and through, and they no longer tolerated another man to speak ill of him. Bill Stumm was their leader, and while none dared speak ill of Jack out of respect for his station as first mate, it was widely known that the captain favored Bill. Fin suspected Bill had eyes for Jack's job as soon as opportunity provided.

Fin, however, took it all in stride. She saw each act of piracy against the Crown as a step closer to home. She even began to look forward to it.

As they slipped among the outer banks of North Carolina, the fears Jack had given voice to came a step closer to reality. A frigate of the Royal Navy came upon them by surprise as it slipped from behind the southern rise of an island. Jack ordered them to quarters, and before they could change tack and get the wind at their backs, the British were nearly in cannon range and testing their long nines against the distance. The *Rattlesnake* was by far the faster ship, and they made flight with ease, but coming face-to-face with the enemy and being the target of cannonshot made Fin's blood chill.

They learned to be incredibly efficient at scaring smaller ships into compliance. Some men made an art of it. Tan had the knack of giving men the evil eye, and they'd quiver in their boots just to know his stare was upon them. Art Thomasson paid a butcher in Baltimore to have blood splashed all over his clothes. He'd stand on deck as near the captured ship as he could, looking like he'd killed five men and bathed in their blood, and he'd taunt waylaid sailors with made-up stories of the men he'd sliced on the last ship to fall victim to the *Rattlesnake*. Jack didn't need to put on a performance; he intimidated men by his very presence. All he needed to do was to stand near a man and look down at him to induce a panicky wave of shudders and obedience. Fin would wave Betsy about with cavalier flourishes to scare the sauce out of whatever poor tar happened to be standing in front of her, and, secretly, she was coming to enjoy the heft of the gun in her hand.

By summer they'd taken only small prizes, and the captain was determined to fill his holds before setting in to port again. When he spotted *The Kingfish* on the horizon he seized the opportunity.

Fin joined Tan on the rail and peered out at *The Kingfish* as they approached. It was large, certainly the largest ship they'd ever attempted. The double gundecks on her sides raised Fin's hackles. Only once or twice had the captain ever dared assail a ship that was anything more than meagerly armed, and each of those times the *Rattlesnake*'s twenty guns easily outclassed the ship they meant to seize. But the ship they were closing on now was not only the equal of the *Rattlesnake*, she was her superior, and they weren't nearly as battle-ready as all their cannons and topside gunmen made them appear.

The *Rattlesnake* was built for a crew of eighty but was manned by less than thirty. There weren't enough men below to man the guns—but *The Kingfish* didn't know that. If it came to cannonfire, they could only get off one full volley before Topper would be run ragged trying to reload. If it came to cannonfire, the *Rattlesnake* couldn't win.

"That's a big ship," said Fin.

Tan raised a worried eyebrow at her. "Sure you can manage that cutlass?" he asked. Fin said nothing.

"Alright boys, same drill, bigger fish. Play your cards, keep your face on, and she'll fry up like all the others," called Jack across the deck. Fin looked back at him. He didn't look as sure of himself as he normally did. Things that scared Jack Wagon were certain to make other men faint cold. She prayed it wasn't fear she saw.

The captain exited his quarters and appraised the ship through his spyglass. Jack approached him, and they spoke in hushed words. Fin couldn't hear what they said, but Creache didn't look happy about it. When they finished, Jack looked more troubled than he had before.

"Swing around and give us a shot," called the captain to the helm. Art spun the wheel and the ship lurched to starboard.

"Ready the guns!" Jack yelled down to Topper.

The *Rattlesnake* tacked around until her gunwales were parallel to *The Kingfish*, offering a clear shot off the starboard.

"Let fly, Topper!" yelled Jack, and seconds later the ship jerked and shuddered as Topper sent a ball across the deck of the other ship. The men on the deck of *The Kingfish* scurried about, some to the rigging, some heading below, but they didn't take in sail, and the ship showed no signs of slowing.

"Warn her a second time," said the captain, and Jack relayed the order. Once again, a cannon boomed and the ship quivered. The shot sailed over *The Kingfish* and raised a plume of water on the far side.

Fin looked around; the crew was tense—scared. They'd never had to fire twice before. If *The Kingfish* tacked around, they might fire back. Fin looked at Tan. He was grinning with anticipation. He noticed her and winked. Tan loved it. Fin looked away and wrung the railing. She wasn't scared, but she certainly wasn't enjoying it like Tan was.

"Ready a volley," ordered Creache.

"Captain?" said Jack with a worried look.

"You heard me, you blithering idiot. Ready a volley and prepare to fire!"

"Aye sir," said Jack. He turned to the hatch and relayed the order down to Topper. Jack was sweating. Topper called up that the guns were standing by.

"Volley away!" snarled Creache. Jack hesitated. The captain's face turned red with anger. "I said volley away!"

Jack didn't move. The captain drew his pistol and cocked back the hammer. "Mr. Wagon, I assure you, I will kill you if you do not obey."

Jack didn't answer. He raised a swarthy arm and pointed behind the captain.

The Kingfish was taking in sail.

The captain's eyes flashed at Jack, and he put his firearm away.

"Prepare to board," Creache whispered. Jack didn't look at him or answer. He turned and prodded the crew into action. Along the rail, men readied their hooks and drew cutlasses. Fin pulled Betsy from her belt.

On the deck of *The Kingfish*, its sailors stood ready with blades drawn. Murmurs of trepidation ran across the deck of the *Rattlesnake*. They'd never been opposed by armed men. These looked not only armed but ready to fight. The situation was far more dangerous than what they were accustomed to. Beside her, Tan was bouncing slightly on his toes. She looked around for Knut and found him against the far rail. He didn't look scared, for which Fin was grateful. If the seizure turned to fighting, she hoped Knut would stay safe aboard the *Rattlesnake*.

Jack called out the order, and hooks flew.

Creache stood at the rail and shouted across to *The Kingfish*, "Call out your captain!"

A large sailor on *The Kingfish* conversed briefly with two of his fellows, nodded, and disappeared into the cabin. Creache smiled with satisfaction and ordered a plank laid across the rail. The sailors aboard *The Kingfish* flourished their cutlasses and glared at their opposition. Tan was making eyes at one of them and twitching his head like a maniac. Dread ran through Fin's veins. The crews of both ships stared at each other in nervous anticipation while waiting for the captain of *The Kingfish* to appear. It was odd that the ship's captain wasn't already on deck given the circumstance. Then the cabin door swung open. From the door came no captain. Out from the bowels of *The Kingfish* issued a red vomit of British soldiers. Fin snatched Betsy into the air and pointed her puckered barrel at the redcoats arraying themselves across the opposite deck. Muskets lifted in answer, and men began shouting. Sabers waved in the air and pistols dared the silence to break.

"Hold your peace!" cried Jack, though which crew he ordered, none could say. Tan glanced from Jack to *The Kingfish* and back, trying to anticipate the next move. Knut cowered behind the mast. Fin was lost in a sea of red. She smelled the burning flesh of a British soldier from a world away, felt a cold knife on her back. She felt a one-eyed man breathing into her face as she thrust a knife. Murder. She saw dead men lying across the dining table, blood spreading across its waxy grain. Ruin. Fear and anger welled within her. She squeezed the trigger and Betsy roared. A cloud of smoke erupted from the barrel and men screamed. The smoke cleared and a man lay dead across the rail of *The Kingfish*. Then musket fire exploded toward the *Rattlesnake*.

Tan leapt the rail, rapier drawn, and began his ruinous work with unsettling grace. The crew fired their muskets and followed Tan. Fin cast Betsy down as if the weapon had burned her. She drew her cutlass and ran after them. A soldier charged with his bayonet, and Fin clubbed it aside. She swung the blade and he fell cloven as she moved to the next soldier in her path.

Aboard the *Rattlesnake*, Jack stood stone-like, firing pistol shot as fast as he could load it while he called up curses and hurled them at the British as if they might flee by the foulness of his insults alone. Creache retreated into his cabin.

Fin's blood was on fire. She lavished vengeance on her attackers like kisses upon a long-missed lover. Jack shouted in the distance, but Fin paid no heed. She cut down a soldier and licked sweat from her lips. She looked around for Tan but he was gone. The deck of *The Kingfish* was choked with bodies, most British, but some she recognized as her shipmates. Jack shouted again from somewhere behind her, but she couldn't make out his words.

A hand grabbed her and spun her around. It was Tan.

"Come on!" he shouted at her and pointed back to the *Rattlesnake*.

"Bloody hell, Button! Get over here or you can join the limey's in Davey Jones' locker!" Jack yelled.

She cast another glance back at *The Kingfish* and saw that Tan and the crew had barricaded the hatches and trapped the British below before reinforcements could make it topside. The soldiers below decks shouted and beat at the hatches. Fin turned and bounded across the plank.

"Now, Topper!" shouted Jack, and the cannons fired into the belly of *The Kingfish*. The *Rattlesnake* rocked hard to port, and Fin grabbed the rail to avoid falling. Sounds of splintering wood and breaking glass echoed through *The Kingfish* as the cannonshot tore through her amidships and left holes the size of barrels down her sheerline. Seawater rushed into her, and the angry shouts of the trapped British turned to screams and cries for help. The *Rattlesnake* righted itself and Jack shouted, "Reload!"

Creache emerged from hiding, livid with anger. "What are you doing?"

"Sending these bastards to the dark below as soon as Topper loads a volley," growled Jack.

"We'll do no such thing until we've plundered her hold."

"Not this time, captain. We was lucky enough we got them by surprise a'fore the entire company made it topside. There's more soldiers below decks. I ain't waiting around for them to bang their way up and bleed us."

Topper called up that the guns were ready.

"Stand down, Mr. Wagon!"

Jack looked at the captain with a stern eye and shook his head.

"Fire!" yelled Jack, and the guns blew. *The Kingfish* shuddered and began to crumple. As it slipped into the sea Tan ran down the starboard rail cutting away the hooks before they could drag the *Rattlesnake* down as well.

The captain and Jack faced each other in cold silence as the remaining soldiers and crew aboard *The Kingfish* sunk to an icy grave. No one spoke a word; all eyes were on the captain. Jack had disobeyed a direct order.

"See Mr. Wagon to the brig. Put him in irons," said Creache to no one in particular. In all likelihood he hadn't any idea who to order. It was Jack who ran his ship, and it was Jack who commanded the men. The crew looked around at each other, each hoping another would be the one to step forward and fulfill the order. Bill stood in the background smiling. No one moved. The captain bristled with anger.

"You, Mr. Bough, is it not?" he asked, pointing his chin at Tan. "Have this mutineer locked away."

Tan looked to Jack, who nodded, before answering. "Aye, sir." He sounded uncertain for the first time since Fin had known him. He motioned for Jack to come with him and proceeded below decks to the brig.

"As for the rest of you cowards, an example will be made."

"Sir, it was an ambush," protested Art. "We wasn't prepared for no fight with British regulars. A trap it was, what with them waiting below."

"Do you presume to *think*," spat Creache with disgust, "that I did not know there were soldiers aboard?" Creache lifted a dangerous eyebrow at Art. He couldn't have known; he simply didn't care. "Sacking a ship of the British Navy and selling off her arms and hold would have turned us more profit than any three pitiful merchant ships. But now, thanks to you lot, our wages are locked safely away at the bottom of the Atlantic." Creache glared around at the crew. He stuck out a crooked bony finger and pointed at a man hiding around the corner of the cabin.

"Bring him!" Creache ordered. No one moved. Creache glared around the deck waiting for his order to be followed. He marked carefully each sailor that defied him, including Fin. Then he spat on the deck and rushed to the man hiding behind the cabin bulkhead. Creache disappeared around the corner as the man shrank away, then reappeared dragging the man, kicking and fighting, across the deck by his arm. It was Knut. The captain threw him against the mainmast, and Knut crumpled into a pile at its foot, quivering and crying. Fin hadn't believed Creache was strong enough to drag and throw a man like that, but she'd just seen it with her own eyes. He tied Knut's hands fast to the mast.

Before she knew what she was doing Fin stepped forward and shouted, "Stop it! What are you doing to him?" Creache's head snapped toward her and he pulled his pistol out.

"I've had enough mutineering for today and will not hesitate to shoot dead the next man that questions me!" He cocked back the hammer.

Fin was horrified. Surely he wouldn't punish Knut for the offense Jack had done him. Creache was not bluffing though. He would shoot her. She was certain of it. She shook her head and stepped back.

Creache stuck his gun back into his belt and turned to the stowage locker behind the mast. He reached inside and brought out a long, stiff cane. Knut pulled and twisted at his bonds in a hopeless attempt at flight. The captain walked slowly around Knut, smiling gently as at an animal caught in a trap. Then he raised his arm and brought the cane down on Knut's back. It made a sharp smacking noise, like the slap of a wave against the ship. Knut cried out. Again and again, Creache let fall the cane, and each time Knut's screams pierced the air.

Fin flung herself to the rail and dared not turn to watch. She couldn't bear it. She convinced herself many times over that she had to run to his aid and cowered as many times from the threat of Creache's pistol. She wailed inside for Knut and fanned into flames a hate for the *Rattlesnake*'s tyrant.

At last, the blows and screams ended. Creache raised the cane like a sword and pinwheeled slowly around the deck, making sure to point it at each sailor.

"Such is the price of mutiny," he said with a nod toward Knut's unconscious and bloody body. "I've no interest in damaging good deck hands, but this worthless half-wit will pay dearly for any breach of my command. His blood is on your heads." Then Creache cast the cane down upon Knut's still body and stalked back through the cabin door.

Fin ran to Knut. His back was striped and split open, cut to the bone. She rolled him over and attempted to rouse him but could not.

"Take him," she whispered. She stood and took hold of him as the men around lifted his body and slowly marched below decks to tend him what care they could.

Chapter XVI

IN THE DAYS FOLLOWING Jack's insubordination, the atmosphere of the ship thickened. The crew's thoughts grew heavy and filled the ship like a vapor. They could feel Jack's presence below, locked away in the dark stink of the ship's brig, and although none spoke of it, the shadow of the captain's accusation was present in everyone's mind. Mutiny, however small or justified, was no light matter. Even the hint of it was enough to win a man a flogging; Jack had done more than hint.

The captain made no mention of appointing a new first mate, so others stepped in to fill the void. Tan gave orders and tried to cover Jack's duties, but he had to contend with Bill. Bill coveted the job and turned his dislike on Tan when Tan stepped in to try to fill it. The reality was that neither of them could. Jack's boots were bigger than his feet suggested, and over the past months the divisions on the ship had become sharper and more defined. No man in Bill's camp would take orders from Tan, and likewise, none of those sympathetic to Jack's defiance would hearken to Bill. Combined with worries over Jack, the splintering of the crew turned the atmosphere of the *Rattlesnake* into an oppressive murk of whispers, suspicion, and distrust.

In the past, the captain was seldom seen about the ship. It was rare for him to leave his cabin unless business demanded it. But after *The Kingfish*, he took to making regular tours. On more than one occasion, Fin felt eyes upon her and turned to find Creache glaring at her in silence. He sent shivers down her spine. Though he never said a word, Creache's eyes told her all she needed to know; he was looking for mutiny, as if Jack's insubordination had spawned a festering mold somewhere in the ship, and he aimed to ferret it out and stamp it dead.

Fin tended to Knut every chance she had, changing his bandages, bringing him water and food, sitting with him when she was able. He would heal up fine, but it would take time. Knut remembered nothing of that day or his beating, and he often asked after Jack and the captain as if they might pop in to see him at their earliest opportunity. Fin would tell him they were busy about the business of the ship, and he'd frown. Fin questioned him gently at times to see if his memory of the event was returning, but he never answered and he never asked what caused his injuries.

Of the rest of the crew, only Tan ever asked after him with anything that seemed more than common courtesy. The other men had always been distant from Knut—he had no real friends except for Fin—but she'd never taken much notice of just how much they avoided him until now. They weren't merely indifferent, though; it was something else. Shame maybe, the same shame she felt that she hadn't stopped his wounding. The shame that kept her cowered on the rail while Knut was beaten and bled for no crime at all.

Fin sat next to his hammock, changing his bandages. She asked him questions to ply his mind for memories of how he'd been hurt, but as ever, he remembered nothing. When at last he fell asleep, she shook her head and continued washing his cuts and wrapping them fresh.

"He never remembers," said Tan from behind her. She hadn't heard him come in.

"He doesn't seem to remember any of it," said Fin with a wrinkled brow.

"This isn't the first time you know. Remember I told you Knut used to be a right good boxer?"

"Yes," said Fin, her curiosity aroused.

"He was more than that. He was first mate before Jack."

"*Knut* was first mate?" Fin was sure he was joking.

"Aye, and a good one." Tan's eyes glazed into memory as he talked. "Ran a tight ship, took lip from no man and gave boot to many a lazy sailor. Most figured he'd be his own captain one day."

Fin's mind boggled. "What happened?"

"Same thing what's happening to Jack in a way," Tan said with a grim look. "We was crossing from West Africa, late summer, must have been two . . . three years back. Captain had us running slaves. None of us liked it, but the captain ain't one for listening to no one but himself. Bad luck running slaves—terrible stink, and diseases, and it hangs darkness on a man's soul. Half the . . . *cargo* . . . was dead before we was halfway to Charleston, and most of the other half was sick. You can't imagine the smell, can't breathe, can't sleep at night listening to the sickness coming up from down below. If death got a sound, I heard it. Every morning we'd throw a net down and the negroes would laden their dead on it. We'd haul 'em up and throw 'em overboard. One time some live ones got in the net with the dead, maybe hoping we'd throw them to the water as well. That got the captain furious mad. He beat a couple of 'em to death to teach the others a lesson. That was the last time talk on the *'Snake* started whispering mutiny. The sickness didn't stay below, see? The crew started to wasting away. Saw twenty mates flush their bloody innards out their bums before they died screaming and bleeding out every hole God give 'em. It was Captain Creache they blamed. Bad luck, hauling the devil's cargo. And hell was the next berth many of 'em seen.

"About two days east of Charleston, the wind and sky turned hellish as well. Knut told the captain we best swing north a ways, 'round the storm, and come in to Charleston on the third day, but the captain wouldn't turn aside. The sooner to port, the more live cargo he'd have to sell off. Captain was more than willing to risk sinking us all to Davey Jones' locker rather than spend an extra day and see his profits sink instead."

Tan paused and considered Knut lying on the hammock in the dark. "That's where Knut and the captain finally parted ways. Knut told him the storm was the death of us all, said it was a great swell of God's vengeance come rolling right at us, said it come to exact payment for the evil Creache had led us into by trading negroes. Knut had the mind of the crew, and the captain nearly did to Knut what he done to those negroes what tried to have themselves drowned. He beat Knut like an animal, and I swear he enjoyed it. Then he hauled Knut below and sailed us through the storm. In all my years of sailoring, I've yet to see a worse one. The ocean jumped up so big it blocked out the sky. Couldn't tell what way was up. The wind grabbed anything on deck—wood, rope, cannon, or crew—and flung it away into the black heart of the storm. The crew wailed and prayed and knew they was sailing straight to hell to drown and burn for Creache's madness.

"But drown we didn't. Though I reckon God got his vengeance on Creache after all. See, every one of them negroes died in that storm, and I like to think God did them a mercy. But the captain was furious mad at losing his entire cargo. He drug Knut up from the brig where he had him stowed and beat him a second time, worse even than before. Somewhere between the blows and the blood, Knut stopped being Knut. 'The price of mutiny,' said the captain. After that, Knut hadn't never been the same." Tan stopped and looked at Knut in a tender way Fin hadn't seen before; it was the same look Sister Carmaline gave Bartimaeus when they laid him in the ground, the look you give a friend that's dead and gone and isn't coming back.

"Why didn't anyone help him?" asked Fin. She hadn't helped him either.

"Knut was certainly guilty of mutiny. Captain would have been right with the law to shoot him then and there."

Tan shifted on his feet and looked at the floor. "But I reckon the real answer is one I don't care to speak." Fin knew the answer. And she felt the shame of it the same as Tan.

"Since then it's Knut the captain beats when a man gets out of line. I tried to stop him once, but it didn't do any good, only got Knut a bloodier beat than he'd got without my help. He ain't Tommy Knuttle no more, just Knut. Makes it easier. That's why the men keep away from him. They figure he's bad luck. Some even figure it was his bad luck brought up that storm and brought down the sickness." Tan's face tightened; he didn't agree. "Lot of the men aboard never come back after that sail though. Deserted for better berth. And then a lot of them figured maybe the captain wasn't so much bad luck after all, seeing how he sailed us through that black storm. Some of us just got no place else to go." Tan stopped and looked at Fin.

"So you see, some of the men aboard, they was there when the captain knocked the thinking out of Knut's head, and them that wasn't, they've heard the tale. So now they're wondering what the captain's got in store for Jack. Most of the men like Jack. Don't think a one of them want to see him get what Knut got. No one deserves that—or else we all do."

"I'll kill him if he touches Knut again," said Fin without looking up.

"I said that once," replied Tan with a cheerless chuckle, "long time ago. Never seems that easy once you're standing in the captain's storm. Sometimes, I think maybe I ought to kill Knut and save him the misery, but that ain't easy either." Again, Tan laid a tender look down on Knut as he slept.

"Were you friends?" she asked.

Tan didn't answer at first; he just stood there, looking down at Knut. Fin was sure he'd heard her. She didn't ask again.

After a quiet long enough to draw the creaks and moans of the ship out into the open, he looked away from Knut and answered, "Aye, good friends."

Fin leaned over and pulled her fiddle case out from its hiding spot among the boxes and crates. She opened it gently and removed the fiddle and bow. She hadn't played it since she left the orphanage, and it felt alien to her. She crooked it up against her chin and let it remember where to sit as she closed her eyes and stroked notes from the wood. She played softly and filled the berth with a gentle cloud of song. The waves beat the hull of the ship like a metronome, and she guided her song to its rhythm. As she let herself fall into the music, she remembered how she loved it and wondered why she'd abandoned such beauty for so long.

After a time, she lowered the violin and looked up to find Tan staring at her with something of sadness and amazement on his face. She blushed and shrugged.

"Fiddler's Green," said Tan with a smile.

"What?"

"Where sailors live the grand hereafter on a wide green field, with nothing to do but fill your cup and bounce a lass to a fiddler's tune. The Green ain't exactly heaven like the preachers preach. They say it's a place for sailors alone: the good, the bad, and all the in-between that ever give his life to the big, blue sea. And here you are—Fin Button, the fiddler himself." Tan smiled and laughed.

"You believe in God, Tan?"

"Ain't no sailor doesn't," answered Tan with a sure nod. "A man don't sail his soul away and give himself to the wind and wave without he believes God above can see him to the other side." He looked at Fin, "Don't you?"

Now it was Fin's turn to be silent. She didn't want to believe in God. At the very least, she was certain he didn't believe in her. All her life she'd listened to the sisters talk and preach about God, Jesus, salvation and the like, but all she could ever account for was God and his sisters telling her where to go and what to do. *All the devils in hell can't come between God and a man he done chose.* No one but Peter had ever chosen her.

"I don't know," she said. "I don't think we like each other." She squinted up at Tan to see if he understood her. He scratched his head.

"The sea's no place for a man that ain't on good terms with the Lord. I'd keep quiet if that's your mind. Other men might take to heaping all their bad luck on you like they do Knut if they knew you and the Lord was in outs." He raised an eyebrow to make sure she understood.

Fin nodded and lifted the fiddle to place it back in its case. As she closed the lid, she stopped suddenly. There in the case was a great long empty darkness in the shape of a gun. Betsy was gone. She thought back—*The Kingfish*, the soldiers. She fired; she cast it away. She could see in her mind where it had fallen to the deck. Then she'd run away across the plank, sword drawn, leaving Betsy where she lay. Fin was instantly angry with herself. It was almost certainly at the bottom of the ocean. In all the commotion and fighting it would have been kicked overboard. The crew knew it belonged to her, and surely anyone would have returned it had they picked it up.

"Problem?" asked Tan.

"Betsy's gone. My pistol. I dropped it during the fight."

"That reminds me, you told me you could manage with that cutlass of yours." Tan was grinning like his usual self.

"I think I managed quite nicely, thank you."

"Managed maybe, but why settle for managing when one can excel, eh?"

Tan pulled his rapier from its sheath and weighed it in his hand, then considered Knut before speaking. "This was Knut's. I keep it for him since he's not one to use it anymore." He twirled the blade about once before seating it back in its sheath. "Back when Knut was Tom Knuttle, my friend, he taught me to use a sword. Remember I told you he was a fine boxer? He was a master bladesman as well." Fin looked at Knut sleeping on the hammock and tried to picture the man Tan had been telling her about, but she still had trouble getting her mind to accept it. "What say I pass a little learning on to you? You could use it now that you're gunless," he said with a chuckle. "You and Knut seem to be good friends. I think he'd bless the teaching if he knew enough to know. What do you say?"

Fin was still kicking herself for losing Betsy, but she couldn't deny the excitement she felt about Tan's offer.

"Sounds like fun," she answered, "but I'd rather have my pistol back." She rummaged around the berthing area on the chance Betsy had somehow lodged herself in a nook. Tan laughed at her.

"Come find me sometime when you've got a mind to learn then," said Tan as he turned and walked away to resume his duties on deck.

After Tan left, Fin didn't have to look long around the hold to decide she'd lost the old blunderbuss for good. She soon enough gave up the looking with a frown and threw herself down in a corner, thinking she ought to find some sleep before her watch.

What felt like little more than minutes later, she was shaken awake by Art Thomasson. His watch was up and hers was on. She grunted loud enough to let him know she was moving, and he stumbled off into the darkness to find his hammock.

Fin climbed up out of the hold to the steady creaks and groans of the *Rattlesnake* slipping south. She preferred the late-night watch duty to any of the other watches. Shifts were set up to rotate, and every month she'd get a week of seeming quiet when she mostly lived in the dark. Ship life never lets a sailor truly off-duty, and a man is as likely to end up working every shift as he is his own, but the work ebbs and flows like the tide below, and getting around to the shift at night always felt like a holiday to Fin.

She padded softly around the deck whispering hellos to the others coming on watch with her. Topper was at the helm, and she snuck up behind him and jabbed him lightly in the side. He jumped sideways in surprise. Even in the dark Fin could see Topper was his typical untidy self. No matter what the occasion, he always seemed to be in the process of becoming dirty. He never looked completely filthy; he merely looked like a recently clean man who had been doused in dirt just before you'd rounded the corner and seen him. He also had a permanent hangover, not the kind that comes from drinking, but the kind that hides a beltline beneath a portly belly. No matter what size clothes he wore, that belly would always find its way out to peek at you from between his shirt and shins. When he jumped aside from Fin's jab his belly danced a little bobble and winked at her in the moonlight.

"Morning, Topper," said Fin. Topper harrumphed and swatted her hand away as she attempted to jab him again.

"Mind your foolin', the captain's about," whispered Topper with a nervous look around. Creache had been out prowling more of late, but to be out at this time of night was unheard of.

"What for?" whispered Fin.

"Damned if he tells me," muttered Topper. "Get aloft before he's got reason to make a fuss." Topper laid a stern eye on her and pointed his nose at the crow's nest.

Fin didn't need to be told again. She was as anxious to keep out of the captain's sight as any man aboard. She climbed down the quarterdeck stair and turned toward the mainmast ladder. The other men were gathered at the forecastle working at something Fin couldn't make out in the dark. She stepped onto the ladder to climb her way up, but before she cleared the boom, a voice broke the night's ease.

"Mr. Button," said the captain's voice. The hairs on Fin's neck shivered and stood. She felt violated just to hear her name from his mouth. She turned her head down toward the deck and answered.

"Yes sir?"

"Join me in my cabin." It wasn't a request. It was an order, and he didn't wait to see it followed. He turned as soon as the words departed his lips and stalked through the door into his quarters. It was a good thing, too, because Fin, in her terror, didn't obey immediately. It took her a few long seconds to gather herself and remind her body to make its way down the ladder, a few seconds the captain might have seen as reluctance to obey at all. An excuse to accuse her of mutinous conduct was the last thing she wanted to present him with. As she dropped to the deck and started toward the cabin door, her blood ran to her feet and her face turned cold. She couldn't imagine any solid reason that he would call her to his quarters. The only person she'd ever seen admitted there before was Jack, as first mate. Fearing she'd delayed too long already, she crossed the final feet as quickly as she could and rapped on the door.

"Enter," came the captain's calm voice from within. She turned the latch and stepped inside.

Lanterns lighted the interior of the cabin and swung gently from side to side with the movement of the ship. The light pitched shadows, long then small, in a hypnotic rhythm across the walls and furniture. An oblong table covered with maps and instruments of navigation dominated the center of the room. The captain sat on the far side of the table, facing her, smoking a long slim pipe as he stroked his mustache.

"Sit," he commanded and motioned his hand toward the chair opposite him. Fin dropped herself into the chair.

For an uncomfortably long time they sat in silence, Creache considering her quietly with narrowed eyes. Fin shrank into her chair. When at last he spoke, his voice was cold and full of breathy pause as if each word had to find its way among the creaks and groans of the ship to fall at last into her ear.

"Why are you here, Mr. Button?" His eyes narrowed again but never let up their gaze. Fin felt naked and alone.

"You called me in, sir," answered Fin with the meekness of a scolded child. The corners of his lips turned up. Once again he breathed words out at her and they stalked their way across the room.

"Why are you aboard my ship, Mr. Button?"

"I was looking for work, and Jack brought me aboard," she said. Fin felt like she was offering an alibi for an unknown crime.

The captain said nothing. Again, they sat in silence for a long time. Fin feared she might cry. Suddenly the captain's hand moved from his mustache into his lap and out of Fin's sight below the table's edge. His eyes grew more intense, never wavering from her face. He was gripping his gun, Fin was sure of it. For no reason she could see or name, she was certain he was about to raise his pistol and shoot her. She froze into the chair. Creache's arm began to rise. Out of the shadow of the table's edge, little by little, his forearm emerged into the swinging light. She couldn't move. She was fixated completely on the hand drawing out of the shadow. The handle of a pistol appeared. Fear and panic hit her like cold water. Still, she couldn't move. Then in one smooth motion he drew the rest of the pistol into the light, pointed it across the table, and laid it in front of her. Delicate engravings ran across the metal. Upon the handle, a large embellished "B" stared at her. It was Betsy.

"Now, tell me why you are here," he said, his voice sharper than before, and quicker.

"I told you, I was—"

"Where did you get *this*?" he pointed a bony finger at Betsy.

Fin was dumbfounded. She gave him the simplest answer she could.

"From my father," she said, if not Bartimaeus then no one was. Creache jumped up, flung the table aside, and picked Fin up by the shirt.

"Twenty years I've wandered the sea looking for that son of a motherless whore and the Crown got to him before I did. Damn his blood!" Creache was seething. He spat each word from his mouth as if it burned him. "But now I've got his brat, and you have your father's debts to pay, Mr. *Button*— or should I say, Mr. *Gann*!"

"You knew Bartimaeus?" Fin asked in bewilderment, still blenching from his stare.

"Don't toy with me, boy!" Creache threw Fin to the floor and drew his sword. He placed the tip against her neck. "Where is the gold?"

"What?"

"Your bastard father made off with more riches than King George himself, and half of it was mine, boy! You think I don't know why you're here? You've come here to seal your claim to it with my blood, eh? You're a damned fool. Did you think I wouldn't recognize the gun? I advise you to start talking, Mr. Gann."

"Captain, I swear, I don't know anything about gold. Bartimaeus was—" Fin screamed as Creache kicked her in the ribs.

"You expect me to believe the son of Bart Gann just happens to be hiding under a taken name, aboard my ship, for no god-damned reason? You mistake me for a fool, child. Twenty years I've been chasing after what I rightly stole, and what Bart wrongly run off with. If you don't want to pay the old pirate's debts in gold, then so be it. But mind your skin, you'll pay in blood before you burn in hell." He pressed the sword into her neck hard enough to draw blood.

"Bart wasn't my father."

Creache pulled his sword away. He picked her up and shoved her against the wall, then laid his sword across her neck.

"Lie to me again, boy," he whispered through clenched teeth. "The only reason you aren't dead already is that I haven't decided which I want more, your blood or my gold. Don't play games with me. I have nothing to lose."

"Let me be and I'll talk"

Creache didn't reply. He considered her, considered the blade at her throat with a grin. The promise of gold won out, and Fin kept her blood. He lowered the sword and dragged her across the room to her chair. He threw her into the seat and ordered her to speak.

"I was raised in an orphanage and Bartimaeus was the cook. He wasn't my father, but he was the nearest thing I ever had. I never knew him for a pirate until the year they hanged him for it, and I swear on Jesus' name he never told me anything of gold. He never talked about his past." Fin spilled all she knew as fast as she could, then sat in the shifting light waiting to see what Creache's cruel mind would make of it.

Creache didn't interrupt her. He stood over her, listening, judging her story, twisting his mustache between his fingers. When she finished, he said nothing. Once again, a long dangerous silence filled the cabin. When at last he broke it, he seemed a different man. His rage was gone, replaced with an uneasy and unnatural calm.

"Well then, Mr. Button, I have decided to believe your story—for the moment at least. If what you say is true, then Bart's hoard—my gold—must be hid within your orphanage. You will lead me there. I will acquire what is mine, and you may keep what is yours—your life." Creache smiled at her, had she not known him she'd have thought it kind and genuine. Fin didn't answer. What had she done? Creache would tear the orphan house to pieces for a treasure that might not even exist. She had to stop him. She couldn't lead him there, couldn't loose him upon her home and the people she loved. But for now there was no defying him.

Fin nodded.

"Good, and should you betray me as Bartimaeus did . . . " he put his hand around her neck and picked her up. His face turned red and he spit his words at her, "Do that and I will flay your skin and damn your heart to flame and the devil's fancy. Now get *out*!" He flung her through the door and slammed it shut.

Fin picked herself up and crawled to the rail. She vomited over the side, then sat shivering in the night air. Her mind struggled to stretch itself around what had just happened. Creache and Bartimaeus. Knut told her when she joined the crew that the captain had suddenly sailed for Savannah and stayed ashore for weeks before she came aboard. He must have heard news of Bartimaeus's execution and come sniffing for his gold. And now he expected her to help him find it. But there was no gold. Bartimaeus never had two coins to rub together. The only belongings he had were Betsy and his fiddle. If he had gold then he'd long since spent it. And if she took Creache to Ebenezer, to the orphanage, he wouldn't find it. He'd kill her.

"Button? You alright?" asked a voice in the darkness. She pulled herself to her feet and turned around. Topper was peering at her in the moonlight.

"I'm fine," she lied.

"Get up to the nest. Captain takes a nasty dislike to sailors sitting around on the watch. Get up a'fore he see's ye."

Fin didn't answer. She turned away and climbed up to man her watch and wait for the dawn.

CHAPTER XVII

KNUT SAT QUIETLY BESIDE Fin's hammock fingering the
hasp of Bartimaeus's fiddle case as if he were trying to work up the
courage to open it. He hadn't noticed she was awake. Fin smiled as
she looked him over. His back must burn like fire, she thought, but at least
he was up and around.

"Morning, Knut."

He jumped nearly out of his clothes at the sound of her voice. Then
he seemed to remember that he'd been thinking about the fiddle case and
frowned.

"Sorry, Fin. I wasn't stealing. I dreamed you was playing on a fiddle." He
raised his eyebrows at her. "I like music," he said as if it explained his entire
thought process.

"I was playing while you were asleep. You didn't dream it." She frowned.
"I haven't played in a long time."

Knut considered the case again. "You should play more," he announced,
then stood up and turned away.

Fin watched him go in sad wonder. He was right. She should play. *Turn
it beautiful*, Bartimaeus would tell her.

She leaned over and opened the case. Betsy's dark absence greeted her,
dominated the space inside. Part of her was glad to be rid of the weapon. She

wished she could forget it, wished she could forget the way it felt when she pulled the trigger. But the absence called her attention to it, reminded her of all she would rather put out of her mind.

Trying to push away the thoughts of her bloody past and dire present, she plucked the fiddle from its nest. Beneath it lay a small, folded piece of paper. It was the *Gazette* from Philadelphia. Georgia War Woman. Murder. And Creache was taking her back there. Even if she somehow stopped Creache, the British would hunt her down like a fox if they got word of her return. The desire to play ran out of her. She replaced the fiddle, and closed the lid.

On deck, the sun was bright and the sea chopped in a light wind. Fin looked for Tan and spotted him on the poop deck conversing with Topper. She walked over and pulled him aside.

"I think it's time you started my lessons."

Tan smiled. "Let's go get you a blade."

THE ART OF THE sword turned out to be hard work and often painful, as the nicks and cuts on her hands and arms bore witness. Tan chose an elegant rapier for Fin to wield and she found it much lighter and easier to handle than the typical cutlasses she used on their boarding affairs. He ordered the men to keep clear the quarterdeck so they could fence, and the crew crowded around the empty space to watch.

Tan was a harsh teacher. He didn't fight light or below his skill to accommodate his student. He gave her all he had, and Fin rose to it. That isn't to say Fin had any notion of what she was doing; she certainly did not. But as with most anything else, she was a fast learner. Tan smiled each time he bested her, and his smile spread wider as Fin's frustration grew. He'd gleaned Fin's feisty nature and taunted the best effort she had out of her. She growled and cursed and scowled and always got back up to have another fence with Tan's tiger grin. She threw herself into the learning powered by all the frustration, rage, and fear she had for Creache and her impending homecoming.

Creache strutted from his lair once and scowled at the goings-on from his cabin door. Fin felt his devil gaze weighing on her and took a deep wound to her right hand for her broken concentration. When she looked again, Creache had retreated to his quarters.

Hours later, the sun sunk into the sea and Fin was exhausted. She stumbled below decks cradling hands bloodied by wayward blades and a sword arm as numb as driftwood. Her hammock greeted her with a quiet nod, and she was asleep as soon as her head found purchase within.

When she awoke in the wee hours for her watch, she felt a little better; she could feel her right arm at least. On deck, she made out Topper's disheveled form in the darkness and greeted him with a moan and a yawn that was mostly lost in the wind.

"The boys tell me Tan give you a thrash today," said Topper. He laughed.

Fin nodded blearily.

"Lot of boys been wanting Tan to learn 'em the sword for a longish time, but Tan never would." Topper looked at her with a suspicious eyebrow. "So why you?"

"I don't know," Fin shrugged, "he offered."

Topper grunted. "Reckon he's got his reasons."

Fin didn't mention the conversation with Tan about Knut. Tan was close to Knut, was pained by his transformation, and was honoring her kindness to him in the best way he knew how.

"Tomorrow you might get a chance to show what Tan learned you. Captain's planning to try Jack for mutiny, and some men are talking they might not like the outcome."

"The captain is going to try him?" Fin was confused. She expected the trying to be done by a court and judge.

"Aye, at the Captain's Mast. A captain is judge, jury, and executioner if need be on his own ship. You didn't think Creache was going to let Jack off easy and ship him home to rot in a jail did you? Can't say as I'd expect much trial though. If I know the captain, the outcome is already come in. He just aims to mete out some sentence. Keep your wits about you. Them loyal to the captain ain't like to swap huggin' with them loyal to Jack, if you know what I'm blowin' on about."

Fin knew. The captain aimed to make an example out of Jack same as he'd done with Knut.

"Get on to your station. That's all in the morning, and we got the night's work to muster. I smell a storm in the wind. See to it the ship's tied fast." Topper turned away and Fin turned to her work.

Fin hadn't seen Jack since the day Creache confined him. The captain kept Bill watching over the door to the little cell the *Rattlesnake* called her brig and permitted no one to speak with him. In truth, she'd all but forgotten about him in her worry over Knut and the captain's suspicions. She felt a tinge of shame about it; Jack had been good to her. Now that he was the main topic of the ship's scuttlebutt however, she was worried for him in earnest.

Discussions were going on all over the ship in hushed whispers. Everywhere Fin looked, men were gathered in huddles, casting about with nervous eyes, speaking in low voices about the captain and Jack, and who would do what and when if such and such was the sentence. Some were even wagering over the affair.

A few hours later, as the sun was still climbing in the east, Tan hopped up the steps and made a round of the deck, checking the conditions of the wind and sails. He conferred with Topper at the helm while pointing away south and west to a huddle of dark clouds and then spotted Fin against the rail and walked over. He looked over his shoulder then lowered his head and spoke in a near whisper. "How's your arm?"

Fin worked her arm around in its socket and winced. "It's alright, better than it was."

"Good, things could get interesting today."

"So I hear."

"Can we count you a friend of Jack then?"

Fin was insulted that he even had to ask. The notion that she might be a friend of Creache made her skin crawl.

"Well I'm certainly no friend of—"

"Thought so, just checking." Tan's grin parted his lips. "The captain will find him guilty, no surprise there. The punishment is what's got everyone on edge. Captain could kill him for mutiny, and he'd be right with the law to do it. The sea's got its own law though, I figure. Jack was doing right by the crew and ship when he crossed Creache—not that Creache cares." Tan's grin was gone. He looked out at the water, saying nothing.

"What if the captain sentences him to death?" asked Fin.

Tan's hand moved to the hilt of his sword. He turned his head and looked at Fin. His grin was like a knife.

"And if not death?"

"A stiff flogging. Jack can handle that himself." Tan looked at the western sky and his eyes darkened. "Whatever he decides, he'll have to be quick about it. Looks to be rough wind to the southwest, and we can't afford to waste the morning listening to the captain blather on."

"Have you talked to Jack?" she asked.

Tan shook his head. "We'll hear from Jack soon enough. Run and give those boys a hand with the sails." He grabbed her arm firmly as she was turning away. "Strap on your sword and sharpen your wits. Like I said, could get interesting." He turned and strode away, barking orders to the deck crew as he went.

Fin hurried to assist in reefing the sails. The men around her were those she considered friends of Jack. There were no more than a handful on board that she suspected were sympathetic to the captain. Bill Stumm, of course, was first among them. Fin could understand Bill siding with the captain; he was a raging idiot. But the other men that tended toward the captain's way were a mystery to her. Certainly, Creache had made them all a great deal of money. Mad or not, Fin couldn't deny that. But that didn't seem to be the whole of their motivation. Tan spoke of the way men interpreted the events surrounding Knut's mutiny, subsequent demotion, and battery. Some had counted their survival to the captain. She was willing to wager those men scried the current situation through the same twisted glass. The few that would back the captain aside, there ought to be an easy majority that would stand for Jack. Good odds.

The captain's door creaked open and Creache walked onto the quarter-deck. Tan piped out the muster on his whistle. Men dropped their business and hurried to gather around. Jack Wagon was about to be tried at the Captain's Mast.

The door to the hold thumped open and a lumbering goon clambered up into the light, tugging on a chain that was attached to something at the bottom of the companionway. Creache hid a satisfied grin beneath his mustache. He strutted across the quarterdeck, looking around slowly at the gathered men. The captain had undoubtedly heard the rumors of trouble among the crew. He knew most of the men looked up to and liked Jack. Surely he considered such things as he weighed crime and punishment. Fin could see which men he counted loyal by the subtle change in his eyes as he looked over the crew. He considered Topper with odium then passed to Bill and his look lightened to something of a disgusted tolerance. Bill grinned back before his gaze passed on. She saw the same story told with several others. There were no surprises. When the captain's eyes made it around to her, there was no mistaking the disdain he glared. Fin was proud of it. She smiled at him slightly and his upper lip curled before he moved his glaring on to the next man.

When at last he'd appraised them enough, he spoke.

"Bring him."

The goon on the steps jerked the chain in his hand. Jack was at the other end. He stumbled up the stairs squinting at the sunlight like a mole. Fin gasped. Jack looked awful. His hair was a matted mess, he was filthy from head to toe, and he stank of long confinement. She saw by Jack's eyes that he could read the crew's reaction to his appearance. He straightened up and set his jaw, then stumbled across the deck in small half steps and leaned against the mast in front of the captain. His body looked overthrown, but his eyes still hinted at the bear.

Creache beheld him with satisfaction and smiled. "Jack Wagon, you are here to answer the charge of mutiny." Creache let the weight of the word settle upon both crew and accused. "How do you plead?" Creache didn't seem to be speaking to Jack. He looked around at the crew, relishing his command of the deck.

Jack straightened himself up to his full height and waited for Creache to look him in the eyes. When Creache tired of smirking around at the crew and became irritated with Jack's silence, he snapped his head toward Jack and asked again, "How do you plead?"

Jack answered in a loud, low growl, "Guilty as all bloody hell."

The captain dropped his smirk, and the onlooking crew erupted in murmurs. "You admit it, then?" asked Creache.

"Admit it? Hell, I'm damned proud of it," Jack growled back.

"Do you know, Mr. Wagon, the price of mutiny?"

"I know it, aye. And I'd sooner be sent to the hungry deep than listen to another order spit from your heathen mouth."

The crew stirred now in earnest. The captain flicked his eyes across the deck and appraised the men. He was worried. There was no smirk on his lips now.

"Very well, Mr. Wagon, you freely admit your guilt, and I shall grant your just reward." Creache produced his pistol from inside his coat and aimed it at Jack. The crew erupted into shouts of protest and anger. Tan stepped forward and drew his rapier. From behind the captain, Bill and two other men stepped forward in Creache's defense.

"Mr. Bough, consider carefully what you are about to do. I can carry out two executions as easily as one." Creache's voice was dangerously metered. Fin didn't doubt he meant it.

"There'll be no executions, Captain. Jack done right by your crew and ship, and I can't stand by and let you kill him for it." Fin and several others walked up and stood beside Tan. "Most of the crew is with me, Captain. I ain't one for mutiny—but what you're up to is murder."

"Stand down, Tan," said Jack. "I knew what I was doing when I give the order."

"And I know what I'm doing now," Tan replied, then he turned his eyes back to the captain. "Either pull that trigger or put it away."

Creache was livid. His pistol wavered from Jack to Tan and back again as if he couldn't decide how he preferred to spend his single shot. He ground his teeth. The *Rattlesnake* awaited his choice.

Then Topper began shouting. "Man-o'-war! Port astern!"

Every head snapped around to look and there, across the water, bore down upon them a warship of the king's navy, a ship of the line. It was less than a league distant and running at full sail. They were caught unawares.

"Man the guns!" cried Tan.

"I give the orders on this ship!" the captain shouted. He cast a nervous glance over his shoulder at the approaching warship. "Turn to your duty, Mr. Bough. We'll settle this business after. He lowered his gun. "Take Mr. Wagon back to his pen."

The man holding Jack's chain tugged him toward the hatch, and with a last look at Tan, Jack followed his jailer below.

The captain and Tan faced each other in silence. Fin held her breath. The captain would kill him the first chance he had. She was sure of it. Creache was no fool; he wouldn't give Tan the opportunity to rally the crew. But for the moment, there were more important problems to deal with, primarily that of the eighty-gun ship crashing through the waves behind them. Tan turned to the maindeck and began shouting orders. As soon as Tan looked away, Creache motioned to Bill. Bill grabbed a pitchpole from the deck and swung it.

"*Tan!*" yelled Fin, too late. The pole cracked across his head and he hit the deck like a coil of loose rope.

"Chain him to the mast," said Creache. "Like I told you—settle up later."

Creache shouted orders. Fin hadn't heard him do so before and often doubted he knew how, but Creache took command without pause and no one dared question him with the Royal Navy chasing down their wake. The *Rattlesnake*'s sails went up, and before the man-of-war could close to firing distance they were running south with the wind.

"We'll not outrun her, Captain!" cried Topper from the helm. "Nor they us, but they'll follow our wake till kingdom come." The ships were in an even match for speed, but the British had the upper hand. They only needed to wait out the *Rattlesnake*. Eventually she'd make a mistaken tack. The *Rattlesnake* was far undermanned. The ship pressing down on them would have a full compliment of crew and could run them to exhaustion with ease.

Creache stood astern and peered at his pursuer through his spyglass.

Then he spun and surveyed the surrounding skyline. His eyes widened and he smiled. The storm hinted at in the early morning had grown dark and hungry. Billowing thunderheads towered like marble columns above a black maw of wind, rain, and wave. The sea below the clouds shunned all light and color. It frothed and boiled like the heaving breast of a drowning man, black-lipped and forsaken.

"Turn her into the storm, Mr. Topper!" yelled Creache.

"Madness, Captain!" cried Topper.

"Madness to follow, says I," yelled Creache as he grinned into the storm. "Turn your course or throw ye overboard. My way lies through the bosom of that yonder black and weeping mistress!"

Creache may have been insane, but he was cunning. The lighter and more maneuverable *Rattlesnake* had a better chance of seeing the far side of the storm in one piece than the ungainly warship could hope for. Topper knew it too. He spun the wheel, and the deck lurched to port as the *Rattlesnake* tacked southwest. The ship rose and fell in hard chops against the sea, sending spray through the air at every fall. Fin and the rest of the crew scoured the deck to tie and stow all loose tackle and, once satisfied, all but the captain and Topper at the helm dove below to wait out the tempest. Tan lay unconscious and chained to the mast.

The pitch and roll of the ship turned the world on its end. Fin stumbled, first one way then the other, one moment trotting downhill, the next struggling up, occasionally being thrown headlong into a bulkhead. She'd been in rough sea, or so she thought, but nothing she'd experienced had prepared her for the spinning world of a ship caught up and laid to the mercy of a real storm. The sounds echoing through the hull made her shudder. The timbers shivered and screamed, and she feared at any moment the hull would give way and the hungry sea would come rushing in to devour them all. Again and again, monstrous waves drove into the ship and the entire vessel trembled. Fin could neither sleep nor find shelter for her mind in other things. The storm consumed her thoughts. *Madness*, Topper had cried to the captain, and madness it was, for no man sane would cast himself willingly beneath the hammering fist of nature.

Topper called down for a furling of sail. Art Thomasson chose a handful of men and climbed up into the gale to meet the order. When they opened the hatch to go out, the entire hold filled with the howl and bluster of the storm. Through the hatchway Fin could spy nothing but a great blackness, even though she knew the hour must be noon or soon after. She thanked God in silence that she wasn't called upon to the brave the deck.

After a time, the men that had gone up returned shaken and tired.

"How bad is it?" asked Fin.

Art made a vain attempt at squeezing the water from his shirt. "Worst I seen since—hell—since a long time. The *'Snake'*ll weather her. Topper's at the helm, and he's been blown far and worse. It'll be a sign of sweet Jesus hisself if Tan see the sun again. Creache still got him chained about the mast, and the waves are like to rip him apart if they don't drown him first. Got him chained 'round backwards where he can't even hold on or keep his feet."

"Damn Creache's heart!" called up a sailor from the shadows.

"Watch yer bleedin' mouth if you don't want the same thing," protested one of Bill's men. "Tan's gone mutinous with Jack and he's getting no more'n he asked for."

The sailor sitting next to Fin stood up and spat on the deck. "Creache is a murdering swine, and what you call mutiny, I calls fair justice!"

Bill's man jumped to his feet and puffed up his chest. The two men circled one another and narrowed their eyes, each quietly daring the other to speak another cross word or turn his back.

Before violence could come of it, a voice came yelling up from the bilge. "Get to the pumps a'fore we're swimming in the berth!" It was Bill yelling from below where he was guarding Jack in his cell. Art and a sailor named Sam Catcher took the first shift, and Fin was glad of the timing. Had Bill not sent up his yell when he did, the situation would have come to blows.

The storm continued to batter the ship without mercy. Twice more, men braved the deck to secure the sails and tackle, and twice Fin was thankful she wasn't called to the work. Two hours later, Art and Sam climbed out of the bilge looking and smelling like drenched rats. Fin breathed a sigh of relief when they pointed a finger at her and Knut, indicating it was their turn at the pumps. They descended into the bowels of the ship to work, and Fin was glad to have something to do. As they entered the bilge, she saw Bill propped comfortably against a bulkhead trying to sleep. Next to him was a door with a chain running through the handle and a lock to fasten it. Jack was inside.

The bilge pumps were spread out along the floor. They were made of two parallel sets of baffles and long wooden handles along the top to work them back and forth. Knut and Fin sat opposite each other. The water was deep enough that they were submerged up to their elbows while sitting. Fin pushed her handle down with a *squeesh* and Knut's handle went up with a *creak*. Then Knut bore down and Fin's handle rose. So began the long rhythm and song of the bilge. *Squeesh, creak, squeesh, creak.*

The smell of the room was nauseating. A bilge was a place never dry and forever in some state of rot. The walls were covered in mildewy slime, and the pungent, musty smell kept Fin on the verge of passing out as she breathed deep of it in her work. Worse, they didn't seem to be making any headway against the ever-spilling water. The storm's beating constantly replenished whatever volume they pushed out with the pumps.

Squeesh, creak, squeesh, creak.

"You tired, Knut?" she asked, barely whispering. The words anchored her mind, stopped it from floating.

"I reckon," shrugged Knut. Fin shook her head at him. Knut lacked extremes, unless extreme apathy for his situation counted. Creache had broken his mind, but Knut was a mystery to her even in that knowledge. Fin's arms burned from the work, and all he did was "reckon."

Fin looked over her shoulder. Bill was still propped against the bulkhead at an angle that, miraculously, the storm did not seem to overturn while he snored. There was a small window at the top of the door he guarded. She peered at it, trying to see Jack within. Only darkness looked back. Then as the lantern next to the door shuddered with a wave, its light led her eye to Bill's belt. There, twinkling like a star, was the key.

Fin turned back around. "Knut?"

"Yeah?" he reckoned.

"We've got to rescue—" She cast a nervous glance back at Bill, then lowered her voice and leaned in close to Knut. "We've got to get Jack out of there."

Knut looked over at Bill with a frown. He considered it for a moment then shook his head. "Captain might get sore about it."

"Knut, listen to me. When this storm is over, the captain is going to kill Jack, and probably Tan too." She studied his face; it was still frowning. "You've got to help me, Knut. You don't want Jack and Tan to get killed, do you?"

Knut slowly shook his head.

"Keep working. It won't do much good to save Jack and lose the *'Snake*. Soon as the storm lets up, we make our move." Fin nodded assurance to Knut and then returned to the *squeesh creeak* of the task at hand.

Having spoken her intent into being, the long time afterward gave her plenty of opportunity to mull over the consequences. If they were caught, the captain would see to it she got the same as Jack and Tan. She knew there were a good many men aboard that sided with her, but she doubted they'd be easily moved to action bereft of Jack and Tan's leadership. The captain would win a swift victory among the crew if he could dispose of them quickly. Without leaders, the followers would soon fall back into line.

If Fin could get Jack free, however, they had a mutinous chance. The men would follow Jack. They'd follow Tan too. But he was beyond her reach, chained to the mast in full view of the captain. Creache had to be stopped, stopped from exacting his cruel sentence on Jack and Tan, stopped from ever again beating Knut like an animal, stopped from reaching her home, Peter, the orphanage.

This time Fin had choices.

They were taking on less water now. She could tell by the way the water sloshed to and fro across the room that the waves were losing their former fury. The storm was letting up. Fin looked across at Knut, who had said nothing since his earlier reckoning. He looked troubled, scared.

"It's time, Knut," Fin whispered. "Wait here."

Fin looked back at Bill; he was still snoring. She stood up carefully.

Her back burned from working the pump for so long, and it felt good to stretch it out. She stepped away from the pumps, moving delicately so that her feet would make no splash in the shallow water. If she could get the key from Bill's belt without waking him, things might go smoothly. The ship rolled without warning and she pitched to the side, flailing for support. Knut gasped behind her. Her hands found wood. She barely caught herself against the bulkhead, nearly falling headlong to the floor at Bill's feet. Bill shifted his weight from the wall to the door behind him, but didn't wake. Fin swore silently—now she would have to move Bill to get the door open. She knelt down in front of him. He still showed no sign of waking. The key was tied to his belt with a small length of cord. Fin took a deep breath and flexed her fingers to wake them up. She took hold of the cord and gently tugged the tassel. The knot slipped with ease, and the key dropped quietly into her waiting palm. Fin breathed in relief. Now she only had to get Bill out of the way.

Fin slunk back to where Knut waited at the pump and pressed the key into his hand.

"Listen to me, Knut," Fin said. "I'm going to lure Bill up into the berth. As soon as he's out of here, you've got to unlock that door and get Jack out." In the back of her mind, memories flashed by, memories of her and Peter playing practical jokes on the sisters or on Danny Shoeman and his friends. This was no different. It was just a game, and she'd played it a hundred times before. Only this time if it didn't go as she planned, there'd be more to pay than a few extra chores after dinner. "Knut, do you hear me?" she shook his arm. "Do you understand?"

Knut nodded, or maybe he was just shaking in fear. Fin wasn't sure, but she didn't have time to wait and find out. She smiled at him then turned and stood up. She faced Bill and squared her shoulders. She was done letting others make choices for her. Starting right now, she was making her own. Jack and Tan had done right by her, looked out for her, and she couldn't stand by and let Creache murder them. Mutiny be damned. If crossing Creache was mutiny, then Fin held it as virtue.

She kicked a splash of water up at Bill. He lurched awake, spitting curses out as if he was choking on them. He looked around bleary-eyed for the source of the splash and had nearly focused on the culprit when the second flurry of water flew up into his face.

"Come have a turn at the pumps, Bill."

"Button?" Bill ventured. "Button, I'm gonna crack you open!"

"If you want to sleep, come have a throw and I'll put you to bed like last time." Fin smiled and topped it off with a wink. She didn't expect she'd need much bait to reel him in. He took the lure and gulped it down as if it was the Last Supper itself. Bill charged at her, and Fin stepped neatly out of the way allowing him to trip perfectly on the pump and fall into the water. When Bill had splashed, screamed, cursed, and dripped his way to his feet he found Fin lighting up the steps and out of the bilge. Bill followed suit, so anxious to corner Fin that he slipped and tripped over his own feet half a dozen times before finally managing to climb the steps on all fours like a beast.

In the berthing area, Fin was standing in the middle of the room, hopping back and forth on her feet with happy anticipation. Bill staggered in, dripping wet, wide-eyed, and spitting fire.

"Damn your blood, Button. I'm going to skin you alive and take a bite out your liver so's ye goes straight to hell."

Fin didn't bother replying. She winked again as the rest of the sailors laid wagers and cheered them on. Bill charged and the blows began. Fin had forgotten how hard the big ogre could hit, but he soon reminded her. She tried to dance about the room and avoid him as she'd done in Philadelphia, but found she'd not taken the size of the ship's berth into account; it was too small and too crowded, and Bill seemed to be able to corner her no matter which way she bounced. She landed plenty of her own blows, but each time one of his huge ham-hands fell upon her she said a prayer that Knut would hurry up and get Jack free so she'd get a little help. But blow after blow landed, and neither Knut nor Jack darkened the door.

In and out, Fin plugged her quick, sharp jabs. Bill was bloodied at the nose and lip but, freshly slept, he showed no signs of slowing and Fin was already weary from the pumps. Another meaty fist landed on her brow and she felt a hot flow of blood stream down into her eyes. Another blow. Her head cracked back against the wall and she slid to the ground. Cheers and boos sounded around the room. Bill stood over her and spat.

"Get up, runt. I ain't done with ye!" snarled Bill.

Fin was mad. She hadn't lost a fight in ten years and didn't aim to start now. Beneath her she felt a crunch from whatever had broken her fall. It took her a couple of hazy seconds to realize that the splintered box she was laying on had a fiddle inside. Now she was doubly mad. She willed herself to her feet, but her body was slow to obey. She faltered and grabbed a stanchion to pull herself up, then wiped the blood from her face and smeared it on her shirt. She shook her mind to rouse it and nudged her fiddle case safely out of the way before squaring off again with Bill. He was the one grinning now. Fin mustered up enough stubbornness from the deep well of it within her to smile at him before launching a new flurry of fists.

Back and forth they traded wallops, blood for blood, bruise for bruise, and Fin began to see signs that Bill was getting winded. Those ham-fisted blows might hurt to catch, but they were hurting him to throw as well. Bill was missing. He'd toss a fist at Fin and she'd dodge it and toss a couple back as she bounced around him. He'd reorient and throw a few more, some misses, some hits, but every one of them was wearing him closer to the floor. Fin's brain was swimming from being juggled this way and that inside her skull, but she saw through enough of the cloudy water in her vision to see that Bill was about done in. She wasn't about to let him simply finish, though. Fin wanted to enjoy the knowledge that it was her that finished him, not just time and his own weight.

Where was Knut? She'd been knocking bones with Bill for what seemed like an hour, and neither Knut nor Jack had come up the steps.

Bill overthrew his last punch. Fin hammered him in the ribs as he stumbled past, smiling at the crunchy sound of a cracking rib, then planted her whole weight behind her right arm and let it fly. Fin's blow caught him under the jaw and removed most of his remaining teeth. He landed in a grunting heap against the timber.

Out of the corner of a blurry eye, Fin saw the doorway darken. She breathed a sigh of relief. What had taken Knut so long?

But something wasn't right. Men should be cheering, slapping her on the back, muttering as they swapped money to settle bets, but the berth was deadly silent. The only sound was a muffled splashing from downstairs. She wiped the blood out of her eyes and shook her head to clear her vision. Every man in the room was silent and staring at the doorway. Fin couldn't figure any reason they'd look at Knut like that and turned to see what all the matter was. There in the door, fire-eyed and poised to pounce, stood Tiberius Creache.

"*What* in the devil's fire is going on here?" he shouted. "I've just sailed you sorry dogs through a black wind from hell herself and saved your wretched skins from the wrath of King George, and here you are playing like whore-born bastards in the gutter!" He glared at them and twitched his mustache. No one moved or spoke. The faint splashes from the deck below drifted up the stairs. "Wake that dog up!" he shouted and pointed at Bill. On the floor next to him was a small folded paper. The *Gazette*, from Philadelphia, knocked out of the case when it broke her fall. Fin bent over and grabbed it, nearly succeeding in throwing herself to the ground thanks to her recently assaulted sense of balance. As she stuffed it into her shirt pocket, Art gave Bill a few kicks in the side. Bill didn't budge.

"Think he's out for a while, sir," Art reported over the sloshing from down below.

"What in the name of God is going on down there?" Creache shouted down the steps in irritation at the splashing noise. As soon as he spoke it the noise stopped, timidly, as a child ceases when it finds itself discovered in mischief.

"Bill! Get up you filthy dog. You're to be keeping guard on that blasted Jack!" shouted the captain. Then he became aware of the implication. If Bill was up here then Jack was unkept.

Creache wheeled around and pounced down the steps. Fin tried to snap her mind back into lucidity. What was Knut doing? He had to have Jack free by now. Then from below, the captain began to roar.

"You! God damn your heart, I should have done with you by now! What in the blue deep are you doing?" he screamed.

Knut's voice floated up soft and full of trembling, "I'm looking for the key, Captain. I dropped it and—" a dull thud interrupted whatever he was about to confess and Knut cried in pain. Fin went cold. They were caught.

"Worthless pig!" spat Creache. A fumbling commotion banged up the steps, and Creache passed the doorway dragging Knut by the hair.

Fin and the rest of the crew rushed out of the berth. The sky was clear ahead of them and the *Rattlesnake* was running south. To the rear, the storm muttered and crackled in the distance. There was no sign of the British vessel; whatever else, the captain had saved them from that doom. Topper, drenched to the bone and looking almost clean from the storm's lashing, stood at the helm like a tide-battered stone. At the base of the mast lay Tan upon his back, still shackled to the mast. He was coughing and sputtering, bleeding from a deep gash on his head and shivering: the storm had pounded him senseless and nearly drowned him on deck.

Knut howled. A harrowing, animal drone issued from his mouth. The captain had dragged him to the quarterdeck and stood above him reigning down blows from a cat-o'-nine-tails. Already, blood was flowing from his arms as he tried to deflect the torment.

"Stop!" cried Fin. She couldn't bear it again. The captain ignored her. "Stop it!" she demanded as she ran across the deck and threw herself on top of Knut's writhing body. "Stop it!" she pleaded. Creache stilled his hand mid-stroke and fumed at her.

"It's my fault. Let him alone!" Fin cried.

"I should have known that ill-born half-wit would be in cahoots with someone," spat Creache.

Fin had received spankings on an almost regular basis at the orphanage. The sisters had occasion to paddle Fin so often that if a day passed and the paddle hadn't been produced, it was simply assumed Fin hadn't been caught. Sister Hilde spanked Fin so hard once, for throwing food at the dinner table, that Fin was sure the shape of her bottom was permanently altered from it. Paddles, switches, belts, canes—Fin had bared her tail for them all during her childhood and was quite fond of showing off the calluses she'd managed to form on her nether cheeks to prove it. But for all the paddlings in her life, nothing had prepared her body or mind for the cruel bite of the cat-o'-nine-tails, a strap of leather roughly cut into many shreds and fixed with barbs and sharks teeth to rend flesh from bone. Creache brought his arm down and the tails bit into Fin's back. Agony wet her vision. He pulled the tails away and they bit again like fire as they tore out of her flesh. She screamed. Creache flailed at her with the cat-o'-nine-tails as he shouted and raved.

"The *price*," he brought down biting pain as he stressed his words, "of *mutiny*!"

Pain.

"The *price* . . ."

Agony.

"Of *MUTINY*!"

Blood.

Fin forgot reason, forgot life, forgot herself. The world existed only as the terrible, gnawing, pain and agony of the whip. She saw Knut crawling away and disappearing into the hold. Somewhere inside she was glad of his escape, then the thought drowned in blood as her flesh tore again.

Creache foamed at the mouth and flung his words about the deck as he rained down his fury on Fin. The crew watched in horrified silence. They had no leader to oppose him. They were broken. Some wept and cried out for mercy. Some grinned malice at the spectacle and saw only Creache's lawful and terrible justice. Topper quivered in helpless anger at the helm. Creache had won. His control was complete; he did as he wished, unhindered.

The tails bit again. Fin groaned in torment. Her thoughts were two: relief that Knut was spared, and anger—anger that at long last, God had finally abandoned her for certain. In her mind she screamed and railed against the choosing that left her bloody beneath the lash. When the tails rose from her back again her shirt caught in the barbs and it tore away. She lay bare-breasted and bloody in the sun.

The blows stopped. All was silent. The apocalypse of her sex washed over the ship.

Creache kicked her over onto her back and confirmed the unveiling, the final naked shame. He stood speechless, hovering over her. Then his eye caught sight of a crumpled and bloody piece of paper lying in the ruin of her shirt. He seized it and looked at it hungrily. His eyes darted from the drawing on the *Gazette* to Fin, then back again.

"Damn your soul!" He spat on her.

Long years past, Fin had cursed her parents for their betrayal and often she had cursed Hilde's rod and staff, but always she held out scant hope that God in heaven would hold for her a place where all others had turned her away. Now naked, bled, and found out on the floor, she cursed God at last and despaired of all hope save one. Her mind turned to Peter, who alone remained. She clung to him like a rock and begged for shelter in his arms.

Creache raised his arm to loose again the tails upon her, but the blow never fell. Huge, hairy fingers reached out and stayed Creache's arm. Fin opened her eyes and saw in blood-washed vision that Creache, sputtering for words, now shrunk in the shadow of a giant form towering over him. Jack. Knut appeared from behind him and dropped to the deck beside Fin.

"I found the key," he wept to her.

Jack's fist descended like a boulder tumbling down a mountain, and Creache crumpled to the ground.

CHAPTER XVIII

FIN OPENED HER EYES in the warm rocking of a lantern's light. She lay upon a soft bed of down. Her back was well bandaged and sore. Around her, a table and chairs, shelves, cabinets, and other accoutrements all looked vaguely familiar. The table dominated the center of the room and was laid up with maps, a compass, and a sextant. She was in the captain's cabin. It was Creache's lair, but somehow the air whispered safety, not savagery. She looked around, confirmed she was alone. Her last memory was the fall of the lash, pain, blood, and something else. Jack. She sat up and winced as the bandages across her back tightened and prickled at her wounds. Creache was gone. She could sense it, as if the air were suddenly cleared of a stench long-smelled.

Sounds drifted through the walls: the gentle creaking of the ship, the soft splash of the sea, laughter from on deck, and the reassuring bark of Jack cursing and calling orders in the wind. There was a new white shirt laid on the table along with breeches and her old leather vest and boots. She eased herself out of the bed and dressed. Pain trickled across her back. She grimaced and walked outside.

The main deck was basked in the dying light of evening. Away to the west, a wavering sun slunk into the sea, spreading long, fading shadows of timber and tackle upon the salt-crusted ship. No one took notice of her. She leaned wearily in the crook of the open door and felt her spirits lift. Creache was gone. For the moment she didn't care how. She simply breathed in the clean air. The wind was light and the *Rattlesnake*, in no hurry to tack a quicker course, drifted south on whatever wind the weather offered it.

Jack's broad shoulders turned her way and, seeing her, he approached. "You ought to be lying down," he said.

"I'm alright," replied Fin. "I'm glad you're back."

Jack didn't appear to share the opinion. He wrinkled his brow at her then took her by the arm and led her back into the cabin.

"How long have I—"

"Two days," answered Jack, "and we got to talk." He carefully guided her to a chair and settled her into it then seated himself opposite and considered her in silence.

"What's wrong?"

"Other than mutiny?" He raised a bushy eyebrow and leaned forward. "I'd say there's a right lot of wrong around the *'Snake* these days, not the least of what is you. If you aim to keep a berth aboard this ship, then I need to know what other secrets you're stowing away besides the ones 'neath them clothes."

Fin blushed as the memory came back to her. "I didn't mean to cause trouble."

Jack frowned at her and scratched his beard. "Fin your real name?" he asked.

Fin balked. "Of course."

He reached into his shirt pocket and produced the *Gazette* with her picture on the front.

"This you then?"

Fin nodded.

Jack raised his eyebrows in a look of surprised satisfaction. "Well, I reckon that's alright," he said as he folded it back up and placed it on the table. "There's to be a meeting, and we aim to decide what's to become of the *'Snake*. We was waiting on you and Tan to come around first. Some of the boys are out of sorts over your little secrets. If I was you, I'd come ready to hear some moaning."

"Is Tan alright?" asked Fin.

"Knocked his noggin' good, but he'll mend. Anyways, you watch yourself till we find out where everyone stands, hear?"

"What happened to the captain?" asked Fin.

Jack regarded her in silence before answering. "I ain't a murderer, Button. Lot of the boys wanted to see him dead, him and them what kept to him, but I ain't one for mutiny if it can be helped, and the same goes for killing folks—especially captains." Fin hoped to breathe relief at news of Creache's death, and robbed of it, her face wrinkled in disapproval. She felt she ought to know better than wish a man dead but couldn't convince herself that he deserved anything less. "We set him and the rest adrift. Bill Stumm, Hatch Calloway, a few others. Like as not, the storm caught them and made a murderer of me anyway." Jack didn't like the situation. He despised the disorder of it, and it wore on him. Beneath his beard, his face looked like a rock that had been beaten against and bore new cracks yet to be weathered smooth by time. "Anyhow, we're rid of him and better off. We're damned shorthanded though, so get your rest. We need every arm on the tackle to keep her running till we can make port in Charleston."

Fin nodded. Jack reached to his belt and pulled out Betsy. "Think this belongs to you." He laid it on the table in front of her. Fin felt a wave of relief. She reached out and picked it up, caressed its elegant curves. She let herself give in to its seductive beauty and was glad to hold it again. Then a tinge of the pistol's darkness crept into her and she shuddered.

Jack stood up and turned to leave, but Fin called out to him, "Jack?"

He turned around and raised his wooly eyebrows at her.

"Thank you."

Jack grunted and walked out onto the deck. Fin thought she saw a hint of a smile under his beard.

Creache was gone, and Fin hoped the storm had swallowed him whole. With the weight of the captain off her shoulders, the worries of him terrorizing her home slid off as well, and she felt almost carefree. Jack said they were headed for Charleston, and Fin determined to write Peter while they were there so he'd not worry after her.

She placed Betsy in her belt, and walked out onto deck. It was darkening to night, and the sails were set on a starboard tack in light wind. She hopped off the quarterdeck and climbed down the ladder into the berthing area. The creaking of hammocks greeted her; everyone that wasn't on deck running the ship was sleeping. As she walked in silence to her corner of the room, her eyes picked out the crumpled form of her fiddle case lying against the bulkhead. With a frown, she pulled it to her and opened it. The lid was crushed and splintered down the right side, the right hinge had broken off, and the top swiveled treacherously on the remaining hinge. Thankfully, the fiddle looked unharmed. She picked it up and carefully turned it over in her hands, inspecting it from scroll to tail, then, satisfied, placed it back in its bed. She pulled Betsy from her belt with a frown and laid it down alongside the fiddle. Part of her had hoped the gun was lost with Creache, but as she had many times before, she hushed that part away and was thankful she hadn't lost it after all.

As she reached to close the ruptured lid, she noticed that down the right side of the box the velvet lining had torn away. A strange thing caught her eye. What lay beneath the torn lining wasn't wood; it was something quite different. She squinted in the dim light of the lantern and wondered what was behind the tear. She took hold of a hanging piece of lining and tugged it gently away to get a better look. The velvet tore easily down the length of the box and exposed an old parchment sealed between the liner and lid. Near the edge, letters were scribed upon it: BARTIMAEUS GANN. Fin's heart quickened. She tore away the rest of the liner and the parchment fell into her hand. She turned it over and gaped in wonder. It was a crude map. There were boxes drawn on it, buildings perhaps, and a river, and roads, but no writing to label them. At the top was written only Bartimaeus's name, and the words:

Standing here I laid me down
Me spoils, me heathen crowns,
To sleep in sacred earth redeemed
Beneath the tower without a sound.

Fin couldn't make anything of it. She turned the paper this way and that trying to find sense in the shapes and lines. When she turned it upside down, the forms drawn on it snapped into place in her mind. It was the orphanage, the dining hall, the chapel, the orphan house, the road into town, the Savannah River; she knew it all. But what did it mean? She studied the map closer and found a small circle drawn in the foyer of what would be the chapel, a mark maybe? Before she had time to consider it, she heard someone approaching and quickly folded it and placed it back in the case.

"What you looking at, Fin?" asked Knut from behind her.

"Nothing. Just about to lay down is all," she lied. Fin stood up and turned. "You did it, Knut! You saved Jack, and me too." Knut blushed red as a beet and kicked at the floor as Fin reached out and pulled him into a soft hug. "Thank you." Knut hesitantly returned the embrace and Fin let out a yelp. "Ow!" She'd forgotten her back was still in shreds. Knut muttered embarrassed apologies. Fin kindly shushed him and bid goodnight.

IN THE MORNING, THE scant crew went about the daily chores of the ship, solemnly considering the events of the past days and their consequences. Fin refused to allow her injuries to hold her back from doing her part, and now that the crew all knew she was a woman, she intended to let no one give witness of her doing less work than any man aboard. If anyone wished to take issue with having her aboard she ensured it wasn't because she lacked the ability or gumption to get the ship's work done. She and Knut climbed aloft to check lines and sail, mending them as necessary, then swabbed the hold and took a shift at the pumps. Fin felt as if she was naked under the eyes of the crew. Some looked at her with narrowed eyes as she passed, and few spoke to her or replied when she greeted them. Art Thomasson frowned and walked away in reply to her cheerful "good morning."

Not all the crew was suspicious, however. Knut seemed to find no reason to act as if anything had changed at all, and indeed, as far as Fin was concerned, nothing had. When she waved at Topper from the quarterdeck, he smiled heartily and greeted her with more cheer than she'd seen him give out in a long time. Jack didn't seem to have decided just what he thought of her yet, but she suspected that the uncertainty itself was proof he'd come around in time. When Tan at last came stepping up on deck, Fin feared to discover whether or not he'd be cross with her. She avoided his eyes and turned her back to him, not wanting to see the same look in his face as Art had given her.

"Can't say as I ever had a lady save my hide before," said Tan from behind her. She breathed relief at the levity in his voice as she turned around.

"It's Knut did the saving, not me," she said. Behind her, Knut blushed like a timid schoolboy.

"My thanks, Tommy," said Tan with pained grin.

Knut shook his head without lifting his eyes and muttered, "Was Fin's idea, Tan. But I dropped the key."

"You did good, mate. I'm indebted to you both. Next time see if you can hurry it up a little though. Storm nearly ended me," he said and laughed. "And Fin, you didn't really think you were fooling anyone, what with the pretty face and all?"

It was Fin's turn to shade red. "You knew?" she asked.

"I knew there was some reason I liked you, and God knows I like a lady a world better than I like most fellas," he said with a chuckle. "Except for old Knut here." He slapped Knut on the back.

Tan seemed his old self, and Fin was glad of it. When she'd seen him last, chained to the mast and bleeding from the head, she was afraid he'd die, or have his wits knocked out like Knut. All he had to show for the bloody wound, however, was a small gash on his forehead that had been stitched up neatly. She related the fight with Bill and the confrontation with Creache at Tan's behest and answered his questions about it all as best she could. She didn't let on about the map. Creache was eliminated, no one was looking for the gold now; no one needed to know.

With the ship running in good order despite the shortage of hands, Fin, Knut, and Tan spent the rest of the morning laughing and enjoying the clean air until, just before noon, Jack sounded his whistle and called all hands to the quarterdeck. Everyone bustled out of hatches and holds and away from whatever they had been working at and gathered close around. Once all were present and quiet, Jack cleared his throat.

"Morning, boys," he bellowed, and a round of greetings muttered back at him. "Reckon we got us a ship!" Laughter and cheers went up. "Now we got to figure what to make of her." Heads nodded all around. "Here's the way I see it. The bloody British got a bounty laid up for our heads, and if word gets out what happened to the captain, we're like as not to get a bounty laid up by the courts in the colonies to boot. If that happens, if word gets round of mutiny, then that means but one bleeding thing: we'll be branded pirates, one and all." He paused so it could sink in. Creache had made privateers of them, but that was legal in the western Atlantic—legal to the colonies and Congress anyway. Out and out piracy was another animal altogether, and it usually ended with a sailor swinging on the gallows' howe. A dark silence hung over the assembly as the men weighed it.

"Now I ain't one to mutiny, less'n it's got to be. And likewise, ain't one for pirating. So here be my thoughts. Right now we're still privateersmen, and no one can say otherwise. The captain rarely poked his head out his cabin, and we can go on letting folks think he's in there yet. We keep right on. We trade sugar, silk, and whatever else in what ports the English ain't infested, and in the othertime, we can lend a hand to the war and see we don't get caught at the wrong end of the winning. But mind ye, boys, we be pirates as sure as Blackbeard hisself so far as British eyes can see. So I'll hold no man to the work what ain't willing to get his neck pulled in a noose."

Fin considered it along with the rest. To her it seemed the same as things had been since the captain first claimed his Letter of Marque in Philadelphia, trading where it was convenient and lightening the loads of British merchants whenever they could to fill out their own hold. The difference now would be in not having to worry after the captain's madness, which made the entire affair seem quite a lot more appealing. The prospect of throwing in with the colonials to help win the war was certainly agreeable to Fin.

Jack pulled a scroll of parchment from his coat and rolled it out on the deck. He barked at Knut to fetch him a quill and ink from the cabin, and Knut returned with it quickly. Jack took the quill, scribed a circle in the center of the parchment, and wrote inside it. When he finished, he moved the quill outside the circle, turned the parchment at an odd angle, and signed his name along the outside curve. He stood and cleared his throat.

"Never thought I'd find myself signing one of these damned things, much less writing it, but here I am. No man that don't sign will be thought less for the lack, and we'll bid you farewell in Charleston if that's your mind." Jack backed away leaving the quill, ink, and parchment lying on the deck in the center of the assembly.

Fin gave Tan a confounded look and asked, "What is it?" in a quiet whisper.

"The Round Robin," was his answer. "Our intent is writ in the center, and every man that'll abide it signs round about. That way if any one finds the vow that ought not, none can say who signed first, nor who was the leader. All take equal share in its record of mutiny."

"Why sign at all?" asked Fin, still unclear.

"To hold men to their word. No one that signs can be held innocent if our mutiny ever comes to light. And no man'll point his finger to blame another while his mark is scrawled round with the rest." Before Fin could inquire any further, Tan stepped forward, knelt down, and signed his name along the curve of the circle. Before he'd finished, Topper had knelt beside him, followed by Sam Catcher. Soon, all hands on deck were huddled around the parchment waiting for a chance to seal their name to the ship. Fin was more than willing to do so as well, and she moved forward to join the huddle, but Jack called for her to hold and motioned her to come to him.

"Listen up, boys," barked Jack. "We got another matter to settle." The huddle turned its eyes back to Jack. "You all know, of course, that Button here is been keeping secrets under her shirt." Jack chuckled at Fin and the crew roared in laughter. Fin tried not to blush. "Now I know some got problems having a woman on board. I hear your grumbling, and we got to make an end of it right here. If the crew agree on the one hand, then she'll be put ashore in Charleston and not trouble us again, or if the crew agree on the other, she can stay aboard and continue the fine job of sailoring she's been at since the day she come aboard."

"Bad luck having a lady on board, Jack!" shouted Art. Murmurs of assent arose here and there.

"Aye, I heard that foolishness, but that bad luck is the only reason we're rid of Creache and the reason I'm here alive instead of feeding the sharks. Tan'll say the same, I'd wager, and Knut." Knut started at the mention of his name and looked around to see whether or not he might be in trouble.

Tan stepped forward and turned to the crew, "Fin's as good a sailor as I ever saw and a far sight better than most. If she goes, I go too."

Topper *here-here*'d his support, and a volley of other cheers backed him up. Fin stood next to Jack, her eyes down. She didn't want to look up and see who wasn't in her favor.

"Well, as ye can see, I think most are agreeable to having her stay, so the question is, can those that ain't, abide it or nay? If it's bad luck you're whining about, then I'd say she's a far sight better than the luck Creache brought. So what of it, Art?"

Fin looked up and discovered Art staring back at her in fierce consideration. Then it seemed a wave washed the disapproval off his face and his lips turned up.

"I reckon it's no further harm." He looked around at the others who had been wary of her and nodded at them reassuringly.

"Alright then, make your mark, Fin," urged Jack as he motioned to the Round Robin. Fin bent down and, with a surge of pride that she'd been found out and found worthy, she signed her name with confidence.

"Last order of business then," continued Jack without waiting for Fin to finish. "We need to elect a captain, and before you even start, don't think for one minute it'll be me!" *Boo*'s erupted at Jacks refusal. "I don't aim to filthy myself by wearing the title. I was born tar, and I'll die tar. So who else?"

Tan stepped forward to speak, "Who says we need a captain, Jack? I don't think no man aboard is anxious to fill them shoes just now. I say we keep on like we been. Besides, we never needed Creache. You're still first mate. You run the ship and we'll run it for you." The crew found this idea a good one and let it be known.

"Well, we got to have someone making the decisions. Where to trade, what to trade—them things don't figure themselves," protested Jack.

"We'll do it democratic then, put the matter to the whole crew. We all signed the robin in kind, and we'll all run the ship the same." Most of the crew enjoyed the idea and stamped and hollered their opinions. Jack raised his hands and hushed them all back down like a conductor.

"Alright, alright. Can't say as I got a good feeling about it, but I can go along since the rest seem willing." A loud cheer of whoops and hurrahs went up and the matter was settled. "I say that since we ain't going to put up a captain, we put Button up in the cabin, for decency and what all. Anyone got a problem with that?" A solid wave of head shaking rolled over the assemblage and Jack looked satisfied. Fin felt relief and was thankful. "Good, the cabin's yours, Button," Jack nodded to Fin. "Our first stop is Charleston I figure. We need food, water, and some good, dry ground to wet with a bottle. Anyone got a say in the matter?" He looked around at the crew, and the crew looked around at each other. No one spoke out. "All in favor of putting in to Charleston for provisions and play, say aye."

"AYE!" sang a chorus.

"Then let's turn to and make it happen. Topper, you and Tan see to the navigation. The rest of you dogs get to work!" The ship jumped to life as the small gathering split to the four corners of the ship like ripples from a stone. Jack wasted no time pondering anything but the eloquence of the next curse to hurl and set to reminding the crew that he was back, he was in charge, and he didn't keen to sloth on his ship.

CHAPTER XIX

AFTER THE SIGNING OF the Round Robin, the *Rattlesnake* enjoyed a prosperous season under the swarthy arm of Jack Wagon. As the crew had agreed, they put in to Charleston for provisions, and while there, Jack and Tan managed to eke out a few good sailors of dubious ethical declination to bolster the crew. When they raised sail for open sea again, they were forty hands strong and felt like new men.

With new sailors aboard, and some green enough to look youngsters even to Fin, she discovered that she felt more weathered and proven among her peers. She wasn't the fresh new tar on deck any longer, and Fin cherished her newfound sense of belonging.

Despite her oft-repeated protests, the entire crew remained adamant that she keep her berth in the captain's quarters. To make matters worse, Topper was calling her Captain Button in friendly mockery and even going so far as to yell, "Captain on deck!" every time he saw her step out of the cabin. Much to her outward dismay, and inward delight, the affection was soon adopted by the entire crew. If a stranger stood on deck and observed, he'd think himself aboard an odd vessel indeed, where the young Captain Button—if the quartered berth and crew's calling were to be believed—was not only often seen with swab in hand or working the ropes like any common tar, but was, of all things, a woman.

With nothing left to hide, Fin stopped minding her hair and cutting it short. It grew wild and hung long about her shoulders if she didn't keep it tied back with a cord. Months at sea had sun-darkened her skin, and she wondered if Peter would even recognize her when she managed to find her way home once again.

After their parting with Creache, she pleaded with Jack to ask the crew about putting in at Savannah so she could check up on Peter. But Savannah, Jack grimly informed her, was now under British blockade, and trying to put the *Rattlesnake* within fifty miles of the port would be asking for more fight than they could fend. So Fin had to console herself with memories far and faint, and she wrote letters to Peter every chance she found. She longed to hear back from him but it wasn't safe to give an address for fear the British would follow, so always her tidings were vague and imprecise.

What news they heard of the war was seldom encouraging. George Washington and his colonial army had met with defeat after defeat and the British were certain of their eventual victory. Rumor hinted at a possible alliance with France that could turn the tide, but as yet no one had seen French colors flying on incoming warships.

If the landward war went ill, however, it wasn't for lack of action by the *Rattlesnake*. They raided fourteen ships in three months. Mainly, their prey was of British merchants, but once they boarded and commandeered a frigate of the Royal Navy when they caught it unawares in a fogbank near Chesapeake. Tan and half the crew sailed it into Plymouth and sold it as trophy to a local politician. Of course, the great success of the *Rattlesnake* in her privateering career did little to endear them to the Royal Navy. They sometimes spent as much time running from the Union Jack as they did running it down. In the late autumn of 1776, the Navy was so thick in the waters of the West Atlantic that Jack sailed them down around the horn of Florida where they peddled in the Caribbean for the winter. But when spring returned to the colonies, so did the *Rattlesnake*. The entire crew missed the waters, small towns, outer banks, and shorelines of the Eastern Coast, and all were glad to return, British or no.

They found upon their return that not only had the *Rattlesnake*'s reputation grown, but so had Fin's. Tavern talk was quick to fix upon something as scandalous as a woman employed as a sailor, and the *Rattlesnake* was rumored to have a woman as captain no less. Some claimed she was Anne Bonny's ghost, and others charged she was Mary Reed's long lost grand-daughter, but all agreed she was a fearsome captain that gave all hell and what-for to the British. Fin rolled her eyes at such things and had to endure constant teasing from the crew. They knew better than to believe the bar-room exaggerations, but they seemed to take great joy in being on the inside of the joke and often furthered the lies themselves.

She once came upon Topper regaling a barroom full of men with ridiculous tales of her ferocity and cunning. He was standing on a table with his hands outspread and his audience gathered around like children listening to a campfire yarn.

"I seen her shot through the heart and fall dead as driftwood! Seen it with me very eyes! We give her body to the deep but the devil himself feared she'd mutiny and throw him down from the throne of hell. So he set her adrift from the burning lake, and she sailed back into the seven seas upon a raft of the damned that was lashed together with nothing but the tatters o' ruined souls!"

The men around Topper gasped and swore and one made the sign of the cross.

"That's right! The Burning Prince of the Pit cast her out of his hall, and her hair still burns fiery red to tell of it. When her gaze falls on a Union Jack, fire leaps from her eyes and she smells of brimstone. When once I was standing too close to her I nearly got burnt myself!" Topper tugged at his shirtsleeve and sniffed it. "Still smells o' the devil's fire! Smell it! You there, smell it for yourself!"

A young sailor stood up and leaned over cautiously to smell Topper's shirt. He took one sharp sniff and his eyes snapped shut and began to water. The men around him looked on goggle-eyed and called on the saints to save them.

"Smells o' the devil, it does!" cried the boy.

Fin rolled her eyes. She had no doubt that Topper's shirt stank badly enough to bring water to a man's eyes.

Then Topper spotted her standing at the back of the room. He jerked himself upright and snapped his heels together.

"Captain Fin Button on deck!"

Every head in the room snapped around, and dozens of wide, fearful eyes stared at her in horror. In the far corner of the room, one poor drunken sailor dropped to his knees and shouted a Hail Mary before begging the Lord to forgive his trespasses and protect him.

Then they began to laugh.

"You had me going, Topper! Thought it was really her."

The fear and terror drained out of their faces when they saw she was nothing more than a slight girl without any sign at all of an aura of fire and brimstone. Within moments, every man in the room was in the throes of laughter.

"Ha! We thought you was Captain Button," they shouted to her. "Burn you, Topper!" Someone threw a mug at Topper's head, and he ducked. He climbed down from the table and hurried out of the room, dodging another thrown mug and a loaf of bread as he went. Fin chased him out and caught up with him in the street.

"Was all that really necessary?" she asked.

Topper giggled and shook with glee. "No, but it surely is fun to get 'em worked up!" He slapped Fin on the back and she caught a whiff of what had already made one man cry.

"You really must wash that shirt."

Topper roared with laughter.

Back aboard the *Rattlesnake*, Fin pestered Tan at every opportunity for further fencing lessons, and he was quick to take up where they'd put off, which more or less meant swatting Fin about like a child. But week after week, Fin improved, and by the time the ship was again prowling the coast of New England she was no longer ending lessons with bruises and bleeding fingers.

In April of 1777, the crew agreed to slip into Wilmington to take on provisions, dry up a tavern, and have news of the war. Jack ordered the anchor dropped in the harbor, and the crew rowed the distance shore to keep the ship as far as possible from snooping officials who might wonder after the captain or seek news of his whereabouts.

Fin's first order of business, as usual, was sending a letter out to Peter. Knut waited quietly as she scratched away at the parchment on the table. She told Peter about the Caribbean and its beaches, long and white as the moon, lapped by clear waters and cool wind. She filled him in on what fortune they'd found in aiding the war and hoped sincerely that the British would be gone soon and she'd be free to come home.

The letters brought back memories that were almost far enough away for her to forget. The writing brought them closer, reeled them in from the grey waves that tried to drown them. Memories of Bartimaeus, Peter, her bell tower. It was a different world to her now, a different life. Peter would have finished building the house long ago, but as much as she longed for it, hoped for it, she couldn't quite imagine herself realizing it. It was too far away, too different. She loved the sea and her ship. She loved the men she now thought of as family. She didn't like to think about leaving them behind when the war ended. She didn't have to consider the breaking away when she left the orphanage, left Peter. At the time it was her only choice. But she had choices now, and she couldn't reconcile the two desires. She shook it out her mind. Such choices were far and away from her now. She finished the letter, wished Peter love, and folded it up.

Tan joined them in the rowboat and they paddled their way toward the waterfront through canyons formed by tall ships; on all sides, ships loomed high like walls of creaking stone. They wended a path to the dockside, tied the boat fast, and climbed up into the city.

Tan grinned them a farewell once they were ashore, and Fin, with Knut in tow, struck off on her own. She made straight for the postmaster to send her letter on its way and then set her mind to leisure and luxury.

The city was full of the smells and sounds of land-bound life that Fin often forgot when far out at sea: the earthy scent of animals and the clatter of wagons, the solid sound and feel of your feet upon the ground, the coming and going of a multitude of other people. The din of thousands of conversations floated up from the streets and out of buildings to form a subtle chorus that one never quite noticed until it was gone in the dark of night or swallowed by the quiet expanse of the sea. The sounds and people made her nervous at times. She'd spent all her life in the country or on the *Rattlesnake*, away from such clangor and bustle. She felt like an intruder in the city and was anxious to be away.

As they crossed the town square, Fin noted on the wind the sickening smell of death. It made her shiver. She looked around expecting to see a dead chicken or dog, even though she knew instinctively it was something else. On the seaward side of the square, framed against the open ocean by two buildings, was the source of the odor. Swinging heavily in the wind like wet flags were the bodies of two men, hanged and decaying. One was little more than a skeleton, desiccated and leathery; the corpse must have been hanging there for months. The other, however, was no more than a few days old. Its eyes were freshly plucked out by carrion and the sockets stared back at her, gaping and empty. The mouth was pulled open in the quiet groan of the dead. Below the corpse, a wet spot spread upon the ground where blood and worse dripped into a fetid puddle. A dog lapped out of it a gruesome meal. Fin shuddered and felt her stomach rise.

Knut stared at the display as if it were no more unusual than sides of beef hanging at market. A makeshift sign hung on the beam that suspended the bodies. It explained simply, PIRATE. A flood of memories came back to her, memories of Bartimaeus smiling as he fell, the rope's cruel jerk. He'd have hung like this, her gentle Bartimaeus. They'd have made a spectacle of him, but Sister Carmaline humbled herself and begged them otherwise. At the time she'd been too stricken and numb to consider what fate Carmaline had begged him away from. Now she understood. Tears rose. How had he been capable of such a life? An outlaw. A criminal. Had he been friends with Creache—friends? When he'd yelled at her—the one time he'd yelled at her—it was because she forced him to dredge up his past, to talk about it. In that one moment, she glimpsed the fire and anger in him. Maybe he had that murderous glint in his eye for years at a time while he worked his piracy with Creache. She tried to imagine him that way, as a man who deserved the same end as the bloated and rotting corpse swinging in the square, but she could not.

Her Bartimaeus was no pirate. Whatever had happened to him in London, whatever blessing Reverend Whitefield had spoken upon him had remade his person entire. Even when he'd come for her in the woods and murdered a man, he never looked the pirate to her. Yet he paid the price of piracy. Even gentle Bartimaeus had not been able to escape his past. He swung like a common criminal. And he smiled. He tried to change himself, but in the end he hadn't changed a thing. And he smiled. Fin pushed away her memory. She had murder in her past too. Somewhere out there British soldiers were looking for her. If they caught her, she'd swing. She'd rot in the town square. She'd be as dead as Bartimaeus.

"Come on, Knut. I don't like the smell." She grabbed Knut and herded him off, away from the dead, and didn't look back until the smell was gone. She wasn't sure she had it in her to smile at that end and never meant to find out.

They shopped the market and gorged themselves on fresh, sweet fruits of every color. Fin stuffed both her pockets and Knut's full of rosy peaches before they wandered on. Knut, stuffed all over with fruit, looked even knobbier than usual. The peaches bulging from his every pocket gave the impression someone had beaten him silly with a stick and raised peach-sized welts all over his body to tell it. His face didn't betray a whit of the ridiculous looking body it was attached to and Fin could hardly suppress her laughter.

They wandered up the street and found a theatre with doors open and a herald announcing the eminent commencement of the latest play by a local playwright, something dubiously hailed as *Petticoats and Corn*. Fin hadn't seen anything of the sort before. She grabbed Knut by a peach-ladened arm and dragged him toward the door.

"*Captain* Button!" called a thick voice from up the street.

"Will you stop that?" Fin said and rolled her eyes at the title. Topper walked toward them swatting at his shirt as if he'd just discovered it was dirty. Small puffs of dust billowed away from him with each swat.

"Fin, there's a boxing ring, and listen here, these boys fighting, they got nary a knuckle to match the way I seen you throw them fists of yours. Come down yonder with me and pick a fight with a few of them old boys. We can lay down our money and collect gold on the dollar when you put 'em in the dirt! What do you say, *Captain*?" He grinned at her and rubbed his hands together as if he could already feel the money rolling in.

"I don't think so, Topper. I'm not in the mood to get my head knocked in—"

"Come on, Fin. You can wallop these boys in no time, not even break a sweat."

The herald at the door of the theatre gave one last call for seating.

"Maybe later. We're going to see a play." Topper's face drooped. "Hey, why don't you come with us? Might be good for you," she offered. Topper raised his eyebrows and looked up at the building, then looked down at the playbill and scratched his ear in consideration.

"A play, huh? Nah, you go on. I can't read anyhow." He looked disappointed and walked off in the direction he'd come from. Fin opened her mouth thinking to tell him that watching a play didn't require that one know how to read but decided it wasn't worth the trouble. She grabbed Knut and pulled him through the door behind her.

A snobbish usher with greasy hair escorted them to their seats and retreated with his nose in the air just as the curtain rose. The stage was set like a cornfield, and a woman in a preposterous yellow dress with half a dozen hoops and acres of petticoats was skipping through the rows and swinging a picnic basket. When she finally came to a stop and set down her basket, she bemoaned her lack of a desirable suitor and was then captured by a man dressed as an Indian who tried very hard but failed to be menacing. Despite the great promise shown by the opening scene, the dark theatre and far away voices put Fin directly to sleep.

She awoke to find Knut poking her in the shoulder and calling her name. Fin rubbed her eyes and felt a rush of irritation that she'd slept through the play. Then she turned her mind to wondering who the man standing beside her with crossed arms might be. It turned out to be the snobbish, greasy-haired usher, and he was overtly vocal about the theatre's policy on sleeping, not to mention snoring, during the performance. Fin also noticed that he seemed to quite despise anyone looking suspiciously vagrant; this qualified him in Fin's regard as someone to be quite despised himself. He attempted to grab her arm to escort her out of the building, and she shook him off with a grumbled curse and explained that had the play been worth anything at all she'd not have been sleeping through it. She exited the theater with a satisfied sniff wondering what the play had been about in the first place. She remembered none of it.

Fin picked a peach from one of Knut's pockets and devoured it as she stomped off down the street in search of the boxing ring. Being kicked out of the playhouse had her worked into a furor, and she was ready to go blows with someone. If she could make some money doing it, then so much the better.

There was a small multitude gathered around a roped-off corral where two unshirted men stood sweating in opposing corners. The cheers from the crowd, however, were not of delight. Someone was interrupting the boxing, and the onlookers were none too happy over the delay. Standing upon a box opposite Fin was a white-haired man dressed in black—the apparent focus of all the unrest. Fin pushed closer to discover what the disturbance was about.

"Oy, Fin!" Topper called through the din. He was supporting Tan as he limped out of the crowd. Tan's face was bloodied and bruised, and if Topper had let him be he'd have fallen over in a heap. "You're too late, Fin," grumbled Topper. "Tan put himself in the ring and the other fella put him right back out. Lost the last dollar in my pocket, and the parson aims to break up the fun a'fore Tan even has himself a chance to win it back. If anyone else is like to get boxed, it's gonna be that preacher."

Topper turned away and half-carried Tan down the street while Fin pushed closer to the ring.

"Throw him in the ring, I says!" shouted a man from the crowd.

"Aye, let's see him turn his other cheek!" called another. As she got closer, she was able to separate the parson's voice from the shouts of the angry crowd.

"Turn every one of you from your evil course. Amend your ways. So says the Lord. But men, they say: 'We will live as we choose, and follow, every one of us our own evil, stubborn minds!' And the Lord declares: 'I know your countless crimes. There will be wailing in all the streets and cries of anguish in every public square when I pass through your midst.'"

The crowd hurled jeers at the parson from all directions, but he would neither flinch nor cease nor speak with anger. He reminded Fin of Hilde and how so often she'd towered over her, and waggled her nose about Fin's fighting with the boys. Fin had rolled her eyes then and all but sworn hate for Hilde in times since, but now she felt a pang of shame that she'd treated her with such disrespect, and was ashamed now that she stood doing nothing to stop the mob from abusing the parson.

Tan had roused and shaken himself away from Topper to come wobbling back toward the ring. The crowd parted and cheered him on. He was clearly in no state to be fighting, though, and Fin intercepted him. She detoured him safely back out of the crowd and away from the boxing ring despite his protests. When they got to the corner, Tan had regained some of his senses and suggested they cure themselves of the parson's sermon by finding a tavern to drain. Fin agreed with a glance back at the parson and then set out with Knut and Tan to secure a table at the nearest establishment and exorcize whatever local spirits might haunt the place.

The tavern they happened upon was the Merry Barrel and Sconce. The shingle over the door depicted a barrel of rum overlit by a candled sconce—though neither appeared terribly merry. It seemed rather a nice outfit, set a few blocks landward of the waterfront. If nothing else, it stank less than the surrounding buildings. Fin ventured to think it might be cleaner as well, but in the torchlight of the evening, she couldn't be certain. At the very least, they found the haunt to be full of all manner of spirits, from Kentucky whiskey to Spanish rum, and no sooner had they knocked back the first round than Tan erupted in an awfully bad sailor's song, and the entire room joined him while Fin sipped her cup in quiet delight. Knut studied the end of his nose, pressing on it now and again as if to test its solidity.

Hours later, after Tan had led the establishment in more choral derangements than Fin was wont to count, Jack stepped through the door and looked over the room. He spotted Fin and dropped into the seat opposite her.

"Seen Tan?" he asked. Fin laughed and kicked at something under the table. A drunken moan answered, and Jack leaned back to look beneath the table. There lay Tan in a happy ale-induced slumber, looking as peaceful as a babe in a cradle. Jack rolled his eyes in irritation and turned back to Fin. He noted Knut's presence with a grunt.

"We got a problem," he said quietly.

Fin set down her mug and leaned in. "What sort?"

"I just come from the dock master's office. They keep a list up of known pirate ships so's they can seize 'em if they sees 'em—reward money and what all."

"What's that got to do with us?"

"Sitting right on top of the list is the *'Snake*," Jack said with a nervous look around.

"We're not pirates!" Certainly, the British Navy had bounties out for them, but those would carry no weight in a port held by the Continentals.

Jack wrinkled his brow at her and shook his head.

"The list says, '*Rattlesnake*: Crew wanted for Mutiny and Piracy.'" Fin felt the blood drain out of her face. "He's alive. Don't know how, but the bastard's alive and he's turned us in for pirates. The *'Snake* will be wanted in every lawful port on both sides of the Atlantic. Pass the word to any of the boys you see to get back to the *'Snake* quick as they can and without making a fuss. We'll slip out just as soft as we slipped in."

Fin nodded.

"I'm going to track down the rest of the boys. Get Tan to the docks. I got a boat waiting to ferry us out to the *'Snake*. Keep quiet and keep your wits. I'll see you there."

Jack stood up, kicked Tan once, and shook his head at the answering groan as he walked out the door.

Fin and Knut spent the next twenty minutes trying to goad Tan back into the world of sobriety. He moaned and snored and protested until, finally, they'd kicked, yelled, and slapped at him enough and he managed to find his feet. With a little help from Knut, he staggered out of the Merry Barrel and Sconce.

The evening had grown full into night, and the dimly lit streets provided them cover enough that Fin's fears were hidden in the darkness. The closer they got to the docks, the more a feeling of rising anxiety grew. Images of dead pirates loomed out at her from alleyways and shadows. More than once, Tan, in his state, would take to shouting at some threatening shadow or just as often laugh at a merry one, and Fin felt sure his noise would give them away to some official stalking them in the darkness. Only a few hours ago, they'd been about town without a worry in the world and no one had known them. But now, with the threat of the law looming over her, she felt that hidden eyes were spying on them every step of the way. When they chanced to meet strangers along the street, Fin bowed her head and held her breath. They were looking at her suspiciously. Surely they knew her. Ridiculous, she reminded herself and forced her eyes up to meet the passersby, smiling a polite hello.

"Ho there!" shouted a voice from the dark. Fin's face went cold. Out of the shadows trotted Topper and she breathed a sigh of relief. What she thought were shadows cloaking his face revealed themselves, upon closer inspection, to be patches of dirt.

"You scared me half out of my wits, Topper!" she whispered.

"You talk to Jack?"

"Aye, we're headed for the docks. You seen the rest of the crew?"

"Yeah, I pointed Jack to 'em, they'll be along. Never thought I'd find myself running from a pirate's bounty, I tell you." He winced that he'd spoken so loudly and looked around to see if anyone had heard. Satisfied they were still alone, he lowered his voice and continued, "I don't deserve this Fin, never did naught but honest sailorin', and damn the blood in Creache's veins if his treachery swings me on a gallows' pole."

In silent haste, they made their way to the docks. When they arrived, they found others of the crew waiting on them in the shadows. Few spoke, but the subject at hand was heavy in their midst. Knut was quiet as ever but clearly addled by the tense atmosphere. He nervously hopped from one foot to the other.

A rowboat emerged from the darkness and slipped up beside the dock. Art Thomasson sat inside and guided it toward them. When the boat bumped along the dock, he threw a rope up to Topper and motioned them to come aboard. Topper flipped a coin to Art and proclaimed the dockside service to be a travesty. Art rolled his eyes as he caught the mock tip. Fin felt a cold chill rattle down her spine. The boatman was paid, and they pushed off into the dark.

"What about Jack and the rest?" she asked.

"He'll be along," said Art. "Soon as you're aboard, I'll head back for the others."

Fin turned away from the dim city and looked out at the darkness of the bay, straining her eyes for the first glimpse of the *Rattlesnake*. Apart from the shore and yet distant from the ship, they floated in a hinterland of shadow and nothingness as if light and earth had been swallowed away. Only the lap of the waves and the splash of the oars gave any assurance that they were still in the corporeal world. The darkness made Fin dizzy. Her mind groped for up and down, for direction, but found only uncertainty in the cloak of night.

At last, against the black sky, a dark hole appeared in the stars: the silhouette of the ship. They were nearly there. The great shadow grew as they approached it, and when they were within a few strokes of the oar, a lantern flickered to life. Art brought the boat along the side and they climbed up.

As Fin clambered onto the deck, she heard a heavy thump against the hull. At first, she thought it was the rowboat, but when the knock came again it felt too heavy for the small craft. It sounded like a larger boat, like the sound the *Rattlesnake* made when it pulled up alongside another ship. The sound came again and she was certain it wasn't the rowboat. She ran across the deck to the starboard side and there, tethered to the railing, was a small frigate, bumping gently against the *Rattlesnake*.

A shout rang out behind her. She turned and her stomach dropped. Coming from every hatchway on the ship were British soldiers. It was a trap. Swords flashed and muskets came to bear. The crew, drunken and unawares, scarcely put up a fight. Fin ran for the captain's cabin to fetch her sword and Betsy. Several soldiers started after her, but she danced around them. When she reached the cabin door it swung open before she could touch it. She took a step backward. Out of the shadows within stepped a tall figure with curly, white hair and murderous eyes. The man's hand held a wrinkled parchment—her map.

"It seems your lies are boundless, Miss Button," he said as he flourished the map in his hand. It was Tiberius Creache. He was sneering.

"You bastard," she seethed.

"Indeed. But save your insults and your breath. I daresay you'll require both when the British have you. And I'll be certain to enjoy the thought as I spend the bounty for your capture." He motioned to a group of soldiers, and they came forward and seized her. Fin fought against them and received only bruises and ill treatment for her trouble. They clapped chains about her wrists and ankles and kicked her to the ground. Creache stood over her smiling.

"Don't worry, Miss Button, you'll have that beastly Mr. Wagon to keep you company in hell just as soon as they stretch his mutinous neck. I expect Mr. Thomasson will be bringing him to me shortly." Fin cursed under her breath. Art had betrayed them. "So refreshing to find good sailors these days. Now, if you'll excuse me, we'll be clearing the deck to await the next catch." He turned away and addressed a British officer, "She's all yours. Get her out of my sight."

As the soldiers dragged her across the deck by her chains, she cried out once, hoping to warn Jack, praying he'd be within earshot. A soldier brought his boot down on the back of her head and the world went dark.

CHAPTER XX

FIN STIRRED TO THE sound of guttural voices.

"Let's have a look at her!"

Her head throbbed with pain, and the voices stabbed into her mind like needles. She drew in a sharp breath and nearly gagged. The air was thick and foul; it smelled of a mouldy bilge. Water sloshed across the floor, ankle-deep and choked with filth.

At least a half dozen men surrounded her. They were scarred, filthy, and in various states of hairy nakedness. The whites of their eyes bulged out at her in the gloom of a single lantern. Only their capacity for language betrayed that they were men at all. Had Fin not heard them speak, she'd have taken them for the apes of an African menagerie.

"Move out, ye dog. We wants a better sniff of her."

"You'd bloody well better move back, mate. Come a shuffle closer and you'll rue it." Tan's voice. She turned her head and looked up. He was standing over her, light on his feet, fists out.

"Boy, ye don't understand. This the rotten belly of the British Empire, the stinking hell where good sailors go to suffer." He paused and grinned. "Well maybe not good sailors, mind ye, but good enough for me, says I. We been here, you ain't; forgot how long, forgot how come, but this is our world, boy. You're in it, and we'll eat ye as soon as beat ye."

The pack of wretched men snarled and whooped and bared their teeth.

"I says move out so's we can get a little taste of your lass, and you'll do it if you know what's good fer."

Tan didn't budge.

"If'n you're worried we'll have all our fun with the lass, then don't ye mind. We'll be having our fun with ye as well." The man let out a sickening laugh and the faces around him broke into unwholesome smiles.

Tan looked down at Fin as she stirred. "Morning, Fin. Might have us a ruckus here. Hope you got your robber-knockers running."

Fin climbed to her feet. She heard a whimper and peered through the dim light to see Knut huddled against the wall hugging his knees. Bruises or dirt covered most of him; she couldn't tell which and would be surprised at neither. Next to Knut lay Topper in an unconscious heap.

"Oh looky, she's up and about," chattered a filthy man, naked to the waist. Fin grimaced in disgust.

"Where are we?" Fin asked as she appraised the room. It was obviously a ship, but no respectable seagoing vessel would allow such filth and disrepair. The wood all around, from floor to ceiling, was rotten and ridden with wormholes. The black, slimy water sloshing about the room was full of a filth Fin didn't care to consider. She was amazed that the ship was even afloat in its state. Men lay all around the room, some living, some apparently dead, some quickly becoming so by the look of them. A few were shackled to the bulkhead, and most had a cannonball chained to one ankle. At the far end of the room, a small stair led up to an iron door. The doorframe was the only wood in the room not decayed to the point of falling apart.

"Prison hulk," stated Tan grimly.

"Prison what?"

"Decommissioned man-o'-war. The English use them as prison ships—until they conveniently sink."

"Aye, missy. This here's the HMS *Justice*. Welcome aboard," said the man standing before them. His lips split apart into a black-toothed smile.

"And who is he?" She asked Tan but the man answered for him.

"You might say I'm the First Mate o' this fair galley, and then," he paused and shrugged, "you might not. But I wager you'll call me anything at all a'fore me and the crew finish with ye."

Tan stepped forward. "I believe I'd have words with the captain, before I box the ears of his first mate . . . mate."

"Hear that boys? Green hand says he wants to see the captain!" The men around him erupted in laughter. "Nobody sees the captain, boy—unless I likes 'em. You ain't been *liked* yet."

Tan hit him under the chin hard enough to knock him over backward and leave him sprawled arms-out and motionless in the murky water at their feet. The rest of the crew boggled at the scene for a moment and then snarled curses and turned on Fin and Tan, their white eyes bulging.

"Here we go," mumbled Tan.

Fin braced herself for a fight she couldn't imagine herself winning, even with Tan's help. There were too many of them, six at least, probably more. The close quarters didn't make things easy. And worse, the floor was slick with mould and rot. Fin marked the nearest growling half-man and kicked him square in the groin. Beside her Tan was busy kicking off two attackers while he held another in a headlock.

"Enough!" boomed a thick French accent. The men around them scurried back into the shadows leaving Fin and Tan alone in the center of the room. Knut retreated farther into the corner, still whimpering to himself. Out of the shadow of the far side of the room came a wiry, grey-haired man with the leathery skin of an old sailor.

"Sorry, sir. We was just messing about—" said one of the half-naked dregs from the shadows.

"Shut up, dog." The man walked slowly across the room and studied Fin with cold, wizened eyes. "Excuse my crew, *cherie*. Sometimes one must tolerate the depravity of such men to maintain proper control over them, *oui*?" He looked briefly toward the shadows, and Fin and Tan's attackers shrunk deeper into the blackness to escape his eyes.

"You the one they call captain?" asked Tan, as he wiped the sweat from his brow.

"I am known by many names," he said with a slight upturn of his lips. "But yes, these"—he motioned to the shadows, his hand was bereft of its thumb and last two fingers—"these call me captain."

Though the old man had called off his dogs, Fin had the impression they were not out of danger. The man's eyes hinted at calculation and sleeping villainy. She preferred a threat she could see clearly to subtleties of deception.

"Suppose we ought to thank you," said Tan.

"I doubt that. You may yet find that a quick death to the dogs is preferable to the slow rot of darkness and time." Fin glanced at Tan. He looked as nervous as she did. He too was leery of this captain's "hospitality."

"Where are we?" demanded Fin.

The captain smiled slightly and answered, "Your friend spoke correctly. You are a prisoner of the king." He spat at the floor. "I am anxious, however, to hear *why*." He narrowed his eyes to study Fin closer. She shivered. "This," he motioned around at the room, "is a place reserved for only the most reviled of prisoners. I consider it a place of honor." Again, he smiled. Fin felt the hairs on her neck stand up. "Murderers, treachers, assassins," he rolled the words off his tongue, enjoying the taste of each one, "and worse." From the shadows came soft laughter. The captain twitched his head in response, and the laughter quieted. "*You*, however, do not appear to belong here, no?" he raised an eyebrow at them. "So, as I said, I am curious. Come, tell me, why are you here?"

"We are arrested for mutiny and piracy," answered Tan.

"Mutiny and piracy! Respectable virtues indeed, but not, I'm afraid, ones that would condemn you to this place. Therefore, either you lie or you have made powerful enemies. If you are lying, then I may kill you. If you have the right enemies, then perhaps I will not. So, come *cherie*, tell me, which is to be the truth." He ignored Tan and looked coldly at Fin, awaiting her answer.

"I'm no liar," protested Tan. The captain's eyes flashed at the tone of Tan's voice and he opened his mouth to speak. Fin interrupted him.

"Tan speaks the truth. We've mutinied and are arrested as pirates. And the English have set a bounty on my head."

The alleged captain's eyes cooled. "And did you wrest your ship free of a tyrant captain and set him adrift? Have you haunted the coast and quickened English hearts with your threats and preyed upon the Union Jack and run the sea red with the blood of king's men?" Fin was baffled. "And tell me, *cherie*, did you kill six soldiers as they sat to dine?"

"How do you—"

"I have many ears—though not my own." He pulled back the hair on the left side of his head. His ear was missing, only a nub of scar tissue remained. He smiled. "So the War Woman of Georgia and the flame-haired captain of the *Rattlesnake* are one and the same, no?"

"I'm no captain."

"Captain or no, the tales name you so. The Flame of the West, they call you across the sea. Terror of the British trade, they say, no? I see that I was wrong. You belong here indeed!" Fin felt sickened by the inclusion. "And tell me, *cherie*, what was the name of the captain you so boldly relieved of his ship?" His eyes were eager now.

"Tiberius Creache."

His mouth opened in a silent expression of pleasure. He closed his eyes and rolled his head back and croaked a breathy laugh. When he looked at her again, his eyes were bright and full of twisted joy. "My name is Armand Defain. I am at your service."

"How can you know—" Fin tried to ask.

"My secrets are mine to keep. It is enough for you to know that I will help you if I can. Go now. Tend to your friends. I will keep the dogs at bay. Rest."

Armand Defain slunk back into the shadows. Tan exchanged a look of hope and concern with Fin. She turned to check Topper.

"Topper found them pawing at you, and they knocked him good for putting himself in the way," Tan explained. Hurt because of her. Fin ground her teeth and moved to check on Knut. He seemed no calmer, but he didn't seem to be hurt. Fin tried to talk to him, to ask if he was alright, but he wouldn't answer.

"What happened, Tan?" Fin asked as she slid to the floor and leaned back against the bulkhead. She tried not to contemplate the stench that choked the air or the content of the murky water she sat in.

"Don't remember much myself, seems I had a mite too much to drink. I recall they chained us and dragged us onto that ship alongside the *'Snake*.

Then, I reckon it was a couple hours before they off-loaded us here."

"Can't be far from Wilmington then," Fin mused.

"Aye. Southport I figure, at Fort Johnston."

"Where's the rest of the crew?"

"They stuck most of them in cells amidships. Don't know why we get the fancy quarters." He chuckled.

"What about Jack?" she asked.

"Not seen him, nor the crew that was with him. If I know Jack, he smelt the trap a'fore he sprung it." Tan raised his eyes to look at her. "Let's hope."

Even if Jack avoided the trap, Fin didn't see how he could know where they were, but scant hope was better hope than none at all.

Armand Defain had disappeared back into his shadowy corner and did not attempt to speak to them again. Fin was glad he was distant. Offer of help or not, she remained wary of him. Defain said he would keep the other prisoners at bay, and certainly they feared him. Nevertheless, she trusted Defain no more than the dogs he kept.

From across the room came intermittent snickers and murmurs from men that long captivity had made beasts of. Their eyes peered out at her from the shadows like animals in the night. She feared to turn her back or close her eyes.

When at last the clanking of chains and bolts on the other side of the door announced dinner, she breathed easier. It shifted the focus away from her, away from her friends. A guard entered and dropped a bucket and a few bowls into the water on the floor. As soon as the guard exited and closed the door, the dogs rushed from the shadows and huddled around the bucket. Defain shouted at them to move away, and they cowered back in obeisance. Then he motioned for Fin to come, and she filled bowls for herself and her companions. The bucket contained a stew of dubious brown liquid that smelled only marginally better than the room. As soon as she moved away, the half-human dogs in the shadows leapt to the bucket and began to feed. No one attempted to feed the men chained to the walls; they stared at the food bucket with hollow eyes. She tried not to think about it.

After dinner, the locks on the door rumbled again and all eyes turned toward it. The prisoners shrunk into the shadows. A tall man entered, dressed in British red and white. He studied the room, his form silhouetted against the light from the door, his face lost in shadow. Only his eyes glinted out of the blackness cloaking his face. They drifted around, picked out each prisoner in turn until they found Fin and stopped. He stepped forward into the lantern light. He had a deep scar running across his face from temple to temple, cutting through his eyes; one was blind and milky white, the other lidless and terrible. She flushed cold as ice. She'd thought this man dead, hoped this man dead. Yet here he stood like a ghost out of nightmare, his mouth twisting to a grin. When he spoke, his sharp dangerous voice brought the past rushing back to her. She heard his words as if from a great distance.

"Here we are again, lass," he said, almost a whisper. He squinted up his cheek to blink his lidless eye. "The knife nearly killed me." The memory flashed in her mind: the kitchen, his hands on her, the knife sliding into his chest, his body slipping to the floor. "Put a hole in my lung, they said. But I ain't dead. Not dead at all. The Governor himself appointed me to your capture—and execution." She deserved it. She killed those soldiers. She was a murderer. But as sure as she was of her guilt, she had no wish to submit to that end. He was grinning wildly now. He affected his unnatural blink again. Fin spat at him. He didn't move.

"Still lively as ever. I'll enjoy watching you kick from the end of the hangman's rope. Not to worry, you've plenty of time to appreciate your new home before that. We'll be towing the *Justice* down to Savannah where you'll be put on trial before the hanging. We've an example to make." He turned and slammed the door shut behind him. As the locks rumbled closed again, Tan stepped up to her.

"You want to explain that?" he asked.

She turned to answer and noticed Armand Defain lurking near the door in the shadows, looking on with narrowed eyes.

"Bartimaeus gave him that scar a long time ago."

"Bartimaeus?"

Tan's question made her realize how much she'd been hiding. Ever since she came aboard the *Rattlesnake*, she'd been hiding—hiding her gender, hiding her past, hiding her fears and worries. She started at the beginning, with her assignment to the kitchen as Bartimaeus's helper, and told Tan everything. She told him about Peter, about the sisters, about Bartimaeus and the soldiers. She recounted his capture and her murderous flight from Ebenezer. Then finally, she told him about Creache and Bartimaeus, even about the map. When she finished, she didn't wait for a reaction, she didn't want approval or comfort or sympathy. She simply sat down, leaned her head back against the wall, and closed her eyes.

"We've got to get out of here," said Tan.

Fin didn't answer. She saw no way out and was too tired to consider the future.

"If we get out, we can get the *'Snake* back," said Tan.

"How? Creache could be anywhere by now. Why bother?" groaned Fin.

"Because we know where he's going."

"We do?" Fin looked up and raised an eyebrow at Tan.

"He'll be headed for Ebenezer, for the gold." Tan was right. Creache would head straight for Ebenezer, for the orphanage. He'd tear the place apart until he found what he wanted, and he wouldn't care who got in his way. Fin stood up and walked across the room to where two eyes had been peering out at them since the soldier left.

"Armand," she called. His face appeared in the half-light. His mouth was turned up in the slightest smile.

"We have to get out of here," Fin stated coldly.

"So it would seem, *cherie*," his eyes twinkled. "Opportunity will present itself. We must be ready. Rest." He retreated into the shadows.

Fin opened her mouth to demand something more immediate, but before she could utter a word, his voice floated back out at her from the darkness.

"Rest."

IN THE GLOOM OF the *Justice*'s brig, the passage of time was marked by meals. Twice a day the locks on the door rumbled and clattered. The guard entered and left behind him a bucket of stew if they were lucky, maggoty bread if less so. Topper was positively miserable and moaned constantly about the lack of proper food. In his sleep, he smacked his lips as he feasted on the ethereal bounty of his dreams. For all Topper's complaint though, Fin didn't worry much for him. He had enough spare blubber around the middle to keep him running a while yet. It was Knut that she worried about. The darkness had a terrible effect on him. He was skinnier than ever, and the dark drew out deep lines and hollows in his face that made him look skeletal. His mood was dark as well; he hadn't smiled or spoken since they were in the tavern on the night of their capture. She tried to talk to him, to cheer him, but her efforts produced no fruit. He simply shivered in the dark and stared into the shadow of the room.

"Why would they put Knut down here?" Fin said. "What's he ever done?"

Tan didn't have an answer.

The four of them were specifically chosen for this section of the prison ship. Tan claimed to have no idea why, but Fin suspected it was because they were her friends. She hoped their friendship wouldn't be the death of them. If the British threw them in with the vilest of criminals simply because they were her friends, might they not also hang them with her? The soldier—she didn't even know his name—said she was to be made an example of. She told herself they wouldn't include her friends in that example, but something in the back of her mind assured her they would.

Water rolled across the room in waves of filth and decay, a rotting metronome marking time in the dark. No ray of sun reached their murk, and the slow wash of salt water patiently eroded away all sense of time and space. Time stretched out, became fluid, lost its form and structure. Fin could no longer discern minutes from hours, hours from days. When the meals came, they afforded a harsh point of reference that forced what felt like days into a reality that insisted only hours had passed. Here and there, now and then, as if stroked by the icy finger of insanity, a muted chuckle, groan, or cry escaped some unseen mouth in the darkness, and Fin shrank away from it into her corner. Madness grew here. It lurked behind the walls, beneath the waves, within the shadows, and in time, inevitably, within the mind.

While other prisoners still stirred and peered at her in the dark, she tried to stay awake, but the absence of light taunted her toward sleep. Her eyes closed and she snapped them open, chased the sleep away, only to find her eyes falling shut again moments later. Out of the shadows crept a man, grinning and naked, stealing closer with each fall of her sleep-heavy lids. Her weary mind ignored the creeping figure. She had only strength enough to fight away sleep, and that for little longer. The man stole closer, slow and intent, a grin of broken teeth and rotting gums spreading wide. Sleep was nearly upon her. The man stretched out a black hand, and the cold fingers closing on her throat snatched her from the descending threat of slumber. Then a thin blade opened the man's throat. His eyes bulged with pain and surprise then closed, and he fell lifeless into the filth of the bilge. Fin's mind came alive and before her stood Armand Defain cleaning his knife.

"I told you I would keep my dogs away, no?" he said.

She shivered at the thought of what might have happened if Defain hadn't kept his watch. She didn't care to take the chance again; sleep was leagues away now.

Defain shrugged as his knife vanished into the folds of his ragged shirt.

"Why are you here?" she asked.

He squatted down in front of her. "Like you, I was put here."

"What did you do?"

He laughed. "Many things, *cherie*. I endeavor to break all laws of both God and man. And in that endeavor I have met success. My sins," he paused and his smile faltered, "are legion. I am sent here, however, for something I did not do. God, it seems, is a clever accountant." He frowned and waved his hand in the air. "It is no matter, *cherie*. In the end we all get what we deserve."

"I don't deserve this." She knew it was a lie.

Defain raised an eyebrow and let his judgment linger. He held up his hand in front of her and stared at the malformed flesh of his missing fingers. No trace of the thumb remained, only a waxen notch of scarred tissue. Of the ring and smallest fingers of his hand, two short nubs stood out from the knuckle like candles burned down to nothing. "My flesh was taken from me. The man that took it will have what he has earned." He put his hand down and looked at her. His grin and laughter were gone.

"Sleep, *cherie*. You need fear nothing here while my vengeance burns. It has chased away madness and death for many years. It will serve you well." He grabbed the dead man lying on the floor and dragged him away, into the shadows. His reassurance didn't comfort Fin, but soon sleep stole upon her and she let herself be taken.

Chapter XXI

FIVE MEALS AFTER THEY arrived on the *Justice*, some two and a half days, the door rumbled and the room scurried to life at the promise of food to come. The door swung in and a sloppily dressed soldier stepped into the room.

"Fin? Tan?" he whispered.

Defain poured slowly out of his shadowy corner and fixed his eyes on her. "Opportunity, *cherie*," he said with satisfaction.

Fin didn't understand. Then the soldier took off his hat and the light shone on his face. It was Sam Catcher.

"Come on!" he said then winced, having spoken louder than he wished. He motioned them over to him. "We're here with Jack. Come quietly." No one argued. "Jack couldn't fit into the uniform," he added with a smirk. "He's waiting in a boat alongside."

Fin pulled Knut to his feet and they made their way toward the door. The room around them crept to life as the men hidden in the shadows caught scents of freedom. Fin eyed Armand Defain worriedly. He too had eyes only for the door. She was anxious to be far away from him.

Just as they slipped through the door, Defain darted past like a breeze, and a snarl erupted behind him as the half-naked prisoners lurched out of the dark and scrambled for the open door. Defain slammed the door shut before any could reach it and threw the bolt closed. The men inside howled and beat against the iron, growling curses at them. Sam swore and looked around in anger.

"Quiet!" he hissed, but too late. A guard had already come to investigate. He trotted down the steps as if expecting nothing more than to yell a threat and put the prisoners back to silence. He was within feet of them before his eyes translated what he saw and a white look of shock blanched his face. He drew his saber and opened his mouth to shout for help. Before he could utter a sound, a shadow flowed from beside Fin and launched itself at the guard. A knife flashed and the guard grunted as Armand Defain pinned him to the bulkhead with a dagger. Defain spat upon the guard and watched him die with satisfaction, then smiled as he retrieved the knife. The soldier slid to the floor in a heap. Fin was sickened. It was one thing to kill a man at need, but Armand enjoyed it; he relished the blood he'd spilt.

"Come on," urged Sam. They sped lightly up the steps into the main hold. Cells lined the entire length. Sam pulled a key from his belt and began opening the locks, freeing the rest of the *Rattlesnake*'s crew. Fin didn't know how many soldiers guarded the ship, but she imagined there were more than just the one Defain had killed. Every second that Sam spent unlocking cells, Fin expected the rest of the guard to burst through a hatchway. Soon, however, Sam had all of them free and her confidence grew. With fifteen able men, Fin felt they surely must outnumber the guards.

Sam gave one last glance around to make certain all were freed, ignoring the whispered protests of those legitimately imprisoned.

"Let's go. Up the back hatch. Jack's waiting." They made for the hatchway, opened it, and climbed out onto the main deck.

The clicking of musketcocks rattled through the night air. A lantern spilled its light over Fin and her men and exposed their escape. The quarterdeck was circled with armed guards, each with a musket aimed. The polished tips of a dozen bayonets glinted in the fiery light, wavering in telltale uncertainty as pulses quickened in the viens of the guards who leveled them.

"Do not move," said the officer. Fin and the crew put their hands in the air. "None shall escape on my watch."

Then Jack stepped into the light behind him. He held a huge piece of timber in his hands, and before the officer could finish turning to see what had come upon him, Jack swung it, catching the man in the chest. The blow knocked the officer across the deck and he tumbled over the rail, disappearing into the darkness with a muted splash.

The crew didn't waste the opening; every man rushed a guard. Muskets fired. Men screamed. At once, the night was full of violence. The soldiers threw their spent muskets to the deck and grappled with the freed crew of the *Rattlesnake* in desperate cries and groans. Tan snatched a saber from one soldier, ran him through, and fenced with another across the deck toward the forecastle. Among them all Armand Defain slid like a shadow of death, his hidden daggers slicing flesh and bone. Fin let her fists fly upon any redcoat in her arm's reach. Jack stood giant-like, swinging his rough timber to and fro, wreaking ruin where it struck. Topper had roused himself to action and held a musket by its barrel, clubbing away at men with the butt. Knut, of all people, had even plucked a baling hook from the deck and flailed it wildly about him with a terrific yell—the fact that no one seemed to be attacking him stayed none of his ferocity.

For all the fight the guards put up, Fin suspected they'd never seen a day of combat in their poor lives. The unfortunate brutes had probably received their stations as prison guards precisely because they hadn't any fight in them—and it showed. The scuffle was over almost before it began. Some of the guards had even jumped overboard to swim for shore at the first sign of violence. When the melee ended, they permitted the wounded and surrendered to escape into the Atlantic with the benefit of a few barrels to keep them afloat until they could be rescued.

The initial musketfire had wounded several men, and Fin rushed to bandage and tend whom she could. Topper had taken a shot to the calf but shooed her away to mend the others when she tried to worry over him.

"That was a buggered mess!" complained Jack. "It was supposed to be quiet-like."

"Sorry, Jack. Done the best I could," said Sam, sheepishly.

"We got to blow out of here quick. The musketfire will have told the garrison there's trouble. They'll be out to see what all, soon enough. Tan, get them boys loaded in the skiff! Let's to shore."

As men moved toward the rail, a bell rang out in the distance, an alarm. They couldn't know what the trouble was yet, but it wouldn't take anyone long to find out. Jack roared curses.

"It's no good, Jack. We can't fit us all in that boat. By the time we get back for the second fill, there'll be redcoats all over the dock and water," said Tan.

"Why don't we raise sail and get out of here on this tub?" asked Fin. The thought hadn't occurred to Jack. The *Justice* was a fine ship-of-the-line when she was young, but she'd been stripped of most of her rigging. Only two of her three masts still stood, and from the looks of what they could see there was precious little tackle aboard to refit her. Jack shook his head.

"She's nothing but a rotten hulk. Hell, they have to tow her wherever she goes. Even if we could get a sail aloft, we've scant men to man her."

"I believe you may be mistaken, *monsieur*," said Armand Defain.

"Who in the rotten hell is this?" demanded Jack.

"Armand Defain," he offered with a bow. "I have been aboard this beast of a boat for . . . quite some time." He said it with pride and a smile. Fin was certain she despised him. He casually cleaned the blood from his daggers as he continued. "The *Justice* happens to carry in her hold all the spare tackle of the ship that tows her, as well as spare sail. She also has ready sail to move her about the bay at need. And you've never an abler or more willing crew accrued. The belly of the *Justice* is filled with sailors. They just need," he smiled, "a little room to grow." The daggers vanished into his shirt.

Tan looked to Jack. There was precious little time to decide. "We better hurry and do something, Jack."

Jack scratched his chin through his beard as he appraised Defain. He looked to the distant shoreline. The sound of the bells ceased and other sounds took their place, the sounds of voices, orders, the splash of oars.

"Free the prisoners, run out the sheets and halyards, get a sail up fast. Fin, you and Knut get aloft and check the mainsail. Get her ready. You," he pointed at Defain, "show Topper where the sails are. Topper, get us moving.

Tan, get these scabs to work. We've a ship to sail."

Without question the entire deck leapt to life, even the wounded found work to assist. Fin bounded up the mainmast with Knut close behind. They found the mainsail furled but ready to fly.

"Mainsail's good, Jack," yelled Fin.

"I'll be damned," muttered Jack.

Fin and Knut set to work and minutes later the mainsail was billowing in the wind. With a dull *whump* it snapped full and the ship lurched into motion. A cheer went up around the deck and the *Justice* lumbered away.

"Don't get comfortable. We can't outrun a dead whale until we get the rest of this rotten heap on the mend. Tan, get below and free what men you think can work."

"Defain, come with me," ordered Tan.

"Hold, Tan," called Jack. Tan stopped as he and Defain turned to face him. "What's the story with this one?"

"He helped us out here a bit."

Jack pondered him in silence.

"I am no friend of the British—" he seemed about to add something more, but tightened his lips and remained silent. Such an obvious admission clearly didn't garner him any trust in Jack's eyes. "I am in your service," added Defain with a slight bow.

"You seem to know quite a bit about this ship. Maybe you know something about the men locked up in her?"

"That I do. A wicked heart in each and every one. Thieves, murderers, mutineers, and worse—good sailors all," said Armand with a grin.

"Then I want you to go with Tan and advise him on which of them we can trust enough to run the ship without giving trouble. I get even a hint of ill-advised action out of any of them, and I'll shoot you."

"I don't want any of those beasts in the bilge let loose, those animals can rot," added Tan. Jack looked at him with a question on his lips but didn't voice it.

"We square, Mr. Defain?" asked Jack. Defain clicked his heels together and bowed.

"Alright then, let's go," said Tan. They turned away and disappeared below decks.

From the helm, Topper waved Jack over and asked him what heading to take.

"East for now, to the open sea. Later, we'll decide what to do."

"Ain't we heading after the *'Snake*, Jack?" frowned Topper.

"The *'Snake*? Hell, Creache is days away and devil knows where by now. He's headed to England if he knows what's good for him."

Behind Jack, Fin dropped out of the ropes and onto the deck. "He's not heading to England."

"And why would you say that?"

"He's headed for Savannah, for Ebenezer."

"Care to explain what the bloody pipe you're talking about?"

Fin told Jack her tale starting with Bartimaeus and ending with the map. Creache was heading straight for Ebenezer. There was no doubt in her mind.

"Thought you said you was done with the secrets," grumbled Jack when she finished. Fin half-smiled like a guilty child. "To the south and Savannah it is then." Jack turned to the open deck and shouted. "Bear her south, Topper. We've a *'Snake* to charm and a serpent to harm. Turn to, boys! Get this rubble running!"

By the time the sun peeked over the far waves, the crew had managed to fit both masts with sail. The *Justice* wasn't fast, but she was moving in the right direction. The rising sun brought bad news as well, though. Away to the north the missing prison ship had been discovered, and the British were mustering a pursuit. The tall sails of two ships of the line stood out sharp against the morning sky. Everyone on board knew they stood no chance in a race, and less chance in a fight against fully gunned men-o'-war. Yet, the mood was somehow both hopeful as well as grim. Hopeful, because they were free and had open sea before them. The men they'd freed from the cells below worked like they never had before in their lives; their freedom depended on it. But they also felt grim. Every heart knew those demons of the British fleet would have to be contended with before any surer freedom was secure.

Although the thoughts and worries of most of the men reached no further than the ships behind them and the sea before, Jack and Fin had further misgivings about what lay ahead. Savannah was but a two-day sail—less than a day and a half away, Jack estimated—but what they'd face when they got there was a grave shadow on any hope they had of reaching Creache and reclaiming the *Rattlesnake*. Savannah was British territory. There would be garrisons of troops and warships patrolling the harbor. What hope they had of slipping in unnoticed was dashed by the two ships that would be chasing them into the harbor. Even if they were lucky enough to make it that far, they'd be hemmed in on all sides with nowhere to go.

"It's damnable suicide," growled Jack.

"We'll figure something out," said Fin.

"Aye, *captain*," said Jack sarcastically. "Some of the boys might call ye captain, but that don't make it so, Button. I hear plenty of scuttlebutt about Captain Button and her pirate crew, but you best see it don't go to your head. What a man brags about in a dark tavern is a different beast than what the day sees him do. So don't you go believing what stories ye hear. Them kind of stories end at the gallows or in the dark below. You got yourself in some trouble back home and run away to the sea—that's fine. But half the men on this ship could tell that story, and none would be lying. So don't go thinking you're special just 'cause the local papers and the barroom poets take you to their fancy. I'm all for getting to Creache, and I'll see him dead if I have my way about it. Didn't want it to come to that, but it's clear now there'll be no rest for us till he's laid below. Don't go thinking this is all 'cause of some fool map. I'm interested in two things: the *Rattlesnake*, and a life free of looking over my shoulder."

Tan emerged from below decks with a troubled look on his face and waved down Jack. "We've got more problems."

"What now?"

"The wind ain't just pushing the ship, it's pulling her apart. The timbers are too old—too rotten. If we don't take in sail and lessen the stress on the masts, she'll rip herself to splinters."

"If we take in sail, the British will be on us by nightfall."

"Jack, we're taking on water. She's leaking like a drunk, and the bilge pumps are useless."

"We ain't taking in sail. Get every man aboard busy bailing. Start a bucket line and keep her emptied as best we can." Tan nodded and walked away shouting orders for anything that could hold water to be hurried below. Jack took a deep breath.

For the rest of the day the ship was abustle with the bailing of water from the hold. The bilge room that Fin and the others had been held in, where they met Defain, was filling with water, and from the far side the wretched prisoners howled and yelled to be loosed. No one moved to their aid, however, and Fin was glad of it. Those men could hardly be called human any longer. There was no telling what they'd do if loosed upon the ship. Armand Defain had somehow kept them in order while he was locked up, but in the open, with weapons of opportunity all about, there was no sure control of the madness that infected them.

All through the night, the bailing continued, and when the sun rose, the ships pursuing them had closed the distance by half. They were no more than a few miles behind them now. Jack estimated they'd see Savannah with sunrise the next morning if the wind held. At the same time, the ships behind would close to firing range. They were going to need a miracle.

By midday, men on the bucket line were passing out from exhaustion. Jack ordered them to split the work so half could rest. The resulting loss of manpower caused the ground they'd gained against the rising water to slowly disappear. Inch by inch, the ship was being swallowed by the sea. What small hopes they had when they first struck for open water were fading. All minds aboard were consumed with wondering which fate would finally claim them: the ships behind, the ships waiting ahead, or the sinking ship beneath their feet. Everywhere was despair. Topper held fast at the helm with his steady eye to the southern horizon.

"We're pickled this time, Jack," groaned Topper.

"Keep her south. Savannah's less than a day ahead. Long as we can keep this tub afloat, we'll be fine."

"What's the good of getting to Savannah if we're stuck when we get there?"

Jack didn't answer; he swung away and shoved himself into the bucket chain.

"Hurry up there, Sam, with that bucket! Somebody sing us a song to keep the time," yelled Jack at the weary crew. Down the line, from somewhere in the hold, where the water was high and the light dim, came back a low booming voice.

Sailed from south sea
gnawin' on a bone
into the North Sea
cold as stone.
Set for the West with
the briny and foam.
Never goin' East 'cause
West goes home.

As the song flowed, the men down the line joined in, and the music grew faster and fuller. The buckets passed from hand to hand in rhythm, and though none could say they were light of spirit, the song at least lightened a heavy mood and kept despair at bay.

Sailed on a high sea,
stormy and mean.
Lost in a far sea,
stars unseen.
Had a keg of rum
but was only a dream.
When I die, I'll head West
to the Fiddler's Green.

All day they sang songs and passed the buckets. Jack called out shift changes, and some slept while others grumbled back to the line to take up the work. Throughout it all, the water continued to rise. The water in the bilge was almost waist high, and the ship was riding visibly lower in the water. Behind them the British were closing, and by dusk they'd come nearly inside gun range. As the first stars were flickering through the amber wash, the first cannon fire boomed. The shot fell well short, perhaps half a mile. The British were testing range. It wouldn't be long. Luckily, however, the night would conceal them. The warships would be within gun range sometime before midnight, Jack guessed, but night would cloak them, keep them safe. Morning would be another matter.

Quietly, Jack called Tan and Fin away from the line.

"We're safe for the night, but come morning the sun's gonna betray us and we'll have a fight. Need you to talk to that Armand Defain bugger and find out what he knows about the ship's arms. I been poking around below, and we got twenty good cannons but no powder or ball that I can see."

Tan nodded and Jack turned back to the line. Fin called over Armand Defain.

"Is there any powder aboard? Any cannonshot?" she asked him.

"We're going to fight them then?" he said, chuckling. "I cannot say I think we have much chance, but it will certainly be . . . invigorating." Fin didn't think dying sounded particularly invigorating at all.

"Is there gunpowder aboard or not?"

"Powder, *oui*. A reserve magazine. Follow me." Defain led them down to the gundeck and along a narrow corridor to a large set of double doors that were chained and locked. Tan retrieved a hatchet from stowage and hacked at the door. He cut away enough to peer inside and saw half a dozen powder kegs sitting peacefully in the dark, waiting patiently for their hour of waking. On the floor beside the kegs lay crates of nine-inch cannonballs, and on the walls hung a complement of muskets and sabers.

"Got plenty of powder and small arms for the crew. Only about twenty cannonshot though. That's enough for one volley," reported Tan.

They finished tearing the door away from its frame and rolled the powder kegs out into the main room. Tan was happy to find the crew's confiscated weapons in the closet, and his rapier was among them. He strapped it on and looked instantly more hopeful. He and Fin picked up what knives and gear they recognized as the crew's and went up on deck to return it. The effect upon the sailors was much the same as on Tan. Having their own weapons at their sides gave them all a bit more hope than they'd had without. Fin thought of Betsy and longed to feel the weight of the old thunder-gun tucked away in her belt, but it was aboard the *Rattlesnake*, along with her fiddle. No comfort for her. She put it out of her mind.

They reported what they'd found to Jack. He'd hoped for enough ammunition to muster a good fight, but there was little to do about it so he ordered them to get some sleep before the sun came up. They'd need all their strength when it did.

Fin crawled wearily into a corner. She curled up on a pile of mouldy rope and tried to sleep but it was long in coming; there was much trouble on her mind. She might not live through the coming morning, but it wasn't the dying she minded. It was the things dying took away. If she died she'd never get the satisfaction of seeing Tiberius Creache dead for his crimes. She'd never get the chance to stop him before he could plunder her home, kill the people she loved, and steal Bartimaeus's treasure. She'd never see Peter again. That aching thought hurt her the most. She wouldn't mind dying if she could see Peter again. If she could tell him how sorry she was for leaving, for all the mistakes she'd made. Did he even care? It had been over two years since she'd seen him. Suddenly, she was sure that all hope of him patiently farming their land and waiting for his lost girl to come home was nothing more than a silly dream in a dim reality. Tears came, and she sobbed quietly into her arm, hoping no one could hear. She wept herself into sleep and dreamed.

She saw a misty wood of pecan and pine that broke suddenly onto a wide green field surrounding a peaceful cabin. Children ran and laughed across the grass, and in the shade of the house was a man tapping the arms of a rocking chair into place with a carpenter's mallet. His face was lost in the shadows. He laid the mallet down and, like a lover, gently traced the lines of the chair with his finger. Then he set himself to rest in his finished piece, and though the shadows hid his face, Fin knew he was smiling. He produced a pipe from his pocket and stoked it to life like an old memory as he rocked in the chair.

Then Fin saw a second chair, in the shadows, more slender and more delicate than the one he sat upon. He reached over and drew it into the light at his side. He looked across the grass at Fin and motioned her to sit beside him. She wanted nothing so much as to join him and sit. She took a timorous step forward, but as soon as her foot touched the grass, the world erupted in thunder. She looked to the sky and saw a great black ship, its sides ablaze with cannon fire. Cannonballs crashed into the cabin, sending splinters across the field. Thunder again, and the children were dying. Thunder again, and all was in ruin. The ship floated off behind a darker cloud, and she fell to her knees weeping. She looked up, and amid the wreck of the scene, the carpenter sat silent and still as an oak, smoking his pipe; beside him still the empty chair waited.

"Fin, come," he said.

"I can't," cried Fin. One step upon that grass had brought ruin and death. How could she bear the many steps to cross the distance?

"Fin, come," he said again and she wailed.

"Fin, *come on!*" said a voice above her, and she opened her eyes. Knut was shaking her shoulder and shouting at her to wake up. Cannons fired in the distance. "Fin, get up!"

All at once, she leapt awake. The sun was rising.

CHAPTER XXII

IN RAN OUT OF her cabin and jerked to a stop. In the dim glimmer-light of dawn she felt immediately that the sea was too near.

At first she thought it was a trick of the light, but it wasn't; the *Justice* was riding perilously low in the water. The sea was patiently rising to consume them. Like a great behemoth, it stretched its maw wide beneath the ship and awaited the fall of its prey.

A flash from the north caught her eye, and seconds later, the report of distant cannons broke the morning. Behind her, she heard a ball splash into the sea. The British were in range. The light didn't permit a good shot yet, but it was only a matter of time.

Fin frowned to herself and felt a pang of guilt that she'd slept so long while others worked through the night baling water to keep them afloat. She rushed toward the chain of men where, despite the encroaching water and cannonfire, the crew still sang and passed the buckets in time. If the sound was merry however, the faces of those singing were less so. They turned and greeted her with mock cheer and the resolution of men marching toward their own deaths. She shouldn't have slept so long.

From down the hatch, raised voices floated up to her: angry, fearful. She lit down into the hold and picked Tan's voice out of the clamor, then Jack's. They were arguing amid many voices.

"Let them rot, Jack!" shouted Tan over the din. He was standing knee deep in water at the top of the steps leading down to the bilge. From behind the locked door, from Armand Defain's lair, came the snarls and yelps of those filthy and barely human creatures that had meant to have their way with her. Fin shuddered at the noise and clamor from behind the door and felt a shameful relief that those dregs were locked away behind it. They would surely drown within the hour.

Jack stood at the door, perplexed, arguing to free the prisoners locked within. Tan was firmly against it. Armand Defain stood to the side observing the discourse with twisted amusement. A few days ago, he'd called those men his crew, but now he was utterly indifferent to their fate.

Jack turned to Defain. "Can you keep these buggers under your thumb?" he asked.

Defain held up his hands, palms outward, and grinned. "They have been kept long, and much abused. They may act . . . unpredictably." The notion seemed to amuse him, and he continued with a smile, "They could be most ferocious if loosed upon the English."

Jack pondered him a moment then turned to Tan, still undecided.

"They're black-hearted murderers, Jack, evil to the marrow. Leave 'em be."

"Don't do it, Jack, don't let them out. I don't trust him," said Fin, her eyes fixed firmly on Defain.

"Alright, the door stays locked—for now. But I don't aim to let men drown, no matter what they've done. Before that room fills to the top, the door opens and we'll deal with the devil that comes of it." He didn't wait for protest; he turned and climbed the steps back onto the deck. Fin and Tan exchanged a worried look. Then Tan, quick as a cat, grabbed Armand Defain by the shirt and hoisted his small frame against the bulkhead.

"If your dogs get out, I expect you to tend them. If they so much as touch one of my mates, you'll answer with blood."

"But of course," nodded Defain with the slightest smirk. Tan pushed him away and disappeared down the hall to the gun deck. Defain didn't appear shaken by Tan's threats. His eyes followed Tan as he departed, then he turned them on the half-submerged door and grinned at the voices thundering through it. The hairs on Fin's neck rose. She turned away to chase after Jack.

The sun was spilling fire into the sky, burning away the last remnants of safety that the darkness had provided. The British ships in chase were within half a mile. A white cloud erupted from the bow of the nearest ship and eclipsed all but the top-most sails. Seconds later, the rumble of cannons rasped across the *Justice*. Two balls splashed into the water less than twenty paces off the starboard. It was only a matter of time before they found their mark and battered the *Justice* into the sea.

Jack belched orders to any man not bailing water. Topper stood at the helm visibly exhausted. He'd been at the wheel since they fled, and he looked like he might collapse if he let go of it. There was no jest left in him; his spirit was consumed by wind and wave, tack and time. Fin ran to the end of the bailing line and relieved a bedraggled looking man dressed in rags, a former prisoner of the *Justice*. The buckets came steadily. She heaved the water overboard and hurried the bucket back up the line for more. Within minutes, her arms ached from the work—work that others had been at for hours.

Again came the sharp crack and rumble of cannonfire, and a ball crashed into the deck, splintering a hole the size of a wine-cask just aft of the main-mast. The song of the bailing line faltered. Shouts of fear and shock arose. Then Topper began yelling. He was pointing across the bow. Away to the southwest rose the sails of two tall ships, heavily armed and apt to war. The men on deck saw them and began to wail.

"We'll be splintered and sunk!" they cried. Another cannonball crashed onto the deck as if in punctuation. Now they were running from danger into despair. Hope of reaching Savannah was gone, and all eyes turned to Jack with angry shouts and fearful pleas.

"Run up the white flag," cried some.

"Damn 'em to fire and the devil's mercy," cried others.

Above the cries Jack shouted, "Beat to arms! We'll not drink the brine before we're drunk on English blood!" Men rushed below and found Tan on the gundeck already passing out what weaponry he'd scrounged. He tossed Fin a cutlass and he was smiling his blood smile. The promise of battle was thick about him, and Tan breathed it like air. Fin had no reason to smile, but danger was afoot and Tan was in his element. She tucked the cutlass into her belt and snatched a battered old pistol off the wall. She wondered momentarily where Knut had got off to and plucked a second pistol off the wall to give to him when he turned up. Tan tossed her a powder horn and a pouch of musket ball before the men behind muscled her out the door, anxious to arm their own defense.

She darted back up on deck and joined Topper at the helm. He looked like the walking dead, like a withered and bloated corpse strapped to the wheel, defiant unto death. The sun had burned his face and chapped his lips. His eyes shone despair like cold moonlight, betraying none of the good nature she'd come to love.

"We'll be alright, Topper. We always have been," she said and smiled at him. He didn't seem to hear her.

Jack's voice boomed across the deck, "Get them cannons loaded, boys!" Then bending low to shout down the hatch, "Tan! See to it!" From below came the dull rumble of cannons hauled into place. "Topper, bring her 'round, and keep her straight down their throats 'til I give the word. Don't give 'em any more target than we got to." Topper didn't move. Jack stepped in front of him and roared into his face, "Topper, I'll box your ears and smack you clean if you can't follow an order and answer an aye!" Jack meant no ill will but he had no choice; he had to lean hard. Topper was a master at the wheel, and Jack couldn't afford to lose him. He needed to push him. Topper blinked and clenched his jaw.

"Aye, Jack. I'm alright."

Jack lingered, appraising his condition. Topper hauled the wheel over, and the ship lurched to port. The *Justice* came around and drove straight into the English cannonfire that they'd eluded all night.

Tan appeared from below and reported the cannons ready to fire. "One volley is all we got, Jack."

"Best make it a good one," he muttered.

Ahead of them, white smoke billowed from the bows of both English ships and cannonshot splashed water onto the deck—near misses. The wind was from the northwest and, unable to tack for want of presenting a broadside target, they all but crawled through the water, sails flapping with slack. Then the ships ahead of them split, one turned west, one east. They were forcing Jack to choose. Whichever he turned to follow, the *Justice* would present her broadside to the other. Jack spat a curse and ordered Topper to keep dead bearing on the easternmost ship. Behind them, the two ships coming up from Savannah were still at a distance but approaching quickly. Fin tried not to consider what would happen when they also came within firing range.

"Tan, get over here," called Jack. "Unload the cannons on the port gunwale. We need two full volley off the starboard." Tan nodded and hurried to make it so. "Every man not on a cannon, get your boots on deck, and make ready to grapple and board." Men lined the rails, loaded their muskets, and brought out hooks and line.

"What are you going to do, Jack?" asked Fin.

Jack didn't answer. He looked as if he were debating whether or not he should reply. After a few tense moments, he looked at her and spoke in a hushed voice. "Make sure you hold on tight, and stay clear of the bow." Fin had no idea what to make of that information, and the look on her face told Jack as much. "Get to the rail, Button." He would say no more.

Fin hurried away to find Knut. He was at the stern peering intently at the ships bearing up from Savannah. She held the extra pistol out in front of him. "Take this." Knut lifted his arm and pointed at the ships behind them. "I know, Knut. Now take the pistol." He didn't seem to hear her. He simply stared south toward the ships as they approached. Cannonshot split the air and the ship shuddered. They'd been hit again. Fin flinched and swore under her breath. She didn't have time or patience for Knut's games. "Fine, suit yourself," she said and rushed away to find a spot along the portside rail.

The two ships in front of them were some four hundred yards apart. Topper steered straight toward one, its masts bloomed with sail, its bowsprit stabbed toward them anxious and saber-sharp, and from her mizzen flapped a massive Union Jack beating the wind like a drummer. The other ship was directly off their starboard; her gunwales were opening up, her cannons running out.

"Tan, as soon as the volley is away I want them cannons reloaded—fast," bellowed Jack down the hatch. Tan's muffled voice shouted back assent. The crew had arrayed themselves along the rails of the ship, a few still packing their muskets. Fin plucked her pistol from her belt and packed the barrel, then readied the one she'd gotten for Knut as well. Two shots, no more, then blades.

"Listen up!" roared Jack over the wind. "We got two full load of cannon to throw at that bastard yonder," he pointed off the starboard side toward the English warship that was now almost within a stone's throw. "Then we ram this tub of rotten timber into the other. We leave the rest to the Lord above and devil below." Around the deck, eyes widened and the collective intake of breath seemed to out-whistle the wind. "Be ready on your hooks. Be quick to board. Give hell with your guns, redden wet your knives, and we'll sing of it when I see ye again on the Fiddler's Green."

He paused and took a deep breath, filling his barrel-chest with the cool air so that when he spoke again his voice exploded horn-like and deep. "We ready, boys?" shouted Jack with a defiant howl.

Sam Catcher raised his cutlass into the air and cursed ruin upon the king and all his men. One after another, the men on deck took to shouting defiance and waving their weapons until the whole ship was a din of hatred raised.

Then the ship off the starboard rail loosed her broadside cannons, and the world exploded in a fury of splinter and scream. Cannonballs punched through the gunwales and deck of the *Justice* with terrifying force, sending men and debris hurtling through the air, landing broken on deck or plunged into the dark Atlantic. In seconds, the *Justice* was riddled with the bloodied and dead.

"*Now*, Tan!" cried Jack, and the guns of the *Justice* answered. Her starboard broadsides detonated and the ship shuddered and groaned under the power of the report. Vast white clouds of gunsmoke billowed from the iron throats of her cannons. The smell of powder woke in Fin's nostrils and stung her eyes. Jack shouted for the reload, and in moments Tan called up the all-ready.

"*Fire!*" cried Jack without waiting for the air to clear, and the guns bellowed again. Through the smoke they heard the impact of ball upon wood and knew the mark was struck.

The men sent up a cheer but in the midst of it came Topper's warning from the helm, "*HOLD FAST!*"

Every head spun around, and for a splinter of time all was silent and still. The ship in front of them was mere feet away, its deck crowded with red-coated British soldiers. An ocean swell heaved the prow of the *Justice* up so that in that moment it seemed they towered over the British warship, descending like a thunderbird from airy heights, talons thrust forth, wreathed in the ancient, red aura of war.

For that singular second, the men aboard both vessels peered across the gulf at one another, rigid with fear and frozen by memories of home, and of women loved and children born, and of all others they might never see again. And in response they called out of the dark reaches of man's collective nightmare that beast that stirs and quickens to violence, that savors the taste of the enemy's throat, the bloodthirst that blinds reason and makes of men a berzerking force of rage with curled lips and bared, animal teeth. Then, like a thunderclap, the ships smashed one upon the other. The aged and rotted timbers of the *Justice* crumpled against the gunwales of the warship like paper. The decks rolled and trembled and heaved and the stacatto popping of wood rattled the air as elemental forces of gravity and inertia and the hoary sea itself took hold of the *Justice* and twisted the ship apart.

Fin ran headlong from stern to bow and leapt as the ships met, letting her momentum throw her into battle. She drew both pistols and spent their issue upon the soldiers doomed below, then lit upon the deck with sword in hand. Her crewmates cried as one and let fly their hooks. They hurtled across the rail in a tide of swinging ropes, whitened knuckles, and thirsty blades. As the crew of the *Justice* fled her groaning hull and boarded the British vessel, they turned their hatred to the work of war. With rusty cutlasses, they drove into the British, painting strokes of crimson across the deck.

The *Justice* was failing quickly; the sea rushed into her, gurgling through the emptiness of her holds like a beast gorging on the blood of its prey. Jack steadied himself on the tilting deck, urging every man to escape the *Justice* before it was too late.

"Defain! Open the bilge!" roared Jack. Armand Defain disappeared down a hatch, and a growl arose from the lower decks. Defain, grinning like murder, reappeared, and from behind him, like a dark cloud, came those mongrels of the bilge: half naked, filthy, and drunken on bloodlust. Defain pointed to the British vessel and commanded them with a word. Like wild animals, they howled and ran with lolling tongues, leaping from the wreck of the *Justice* to assail the British with bare hands and teeth. Horror and disgust took what men they flung themselves upon, and they preyed easily. Defain looked on, laughing with wicked glee. Then, fetching daggers from his shirt, he darted in amongst them.

Fin parried and dodged, agile and untouchable amongst the stiffly uniformed soldiers. Tan was beside her, his grin as quick and sharp as his blade. Her long hours of fencing lessons came unbidden to her sword arm, and she carved her way through the enemy in a fury of steel. She glimpsed Armand a few yards across the deck, swirling among the British like a mist, his daggers flashing in a grim coalescence of death. Each bite of his daggers fed the villainous smile upon his face. But it was far different from Tan's smile. Tan's pleasure arose from challenge and action, Armand's from cruelty and death. Armand's eyes found her suddenly, and with horror, Fin realized she also was smiling. His eyes shone and his smile deepened. Fin wrenched herself away from his stare and ground her teeth to quench the smile.

A figure rose in front of her, dark and terrible, snarling like a beast. One of Defain's dogs. He twisted up a licentious grin and lunged at her. Then an arm seized him by the throat, snatching him from midair, and pinned him to the deck. Daggers opened his throat, and Armand looked up from his work and winked at her before spinning away and hurling himself back among the British.

Behind her, the last groans of the *Justice* followed the ruined ship as it slipped beneath the waves. Jack and Topper were the last to come aboard and stood back to back: Topper, swinging his cutlass in wild, bloody arcs; Jack, hammering blows upon men with fists like stone.

The British ship didn't appear to have suffered at all from the collision. Its stalwart timber was more than a match for the rotten hull of the *Justice*. Then, with dismay, Fin saw across the water that the other British vessel, the one they'd fired upon, had also suffered little damage. It was bearing straight for them. In minutes, it would be alongside and her complement of soldiers would join the fight. Fin recalled Knut pointing ominously at the two ships approaching from the south. She jerked her gaze around and beheld their last despair. Those ships also were only moments away. No matter what the outcome of the battle on deck, they would never survive whatever fate the remaining three ships offered.

Fin clenched her jaw and launched herself at the nearest soldier with renewed fury. She spewed curses as she fought, cursing Creache for his cruelty and greed, cursing herself for being helpless to prevent his violation of her home.

She slew two men and three appeared to take their place. She saw red-coated soldiers streaming out of every hatchway like blood from an open wound. Even this victory would be denied her. Fin and her company of desperate sailors couldn't hold the deck for more than a few more breaths. They were too few.

They gathered in a small circle with what remained of the *Justice*'s make-shift crew. Jack was on her left and Tan, her right. Topper was there also, along with Armand Defain, Sam Catcher, and few others. All around them circled more British troops. She cast around franticly looking for help, for hope, but there was none.

"We made a good run of it, boys," said Jack. No one spoke. Around them, soldiers brought forward muskets and leveled them at Fin and her companions, ordering their surrender. Jack was the first to drop his sword and raise his hands. Reluctantly, the others followed suit.

A dull thump shook the deck as one of the two ships from the south knocked alongside.

Jack swore, and his eyes widened in disbelief. "By the milk of a mermaid's blessed breast!"

Musket fire crackled through the morning air, and three British fell dead at Jack's feet. Fin looked around in confusion. From the ship alongside she saw a wave of blue-coated soldiers leap onto the deck with flashing swords. First among them was Ned Smithers and behind him, Fred Martin. Their muskets spat fire and belched smoke, and British soldiers all around fell dead.

"Ho! Jack Wagon!" cried Ned with a laugh. Then a flurry of red-haired O'Malleys dressed in blue uniforms came crashing onto the deck and, with a loud cry, set themselves to war.

Fin looked up the mast of the ship alongside. Atop it flew a flag she'd never seen. Stripes white and red ran across its flanks and a crown of white stars adorned its deep blue shoulder. Not a British flag at all. Then the report of cannons rollicked across the waves, and she looked around to see another ship borne from the south, the same flag raised above her, assaulting the other British vessel. The Continental Marines had joined the battle.

Chapter XXIII

THE MARINES STREAMED ABOARD the British warship, and Fin and her companions charged back into the fight. Jack laughed loud and threw himself at the British. His laughter spoke what was in all their hearts: hope, amazement, joy. Ned Smithers and Fred Martin. The last time any had seen them was in Tun Tavern, Philadelphia, when Jack had tried to knock them flat for jumping ship. A fortunate twist of fate is never ill-spent upon an old sailor, so Jack bellowed a laugh to quake the timbers of the earth. Over the screams and sounds of war rose the resounding peal of his laughter like a call to battle and a cry of victory.

The solid reinforcement of marines boarding the ship struck fear into the English, but they had no avenue of retreat. As the O'Malley brothers gleefully fought their way across the deck, their ferocity turned English faces white with terror. When they reached the forecastle, the last Englishmen, trapped between the Irish and the rail, threw themselves overboard to escape. Tan led a group down the hatch into the belly of the ship and flushed out what men remained below. They emerged, fleeing Tan and his men, to find Ned Smithers and a group of marines waiting with muskets. Soon the clatter of surrendered arms falling to the deck rattled around the ship as British soldiers and sailors flung them away and begged for mercy. Of the few British who still breathed, some quivered and prostrated themselves before the company, and many more flung themselves into the sea rather than beg succor.

Across the waves, a mile distant, the marines' sister ship harried the remaining British vessel with cannonfire as it fled east. A riotous cheer arose from Fin and all those around her. A smile that she could wear without shame spread across her face.

"Lucky for you lot, we happened along," said Ned Smithers with a raised eyebrow and a grin. Jack bellowed another laugh that split the air like a cannonade.

"Lucky I let you go in Philly," said Jack. The crew gathered round and laughed. "Just what in bloody hell are you boys doing out here, Ned?"

"It's no accident. We're bound north with dire news of the war. The English are moving out of Savannah, sweeping north, burning and pillaging as they go. Word is they aim to take Georgia and the rest of the South while Washington is busy in the North. We make for Philadelphia for reinforcements."

"Bloody hell. How far are we from Savannah then?" asked Jack.

"We just run north of the river when we saw your sail. Savannah's right 'round the hill there." Ned pointed southwest. "Now you want to tell us what you're doing here?"

"You seen the 'Snake?" asked Jack.

"No, but I heard from others it passed up the Savannah sometime yesterday."

"We aim to take her."

Ned eyed him warily, as if he wasn't sure how much he wanted to know. Jack stared back, quiet a moment, before deciding to elaborate. "We set Creache adrift. Reckon you heard about that."

"Aye, we heard. Can't say I believe everything I hear, though."

"Believe it. Had it coming, he did."

"I don't need convincing. He's the reason me and Fred run off."

"Aye. Now the bastard's got us on the run. Turned us in as pirates. Ain't but one way to put an end to it."

"You'd best keep your head down. You and your crew are wanted men and not just by the British. Your name's up for bounty in every port from here to Boston. What do you aim to do, Jack? We'll help if we can, but we're in the middle of a war."

"Think we can sail this tub up the river without raising too many questions?"

"Well, you don't want to put in at Savannah, that's for sure. You lot walking off a ship o' the line would draw more attention than you want to deal with. And the British have the mouth of the river blockaded. They'll board and search any vessel going upriver."

"Any vessel except one of their own," said Tan with a devilish grin. Ned and Jack considered it in silence.

"Might work. Might get you dead all the same," said Ned.

"If we get through, you got any idea what's waiting upriver?" asked Jack.

"Well, so far the British haven't bothered much with Georgia. Been satisfied to sit in Savannah and control the river. But they aim to change that. They're headed toward Ebenezer, we reckon, and like as not, the British will be there within a day. Augusta within the month."

"Ebenezer?" exclaimed Fin.

"A little town a few miles upriver."

"That's where Creache is going!"

"Aye, seems so."

"Creache is going to Ebenzer?" asked Ned.

"Long story—but Fin's right."

"Fin?" asked Ned with a confused look. The last time he saw her, he thought her a man. Ned didn't even recognize her. "The Fin Button that's got the British trade running like scared goats?"

Fin blushed.

"Aye, that's the one. Not that she done a fat lot of scaring without the rest of us," muttered Jack. Fred's eyes bulged and Ned's mouth dropped open.

"Don't believe everything you hear," added Fin.

"Well, bloody hell!" cursed Ned, and both of them broke into belly laughs. Fin rolled her eyes at Tan, who smiled back and laughed at her.

"Alright you two, off to your ship. We're making for Savannah, then upriver."

"Best keep that Union Jack waving if you aim to slip past the blockade without trouble."

"What's the name of this tub anyway?" Jack wondered.

"The *Monarch*," said Fred.

Jack chuckled and spit on the deck. "Always wanted to spit on a king." Tan shook his head and groaned at Jack's humor. "Alright then, off with you. Let's go."

Jack wasted no time. He swung around and spat his orders to the crew. Of the fifty or more that had climbed aboard from the *Justice*, less than thirty remained. Ned and the other marines bound what British still lived and hustled them across the rail onto Ned's ship, the *Constellation*, where they disappeared below decks—prisoners of war.

Fin and the crew followed Jack's orders and commenced to clearing the *Monarch* of bodies. The deck was slick with blood, and it was a gruesome task. Those of the crew that had died, they carried below to await an honorable burial at sea; the British dead they threw overboard. Fin spotted Armand Defain against the rail, rifling through the pockets of a dead British officer. He happily slipped a pocket watch and ring into his shirt. She wrinkled her nose in disgust and then noted with satisfaction that all of Defain's "dogs" seemed to have perished in the fighting. Defain raised his head and caught her looking at him. He grinned at her as he pushed the officer's body over the rail.

Fin and Sam Catcher worked their way aft cleaning off the deck. As they picked up the last dead soldier and tossed him over the rail, they heard a curious thump and a grunt before the body splashed into the water. Fin stuck her head out over the rail and looked down. Clinging desperately to a rubbing strip, just above the waterline, was Knut. They'd thrown the body on top of him.

"Howdy, Fin!" he called, as if nothing of any import were taking place. Sam fetched a rope from the deck and threw it down. They hauled him up and checked him over for injury as he sat and shivered like a drenched rat.

"Are you alright? Are you hurt?" asked Fin as she inspected him bodily like a mother.

"I'm alright, Fin. I couldn't find nobody. The ship—I think it hit something. Then I fell in the water and couldn't find nobody there either. Then I couldn't find the ship no more even. I was scared you guys was some of them English fellas. So I was trying to be quiet for I wouldn't get killed like that man that just jumped on top of me."

Fin and Sam looked at each other and shook their heads in amazement.

When the deck was clear, Jack ordered every man below to find himself a British uniform. If they were to slip by the blockade, they were going to have to look the part.

"Let's find you some dry clothes, Knut," said Fin as she pulled him across the deck by the arm.

There were plenty of clothes to choose from; a full crew and compliment of British marines had manned the *Monarch*. She found him some breeches and a plain shirt and coat and then left him to change. A few minutes later, she returned to check on him and found he'd fallen asleep on the floor where she left him. At least he put the clothes on first. She left him sleeping and scurried back to the main deck.

While they sailed the short distance to the Savannah River, the crew adorned themselves in red coats and tricornes. Jack slipped a coat over his bulky frame, but, as none on the ship were even close to his size, there was no hope of him looking natural in it. The sleeves ran only to his elbows, and it was so tight that his arms refused to hang straight. Instead, they arched out from his body, making him look like a giant red penguin.

"Damned skinny limeys," Jack muttered. "Not a word, Tan."

Tan burst into laughter, and Jack's face turned as red as the coat. He reached out to swat Tan, and the seams of the coat split clean apart. Jack ripped off the tattered pieces of the coat and threw them onto the deck, then kicked them across the rail.

Fin found clothes of a much better fit. She felt strange wearing a dead man's clothes—and an Englishman's at that. Like the Union Jack flapping in the wind overhead, it was too big a lie. It made her feel unclean. Tan snapped his heels together and saluted when she walked onto the deck. Jack rolled up his eyes.

From the helm, Topper yelled, "Captain on deck!" Fin glared at him and everyone around broke into laughter.

Topper eased the ship around the southern shoulder of South Carolina and approached the mouth of the Savannah River. A British frigate in execution of the blockade was waiting to greet them.

"Alright, boys, keep your wits—and no horsing around," said Jack.

"Jack, you best get in the cabin," said Tan. Jack's size and lack of proper dress made him suspicious. Jack grumbled under his breath, and then ducked through a hatchway to watch the passage through the porthole.

"Steady, Topper. Act like we're supposed to be here," said Tan over his shoulder.

The British frigate in the mouth of the river ran up signal flags.

"What's that mean?" asked Fin.

"They mean us to give way and let their captain aboard—to check papers and ask questions most likely," replied Tan.

"What do we do?"

Jack called Tan to the hatchway. They talked quietly for a moment, and then Tan gave orders for two men to help him look for the ship's signal flags. They found the flags stowed in a locker, and Tan found what he was looking for. He ran up two flags and then came back to the rail to wait.

"What are we telling them?" asked Fin.

"Told them to stay clear, said we're having trouble maneuvering."

"Will that work?"

"We'll find out."

The other ship was only a couple hundred yards off the port rail. Tan raised a hand in friendly gesture. On the deck of the other ship, Fin could clearly see their captain peering at them with his spyglass.

"Easy boys, look natural," said Jack from the doorway.

Another signal flag ran up the mast of the blockade ship.

"They're asking if we require assistance," explained Tan. He turned and ordered Sam to signal back that they did not. Sam ran the flag, and they waited. Aboard the other ship, the captain consulted with another officer. The captain handed the spyglass over, and the other man peered at them.

The two men consulted again while Fin and the crew waited. Sweat rolled down Tan's face. The deck was silent; every breath was kept long, and drawn through gritted teeth. Then the blockading ship gave way. Her captain waved, and Tan returned the gesture. They were through. Tan wiped the sweat from his face and grinned.

"Nothing to it," he said.

Chapter XXIV

THEY SLIPPED QUIETLY PAST the city of Savannah and saw along the banks that the British were well prepared for war. Soldiers had overturned boats and small ships at regular intervals to use as defensive positions, and all the marshy land between the riverbank and the higher ground of the city proper was speckled with wooden fortifications to hinder any ground advance. It wasn't the Savannah she'd left behind. It was darker, as if war had pushed the light from it, leaving a desolation of brown and grey where once had been green. The sounds of life were gone. The country near the city held its music back, waiting, wondering when the crouching beast of war might stir.

Fin's eyes turned northward, toward home. Two years had passed since last she saw it. She prayed the shadow cast on Savannah hadn't stretched so far as Ebenezer. She leaned against the rail and looked out at the familiar pines and cypress of the Georgia riverbank. The city slipped away to the southeast, and gradually the land emerged from the grey cast of war and became itself again. It hadn't changed, not yet. The trees still rose straight and thin; they still shed their leaves and straw to carpet the forest in shades of autumn and rust. The same wet smell of pine and mud filled her nose. The birds singing and the sounds of animals splashing in the river were no different now than when she and Peter walked in silence and threw stones to pass the time. No shadow here, not yet.

When she left, she was a scared girl, running from the consequences of a scared girl's actions. *Murder*, whispered a voice inside her. Bartimaeus's smile erupted in her mind as the rope snapped his neck. She shut her eyes. What would he think of what she'd become—a pirate, a murderer. *Terrible things.* He gave up all of that, and even though he left his old life behind, he hadn't hesitated to step forward and place his neck in the noose when they came for him. All because he'd protected her—and now she rendered his sacrifice worthless by her actions.

She hated herself. She'd been smiling as she killed soldiers today. Defain had seen her; he'd approved. Something inside her enjoyed it. No matter how far she ran from it, that smile lurked in the darkness, waiting patiently to rule her like a tyrant. But at this very moment, Creache was in Ebenezer, wreaking what havoc she couldn't imagine. If that smile could help, if that murderous tendril of spirit inside her could stop him, she would embrace it.

The river wound inland like a snake. Topper, renewed by the morning's action, no longer showed signs of exhaustion and worked fervidly steering the ship around the curls of the river. Even a mighty ship of the line could appear small and insignificant out on the open sea, but here, constricted amongst the trees, banks, and bends of a land-bounded world, the ship was unwieldy, awkward, out of place. It made the men nervous.

Fin stood near the prow, straining her eyes through the trees, looking for any familiar stone, bank, or grotto that would tell her she was home. The ship crept along in silence. Every tree that slipped past pulled the invisible knots in her stomach tighter. Fin needed to see what was coming. She needed a better view, needed to know what to expect. She ran to the base of the mainmast and hauled herself up the ladder to the crow's nest. Topper's voice called out, asking if she was alright. She didn't answer him.

She reached the top and looked fearfully out across the canopy of the forest. She didn't know what she expected to see, didn't know what she feared to find. Only a riddle of mottled brown and rolling yellow treetops greeted her. She felt better though, more at ease, more ready to meet what awaited her. From up here she could see. She breathed deeply and dared to think that maybe everything would be alright after all. Peter was out there somewhere, in these very woods. She traced the line of the river northwest to a point where something stopped her eye. In a small bend of the river, some few miles ahead, she picked out a straight brown line jutting up just above the treetops. A mast. The *Rattlesnake*. Her breath caught in her chest, and she searched the line of the treetops south of the mast. She couldn't be sure she saw it at first, but the more she stared, the more certain she became. Rising just above the trees was a white swan perched on a bell tower. The chapel. Home came back to her in a rush, and suddenly every smell and stone was familiar. She dropped through the gate of the crow's nest and swung down the ladder.

"We're almost there, Topper," she said.

"Best go find Jack."

RE-ARMING THE CREW WAS easy. All they had to do was report to the armory. Every man took a musket, a pistol, and whatever blades he found that suited him best. Topper put the *Monarch* at anchor downriver from the *Rattlesnake*, out of sight.

Jack urged everyone to silence. They lowered the rowboats into the river and rowed to the shore in an uneasy silence, all eyes and ears strained for signs of trouble. Once they reached the bank, Jack climbed up into the cover of the woods and motioned everyone to gather around.

"Alright boys, I know you're tired." A collective groan seeped out of the crew. Most were running on nothing more than hope and adrenaline. "Stay lively a little while longer," said Jack. "Soon as we get the *'Snake* back we'll make for open sea and find us a quiet port to disappear into. But first things first. There's no telling how many hands Creache has on board the *'Snake*. But he didn't waste time pulling out of Charleston, so I'm guessing the *'Snake* ain't full. Likely a skeleton crew." Heads nodded. "Creache'll be anxious to get underway soon as he's done with business ashore, so odds are most of the crew's waiting for him aboard ship. We're going to sneak up— quiet like—right down the shore here, board the *'Snake* and take her quick as we can. After that's settled, we can look to settling up with Creache. Any questions?" He looked the men over. When no one spoke, he turned to Fin. "Button, this is your stompin' ground. Lead the way." He thumped her on the back and pushed her out in front of the group.

There were twenty-eight of them in all. Half were remnants of the *Rattlesnake*'s crew, the other half were the prisoners freed to man the *Justice*. Fin didn't know any of the prisoners by name, but so far none had given any reason not to be trusted. Armand Defain crouched at the rear of the group, in the shadows, uncharacteristically somber. Fin hadn't thought him capable of anything other than murder and gloatish amusement, but here he looked almost nervous. Tan nudged her shoulder and urged her to action.

She led the crew down the bank to the water's edge and then quietly upriver toward the *Rattlesnake*. The fallen leaves on the ground caused her boots to slip on the sharply rising bank, and she stumbled along with one hand to the ground to stop herself from falling completely. Troubled footsteps from behind told her the others fared no better. She'd walked through these woods, down this very bank a hundred times with Bartimaeus, foraging herbs among the grass and growth, never once worrying over how much noise she might make or who might see her coming if she didn't stay low. The effect was unsettling. She was a stranger in her own home. Her stomach churned with every step. She strained her ears, listening for even the slightest sound that might warn her of violence or alarm from ahead.

The river wound to the left, and they followed it around the bend. It turned sharply to the right, then curled back to the left again where it ran nearest the orphanage. They could see the *Rattlesnake* anchored upriver around the curve. Now exposed along the riverbank, Fin climbed back up into the woods where they would have less cover from landward eyes but more concealment from the ship. She led them through the pines and out across the river-carved shoulder of land that lay between them and the ship. To her left she could see the outer walls of the orphanage. More than anything, she wanted to run straight to the front gate to see what was going on behind that wall. But they needed to secure the ship first. She tried to put it out of her mind and kept her eyes fixed on the *Rattlesnake*.

When they approached to within a hundred yards of the riverbank nearest the ship, Fin caught the sounds of harsh voices on the wind. The sounds came from the chapel. The wind changed again, and the snippets of sound were whisked away, replaced by the chirping of birds and the low babble of the river.

She stopped behind a large, fallen cypress and deferred to Jack. He crawled forward and peered over the tree, across the last few yards toward the ship. Fin forgot all about the *Rattlesnake* and fixed her attention up the hill, toward the chapel. She caught hollow thumping sounds: feet on a wooden floor. She picked out a woman's voice: loud, in anger—or fear.

"Button, pay attention!" spat Jack in a harsh whisper. He was talking to the group, explaining his plan of action. Fin didn't care. The sounds coming from the chapel consumed her thoughts.

Tan nudged her. She turned and saw Jack stooped low and creeping through the brush, leading the men down to the river, toward the *Rattlesnake*. Tan nudged her again, beckoning her to follow but she held back. Jack and several others crawled into the rowboat that Creache must have used to come ashore. Those that didn't fit in the boat clung to the side and held their muskets and powder-horns out of the water. Fin watched as Jack quietly rowed the boat toward the ship. Tan beckoned again and she moved to follow; she could still catch up with Jack and the boat. Then once more, the harsh tone of a male voice rang out from the direction of the chapel. Fin jerked her head away from Tan, away from the river, away from the *Rattlesnake*. The voice came again and she made up her mind, small steps at first, then she broke into a run. Tan called out for her to stop, but she ignored him.

The chapel was a hundred yards away; it was a world away. As she ran across the distance, she felt as if she were violating something sacred. She'd dreamed that when she came home, came back at last, that she would do so having put who she'd become behind her. She didn't want the sailor, the pirate, the murderer, following her—not here. She left home to keep those things from this place, from these people, from Peter. Now she was bringing it all back. Worse, she wouldn't be able to hide it, to lie about it, to cover it up. If she meant to stop Creache, then she meant to bring death where innocence slept. She felt her blood rising; she meant to fight. And with it rose her shame, her guilt. Then she felt what she hated most: a rising sense of excitement. She was looking forward to it. She imagined Armand Defain smiling at her in approval. She didn't care anymore.

She reached the chapel and flattened herself against the wall. Tan emerged from the trees and ran to her. Fin gritted her teeth and prepared a protest. He wasn't going to stop her now.

"What's the plan?" asked Tan. Fin relaxed and unclenched her jaw. He wasn't here to stop her.

"Kill Creache."

"Simple. I like it."

Tan smirked and drew his rapier. He edged his way down the building, and Fin followed. They slipped around the corner and sidled up to the first of the tall arched windows that marched down the flanks of the chapel.

Inside was everything that Fin feared. Orphans filled the pews, more of them than Fin expected. In the past there were rarely more than twenty; now there must be fifty, quiet and meek in the pews, driven here by war no doubt. Standing near the rear of the sanctuary, clothed in grey, hunched and crooked like a gargoyle, stood Sister Hilde. She guarded the children, her hands on the heads of those around her, channeling comfort and discipline. Her eyes, though, were turned away. Fin was thankful. She wasn't ready to confront that gaze; she wasn't sure she would ever be.

The focus of Hilde's attention was Carmaline. She was standing awkwardly, as if off balance, near the front door. Her arms struck out at right angles, and her head was thrown back as if in the middle of a great laugh. Then Carmaline turned, and Fin saw the figure behind her. Carmaline's immensity had hidden him. It was Bill Stumm. He had one arm wrapped around her waist and the other held a knife. He pressed the blade against Carmaline's throat, and it was nearly lost in the folds of her neck.

Silhouetted in the door was Creache. In front of him, the floorboards had been ripped up and cast aside. Piles of dirt filled the doorway. Now and then, a shovel tossed a new cloud of dirt out of the hole in the floor. It was deep enough that only the diggers' heads and shoulders were visible above the rim of the hole. The shovelers were two teenaged boys. Orphans.

"Deeper!" shouted Creache.

"There ain't nothin' down here, mister—" argued one of the boys in the hole.

"Do as he says, child!" snapped Hilde. Her voice was thinner than Fin remembered.

Fin turned away from the window and crouched down, out of sight. She pulled her cutlass from her belt and took a deep breath. It was time. She had to act. She started to rise, but Tan pulled her back down.

"Let him dig up whatever's down there. Then he'll leave on his own, and we'll be waiting."

Fin hadn't considered that. She didn't care for whatever Bartimaeus had stolen and buried. Creache, on the other hand, was ready to kill for it. If she rushed in to stop him, too many people were in a position to get hurt. Tan was right. They peeked through the window to watch and wait.

"If you'd care to tell us just what it is you're looking for, we might be able to help you find it," said Hilde.

Creache turned to face her. "Do you know the name Bart Gann?" he asked.

"Bartimaeus? Of course. He was our cook for nearly twenty years. What of him?" said Hilde. She wasn't intimidated and held back none of her usual venom.

"Your *cook* stole a great deal of gold from me—nearly twenty years ago."

"Nonsense. Bartimaeus wouldn't steal a crumb. He was as penniless as any orphan that ever darkened our gate, and that till the day he died."

"Bart Gann was as malicious a pirate as ever set blade to flesh. He was a thief, a murderer, and a lover of cheap wine and cheaper whores. Have any orphans here from the brothels of Savannah?" Creache raised an eyebrow and a smirk threatened his lips. Hilde didn't answer. "Perhaps he came here out of pity, looking for one of his bastards. As ironic a place as any to hide, I suppose."

"He was a good man," protested Hilde.

"Aye. Good sailor, good pirate—good traitor. I never saw him coming, I'll give him that. When he made off with the gold, he caught me perfectly off my guard. Once you've debauched with a man, pirated with him, warred and whored with him, you come, at last, to think you know him. Perhaps even trust him. But Bart was far more wicked than I. Often I wonder when it was that he decided to turn. What was the precise moment his treachery was born? I never had an inkling of it."

Creache paused and preened his mustache in silence. "Then, when he'd stolen our fortune, he disappeared. Twenty years I searched for him. Twenty years poking in rotten little towns up and down the coast, and never once a whisper, never a hint. Made myself an honest man, put away the pirate, and turned all my purpose to searching for him unhindered by the hangman's threat. To give up being a pirate is no small thing for a man who gives himself to the life. Such was my hate that I cast it away. And then for years, nothing. Until at last, the British caught up with him. I sailed to Savannah the moment I heard. But when I got here, what did I find? The bloodthirsty bastards had already dangled him. I was furious, demanded they tell me where he had been hiding—but they starting asking questions—about me, about why. And I couldn't let them connect us could I? No." Creache paced the chapel floor in front of Hilde as clumps of dirt flew up from the hole in the floor.

"Then Bart's deception unraveled itself when that little whore of yours— that Button—had the nerve to come aboard my ship."

"Phinea?" said Hilde with disbelief. "You're mad."

"Quite," he said with an arrogant sniff. "I can't imagine what she thought to gain by coming out to find me, but whatever her little plan, it failed. I expect the British will be sending her to join old Bart any day, if they haven't already."

Carmaline swooned, and Bill staggered against her weight to keep her upright. Sister Hilde's face turned a shade whiter. "You *lie*," she hissed at him.

Creache turned on her with an amused smirk. Before he could answer, one of the boys in the hole threw his shovel out. "We can't dig no more, mister. There ain't nothing down here. We dug so far we hittin' water."

Creache kicked the shovel back at him. "You don't stop until you find what's mine!" he shouted.

"We can't dig no more! Ain't nothing but mud!" hollered the boy back at him.

Creache walked to the hole and looked down into it. The muscles of his shoulders twitched in anger as he glared into the muddy pit. The bottom was flooded with water. The boys stood in it up to their knees. He spun around and grabbed a child from the nearest pew. Sister Hilde's nose quivered in anger as he dragged the scared little girl in front of her and pulled a pistol from his belt. Fin's eyes widened; it was Betsy. He jerked the girl by her arm and rammed the blunderbuss against her temple. His face twisted into a snarl of rage.

"Where is it?" he said to Hilde through clenched teeth. Sister Carmaline worked her mouth open and closed like a fish, her face white with fear. Hilde matched his gaze.

"Where is what?" she said coldly.

"He lived here twenty years, and you expect me to believe that he never said a word or spent an ounce?" The small girl in his grip began to cry as he pressed the gun into her temple. "It's not where the map says it is, so that means one thing: someone took it. Where is it?"

Fin considered that Creache might be right. Would Bartimaeus have kept a fortune in gold secret from the sisters for so long? Surely they could have put the money to good use, rather than let it lie in the ground for twenty years. If Hilde knew, she would certainly give it up before she let Creache harm one of the children.

"I told you. Bartimaeus was poor when he came and poor when he went. He never owned anything but the clothes on his back and that blasted fiddle."

Creache didn't like her answer. He cocked the hammer of the gun. Hilde's nose froze. So this is what she looks like when she's scared, thought Fin. Carmaline staggered backward, threatening to faint. She forced Bill up against the wall, and he grunted and cursed while she mashed him against it in her infirmity.

"You'll answer me this time or the runt dies," said Creache.

Then three things happened in succession that caused the room to explode into chaos.

First, Sister Carmaline fainted away cold. She fell backward and pinned Bill against the wall with such force that all he could do was sputter, moan, and gasp for air. After a struggle, he managed to shift her weight away. She rolled forward and hit the floor with a thunderous boom that shook the building. Bill collapsed on top of her, groaning curses as he fought to regain his breath.

Second, as Creache gaped wide-eyed at the ruckus caused by Carmaline's faint, Knut walked through the front door of the chapel and said, "Hey Captain, you seen Fin?" just as plainly and calmly as if it were the most normal thing in the world. The expression on Creache's face at Knut's appearance could only be described as groping—groping for some way to explain the sudden appearance of someone he knew to be far away, locked up, and possibly even hanged. Fin was scarcely less surprised than Creache.

Before Creache could finish reacting to Knut's entrance, the crackle of musket fire echoed through the woods as Jack commenced his attack on the *Rattlesnake*. Creache's eyes snapped toward the sounds of battle coming up from the river and fell upon Fin and Tan peering in the window. Bill snatched a pistol from his belt and fired. The window shattered, and Fin heard the sharp crack of the ball as it pierced the air above her head.

"Phinea!" shouted Hilde. Her voice was a mix of surprise, disdain, and anger.

Fin and Tan ran to the front of the building and through the open doors. Bill was red-faced and sweaty from his battle with Carmaline's bulk and he crouched behind her unconscious form as if she were a fortification of war. He was trying to pack his pistol. Fin ran at him headlong and knocked the gun from his hands before he could finish reloading.

The children screamed. They crowded to the far end of the sanctuary, hid beneath the pews, crouched in the corners. Hilde hadn't moved; she stood between Creache and the orphans like a bulwark, upthrust and defiant. Her eyes lay steady on the girl in Creache's grip as if she might stay his hand by will alone.

Tan leapt across the hole in the floor, knocking Knut into it in the process. The two diggers cowered with their shovels held like weapons, fearing

Knut might attack them at any moment. Knut lowered his head and tried his best to disappear into the mud. Tan raised his rapier to Creache, and Fin drew her cutlass. She felt the eyes of the orphans upon her. She knew some of them, and those she didn't surely knew of her. They were staring, open-mouthed.

"Loose the girl," demanded Tan.

Creache smiled. A chill prickled Fin's spine.

"Gladly," he said. In one swift motion, he thrust the girl at Sister Hilde, tucked Betsy into his coat and drew his sword. The small girl fled into Hilde's skirts, and Hilde's eyes turned on Fin. There was no welcome or thanks in them. Her nose quivered. Then the little girl clutching at her skirts looked toward Fin and screamed. Fin stared at the girl with a puzzled look before realizing the girl wasn't looking at her, she was looking behind her. She turned and felt a sharp pain in her left arm as a knife sliced it open. It was Bill. If she had turned a moment later, his knife would have been in her back. Before he could stab at her again, she swung her cutlass. He leapt to the side and swiped at her again with the knife.

Tan took a step toward Fin, his instinct compelling him to act. Creache saw his opening and took it. He ran forward, sword held high. But Tan was no easy prey; he parried the blow. The two swordsmen squared off, each judging the other, placing upon the mind's scale weights of size, speed, experience, and cunning. Each calculated his oppenent in the beat of a heart and then they began a dance of savage grace. The clash of steel resounded through the chapel like music. Tan and Creache stepped in and struck, fell back and parried, a wicked parley of ringing steel and knuckles white. For all Tan's skill, he found Creache an even match. Creache had fenced and slain when Tan was no more than a child, and though he hadn't called his sword to action in many years, his blade was wakened now to evil deed: deadly, swift, and sure.

Fin drove herself after Bill. She'd beaten him soundly twice before with nothing more than fists and meant to end it now in blood. Bill frothed at the mouth like a dog. His hate for Fin was long nurtured; he wore it on his face like a mask. Again and again he sliced at her with his knife. Each time she dodged him and swung her cutlass back. He rolled and leapt always narrowly evading her attacks. He was beyond his skill, beyond his endurance, urged on by rampant, seething hate. He'd hated Fin since Tun Tavern, hated her more since she'd bested him on the day of the mutiny. Here and now, he meant to complete his hatred in death. Fin was desperate to be done with him.

As she fought, she cast glances toward Tan. His fight with Creache raged across the chapel, overturning furniture, sending orphans fleeing from corner to corner. Both men had wounds open and bleeding. Tan bled from the forehead and left arm, Creache from his left side and cheek. Fin feared for Tan for the first time. Never before had she doubted he'd still be standing when the battle was done, but now she feared for him. Tan was no longer smiling.

She flung herself at Bill again, and his boot slammed into her stomach. She doubled over and fought for breath. She would be no help to Tan if she didn't focus on Bill first. It was a stupid mistake; she was taking him for granted. His knife whistled through the air and she rolled to the side, swinging her cutlass wildly. The blade caught his elbow and he cried out in pain. Before she could gain her feet, Bill was on top of her, his blade descending toward her chest like a stab of lightning. She dropped her cutlass and flung both hands up to stop his attack. As his weight crashed down on her, a sickening moan blew out of her mouth and he crushed the breath from her lungs.

The blade stopped, inches from her neck. Bill's face was flushed red, his lips curled back in a snarl of yellowed teeth and cancerous gums. His breath stank of tobacco and drink. Thick drops of sweat rolled off his nose and spattered on her face. All his weight was gathered behind the knife. She had no hope of holding back the blade for more than seconds longer. Something hard was biting into her hip. Fin cursed whatever was causing the pain; it was drawing her mind from the fight to keep the knife away. A fight she was losing. Slowly, inexorably, the tip of the blade was closing distance. The flesh beneath it crawled and prickled as if it could avoid the pierce. Pain in her hip again. She tried to call for help but she had no breath to utter the words. Her mind wandered again to the hard object pressing into her hip. It was her pistol.

The blade slipped closer, less than an inch now. No time to think about it. She dropped her hand to her side and found the pistol. With only one hand holding back Bill, the knife closed its distance. The tip of the blade pushed through her skin and into her sternum. She loosed a ragged scream at the pain. Her hand fumbled to find the trigger of the pistol. Bill's snarl was turning into a smile. The pressure in her chest was excruciating. She could feel the warmth of blood spilling across her skin. Her hand found its prize. She squeezed the trigger and the hammer fell. *Clack.* Nothing. She squeezed again. *Clack.* There was no powder in the pan. She dropped the pistol and beat at Bill's back. Then a loud clang sounded in her ears, and Bill went limp. She screamed again as the knife twisted out of her skin and fell to the floor. Knut was standing over her holding a shovel in his hand. A clump of hair clung to the spade.

"Help Tan!" she yelled to Knut.

Knut's usual stupor washed away. He turned his face to Creache. Fin stared up at him in awe. This wasn't Knut. It was Tom Knuttle, first mate of the *Rattlesnake*. His back was straight, his head held high. His face was taut and angry as necessity called up from inside him what had so long been hidden away. He walked toward Creache with the shovel cocked back to strike.

Creache was focused solely on Tan. The rhythmic peal of their blades dominated the room. Creache advanced on Tan again and again, pushing him, tiring him, waiting patiently for his defense to wane. Tan could make no advance. Creache was too fast.

Then Knut was within striking distance. He lifted the shovel.

"Captain, that's enough!" said Knut. His voice was strong and filled with authority.

Creache turned and saw the shovel raised to deal its blow. Fin thought she saw fear in his eyes. Tan leapt forward to take the opening, but Creache was ready. He riposted Tan's attack and turned his eyes back to Knut. It wasn't fear in them. It was hatred.

"Damn you," he shouted at Knut. He pulled Besty from his belt and took aim. Knut faltered. Fin's face turned white with horror. She was pinned to the ground under Bill's body. She struggled to roll him away, but there was no time. A heartbeat was all that stood between Knut and Betsy's waking. Tan stepped wide around Creache and swung his rapier. The blade sliced through Creache's forearm with sickening grace, and his cloven arm fell to the ground. Betsy, still sleeping, lay clutched within the hand.

Tan didn't waste the momentum of his attack. In one swift motion he spun and brought the blade high overhead to kill. But the stroke never fell. Creache hadn't given the loss of his hand a second thought. He tucked the stump of his arm into his side to staunch the flow of blood and drove his sword hilt-deep into Tan's chest.

Fin screamed.

Tan stood motionless, his rapier held overhead, his mouth open, his eyes wide. Creache jerked the blade from his chest and Tan took a step backward, then fell to the floor with his hands pressed to the hole in his bosom. The wails of crying children resounded throughout the chapel.

At the sight of Tan dying on the floor, Knut stooped. His features softened, and his eyes glazed over as the part of him that had briefly awakened retreated back into the depths of his mind. Creache swung his sword, and Knut dropped the shovel and fell to the floor to escape the blade. He curled into a ball and trembled like a child.

Fin wrestled Bill's body away and crawled toward Knut.

"Damn you, Tom Knuttle," shouted Creache. "Damn the day I took you on, and damn the day I let you live."

Creache cast his sword aside. He plucked the shovel from the floor and raised it.

"Damn your willful soul!"

He swung the shovel upon Knut.

"I'll knock more than your wits loose this time!"

The captain rained down a volley of blows, and Knut threw up his hands and caught the shaft as it fell. Creache kicked Knut's arms away and wrenched the tool from his grip. He jammed the heel of his boot against Knut's neck and lifted the spade of the shovel to deliver his final blow.

Fin scrambled across the ground toward Knut and saw Betsy lying on the floor, still held in Creache's fallen hand. But she wasn't close enough. Even as she reached out and took the blunderbuss from the hand, she knew she was too late. Creache's blow was already falling.

Then from the doorway a voice. "*Tiberius Creache!*" it shouted.

Creache froze.

Armand Defain stood in the doorway. His face was filled with wicked glee. Topper and the others from the *Monarch* stepped into view.

Creache's eyes were locked on Defain. "*You*" he said, his voice dripping with hate. Defain sneered at him.

Fin cocked Betsy and raised her arm.

Creache cast the shovel away and lifted his remaining hand in surrender. His life hung upon her choice. On the floor between them Knut shivered and cried and cradled his head in his arms. Creache was smirking.

Fin closed her eyes. She made her choice. The gentle twitch of a finger and it was done. Betsy awoke and spat hellfire.

The blast threw Creache against the wall and shook the building. He slid to the floor and lay still beneath a red stain on the glimmering white sanctuary wall. Fin dared not look at Defain; she could feel his wicked smile upon her.

She ran to Tan and knelt beside him. His skin was sallowed, and his breath came in ragged fits and jerks. Blood was everywhere.

"You bring your fiddle, Fin? To see me to the Green?" he said.

Fin wept. Topper and the crew gathered around her. They bowed their heads and looked away when they saw Tan's wound. They knew what it meant.

"Tell Knut—tell Tommy—I'll see him there," he whispered. His smile found his lips once more, and he died.

Fin tried to quiet the sobs welling up inside her while Topper and the rest of the crew lifted him up and carried him out of the chapel. The white floor where he fell was puddled thick with blood. Fin wiped her tears away and pressed her palms to the floor. Blood she had spilled, caused to be spilled. Everything, everyone she touched turned to blood. She lifted her hands and wiped them across her shirt. If she couldn't escape it, then she would accept it, embrace it, use it. Tan's rapier, Tom Knuttle's rapier, lay on the floor in front of her. She picked it up and wiped the blade clean, then stood and tucked it into her belt.

The inside of the chapel was wrecked. Pews were cast aside and over-turned. Blood was splattered on the white of the walls and floor. Huddled in the corners, the children were quiet now. They were staring at her. Fin found Hilde's gaze at last.

"What have you done?" whispered Hilde. "What have you *done*!"

After all the time that had passed since she'd walked away, Hilde still knew no forgiveness. Deep inside her heart, Fin longed to mend the wounds between them, longed to be welcomed, comforted, embraced, even by Hilde—especially by Hilde. But that crooked face stared back like graven stone, dry and cold. Hilde's eyes offered nothing but disdain.

Carmaline stirred, and Hilde rushed to her sister and fell to her knees. As Fin approached, Hilde stopped her with a word.

"Leave," she said with the slightest turn of her head.

Fin stopped. Carmaline groaned as she returned to conciousness. Fin started toward her again, wanting to help, to see her, to be seen by her.

"Get out!" ordered Hilde.

Fin obeyed. She turned to leave and found Defain crouched on the floor clutching Creache's severed arm in his hand. He pulled out a dagger and cut off the last two fingers then tossed the wasted arm into the hole. Fin wrinkled her nose in disgust. Then he grabbed Creache's body by the ankle and dragged him across the chapel floor.

"*Au revoir, capitaine.*" He flung the body into the pit and spat upon it. "Bury him."

As Fin walked out of the chapel, two boys were already at work filling in the hole Creache bade them dig. His own grave. They lowered their eyes as she passed, as if afraid to look at her. This was what she had become, a terror to children. Feared, not loved. Would Bartimaeus fear to look at her now? Would he order her away? The memory of him hurt, but she was thankful he wasn't here to answer her questions. She dreaded what answers he might give.

Outside the building Topper and the crew were waiting. Most were either bruised or had some extremity wrapped in fresh bandages—or both. Despite the injuries, the fight aboard the *Rattlesnake* must have gone well to have been so short.

"Where's Jack?" she asked Topper.

Topper frowned. "He's on the *'Snake*. Got himself hurt."

Fin cursed herself. Another friend hurt. "Will he be alright?"

"He won't die, but he won't be the same."

Before Fin could make sense of his answer, a horse and rider galloped around the corner. In all that had gone on, she hadn't had time to think about him, hadn't dared to hope he'd still be here, still waiting. But the sound of the hooves behind her brought years of hopes and longings thundering to the surface like great whales breaching and gulping in life, rising from an ageless and unfathomed sleep. Why was it so hard to turn around? One foot at a time. Steady. She turned.

It was Peter. Fin stared at him, willing it to be true and fearing to believe it. She couldn't speak, and for a long time Peter didn't come down. After waiting so long to see him, she couldn't bring herself to violate the moment with words. It was perfect now, just the seeing of him; words might tear it all away.

"Fin," he said at last and climbed down.

Fin didn't move, feared to speak even his name.

"The British are coming," he said. Then, looking at the entire group as if he had only just discovered them standing there, he continued, "Hundreds, coming up the road. They've burned the Dorst and Koerner homesteads."

Topper's eyebrows went up, and he ordered the crew to the ship. He slapped Fin on the back and turned to the river, yelling orders to get underway as he ran.

They were alone. The sounds of the world around died away, faded into the background of things that no longer mattered. They stood too far apart to touch and too near not to want to. It was as if all the miles and time and tears that had kept them apart had now come thick into the air like a wall, and both feared to try themselves against that last invisible barrier. He was grown now, larger, taller, but weathered, as if time and memory had eroded him, worn him smoother. The skin of his face was pulled taut across his cheeks by long hours in the sun. The creases on his forehead ran deeper than those around his mouth, telling of more worry than mirth. His smile was closely kept, as it always had been. She missed it. The smile he kept only for her.

At last, Peter stepped forward and pulled her into an embrace. The distance was crossed. Fin shuddered and cried. She buried her face in his chest and let herself rest against him. His hands were rough, calloused, and scarred. The boy was gone, and she knew the moment he touched her that the man would send her away. He was holding part of himself back because he knew the giving couldn't be complete. He would send her away as surely as Hilde had. But unlike Hilde, his sending was a plea, not an order.

"You should see it, Fin." She could hear it in his voice. He didn't know how to say it.

"See what?" she asked.

"Our home. Finished and waiting."

Though she knew every board and batten, every nail and joint, she'd nearly lost it in the blurry dwindling of memory. "Tell me," she said and quieted to hear Peter build it anew in her mind.

"It's framed of an old oak, gnarled and bent, but strong as the roots of Georgia itself. It's sided of cypress and pine, and rain brings the scent of it into the air like perfume. The field grows green and so soft that the scythe cuts it like a whisper. When I sit on the porch at sunset, I can almost hear the laughter of children in the wind." He lifted her chin and turned her face up to see him. His fingers were rough against her face, like braids of rope, and smelled of new-turned earth, but they were gentle, deliberate, and patient. "It's no home 'til it's our home, Fin. It's only half a place."

They both knew she couldn't stay. Both refused to speak it. She could smell the grass, see Peter working in the field, hear their children playing in the heather. But she could also hear the march of British boots. There could be no peace and no home while war endured.

"I call it Shiloh," said Peter, breaking the silence.

"What does it mean?"

"Harbor of rest."

In the distance, a musket fired.

Peter looked up and turned in the direction of the shot. "They'll burn it," he said.

"Come with me, Pete," said Fin pulling his face back toward her.

Peter shook his head. "Mr. Hickory died last winter. After the British have come and gone, the town will need me, to rebuild." She knew he would refuse.

"Don't fight, Peter. Promise me you won't try to fight them."

"I'm not a soldier; I'm a carpenter," he said. Then at last, he smiled. "Don't suppose it would do any good to tell you not to fight, would it?"

Fin didn't answer. Musket fire again, closer this time.

"Don't wait for me, Peter. You don't know who I am anymore." She tried to push him away, but he wouldn't be driven. When at last he let her go, he mounted his horse and looked down, smiling and sad.

"I've been waiting for you my whole life, Phinea Button. Wouldn't know how to stop now." He pulled on the reins and turned the horse toward Ebenezer. More musket fire popped and snapped in the distance, and the horse shifted nervously. "I have to warn the rest of the town. Go Fin, before they get here. Come back when it's all over and done. Come home. I'll be waiting." He didn't give her a chance to answer. He kicked his heels and galloped away. Fin stared after him, committing everything about him to memory. If she never came home again, she wanted at least to have the memory of him perfect in her mind. She'd take it with her to the ends of the sea.

FROM THE RIVER, THE sound of Topper shouting orders wove its way through the trees to find her, to pull her back from a world that belonged to her and Peter alone. Tears were drying on her face. She wiped the last of them away with her shirtsleeve and turned away from Peter, away from the orphanage, toward the ship. She felt she had betrayed everyone by failing to stop them from being hurt. Bartimaeus's voice floated back to her, *terrible things.* She shuddered. He had tried to warn her. Then she remembered Betsy. She ran back into the chapel and there on the floor it lay, silent and awful. Its barrel was still warm with murder. She took it up. She needed it. She couldn't stand by and let the world decide her fate. To make her own way she needed action, and action in war meant death, violence, murder if need be. Such were Betsy's gifts. She pushed it into her belt. One day, like Bartimaeus, she'd put it down, but not yet.

As Fin walked out of the chapel, thoughts of Bartimaeus continued to come back to her. He was the one who had drawn her here, drawn Creache here. And for what? Nothing. The map had led to nothing. Then she recalled the words scrawled on the map.

Standing here I laid me down
me spoils, me heathen crowns,
To sleep in sacred earth redeemed
beneath the tower without a sound

She held her breath as the tumblers in her mind clicked into place. Bartimaeus couldn't possibly have buried anything under the chapel—not the new chapel. *Beneath the tower without a sound.* The old chapel had no bell in its tower.

She closed her eyes and let herself drift back. Back through time, to years ago. How many times had she run to her old bell tower for quietude and solace? Hundreds? Thousands? She let herself remember them. Then, without thinking, she let her feet guide her. Her eyes were still closed as she began to walk, slowly at first, then faster, finally breaking into a run, through the gates of the orphanage, past the dining hall, down the length of the orphan house to the door—the space that had once been a door. She opened her eyes. She stood in the courtyard, now empty and plain. She looked around and knew for certain her feet had not failed her. This was the place. She took a few steps forward then one to the left. The ladder to her bell tower would have stood right here, she thought. This was where the map pointed. She could almost feel something hidden in the ground, calling up to her, crying out to be found.

She dropped to her knees and felt the ground with her hands. Yes, it was there, she felt it, she knew it. Right where Bartimaeus had put it. She nearly cried out with excitement, but stopped herself. Why hadn't Bartimaeus spent the gold if it was here? He could have been rich. But she knew the answer before the question had fully formed. *Me spoils, me heathen crowns.* It wasn't a treasure to Bartimaeus. It was the past. Bartimaeus hadn't hidden out here to escape Creache; he hadn't died a pirate in hiding. He had told her the truth: he became a new man the day Reverend Whitefield saved him. The only cent of the treasure he'd ever spent was to buy the fiddle. What remained, he buried, not to keep it hidden but to put it to rest. To bring it up now would be the ultimate betrayal. She smiled. No, she wouldn't cry out for shovels and picks. She wouldn't breathe a word of the place that she among all others was able to find so easily. The gold would lie in the earth, and Bartimaeus with it, until the faithful were called into the sky.

Fin stood and wiped the dirt from her hands. She looked around the courtyard one last time, scoring the place upon her memory, and then she left with a smile on her face. The sea was calling.

Chapter XXV

DOWN THE HILL AND to the bank she ran. Topper was waiting with a rowboat and ferried her out to the *Rattlesnake*. She climbed aboard and felt like she was home. The crew was busy about the deck and tackle. Sam Catcher was calling orders. Somewhere in the tops, men were singing. And from the cabin came the angry growls of Jack Wagon.

She ducked through the hatchway and found him laid in the bed with a thick bloody bandage on his leg. Something didn't look quite right about it, and it wasn't until Topper's comment that he "wouldn't be the same" came back to her that she realized what the problem was. He was missing his left leg from the shin down. Her jaw fell open, and she thought she would be sick. One of the men that had joined them from the *Justice* was arguing with Jack, trying to convince him to stay in the bed.

"Bloody hell, Button. What are you gawking at?" growled Jack. "Tell this bugger to leave me be. I'm fine. Never used that leg much anyway."

Fin couldn't help but smile. The leg had to be hurting like the devil, but somehow it didn't surprise her that Jack didn't care. The man trying to keep Jack in bed turned to look at her for advice. She shook her head.

"Let him alone. He learns the hard way." The man shrugged and walked out the door.

Jack swung himself around and sat up with a wince.

"Heard from Topper about what happened. Damned shame about Tan.

Gonna miss him more than my blooming leg." He wrinkled up his face and reached down to touch his stump. "Some bugger got lucky with his musket and blowed the thing clean off. Wouldn't mind so much, but he took off running after he seen I wasn't happy about it and there wasn't no way for me to chase after him. Last I seen he was swimming down river toward Savannah." Fin didn't blame him.

"Me and the boys had us a talk while you was dallying ashore. The whole lot of 'em seen you give the captain his due, and of course no one thinks worse of you for the doing. But seeing how we're all pirates now, the boys seem to think we ought to go about things like proper pirates, which means having a captain for the ship. So like any good pirate ship, the man what killed the captain gets the job. So, Captain Button, take us to sea. I believe I'd like to take a little nap." Without another word, he laid back and passed out.

Fin wasn't sure what exactly had happened. It sounded like he just told her she was the captain. A clear mistake, probably brought on by delirium from the pain. She left him to rest and walked back out on deck.

"Captain on deck!" shouted Topper from the helm. The crew turned and cheered.

"Captain on deck!" they shouted. Fin flushed red and hurried over to Topper.

"How many times do I have to tell you to stop that?" she chided him.

"At least a few more, Captain," he said with a grin. She gave him a sharp look. "It's official now. The crew voted on it. Fair earned or not, you've got the reputation, Fin. And the whole crew seen you give Creache his comeuppance." Fin rolled her eyes. "Stop fighting it. These boys will follow you, and you got me and Jack to help you out when you need it." He winked at her. "What's our course, Captain?"

She didn't deserve it. She didn't have the slightest idea how to be captain. But Topper was right. It was a gift and she should use it. Just as she had embraced Betsy, she made up her mind and took what she was offered. Flame of the west, they said. Terror of the British trade. So be it. Until she could return home in peace and give herself to Peter with no fear or regret, she would take up war, piracy, and whatever else she must.

"South, to open sea," said Fin. "Then wherever the wind wills. We bury Tan and the others at sunset." Topper nodded and called out the order. The sails unfurled and the *Rattlesnake* groaned to life. The crew sent up a cheer.

"Defain!" Fin called.

He presented himself with a measured bow. "*Oui?*"

"Take what men you need and precede us in the Monarch. We'll need her to run the blockade."

"Aye aye, *capitaine*." He clicked his heels once then turned and assembled a crew. The knowledge that he had known Creache didn't garner him any trust in her eyes. She intended to have answers out of him, but right now the crew needed open sea, room to breathe, time to bury the dead. Answers would have to wait.

The *Rattlesnake* and the *Monarch* pulled away, and the sounds of British muskets filled the air. Here and there along the treetops, pillars of smoke rose like tombstones marking each homestead razed in the British passing. As they rounded the bend of the river, Fin could see flames through the trees. Ebenezer was burning.

To be concluded in Book II:
FIDDLER'S GREEN

Special Thanks
&
Acknowledgments

The classic stereotype of the author is that of the lone, grizzled recluse sequestered in a dingy one room apartment of some Manhattan brownstone. He's barely visible in the smoke-filled room. Empty bottles clutter a hardwood floor carpeted by cast away pages and a lamp throws a dim cone of light across a typewriter set on a rickety wooden desk. This mythical author emerges from his cave after some years with a coffee-cup ringed manuscript in his hands like Moses descending from Sinai carrying stone tablets still smoldering from their encounter with the finger of God. The author delivers this paper-borne slab of genius to a publisher and the rest is lost in a whirlwind of tired cliches.

Try to imagine the exact opposite of all that and you have a more accurate picture of the writing and publication of The Fiddler's Gun.

I owe a great debt of thanks to my brother for threatening several times to visit bodily harm upon me if I didn't pull this manuscript out of the drawer and publish it. This, I think, is a prodigious arrangement because if readers decide that it ought to have stayed in that desk drawer after all, then I can confidently point my finger and proclaim, "He made me do it." (And thus shall all hate-mail be forwarded.)

Once I did decide to avoid this threat of harm, the road to publication was no easy journey and, humbly now, I wish to extend my debt of gratitude to those who helped me along the way, to Kate Etue, my editor, who did a wonderful job and did more than I ever asked of her, to Evie Coates who was able to capture the vague images in my mind and illustrate them into a beautiful cover, to the members of the Rabbit Room Writer's Fellowship who critiqued and encouraged me, and finally, to my gracious patrons—those who believed in me and in my writing and, more importantly, had faith that I would not let them down. The book you hold in your hands would not exist without these fine people and thier blessed offerings.

Patrons of The Fiddler's Gun

Matt McBrien, Cris Jesse, Steve and Kathy Fronk (double thanks), Dieta Duncan, Quirky Kate Hinson, S. D. "Sam" Smith, Matthew Radzius, Kathryn Berryman, Paula Shaw, Laura Preston, Sha-Una Peterson, Jeannette McIntyre, Jerry Hampton, Tony Oakes, Michelle O'Shea, "The" Carlen Groce, Kristen Kopp, Jodi Kiffmeyer, Amy Riley, Eric West, Shannon Craig, Malia Mondy, Sharon Frazier, Marit Aanestad, Hannah Holman, Toni Whitney (glad you found your boat), Meg Hinson, Eddy Efaw and family, Richelle Maki, Linnea Lewis, Bruce Hennigan (double thanks), Peter Brunone, Angela Day, Larry Olson (many thanks), Hannah Nesmith, Kirk Plattner, Margaret Bull, Stephen Lamb, Christopher Rule, Bob Soulliere, Keith Schambach, Kristal Ragsdale, Curt McLey, Cyndi Sager, Trenton Gibbs, Lance Anders, Chad Ethridge, Tim McMillan, Connie Solomon, Lyndsay Slaten, John Barber, Kelsy Hill, Katherine Schultz, Yvan Rey (all the way from Switzerland!), and Arthur O. Peterson (thanks Dad)

A Brief Guide to Terms
of Nautical Significance

-A-

ABOARD: on or in a seagoing vessel

ADRIFT: afloat, unattached to either shore or seabed, and uncontrolled, therefore going wherever the wind and current command

AFT: toward the stern of the vessel

AGROUND: resting on or touching the ground or sea bottom

AHEAD: forward of the bow of the vessel

ALL HANDS: the entire population of a ship's crew

ALOFT: above the vessel's uppermost solid structure; in the rigging of a sailing ship

ALONGSIDE: parallel to a ship or pier

AMIDSHIPS: the middle portion of a ship

ASHORE: on the beach, shore, or land

ASTERN: toward the rear or transom of the ship

AWASH: dangerously low in the sea, such that water is constantly washing across the deck

AYE, AYE: reply to an order indicating, firstly, that it is heard and, secondly, that it is understood and will be carried out

-B-

BEFORE THE MAST: often used to indicate the area in the forecastle of the ship where sailors of the lowliest rank lived. Once promoted, sailors moved amidships (hence midshipmen), and when granted officer standing, moved once more to the rear nearest the quarterdeck.

BERTH (as mooring): a location in port or upon the quay used specifically for mooring vessels while not at sea.

BERTH (as sleeping): a space used as sleeping accommodation on aboard a ship

BILGE: compartment at the bottom of the hull of a ship where water collects so that it may be pumped out of the vessel

BOWSPRIT: a spar projecting from the bow used as an anchor for the forestay and other rigging

BULKHEAD: a load-bearing wall within the hull of a ship

-C-

CAPSTAN: a waist-high cylindrical device operated by a number of hands each of whom, working in concert, inserts a capstan bar into a hole in the capstan and walks in a circle. Used to wind in anchors or other heavy objects.

CAT O' NINE TAILS: a short nine-tailed whip used to flog sailors in disciplinary measure

CLEW: the lower corners of square sails or the corner of a triangular sail at the end of the boom

COMPANIONWAY: a raised hatchway in the ship's deck, with a ladder leading below

CROW'S NEST: a masthead constructed with sides and sometimes a roof to shelter lookouts from the weather

-D-

DAVY JONES' LOCKER: a sailor's idiom denoting the bottom of the sea

-F-

FIRST MATE: the second in command of a ship

FORECASTLE: a partial deck above the upper deck and at the head of the vessel; traditionally the sailors' living quarters. Often contracted and pronounced "fo'csle".

-G-

GALLEY: the kitchen of the ship

GANGPLANK: a movable bridge used in boarding or leaving a ship

GUNWALE: upper edge of the hull

-H-

HAMMOCK: canvas sheets, slung from the deckhead, in which seamen sleep

HELMSMAN: person who steers a ship

HOLD: the lower part of the interior of a ship's hull, considered as storage space for cargo

-L-

LADDER: aboard a ship, all "stairs" are called ladders. Most "stairs" on a ship are narrow and near vertical, hence the name.

LETTER OF MARQUE: a warrant granted to a privateer condoning specific acts of piracy, usually against a foreign power during time of war

LINE: the correct nautical term for the "ropes" used on a sailing vessel. A line will always have a more specific name describing its function, such as "mizzen topsail halyard".

LUFF: the forward edge of a sail

-M-

MAINMAST: the tallest mast of a sailing ship

MAN-OF-WAR: a warship

MARINES: soldiers afloat

MIZZENMAST: the third mast of a ship, or mast aft of the mainmast

-P-

POOP DECK: a high deck on the aft superstructure of a ship

PRESS GANG: personnel from a ship, usually of the Royal Navy, that would force men into maritime service against their will

PORT: refers to the left-hand side of a vessel as perceived by a person on board and facing the bow

PRIVATEER: privately-owned ship authorized by means of a Letter of Marque to conduct hostilities against an enemy

-R-

REEF: to reduce the area of sail exposed to the wind in order to guard against the effects of strong wind or to slow the vessel

RIGGING: the collective system of masts and lines on a sailing vessel

-S-

SCUTTLE: to cut a hole in an object or vessel, especially in order to sink a vessel deliberately

SCUTTLEBUTT: slang term used by sailors to mean gossip or rumor

SEXTANT: navigational instrument used to measure a ship's latitude and longitude

STANCHION: a timber fitted between the frame heads of the hull

STARBOARD: refers to the right-hand side of a vessel as perceived by a person on board and facing the bow

STERN: the rear of a ship

-T-

TACKING: zig-zagging so as to sail directly toward the wind

TOPSAIL: the second sail on a mast (counting from the bottom)

TOPSIDES: the part of the hull between the waterline and the deck

-U-

UNDER WAY: a vessel that is moving under control

-W-

WATCH: a period of time during which a part of the crew is on duty. Changes of watch are marked by strokes on the ship's bell.

-Y-

YARD: the entire spar upon which a sail is set

A Brief Account of the Salzburger Flight, the Orphan House, and an Unsettling Songstress

❧❧

Author's Note: What follows is material that, while considered extraneous to the narrative of The Fiddler's Gun, *may be of some interest to the reader wishing to discover what mysteries lie just beyond the boundaries of the story proper. Said material refers chiefly to the arrival of the Salzburger Germans in the New World and their subsequent founding of the Ebenezer settlements.*

Also included is a brief and chilling account of the vocal terrors that Sister Carmaline is known to have visited upon the orphans in her care, as well as an accounting of select and sundry details surrounding the life of the Ebenezer orphan house itself.

THE SALZBURGERS, AS THEY came to be called, hailed from far Germany. They fled the bloody wake of Martin Luther's ninety-nine theses when the Catholics of Salzburg took it in mind that excommunication was too good for their Protestant brothers-in-Christ and determined that killing them off was a more proper solution—if not exactly scriptural. This protestant remnant of Salzburg embarked on a long exodus across Europe, through England, and landed itself at last upon the promised land of a place called Georgia. The place they founded they named Ebenezer, from the Hebrew for 'Stone of Succor'. But like the Israelites of old, the Salzburgers learned that the world had plenty of pain and trouble left to offer, even after the Exodus. The first winters in the new world aligned themselves with scurvy and dysentery to rob them of half their number right off the boat. Such heavy losses moved them to abandon that first settlement and once more they went to the wilderness, down to the river, the Savannah River, and found a new place, a better place, along its high green banks. They tried again, calling it New Ebenezer. The world and the weather had whittled them down to the quick and what it left behind was a hard, determined people—and a lot of orphans.

The Ebenezer orphan house was the first to lay its foundations in America. It sat upon a small knoll on the south bank of the Savannah River and looked east toward the sea like some age-old wooden battlement of the fatherland commanding the attention of all the nearby woods. The children, to whom the world itself is a place of giants and wonders, saw it in far greater terms than any of its architects could have dreamed. By the mouths of castaway babes it was christened the Castle, for unlike the orphans of the Old World, those in this new one had only tales and stories of such ramparts to quicken their imaginations.

The most impressive structure and the chief battlement of the fortress was the chapel. It was made of pine timber and rose to a sharp steeple set atop the bell tower. Inside lay ten rough benches, without backs of course, to dissuade any temptation of napping during vespers. There was no pulpit for the chapel had no preacher, though from time to time itinerant speakers of varying renown graced the podium. Near the front door was a narrow ladder that led up to the bell tower, but from its hollow no toll rang; bells suitable for calling the Lord's worship were found to be too costly for the small town and so for all it's many years the tower stood hollow and empty.

Surrounding the chapel lay the lower fiefdom of its little kingdom. The dining hall flanked the left: a small building that could only be called a hall in the most removed of fashions. Indeed, there was nothing grand or impressive about the building itself, made as it was of pine logs cut from the surrounding wood and harboring a cooking area at the rear filled with all manner of potions and reagents with which the cook, Brother Bartimaeus, invoked culinary magic three times a day.

Set in the center of the hall, however, was the one thing that broke up the monotony of its rough wood and stone: a long dinner table of polished red cedar. The red and vanilla grain of the wood played together along its length like bread dipped in wine. Every morning before the meal Brother Bartimaeus hovered over the table, polishing it with beeswax, muttering to himself over the small nicks, scuffs, and scratches left by the previous day's dining. He'd rub them furiously until it was all shine again and then disappear into the kitchen to work his craft.

Directly behind the chapel sat the actual orphan house. Much like the dining hall, it was of log construction and had a fireplace at either end to chase off the assault of a chilly night. The lower, boy's floor was only accessible from the north end and the upper, girl's area, only from a stair at the south. Ten straw beds marched down the length of each floor, five to a side, and nearly every inch of the lower interior was carved and whittled at by boys with too much energy to sleep.

There was a stable for the wagon and horses, a chicken coop, and of course the headmistress's chambers. And the whole of the compound was guarded well by a high surrounding fence that obscured the view to all but the empty bell tower.

When Hilde and Carmaline Baab crossed from Germany in 1748 they brought with them dreams of starting over and raising their children in Protestant fashion without the menace of the Pope lingering at the back door like a wolf. But the Georgia wild claimed the Baab men in the first winter and made widows of them both. So the Baab sisters took charge of the orphan house. The first orphans in their care were Salzburger Germans, but the good graces of sister Carmaline didn't let her turn down a child. Soon there were children at the Castle from backgrounds as different as the whole of Europe and the colonies.

Each day after breakfast, the Sisters herded the children into the chapel for morning prayers. Aside from prayers, this service consisted of Sister Carmaline terrifying children—which is to say, singing. She'd pitch a tidy devotion to the captive congregation and then the tone of her voice would take on a subtle change, hinting to the orphans that she was about to break into song. Every child in the room bristled and squirmed when they caught wind of it, darting their eyes about like trapped animals, desperate for a means of escape. Then she'd open her mouth and confirm all fears.

"This morning I'd like to sing you a song, one the Lord has blessed me with."

A sharp intake of breath would split the air as the room full of children braced themselves for the coming onslaught. Fists would clench, shoulders stiffen, and faces quiver, some on the verge of tears. Then it would happen. The first notes would break on the fold like a wave—a wave that smothers you and drags you straight to the bottom of the sea. To Sister Carmaline all the quivering and quaking in the pews looked suspiciously like the manifest of the Holy Ghost, so she'd praise God for it and sing all the more.

In the aftermath of the song, she'd ask her congregation to bow their heads in prayer. It really didn't matter what Sister Carmaline prayed about because no one ever heard it. Every soul in the chapel was too busy thanking God that the singing was over and begging Lord to spare them an encore. Quite possibly, Sister Carmaline's singing saved more souls than her sermons ever did. Her singing, you see, brought many a young man and woman close to the Lord much as soldiers on the battlefield often find salvation in the face of their own mortality.

On a few dreadful occasions, Sister Carmaline felt especially blessed and passed that on to those in attendance in the form of a second song to dismiss the children to their daily chores. On at least one occasion, this caused nine-year-old Delly Martin to faint cold.

After the retreating from Carmaline's singing, it was time for chores, and while normally dreaded by children, chores seemed almost an escape for the orphans at the Castle. They'd come fleeing out of the chapel like scared goats and head straight for the nearest broom or water bucket or feed pen, throwing themselves at their work as if trying madly to erase some terrifying vision from their minds. Chores, however, were the domain of Sister Hilde, and hers was another form of combat all together.

Now Hilde wasn't all monster and no mouse. She managed to be positively pleasant during school studies. There was something in the act of teaching that seemed to calm the beast inside her. She'd talk passionately for hours about history, grammar, and mathematics and seemed to grow larger with the imparting of information, as if she could somehow straighten her crooked body simply by the filling of young minds. But no child lived long with out learning that pleasant in class in no way implied pleasant during chores.

The raising of orphans is a business of controlling the chaos that a storm of children tends to muster, and if the Castle was often the site of storms, then the dining hall was certainly the eye, and Brother Bartimaeus its keeper. He didn't so much cook as work magic on food. A squawking chicken would disappear from the coop into the back of the dining hall and a few hours later that chicken would be miraculously transformed into the smell of home. Hints of rosemary and onion would come wafting out of the hall and find their way into every last nostril in the Castle. Yes, Brother Bartimaeus was a master of the cook pot, and when the place fell under his spell all sins were forgiven for a time. Argument would end, enemies would truce, and enmity turned to amnesty all for the love and savor of supper.

Such was the state of the world into which Phinea Button found herself fallen as a babe, and such was the place that raised her up to the woman she became, whether for good or ill. And from that same did she sail away, years later, her heart all torn and somewhat twisted by the great deep sea ahead and the ruin and flames behind.